PENGUIN BOOKS

Tom Clancy's Full Force and Effect

Thirty years ago, Tom Clancy was a Maryland insurance broker with a passion for naval history. Years before, he had been an English major at Baltimore's Loyola College and had always dreamed of writing a novel. His first effort, The Hunt for Red October, sold briskly as a result of rave reviews, the catapulted on to the New York Times bestseller list after President Reagan pronounced it 'the perfect yarn'. From that day forward, Clancy established himself as an undisputed master at blending exceptional realism and authenticity, intricate plotting and razor-sharp suspense. He passed away in October 2013.

Mark Greaney has a degree in international relations and political science and is pursuing his master's in intelligence studies with a concentration in criminal intelligence. He is the author of The Gray Man, On Target, and Ballistic.

www.tomclancy.com
facebook.com/tomclancyauthor

Also by Tom Clancy

FICTION

NONFICTION

Tom Clancy's
Full Force and Effect

MARK GREANEY

PENGUIN BOOKS

PENGUIN BOOKS

UK | USA | Canada | Ireland | Australia
India | New Zealand | South Africa

Penguin Books is part of the Penguin Random House group of companies
whose addresses can be found at global.penguinrandomhouse.com.

First published in the USA by G. P. Putnam's Sons 2014
First published in Great Britain by Michael Joseph 2014
Published in Penguin Books 2015

001

Text copyright © The Estate of Thomas L. Clancy Jr; Rubicon, Inc;
Jack Ryan Enterprises, Ltd; Jack Ryan Limited Partnerships, 2014

The moral right of the author has been asserted

Set in 12.5/14.75 pt Garamond MT Std
Typeset by Jouve (UK), Milton Keynes
Printed in Great Britain by Clays Ltd, St Ives plc

A CIP catalogue record for this book is available from the British Library

B FORMAT ISBN: 978-1-405-91926-5
A FORMAT ISBN: 978-1-405-91927-2

Tom Clancy's Full Force and Effect

THE KOREAS, CHINA, AND JAPAN

N

RUSSIA

Vladivostok

Beijing

NORTH KOREA

Pyongyang

Seoul

SOUTH KOREA

Sea of Japan

Tokyo

JAPAN

Yellow
Sea

CHINA

Shanghai

East China Sea

Pacific Ocean

© 2014 Jeffrey L. Ward

Principal Characters

Sam Driscoll: operations officer

Jack Ryan, Jr.: operations officer

Gavin Biery: director of information technology

Adara Sherman: director of logistics/transportation

THE NORTH KOREANS

Choi Ji-hoon: Dae Wonsu (grand marshal) and Supreme Leader of the Democratic People's Republic of Korea

Ri Tae-jin: lieutenant general in the Korean People's Army and director of the Reconnaissance General Bureau (RGB), foreign intelligence arm of North Korea

Hwang Min-ho: director of Korea Natural Resources Trading Corporation, North Korean state-owned mining arm

OTHER CHARACTERS

Wayne 'Duke' Sharps: former FBI agent, and president of Sharps Global Intelligence Partners

Edward Riley: former MI6 station chief, and employee of Sharps Global Intelligence Partners

Veronika Martel (aka Élise Legrande): former French intelligence officer, and employee of Sharps Global Intelligence Partners

Colin Hazelton: former CIA case officer, and employee of Sharps Global Intelligence Partners

Dr. Helen Powers: Australian geologist

Óscar Roblas de Mota: Mexican billionaire and president of New World Metals LLC

Daryl Ricks: chief (E-7), Naval Special Warfare, SEAL Team 5, Echo Platoon, NSW Group One

Marleni Allende: Chilean legal counsel of the United Nations Security Council Sanctions Committee

Santiago Maldonado: leader of the Maldonado cartel

Emilio: Maldonado cartel member

Adel Zarif: Iranian bomb maker

Cathy Ryan: First Lady of the United States

Prologue

John Clark didn't give a damn what anybody said – this was still Saigon.

He knew history, of course. Forty years ago the communists came down from the north and they took the place. They renamed it Ho Chi Minh City in honor of their conquering leader. To the victors the spoils. They executed collaborators and imprisoned unreliables and they changed the politics, the culture, and the fabric of the lives of those who lived here.

It looked a little different now, but to John it felt the same. The cloying evening heat and the smell of exhaust fumes mixing with the pressing jungle, the incense and cigarette smoke and the spiced meat, the buzz of the stifling crowds and the lights from the energetic streets.

And the sense of pervasive danger, just out of sight but closing, like an invading army.

They could name this city after his sworn enemy from the past, they could call it whatever the hell they wanted, but to the sixty-six-year-old man sitting in the open-front café in District 8, that didn't change a thing.

This was still *fucking* Saigon.

Clark sat with his legs crossed, his shirt collar open, and his tan tropic-weight sport coat lying across the chair next to him because the slow-moving palm-frond fan above him did nothing more than churn the hot air. Younger men and women swirled around him, heading either to tables in the back or out onto the busy pavement in front of the café, but Clark sat still as stone.

Except for his eyes; his eyes darted back and forth, scanning the street.

He was struck by the lack of Americans in uniform, the one big disconnect from his memories of old Saigon. Forty-odd years ago he'd trod these streets in olive drab or jungle camo. Even when he was here in country with the CIA's MACV-SOG (Military Assistance Command, Vietnam – Studies and Observations Group), he'd rarely worn civilian clothing. He was a Navy SEAL, there was a war going on, battle dress was appropriate for an American, even one in country working direct-action ops for the Agency.

Also missing were the bicycles. Back then ninety percent of the wheeled traffic on this street would have been bikes. Today there were some bikes, sure, but mostly it was scooters and motorcycles and small cars filling the street, with pedestrian throngs covering the sidewalks.

And nobody wore a uniform around here.

He took a sip of green tea in the glow of the votive candle flickering on his bistro table. He didn't care for the tea, but this place didn't have beer or even wine. What it *did* have was line of sight on the Lion d'Or, a large French colonial restaurant, just across Huynh Thi Phung Street. He looked away from the passersby, stopped thinking about the days when twenty-five percent of them would have been US military, and he glanced back to the Lion d'Or. As hard as it was to divorce himself from the past, he managed to put the war out of his mind, because this evening his task was the man drinking alone at a corner table in the restaurant, just twenty-five yards from where Clark sat.

The subject of Clark's surveillance was American, a few years younger than Clark, bald and thickly built. To Clark it was clear this man seemed to be having issues this evening. His jaw was fixed in anger, his body movements were jolting and exaggerated like a man nearly overcome with fury.

Clark could relate. He was in a particularly foul humor himself.

He watched the subject for another moment, then checked his watch and pressed down on a button on a small wireless controller in his left hand. He spoke aloud, albeit softly, even though no one sat close by. 'One-hour mark. Whoever he's meeting is making him wait for the honor of their company.'

Three stories above and directly behind Clark – on the roof of a mixed-use colonial-style office building – three men, all lying prone and wearing muted colors and black backpacks, scanned the street below them. They were connected to Clark via their earbuds, and they'd picked up his transmission.

Domingo 'Ding' Chavez, in the middle of the three, centered his Nikon on the man in the restaurant and focused the lens. Then he pressed his own push-to-talk button and answered back softly: 'Subject is not a happy camper. Looks like he's about to put his fist through the wall.'

Clark replied from below. 'If I have to sit here in this heat and sip this disgusting tea much longer, I'm going to do the same.'

Chavez cleared his throat uncomfortably, then said, 'Uh, it's not too bad up here. How about one of us take the eye at ground level, you can make your way to the roof?'

The reply came quick. 'Negative. Hold positions.'

'Roger that.'

Sam Driscoll chuckled. He lay on Chavez's left, just a few feet away, his eye to a spotting scope that he used to scan to the north of the restaurant, watching the road for any sign of trouble. He spoke to the men around him, but he didn't transmit. 'Somebody's grumpy.'

Several yards to Chavez's right, Jack Ryan, Jr., peered through his camera, scanning the pedestrians on the sidewalk to the south of their overwatch. He focused his attention on a leggy blonde climbing out of a cab. While doing so he asked, 'What's wrong with Clark? He's usually the last one of us to bitch, but he's been like this all day.'

There was no one else on this rooftop other than the three Americans, but Chavez had been doing this sort of thing for most of his adult life. He knew his voice would carry through the metal air-conditioning duct behind him if he wasn't careful, so he answered back as if he were in a library. 'Mr C's got some history around here, is all. Probably coming back to him.'

'Right,' Ryan said. 'He must be reliving the war.'

Ding smiled in the darkness. 'That's part of it. Clark's down in that café thinking about the shit he saw. The shit he did. But he's also thinking about running around here as a twenty-five-year-old SEAL stud. It probably scares him how much he wishes he was back in the groove. War or no war.'

Ryan said, 'He's holding up for an old guy. We should all be so lucky.'

Driscoll shifted on his belly to find a more comfortable position on the asphalt mansard roof, though he kept his eye in his optic, centering now on the man at the table. 'Clark's right. It doesn't look like this meet is going to happen, and watching this guy through a ten-power scope while he drinks his liver into oblivion is getting old.'

While Sam focused on the subject, Ryan continued following the blonde as she pushed through the foot traffic heading north along Huynh Thi Phung Street. He tracked her to the front door of Lion d'Or. 'Good news. I think our evening just got interesting.'

Chavez followed Ryan's gaze. 'Really? How so?'

Jack watched the woman as she turned sharply into the restaurant from the sidewalk and moved directly toward their subject's table. 'The meet has arrived, and *she* is hot.'

Chavez saw her through his own binos now. 'I guess it's better than watching another fat dude slurp gin.' He pressed the push-to-talk button again. 'John, we've got a –'

Clark's voice crackled over Chavez, because he had the command unit on their network and could override other transmissions. 'I see her. Too bad we don't have any fucking audio.'

The men on the roof all laughed nervously. Damn, Clark *was* grouchy tonight.

I

Colin Hazelton made a show of checking the time on his mobile phone as the woman sat down. She was an hour late and he wanted to indicate his displeasure, even if only passive-aggressively.

She fixed the hem of her skirt and crossed her legs, and only then did she look up at him. She seemed to notice the phone and his focus on it, then she lifted the sweating water glass in front of her and took a sip.

Hazelton dropped his phone back into his pocket and drank down half of his gin and tonic. He had to admit she was every bit as attractive as advertised. It was virtually all his control had said about his contact tonight. Statuesque and blond, with mannerisms that transmitted refinement and poise. Still, Hazelton was too pissed to be impressed. Not pissed at her, exclusively, but generally angry, and he certainly wasn't in the mood to ogle his contact tonight.

That she'd made him wait a goddamned hour took even more of the luster off her splendor.

Before either spoke the waiter appeared. It was that kind of place, not like the dive bars and tea shops that populated the rest of this part of Huynh Thi Phung Street.

The woman ordered a glass of white wine in perfect French. Hazelton could tell it was her native tongue, but his control officer had mentioned this fact as well, between

7

breathless comments about her almond eyes and her lithe body.

He assumed she was a former French spook, either DGSE or DCRI, although she also could have been from DST, which became DCRI in 2008. Virtually everyone Hazelton met with in the course of his work was a former intelligence officer, so this was no stretch.

She did not introduce herself, though he wasn't surprised by this. He had, however, expected some contrition for her late arrival. But she didn't mention it at all. Instead, she opened with, 'You brought the documents?'

Hazelton did not answer her directly. 'What do you know about the circumstances of the operation?'

'The circumstances?'

'The client. Have they read you in on the client?'

She showed a little confusion now. 'Why would they do that? The client is not relevant to my brief.'

'Well, let me fill you in. The client is –'

The woman held a slender hand up. Her nails were perfectly manicured, and her skin glowed with lotion. 'When they don't brief me, I take that to mean I am not supposed to know.' She looked Hazelton over. 'You don't appear to be new to this work, so surely you understand this.' Her French accent was thick, but her English was flawless.

He took another gulp of gin. 'Sometimes it's best to know.'

'Perhaps that is your philosophy. It is not mine.' She said it with an air of finality. She wanted to move on. 'So . . . do you have them or not?'

Hazelton spoke slowly and softly, but stressing every word through a slur from the alcohol he'd been consuming all day, both here and in the lobby bar back at his hotel. 'North . . . Fucking . . . Korea.'

No response from the Frenchwoman.

He said, 'You *did* know, didn't you?'

She did not answer. Instead, she replied, 'You are very emotional, aren't you? This surprises me. I know you were given a rush assignment, someone took ill and they pulled out and then you were called over, but New York should know better than to send in an emotional traveling officer.' Below the table, Hazelton felt the tip of her high-heeled shoe as it ran along his leg, just next to his ankle. There was a time in his life when this would have excited him, but that was long ago. This was work; he knew she was just feeling around to see if he had a briefcase. Soon he heard her toe thump his case, next to his leg.

She said, 'Slide it to me, please.'

The big American just sat there. He drummed his fingers on the table. Considering.

He expected to see frustration on her face, but she was oddly cool about his delay. After several seconds she repeated herself with no change in tone. 'Slide it to me, please.'

He didn't know what he was going to do tonight. Would he pass the items or shred them and dump them in a river like fish food? The ramifications for each course of action had been weighing on him all day. But now a sense of composure came over him, and he heard himself say, 'You know what? I didn't sign on to this job to be an errand boy for a bunch of murdering psychos.' Then, 'There is other work to be had without stooping this low.'

9

'I don't understand,' the woman said, and while speaking she glanced into the street, a casual gaze. She looked bored, but Hazelton knew she was simply keeping an eye out for surveillance.

Hazelton waved his arm in the air angrily. 'To hell with this. I'm out.'

The woman, by contrast, displayed no emotion. '*Out?*'

'I'm not passing the documents on to you.'

She sighed a little now. 'Is this about money? If so, you will need to talk to New York. I have no authorization to –'

'It's not about money. It's about good and evil. That's completely lost on you, isn't it?'

'My job has nothing to do with either.'

Hazelton looked at the woman with complete derision. His decision had been made. 'Tell yourself that if you need to, but you're *not* getting these docs.' He kicked the briefcase loud enough for her to hear it.

The woman nodded. A countenance of calm. Her detachment was odd to Hazelton. He'd expected screaming and yelling. She just said, 'This will complicate things. New York will be angry.'

'Screw New York.'

'I hope you don't expect me to join you in your moral crusade.'

'Doll, I don't give a damn what you do.'

'Then you won't give a damn when I walk out of here and make a phone call.'

Hazelton paused, the strain of his work and the travel evident on his face. 'Call him.'

'He will send someone to take that case from you.'

Hazelton smiled now. 'He might try. But like you said, I'm not exactly new at this. I have a few tricks up my sleeve.'

'For your sake, I hope you do.' The Frenchwoman stood and turned away, passing the smiling waiter approaching the table with the wine on a silver tray.

Jack Ryan, Jr., watched it all through his camera from the rooftop across the street. He couldn't hear the conversation, of course, but he correctly identified the body language.

'If that was a blind date, I don't think they hit it off.'

Ding and Sam chuckled, but everyone stayed on mission. They watched while the tall woman pulled a phone from her purse and spoke into it, then began walking north.

Driscoll depressed his PTT controller. 'Clark? Are we staying with Hazelton or do you want someone on the woman?'

Clark replied quickly. 'She was after whatever is in that briefcase, so that case is now part of our mission. Still . . . I want to know more about her. One of you go with the blonde. The others stay put, eyes on that case.'

Jack and Sam took their eyes out of their optics and looked to Chavez, between them on the roof. Chavez said, 'I'll stay. You guys fight over it.'

Now Jack glanced to Sam, who slowly put his eye back in his spotting scope to watch the subject. 'Go.'

Jack gave a big smile; it was the brightest light on the rooftop. 'I owe you one, Sam.'

He was up and moving toward the fire escape in

seconds, putting his camera into his pack as he walked through the dark.

Sam and Ding watched while Colin Hazelton drained the last of his gin and tonic, then gestured for the waiter to bring him another.

'What's he hanging around for? He's got another shitty date?' Sam asked rhetorically. Downstairs Clark was thinking the same thing. His voice was gravel, all annoyance and frustration. 'Looks like we're stuck here for a fourth round of g and t's.'

The drink came and Hazelton let the waiter put it on the table in front of him. He said something to the waiter; all three Americans watching across the street thought he was asking for the bathroom, because the waiter pointed toward the back of the establishment. Hazelton stood; he left his drink, his coat, and his briefcase; and he headed to the back.

It was quiet in all three headsets for a moment. Then Ding said, 'John? That look right to you?'

Clark understood what his second-in-command meant, but instead of revealing what he was thinking, he put it as a challenge to Driscoll. 'Sam? What do you see?'

Driscoll adjusted his eye in his scope, looking at the empty table, the coat over the back of Hazelton's chair, the briefcase on the other chair. He looked at the other tables in the restaurant, the well-heeled clientele seated or milling about. After a moment his eyes went back to the briefcase. He said, 'If something was so important in that case that he refused to pass it to his contact, why would he leave it unattended at the table while he goes to take a leak?'

Clark said, 'He wouldn't.'

'Then the case is a decoy.'

'That's right.'

'Meaning . . .' Driscoll had it in another second. 'Hazelton isn't coming back. He suspects surveillance on the front so he's slipping out a rear exit.'

Ding confirmed this with 'The old dine-and-dash routine.'

Clark said, 'Bingo. I'm going to head through the restaurant and come out the back. It's a north-south alley, but his hotel is behind us. You two stay on overwatch and keep an eye on the intersections to the north and south. Unless he can teleport, we'll pick him back up.'

In the tea shop Clark dropped a few wadded dong notes on the table, paying for a drink that made his stomach churn, then he grabbed his jacket and headed toward the Lion d'Or across the street.

He'd just stepped off the curb when he saw something that made him pull up short. He backed onto the sidewalk, then looked around in all directions.

Softly he spoke over the communications net. 'Ryan. Hold position.'

Jack Ryan, Jr., had been moving up Dao Cam Moc, but on Clark's order he stopped. 'Holding,' he replied. He turned toward the alcove of a closed electronics retailer and pretended to window shop.

'What's your location?' Clark asked.

Jack looked down to his phone to a map of the area. Tiny colored dots displayed the position of the four men on the team, or more precisely, the position of the GPS tracker each man wore under the belt loop in the small of his back. Clark's green dot was two blocks to the south-east, still in the open-air tea shop.

Ryan said, 'I'm two blocks northwest of your poz.'

Over the earbud Clark explained himself. 'I've got eyes on four unknowns on motorcycles approaching from opposite ends of the street. They look like a team.'

A moment later Chavez, who was still on the roof with his camera, transmitted. 'Black Ducatis?'

Clark said, 'Roger that. They came from opposite directions and have different clothing, but it looks like they are riding identical bikes and wearing identical helmets. No coincidence.'

Ding picked all four bikes out of the traffic below. It took him several seconds, because they were spread out. 'Good eye, John.'

'Not my first visit. I know when something doesn't look right around here. Jack, I want you to continue north of your poz. If he takes that alley all the way through the district you can get ahead of him when he comes out on Pham The Hien, but only if you double-time it. Watch for these bikers, don't let them catch you eyeing the subject.'

Ryan was still pretending to look over a shelf of high-end cameras in the shop window. He felt the blood pumping through his heart for the first time on this trip. His boring evening was suddenly building in intensity.

Jack took off in a jog. 'On it. I'll stay parallel to the bikers and get to the mouth of the alley before Hazelton exits.'

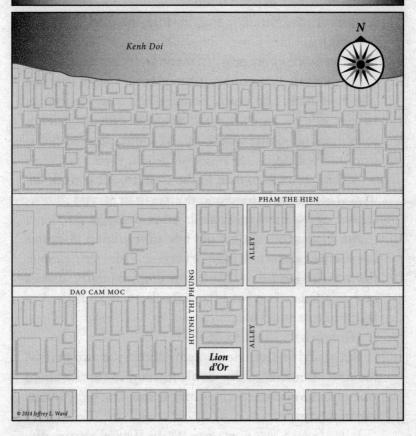

Clark said, 'Sam and Ding, do what you can to catch up to Ryan.'

'We're en route,' said Chavez. 'A minute to get off the roof, that puts us three minutes behind you, Jack. Keep it loose till we catch up.'

Colin Hazelton stepped out into the alleyway behind the restaurant and headed due north, his hands in his pockets.

He was well aware he'd just made a very costly decision. Costly because he wouldn't get paid for his work over the past four days, and costly because he'd lose his job for his decision to abort. But also costly because he'd left a three-hundred-dollar sport coat and a four-hundred-dollar briefcase behind.

All bad news for a man in the twilight of his work life who was also sixty thousand dollars in debt, and in possession of few marketable skills other than spycraft.

But in spite of this, for the first time all day, Hazelton felt a sense of peace. It even occurred to him that, despite the valuable property he'd left in the restaurant, at least he'd skipped out on his fifty-dollar bar tab, so he had to factor in that small win.

He managed a half-smile.

But it didn't last. He thought about the events that brought him here, to this dimly lit alley, to this decision, and his mood darkened to match the low light of his surroundings.

It had been a year now since Wayne 'Duke' Sharps, director of Sharps Global Intelligence Partners, interviewed Colin Hazelton in his Upper West Side Manhattan office about a job in 'corporate intelligence.' Sharps had made it clear to the ex – CIA officer that the work at Sharps Partners would be safe, low-key, and nonpolitical, but it would also require Hazelton coming to terms with the fact he would no longer be working for the United States. He would, instead, be working for a paycheck.

Hazelton pushed back at this, insisting he'd never do anything against the red, white, and blue, but to that Sharps replied, 'We don't operate against US interests.' He laughed at the thought. 'We're not devils here at SGIP, we're just not angels.'

That sounded fine to Colin Hazelton. He was ex-CIA after a career as an Air Force pilot. He bled red, white, and blue, yes, but the times dictated his actions. He'd made a string of speculative international investments in emerging markets, mostly in North Africa, and they had all gone belly-up during the unexpected events of the Arab Spring.

Hazelton needed the work, so he took the job.

And Sharps's promise of apolitical corporate intelligence work had proven true. For the past year Hazelton had not thought twice about his assignments or his clients.

Until this week, that is.

On Monday Hazelton's employer had rushed him to Prague to meet with a government official to pick up travel documentation for five individuals. There wasn't much exciting about this sort of thing; as an operations officer in the CIA, he'd secured alias travel for hundreds of agents around the world. Even working for Sharps this was not out of the ordinary; Hazelton had been involved in moving highly skilled foreign professionals who'd been unable to obtain US work visas into the States. He saw it as a good thing; he was subverting American bureaucracy, not America itself.

Normally it was part of his job to inspect the documents. But not this time; for some reason, when the docs were presented to him in Prague they were sealed in a laminated pouch and his instructions were to deliver the package to a contact in Ho Chi Minh City, and then to return to New York.

He assumed the five sets of documents were for five Czech professionals, and they would be heading to some other country via Vietnam, not the States, as that would be an odd connection from Prague. Hazelton guessed the travelers would be going to work in Japan, or Singapore, or maybe even Australia.

It was strange he wasn't allowed to see the documentation, but he let it go.

That was until last night on the flight over from Prague. With an hour and a half till landing, the burly American polished off a gin and tonic and began securing items in his roll-aboard and his briefcase. The laminated package full of docs was stowed under the fabric lining of his carry-on, but as he moved a pair of shoes to make room for his jacket, to his horror he realized there was a small tear in the lining of the case. He'd been using the luggage since the late eighties, and the secret compartment had finally given out. He tried to fix it, but this only made it worse. It was a rookie mistake for a spook, and Hazelton was no rookie, but he had been drinking, and that, along with Murphy's Law, had worked against him.

As he sat in his first-class seat he thought about going through immigration in Vietnam and he began to sweat. If his carry-on was searched at all he knew they would find his stash. But thinking it over quickly, he realized he couldn't remember a single visit to Vietnam where his person had been searched. If he removed the documents from the hidden compartment and simply stored them in a money belt around his waist, he'd be fine.

But to do this he knew he'd first need to remove them from the large square laminate package.

Hazelton took the document package into the lavatory, sat on the toilet, and tore it open with his teeth. Inside he found five plastic bags, each one containing a passport, a driver's license, some credit cards, and a folded letter. Despite a strong presumption he was not supposed to look, he began thumbing through the documents.

A flight attendant knocked on the door to the bathroom, telling him to return to his seat because the pilot expected unstable air ahead.

But Hazelton ignored her; all his attention was concentrated on the travel documents. He was not surprised to find the black diplomatic passports. They were not fakes, these were legit, although he assumed they had been altered somehow. He looked at each of the photos. Four Caucasian men and one Caucasian woman.

He couldn't be sure if they were Czech just by looking at them, but where they were from was *not* the issue.

It was where they were going. The letters in each person's possession were travel authorizations, given by the Czech government, allowing the diplomat holding the corresponding passport to travel to North Korea to work in the Czech consulate there.

North Korea? Hazelton had spent the last year doing corporate intelligence work for Siemens, for Microsoft, for Land Rover, and for Maersk.

Now I'm working on behalf of the most brutal and repressive regime in the world?

As he sat on the toilet, his shoulders slamming from one wall to the other with the turbulence, Hazelton decided these five individuals were nuclear scientists being snuck into North Korea. What the hell else could be going on? DPRK had been caught trying to move nuke experts before, and they had no major industry to speak of other than mining, which was handled almost exclusively by partners in China. He couldn't be certain these were nuke scientists, of course, but he could damn well tell they weren't Chinese miners.

And he knew this wasn't some operation Sharps was running against the North Koreans. Duke Sharps wasn't in the business of taking on despotic regimes for noble aims. He worked for money, there was money in getting brainpower into North Korea, so that had to be what was going on here.

He closed his eyes and leaned back against the bulkhead of the plane, still sitting on the toilet. 'Son of a bitch,' he whispered to himself.

The fact Duke Sharps was shipping nefarious characters into the Hermit Kingdom of North Korea pissed Hazelton off, but the fact Hazelton was helping Sharps do it made him shudder.

Hazelton made it through airport immigration with

the docs strapped to his midsection, and then an hour later he arrived at his hotel from the airport, salty remnants of dried sweat covering his body. He spent the afternoon in the lobby drinking, thinking about the money and the job and his need to make his financial problems go away, hoping against hope there was some sweet spot of inebriation he could find right as the time came to pass the docs off to the cutout here in Ho Chi Minh City so he wouldn't feel like he was doing anything wrong.

Now Hazelton knew . . . a half-dozen Tanquerays at the lobby bar and three more at the restaurant – more than a *pint* of gin – this wasn't even close to enough to washing away the stench of working for the North Koreans.

He'd balked tonight in the restaurant, refusing to give the docs to the gorgeous French spook, his cutout who would have taken them to the five travelers, probably lodged somewhere in the city. Then the French bitch had probably run off to tattletale to Duke Sharps, and now sixty-one-year-old Colin Hazelton found himself stinking drunk, staggering through a Third World back alley dodging whoever Sharps would send to find the dirty docs that Hazelton now held in a large money belt around his waist.

While he stumbled along he kept an eye out for any surveillance, but he didn't really expect anyone on him for a day or two. He planned on walking a couple blocks through these back streets to the Kenh Doi, one of several brackish canals that ran through the city, tying his money belt around a loose brick, and then dropping the five sets of dirty documents into the water. From there he'd head to the airport, he'd be on the first plane back to the United States in the morning, and he'd wait to get fired by phone, no doubt by Duke himself.

He'd go back to flying planes for a living. At his age and with his lack of recent flying time he might be able to scrounge some work flying beat-up cargo props in the Third World. He'd die before he paid off his debt, but at least he wouldn't be a bag man for the Asian Dr. Evil and his murdering minions.

Hazelton walked on. There had been a flurry of activity in the streets – this was District 8, full of French colonial architecture and active nightlife – but now he passed through the darkness in a commercial area near the canal. A restaurant worker carried garbage by him, and an old woman on a scooter putted through the alley.

As he made a left toward the water a pair of men on whisper-quiet black Ducati Diavel motorcycles rolled into the alleyway he just vacated, but he neither heard nor saw them, nor did he have any idea two more similar bikes were already positioned ahead of his route, and waiting for him to walk into their trap.

2

Jack Ryan, Jr., moved in the darkness, east on Pham The Hien. In front of him he saw Colin Hazelton appear from an alleyway across the street. Jack had expected him to turn to his left and head back to his hotel, but to his surprise the American in the white button-down shirt and loose necktie stepped into the road and began heading over toward Ryan's side of the street.

Shit, thought Jack. He kept walking, looking away from Hazelton and taking care not to alter his gait. He wondered for a moment if he might have been burned, but Hazelton didn't seem to pay any attention to him.

To Jack's surprise Hazelton stepped onto the pavement forty yards in front of him, then entered another narrow, dark alleyway. This would lead him directly to the Kenh Doi, an east-west canal that served as the northern border for District 8, and from Jack's study of the map of this district, there was nothing there but docks and houseboats and ramshackle apartment buildings.

Confused as to why the man wasn't going back to his hotel, Jack decided he would walk on a few blocks and then try to move up a parallel alley.

Jack picked up the pace, took a second to orient himself with the map on his phone, and then he spoke over the net. 'This is Ryan. I've got the subject. He's moving north. Two blocks south of the water. Unless he's got himself a dinghy tied up somewhere, then he's going to run out of road here in a minute. I'm going to try to get ahead and see what he's up to. I'll move parallel to his –'

Jack stopped transmitting when, directly in front of him, two black Ducati bikes rolled out of the alley ahead and crossed the street. They were just a couple hundred feet behind Hazelton. Here in the quiet sector near the river they couldn't hope to remain covert from a trained CIA veteran.

Nothing about this looked like a surveillance exercise by the men on the bikes.

'Ryan?' Ding called over the network. 'Did you lose comms?'

'Negative, I'm here. But a pair of Ducatis are here, too, and they are definitely following Hazelton. Not sure where the others are. This looks too aggressive for surveillance. I think they are going to confront him.'

Driscoll spoke over the net now. 'Unless they've got cars involved in the pursuit that we haven't spotted yet, they aren't planning on an abduction. This might be something worse.'

Jack confirmed, astonished that the stakes of this operation seemed to be rising with each moment. 'Holy shit, this could be a hit.'

Ding broke into the conversation. 'Hang on a second. Hazelton is supposed to be over here on a corporate intelligence job. His last op was for Microsoft. Nothing we've seen indicates he has any concerns about a lethal adversary. A hit would be one hell of an escalation.'

Jack saw the two other bikes now, entering Pham The Hien from the east and then racing past Ryan and separating. One turned into the alley that ran parallel to the east of Hazelton's path; the other turned into the alley to the west, the one Ryan had planned on taking.

Jack passed the road Hazelton took. He just caught a glimpse of the first two bikers as they turned between a pair of long two-story warehouses that ran all the way to the water's edge. He picked up the pace, thinking any confrontation would have to be soon, because Hazelton was running out of alley before the canal, and then he would have to retrace his steps back in this direction.

As he jogged to the corner to get a look between the buildings, he said, 'I agree, Ding, but now four guys have him boxed in with nowhere to run. Something is about to go down.'

Now John Clark came over the line. 'I'm getting the car in case we need to make a hasty exfil with Hazelton. Traffic is tight, though. It's going to take me some time. Ding and Sam, get to Ryan's poz on the double. Jack, you do *not* intervene, no matter what. You are unarmed.'

Jack replied softly now. He'd reached the corner and he was about to lean around to take a peek at what was going on. 'Understood.'

Hazelton approached the Kenh Doi, a dense blackness fifty yards in front of him. There were a few twinkling lights of District 5 on the far bank, but there was also a group of warehouses there, without much going on at this time of the evening. And this stretch of canal, though nearly in the center of the city, had next to no boat traffic at night.

His plan had been to tear up the documents to the best

of his ability and then drop them in the Kenh Doi. They would separate as they flowed downstream, and they would be rendered useless to the North Koreans.

But he knew that plan was shot now, because of the sound of finely tuned motorcycle engines behind him.

He understood the bikers were here for him. They made no secret of their presence. And they weren't alone. He hadn't seen any more followers, but the slow approach from the men behind him gave the distinct impression they were waiting for someone else to get into position.

Colin Hazelton was drunk, but he was still perceptive; after all, he had been doing this sort of thing for a very long time.

And just like that, his suspicions were confirmed. A pair of headlights appeared in front of him, one coming up the riverside path along the docks from the east, the other from the west. They turned in his direction and approached at a steady pace.

They had him and he felt he knew who *they* were. They were more of Duke Sharps's men. That French bitch had had confederates here in town, and they'd swooped down on him not in days, as he'd anticipated, but in mere minutes.

The two bikes in front of him pulled up to within feet, and then they turned off their engines. The men kept their helmets on and their mirrored visors down. The pair behind had stopped twenty yards back, their soft motors reverberating confidently, announcing to Hazelton that he had nowhere to go.

He knew he was going to have to talk his way out of this.

Hazelton looked to the closest biker, taking him for the leader. He managed a little laugh. 'Figured you wouldn't be in position till tomorrow. I underestimated the hell out of you guys.'

None of the bikers spoke.

Hazelton continued. 'Well done. New York sent you in early, I guess? They expected me to waver? I'm impressed. That's what we used to call "anticipating surprise."' He chuckled again, and repeated, 'Well done.'

The closest biker climbed off his motorcycle, and he stepped to within arm's reach. His mirrored visor gave the man the appearance of a robot.

Hazelton shrugged. 'Had to make a stand. You get it, right? The client this time is the DPRK. I don't know if you knew it, but Duke is in bed with the worst people in the world.'

The biker reached to his helmet and lifted his visor now. Hazelton was surprised by this a little – the man initially seemed content to keep himself masked – but Hazelton thought it possible the man was showing his face because they were acquainted. He knew Sharps hired a lot of ex-Agency assets, after all.

Colin Hazelton leaned forward a little to get a look at the man in the light, but as soon as he saw the face, he recoiled back.

He did not know the man. It was an Asian face. Hard. Cold.

North Korean.

'Oh,' he said. 'I see.' Then he faked another little laugh. 'You ever had one of those days?'

'Give me the documents,' the North Korean said.

Hazelton felt around on his body. He shrugged. 'Would you look at that? I left them in a briefcase back at the –'

'The case was empty!' An automatic pistol appeared in the North Korean's right hand. Hazelton knew little about weapons, but he had no doubt it was real. The pair behind him began revving their engines, and the other man in front of him stood up taller on his bike.

After watching the entire confrontation, Jack Ryan, Jr., pulled his head back around the corner of the warehouse. He dropped down on one knee, and he tapped his PTT button. 'This is Ryan with eyes on. All four followers are around the subject, and they have him at gunpoint.'

Ding replied; it was clear from his breathing he was running. 'So much for this being an easy corporate gig. Stay covert. We are on Tran Xuan Soan, about ninety seconds from you.'

Jack said, 'If this is a hit, Hazelton doesn't have ninety seconds.'

Clark barked over the net now. 'And if that's a hit you aren't stopping it unarmed. I'm en route with the car. Three to five minutes back.' Through the transmission Jack could hear Clark honking his car horn at traffic ahead of him.

Ryan's impulse was to run headlong into the alley, but he knew Clark was right about his chances if this turned into a real fight.

But Jack had an idea. 'I don't have to engage, John. I can try a diversion.'

Clark replied quickly. 'You are on your own, son. Use extreme discretion.'

Ryan did not acknowledge the instructions; he was already looking at the map on his phone, formulating a hasty plan of action. He pulled his camera from his backpack and took a few breaths to ready himself.

The North Korean biker leveled the gun at the American's chest. He did not say a word.

Hazelton raised his hands slowly, panic welling within. 'There is absolutely no need for that. I'm no threat to you. Let's keep this civilized, at the very least.' The American looked around him. Through the fear coursing through his body he realized he'd put himself in a terrible situation. Had he not been three sheets to the wind he knew he never would have wandered down a dark street like this, especially while harboring concerns someone was after him.

Of course, had he known DPRK agents were on his tail, no amount of alcohol would have caused this breach of tradecraft.

The North Korean pulled the hammer back on his pistol. Hazelton stared into the black hole of the muzzle, not quite past the disbelief of what was happening. He'd never faced a gun, he'd never faced any real danger in his career other than an incident once when he was roughed up by street hooligans in Denmark, hardly comparable to his present circumstance. His mind was overcome with the terror of the moment, but he did retain the presence of mind to know he was beaten. With a cracking voice he said, 'Money belt. Around my waist.'

Just then the door to an apartment building opened twenty-five feet from Colin Hazelton's left shoulder. Two women stepped out carrying large bags, and they immediately glanced up at the men in the middle of the little street in front of them. The North Korean turned his pistol in their direction, and they screamed, leaping back inside the building.

The North Korean heard a shout behind him, his man there alerting him. He looked up and saw the burly American running past them up the street, lumbering toward the water.

He fired up his bike, preparing to take off after the American; the other bikers revved their engines as well.

'Hey! Hey!' someone shouted in English a half-block behind at the corner of a corrugated tin warehouse. All four bikers turned to look and they saw a young white man with dark hair and a beard. He held a camera up in their direction. 'Everybody smile!' The camera flashed a dozen times, strobing the men in the dim alley.

The two bikers closest to the cameraman throttled their engines and burned rubber as they turned around on the street, then began racing toward the white man with the camera. The leader and the man with him went off in pursuit of Hazelton and his money belt.

As he accelerated, the lead North Korean stuck his pistol back into his jacket, then reached to his waistband and pulled a long stiletto from a sheath.

3

Colin Hazelton hadn't broken into anything more than a light jog in nearly thirty years, but the adrenaline in his body put enough spring in his step to get him down to the river in twenty seconds. Here he made a right on the path, the two bikers close on his heels. He thought about running across the dock and diving into the water, but he knew nothing about the current and he felt sure the younger men after him would just fish him out soaking wet, or else drown him there and take his money belt. So he raced along the path for a block, then made a right up into another dark and narrow street.

The bikes approached confidently; he could hear that the throttles weren't having to work very hard at all.

'Help!' he shouted to the apartment buildings around, his eyes scanning balconies and windows, desperate to find anyone who could save him. He thought about the gun behind him and wondered at any minute if he was going to take a bullet in the back of the neck. He knew he just had to get into a public space, but he also knew the area. He had several blocks to go before finding any sanctuary of community.

Domingo Chavez and Sam Driscoll sprinted through the darkened streets of District 8, closing on the gray GPS beacon on their map that represented Jack Ryan. Ding glanced down at the electronic map for the first time in thirty seconds, making sure they made the correct turn off the two-lane street, when Ryan's voice came over his earpiece.

'Ding, you guys have me on GPS?'

Chavez responded, still looking at the dot on the map. '-Affirmative. Looks like you're running.'

'Damn right I am! Two armed bikers on my six.' Chavez could hear the roaring engines through the warren of apartment buildings off his left shoulder.

'We'll catch up with you.'

'I need one of you to go for Hazelton. He took off to the water. He's not over here to the west, so try to the east.'

Ding called to Sam as he ran on. 'You go for Ryan! I'll grab Hazelton!'

Colin Hazelton never stood a chance. The lead North Korean biker raced up behind the big, aging American, positioned his flat stiletto down by his side, and then thrust his arm out, stabbing the man from behind, once under the left shoulder blade, then quickly on the right side in the same place.

Both of Hazelton's heaving lungs began deflating almost instantly, and blood pumped into the damaged organs. He ran on a few feet, no reaction in his stride to what he thought were just punches into his back, but soon he toppled over in the middle of the dark street, gasping. The bikers slowed and stopped, then both men dropped the kickstands on their Ducatis and climbed off, quickly but still casually. They stepped over to the wounded man, who was now trying to crawl away, and they knelt over him.

The leader began feeling through Hazelton's pockets and then his shirt, finally laying his hand on the money belt hiding there. He yanked the hem up over the man's corpulent midsection, used his stiletto to cut free the sweaty and bloody white Velcro money belt, and he quickly checked it to make sure the documents were inside. There was blood on one of the passports, but everything was there.

Hazelton lay on his side now, and he reached up for the documents weakly, his right arm extending fully and the whistling wheezes out of both his mouth and the holes in his back changing in pitch as he tried to yell.

The North Korean biker knocked the American's feeble grasp away and stood up, then he turned back to his motorcycle. His partner joined him, his handgun low by his side and his helmet turning in all directions as he scanned, making certain no threats appeared in the street.

They started their engines and turned back in the other direction to join the hunt for the white photographer.

Ryan was five blocks away now, still in the warren of darkened streets and parking lots around the apartment buildings here by the Kenh Doi. He wondered what had happened to Hazelton. He had done all he could for the man, but he feared it hadn't been enough. He'd seen the two women step outside the apartment building and in so doing distract the bikers. To his shock Hazelton took off toward the water. Jack thought this to be a terrible idea, unless of course Hazelton had seen something that gave him no hope he'd survive the encounter with the armed men.

Or else he was just drunk and he freaked out and he went for it, decided he was smarter, stronger, and faster than he actually was.

Ryan was betting on the latter.

To give the American ex – CIA man a fighting chance, Ryan had darted into the alley, demanded the attention of the bikers, and flashed his camera as a distraction, then he turned and ran for his life, hoping to draw at least some of the men off the older, slower Hazelton.

That part of Jack's plan had worked. As he leapt over a pair of aluminum trash cans on the sidewalk he could tell from the lights and noise of the two Ducatis on his tail that they were no more than fifty feet behind. They crashed through the cans just three seconds later, sending them and their contents flying. Jack leapt over a wooden pallet lying on the curb and then turned, flicking it up into the path of the bikers, but the pallet shattered against the bikes and didn't slow the men down at all. He ducked around a tree in a planter, then changed direction again.

The Ducatis spun toward him and increased speed again.

Ryan worried the men might tire of the chase and just open fire, so he tried to keep his sprint erratic, moving from left to right, leaping over garbage or parked scooters or boxes on the sidewalk, racing around electric poles and switching direction unpredictably.

But the bikes stayed on him, he wasn't going to shake them as long as he stayed on the road.

Sam Driscoll came over his earbud, yelling at Jack to stand still a minute so he could get a GPS fix on the map long enough to find him in the narrow alleyways. But Jack was hardly in a position to comply; he just kept running, ducking under low wires that hung over a narrow pathway next to an office building. He made a hard left, then took a flight of concrete steps that ran down to a parking lot alongside an apartment complex. The bikes took the steps down as well, and they closed to within feet of their prey.

The crack of a gunshot and the flash of sparks on the ground at the bottom of the stairs told Ryan the men behind him had been given the all-clear to use lethal force by whoever the hell was controlling them. Of course Ryan had no idea why these men were trying to kill him. He and his mates had stumbled onto something big here in their tail of Colin Hazelton, but Jack didn't have time to think about it now. He had to get out of the line of fire.

A satellite dish stuck out from a second-floor balcony at the bottom of the long flight of concrete steps. It was eye level in front of him now, but if Jack wanted to grab hold of it he'd have to make a running jump of nearly fifteen feet. Jack leapt off the stairs, using the momentum of his run, the kicking of his legs in the open air, and his high position on the staircase to give him as much distance as possible.

His hands just grasped the metal arm of the four-foot-wide satellite dish, his legs swung out below him from the momentum as if he were an Olympian on the horizontal bar.

The two riders on their bikes raced down the staircase below him. When they reached the parking lot at the bottom of the steps, they spun around on their front wheels to face him. Their tires screeched in unison.

Jack's legs had gone horizontal to the ground during

his swing on the sat dish's arm, but he was unable to kick high enough to climb up on the balcony. Instead, he swung back down, tried to pull himself up to take hold of the metal balcony railing.

Suddenly the mount for the arm gave way under the strain of Ryan's weight, tearing off from the balcony railing and breaking free, attached only by a thick band of wiring.

Jack dropped ten feet to the steps below. The satellite dish fell part of the way with him but was then caught by the wiring. Jack landed well initially but then tumbled forward and down the steps, ending up dazed on his back in the parking lot, just twenty feet from the bikers.

Jack looked up at the armed men. The bikers glanced at one another quickly, as if to marvel at their luck, then one man raised his pistol.

But before he could fire a bearded man dressed in black appeared on his right at a sprint, slamming into him like a linebacker making a tackle in the open field, and knocking both the rider from his bike and the gun from his hand.

The second helmeted man on the other Ducati spun his arm around toward the movement, but the bearded man – he was clearly a Westerner – swung his backpack off, hurled it overhand, and it connected with the biker's firing arm, knocking it down. A gunshot ripped through the night, the entire parking lot exploded with an instant of light, and the biker fell back onto the pavement. He rolled quickly to his knees, but before he could stand the bearded man was on him, kicking him once in the visor of his helmet. The padded ballistic plastic absorbed the impact, but the blow torqued his neck back and he fell hard onto his back, slamming his head onto the unyielding surface of the parking lot and knocking him out cold.

Sam Driscoll was glad he was wearing his big Salomon boots this evening. Otherwise he was sure he would have broken his foot on the helmet of the prostrate man in front of him. Still, the top of his foot hurt like hell from the impact.

He'd been running full out for five minutes, with only a couple breaks to slow in order to check Ryan's GPS locator on the map on his mobile phone. Now that both threats were down and Ryan was safe, Sam kicked his foot out to shake away the pain, picked his backpack up off the ground, and began looking for some zip ties to restrain the two attackers.

'Thanks,' Ryan said, still looking at the men on the ground.

Sam wasn't reveling in his handiwork at all. Between gasps for breath he said, 'Asshole shot my backpack. The camera and spotting scope belonged to the company, but the tablet computer in here is mine. Took a round right through the screen.' He looked to Ryan. 'You gonna buy me another?'

Ryan had his hands on his knees; he was still heaving from the action of the past few minutes. He managed a laugh. 'Sure, man. I owe you an iPad. If you want I'll throw in –'

Ding Chavez's voice came over the network now. 'Clark? Hazelton is down and critical! I need wheels. Now!'

As one, both Jack and Sam hefted pistols off the pavement, left the two unconscious men where they lay, and leapt on the downed Ducatis.

Sirens filled the air in the distance as they began racing back to help Chavez.

Seconds earlier, Ding Chavez rounded the corner of a building at a full sprint only to find a large man crawling in the middle of a dark and otherwise empty two-lane street. He recognized the white shirt and bald head of Colin Hazelton, and he raced over to him. 'Come on, Hazelton! Let's move!'

Ding tried to help the man back to his feet, but Hazelton could not put weight on his legs.

Ding heard the hissing sound of air leaving the man's lungs. The back of the ex – CIA officer's shirt was soaked in blood. It took another second to find the wounds, but through tiny tears in the shirt his fingers felt the damaged flesh. Ding ripped Hazelton's shirt open, exposing the man's back and the pair of small, deep slit punctures below his shoulder blades.

'Shit,' Ding said. He knew all about deep injuries to the torso. Holding pressure on these two holes would do nothing for Hazelton, because he was bleeding internally, and his deflated lungs were far away from the surface wounds on the skin. They were behind the rib cage, spurting blood and functioning at ten percent efficiency at best. Ding needed to seal the holes and try to reinflate the lungs.

While still on his knees in the middle of the dark street, he reached into his backpack and retrieved a tiny black pouch. It wasn't much, just a personal first-aid kit that each man on the team carried with him at all times. From it Ding pulled a pair of occlusive dressings, ripped them out of their packaging with his mouth. He used his fore-arm to wipe blood away from the sucking wounds, then he affixed a dressing over each hole. He pressed them firmly on the skin, knowing he needed to completely seal the breach before he could do anything else.

Chavez rolled the man onto his back. He saw Hazelton's eyes were open and unfixed. Hurriedly he performed rescue breathing, more commonly known as mouth-to-mouth, trying to get enough lung function going to keep the man's blood oxygenated.

He stopped only long enough to shout over the commo net. 'Clark? Hazelton is down and critical! I need wheels. Now!'

Clark responded quickly. 'I'm on the way!'

'Are you clear of the opposition?' Clark asked.

Ding started to reply in the affirmative, but he looked up when a single headlight appeared far up the street. It wasn't moving, but he heard the revving engine of a finely tuned motorcycle.

'Negative,' he said. 'At least one of the bikers is back. Probably trying to figure out how help showed up so fast.' Ding could run, but he didn't want to leave Colin Hazelton here in the middle of the road. The man needed attention this second. Without someone to keep his heart beating he wasn't going to make it more than a minute.

Jack Ryan, Jr., came over the net. 'Jack and Sam coming to you with bikes and guns. Find some cover till we get there, Ding.'

But Ding stayed right where he was in the middle of the road, continuing the rescue breathing, a valiant attempt to keep Hazelton's heart beating.

The motorcycle lurched forward and began heading up the street in his direction.

After five breaths Ding transmitted while listening to Hazelton's mouth for sounds to confirm the man was still breathing on his own. 'Biker heading my way. I don't know what this guy's going to do, but if I run, Hazelton's dead.'

Clark said, 'I'll be there in twenty seconds.'

Ding watched the approaching headlight. It passed under a street lamp at the intersection three blocks away. In the light he saw a black Ducati and the biker was holding something out in front of him, pointed at Chavez and Hazelton in the middle of the road.

Ding spoke softly, a twinge of resignation in his voice. 'Ten would be better.'

Chavez was unarmed. His mission had been to ascertain just what a former mid-level CIA exec was doing here in Vietnam. Moving through the country with firearms didn't seem prudent, considering the threat matrix.

It was clear now, however, *that* had been the wrong call.

The bike raced up the street, approaching the intersection at speed; the rider kept his pistol out in front of him, aiming it at Chavez.

He fired, a flash of light and the gun's recoil snapped it up. Chavez could only drop low to the pavement, tucking over Colin Hazelton. He felt the round pass just high.

Another shot sparked the pavement just to Ding's left. He began chest compressions now, but he felt sure that as the attacker closed on his bike, the next shot would find its mark.

Ding saw the pistol level again, and he saw no way out of this. He was about to take a round.

A gray four-door sedan raced into the intersection from the east, its headlights off and its engine screaming at full throttle. The man on the Ducati sensed the movement on his left and turned to look a half-second before impact; he pulled his gun arm back in and tried to turn the motorcycle, but before he could take any evasive action at all he was flattened by the sedan. Sparks and wreckage arced into the air, smoke billowed in all directions at the point of impact.

The biker was crushed under the sedan. His helmet bounced down the street. Ding was reasonably sure there was no head inside the helmet, but he could not be certain. The impact had certainly been violent enough.

Chavez winced but immediately went back to giving Hazelton mouth-to-mouth.

The sedan came to rest just as Ryan and Driscoll appeared behind Chavez on the two Ducatis. They climbed off the bikes, helped their teammate to his feet, scooped Hazelton up by his arms and legs, and then carried him to the sedan.

John Clark waited behind the wheel. His airbag had deployed and his windshield was cracked across the entire length of the glass, but the vehicle remained operational.

Sam climbed in front, and Jack and Ding pulled Hazelton into the backseat with them. Clark took off before the doors were closed; behind them sirens neared and flashing lights reflected off wet streets and the window glass of apartment buildings.

Clark called out to the men behind him, 'Anyone hurt?'

Ding said, 'Just Hazelton.'

'Is he going to live?'

Ding made eye contact with John in the rearview, and he shook his head. But he said, 'Let's get him to a hospital.'

The intimation was clear from the tone in his voice. Nobody was going to save Hazelton at this point, but they had to try.

Driscoll was already on the phone to his organization's Gulfstream jet. 'Sherman, Driscoll. En route to airport, ETA twenty-five mikes. Four pax in total. In extremis exfiltration, negative contraband. Negative injuries. Threat condition red. Confirm all.'

Over the phone Adara Sherman, the transportation and logistics coordinator for the team, repeated everything back to the operator in the field and let him know the aircraft would be ready for them when they got to the airport.

The men were quiet for a moment, the main sound in the sedan coming from the heavy breathing of exhausted men and the chest compressions Chavez continued on Hazelton's thick torso, as well as the soft wheezes coming out of the wounded man's mouth and nose. Foamy blood had formed on the ex – CIA man's lips, and this told Chavez the internal bleeding in the lungs was as bad as he'd feared.

Ding had called this one correctly. Hazelton wasn't going to make it.

As Chavez looked down at the man he was surprised to see Hazelton's eyes open. Beneath a thin wheeze he made another sound, like he was trying to form words.

Chavez leaned over closer. 'What's that?'

Hazelton tried again. 'Sh . . . Sharps.'

Chavez nodded quickly. 'We know. You were working for Duke Sharps. Do you know who attacked you?'

Hazelton nodded emphatically, did his best to speak again, but just a pathetic croaking rasp came out of his mouth.

His arm reached out and began flailing around the backseat.

Ryan figured out what he was doing. 'He wants a pen. Hurry!'

Driscoll found a pad and pen in the glove compartment and he passed them back. Ding held the pad for Hazelton, who took the pen and began furiously scratching with it. It was too dark to discern the writing here in the sedan, but Ding was able to see that all the blood on the man's palm was also smearing the page.

In fifteen seconds Hazelton stopped. The pen fell from his hand and his head lolled to the side.

Ding put two fingers on the man's carotid artery. After a half-minute he said, 'John . . . to the airport.'

'Got it,' said Clark, then he turned at the next intersection. No use wasting time on a hospital drop-off now.

Chavez collapsed back in his seat, the dead man lying across his and Ryan's laps. For the past ten minutes Chavez had worked as hard as he could to save the man, even risking his life to do so. Now he was wasted and worn out, both mentally and physically, from the strain of his efforts.

Ryan took the pad and held his flashlight's beam up to it. 'Fucking chicken scratch.'

Clark said, 'Let's worry about that when we're wheels up.'

43

4

Veronika Martel took one more glance into her rearview mirror before turning her two-door Hyundai through the gates of the safe house. She'd checked the traffic behind her one hundred times during her drive; it was hard enough to do in the dark, but since the rain began a few minutes earlier, identifying any vehicles that might be following her had become all but impossible. Still, she told herself she was clean, she'd seen not a hint of a tail during her circuitous drive from central Ho Chi Minh City to Thu Duc, so she pulled up the drive of the two-story villa with little concern for her operational security.

A gravel parking circle sat to the side entrance of the villa and she took advantage of this, turning around to position her Hyundai so it was facing the road and ready for a fast escape. Martel was aware of no specific threats, but she was operational, and this sort of tradecraft was second nature to her.

It had been an hour and a half since meeting with the American at the Lion d'Or in Ho Chi Minh City. Thu Duc was only a dozen miles from the city center, but she'd been running a long surveillance detection route, stretched even longer by her control officer's orders to take her time.

She sat in the Hyundai in the parking circle, listening to the rain on the roof of the vehicle. She could have gone inside the villa but she decided against it, since going inside would have entailed being around others, making small talk with people who were neither friends nor family while she waited for a call from her control officer. Martel had no interest in this. She wasn't particularly friendly, and she most certainly could not be characterized as chatty. So she sat alone, enjoyed the patter of rain on the roof, and focused her thoughts.

North Korea. Christ.

She closed her eyes and leaned her head back against the headrest.

Have you really fallen this far?

Veronika Martel was thirty-eight years old, an employee of Sharps Global Intelligence Partners of New York City. Duke Sharps had headhunted her after she left DGSE, the Direction Générale de la Sécurité Extérieure, French foreign intelligence, where she had spent more than a decade working as a case officer in embassies in the Middle East and Europe.

Now she was based at Sharps Partners' European satellite office in Brussels, but her work in the corporate intelligence field took her all over the globe. In the past six months she'd served on operations in Mumbai, in Osaka, in Moscow, and in Madrid.

And now Vietnam. Ho Chi Minh City was unfamiliar turf for her, but Veronika went where New York told her to go, and this assignment was similar to ops she had done in Europe. Or at least it had been until her contact this evening made the unilateral decision to derail the operation by not handing over the documents he'd been tasked to bring with him from Prague.

She'd reported him to her New York control officer immediately – she wasn't going to take the blame for the op falling apart. New York told her to head back to the safe house, but to take her time doing so, while they did what they could to rectify the situation.

Short of arranging a street mugging to get the package from Hazelton, she didn't know what the hell her control officer in New York could do about it, but she did as ordered.

As she sat with her eyes closed her phone chirped, the sound louder than the pattering rain on the roof of the Hyundai. *'Oui?'*

'This is control. I'm connecting you to a local agent.'

Local agent? As far as she knew, Veronika Martel was the only Sharps employee in the area other than the pretentious bald-headed American who had ruined her evening.

There was a delay on the line, then a heavily accented Asian voice came over the speaker. 'I have the package. I will be arriving at your safe house in five minutes.'

She felt certain the man was North Korean. Not a local agent, but an interested party in her mission nonetheless. She knew better than to ask any questions.

'I'll be here,' she said.

The man quickly asked, 'Was he alone when you met with him?'

'The contact? I only presume so. It was not in my brief to establish whether or not he had any coverage on him. Why do you ask?'

'Five minutes,' came the non-response to her question, and the line went dead.

Veronika climbed out of her little Hyundai and walked up to the front door. She had a key to the villa, she'd been living here for several days, but she knocked on the door nonetheless, as per the arrangement. She waited for a moment on the porch, then heard the door unlock from the inside.

She was met by a North Korean. He was one of three security men who had been watching over the occupants of the safe house. Again, not Sharps employees, but interested parties in the operation. The three men had kept their distance from her, and she from them. This one said nothing at the door, she was certain he spoke neither English nor French, and he left the entryway, heading back into the living room.

Veronika folded her umbrella and hung her coat, then she stood alone, looking out the window at the rain, waiting to see headlights in the driveway.

Her plan was to avoid the others until the package arrived, but after a few minutes she decided that as much as she didn't want to get into a conversation with anyone right now, it was her responsibility to check on the subjects of her work here in Vietnam.

She walked into the living room and found the three security officers standing along the wall behind four men and one woman, who sat on sofas and chairs. These five were all Caucasian; they looked straight at her as she entered the room, their faces illuminated by candlelight. Even in the amber glow Martel saw the apprehension in their eyes.

She felt obligated to make some remarks to calm the group down. In English she said, 'Everything is in order.

47

I am waiting for a visitor to arrive, and then we will proceed.'

Before anyone spoke, there was a knock at the front door. The three security men looked up and started toward the entryway, but Martel waved them back into their places and went herself.

She opened the door to find a man in a black motorcycle jacket. He was Asian; she assumed he was North Korean like the others, but she sure as hell was not going to ask.

The man carried a folder in his hand. He held it out and said, 'You saw no one?'

She took the folder. 'You already asked me this. What is wrong? What happened?'

She looked past him and into the parking circle. Two men sat in the rain on motorcycles. A third bike, presumably belonging to the man in front of her, was parked alongside them.

The North Korean stepped into the entryway and shut the door. 'The American had men with him. We were not notified of this.'

'Nor was I. As I said before, it wasn't my job to identify surveillance.' The man did not seem satisfied with her answer, so she added, 'Call New York if you'd like to make a complaint about my performance.'

The North Korean's nostrils flared. Martel presumed he wasn't accustomed to being spoken to like this, but she couldn't care less. She ignored the man's glare and began looking through the folder. Inside she found five smaller manila folders. Opening them one at a time, she fanned through five complete sets of documents: EU diplomatic passports. Czech diplomatic assignments to Pyongyang. Credit cards bound with rubber bands.

She returned to the living room; the North Korean in the black jacket followed behind. Veronika looked at the photo page of each passport and each visa, and she took her time to match the documents to the five sitting in front of her. They sat quietly, nervously waiting for her to say something, but she did not rush herself.

All the documents looked perfect, except for the last of the passports. The cover appeared to be stained with red ink. Martel ran a thumb over the embossed cover and she realized the color was no stain, as it came off easily.

Looking at her thumb, she saw it was fresh blood.

Mon Dieu, she said to herself. These men had taken these by force from the American agent.

She glanced up at the North Korean. His eyes remained on her – surely he had seen her notice the blood. She thought he was enjoying her discomfort.

'Everything is in order,' Veronika Martel said. The North Korean left without another word, and within moments she heard three motorcycles firing up and driving off.

Martel put the documents on a table and moved a lamp closer. To the entire group she said, 'Your flight leaves at nine-thirty a.m., arriving in Pyongyang at eleven thirty-five. I'll go over your legends with each of you, and then you should try to get a few hours' sleep. I will wake everyone at six.'

The one other female in the house, a redhead in her forties, stood up from the sofa and approached. Her

49

Australian accent was obvious. 'Would you mind it if I spoke to you in private?'

Veronika Martel just shrugged and moved into the kitchen. The woman followed. She was much shorter and a little heavier than Martel, and the lighting here did her no favors. Martel thought the redhead looked as if she hadn't slept in days. It had been rough for all five of the Australians, she knew, as she had been with them all week.

The French intelligence agent said, 'What can I do for you, Dr. Powers?'

The Australian closed the door all the way. She spoke softly. 'Look. I . . . we agreed to come. The money was incredible, obviously, but it seemed like an adventure, you know?'

'What is your question?'

'I left a family behind back in Sydney. Six months' work, and I'm back home. That's what was agreed on.'

Martel put a hand out on the counter, strummed her perfect nails on the tiled surface.

Dr. Powers continued, 'I . . . I just want to make sure the terms promised me are honored.'

Martel made no attempt to whisper. 'Dr. Powers, my job is to facilitate your clandestine travel safely from Sydney to Pyongyang. Nothing more. Whatever agreement you have with the DPRK, it is between yourself and the DPRK.'

Powers looked to the door to the living room nervously. 'I don't trust them. They watch over us like we are prisoners. They won't answer my questions. I just thought . . . you are working with them. Can you help me?

Maybe just ask them to be a little more forthcoming about the arrangements in place. Please?'

Martel took her hand from the counter next to her and placed it on the smaller woman's shoulder. With a little smile she said, 'Doctor. I understand.'

The older redhead looked relieved. 'I knew you would.'

'I understand that the fact I am female and I have round eyes, to you, means I should be more sympathetic than the North Korean men acting as security here. But nothing could be further from the truth. *They* have use for you, *I* do not.' She lowered her hand and headed for the door. 'When you get to Pyongyang, I'm sure your concerns will be alleviated.'

Powers all but shouted, 'Do you have any idea how ridiculous that statement sounds?'

Martel was unfazed by the redhead's anger. 'I didn't agree to work for the North Koreans. *You* did. Your decision is made, and you would do well to make peace with that decision, because they are not going to allow you to change your mind at this juncture.' She returned to the living room without another word.

As she passed out the documents and went over the individual legends for each of the five, she let herself wonder what would happen to these Australians. Working with the North Koreans certainly would be fraught with legitimate concern, but she expected all five of them to fulfill their contract with Pyongyang and to return home much wealthier than when they left. It was, of course, illegal work, and they were being paid with this in mind.

Martel knew very little about what these five would be doing for North Korea, but even so, she wasn't worried about this operation from any sort of a moral standpoint. It wasn't as if these people were nuclear scientists or rocket scientists. They were geologists, that was all. No threat to anyone, certainly, even if they were working for the North Koreans. No, this was just some industrial commercial and diplomatic subterfuge, nothing dangerous.

And then she paused for a moment, thinking about the blood on the passport and the annoying American who had no doubt shed it. If the North Koreans were willing to use violence in a foreign nation to secure the travel of these geologists, perhaps the stakes were higher than she thought.

She pushed the misgivings out of her mind, a skill she had developed and honed over her intelligence career.

Right now she just wanted to get these five on the nine-thirty flight tomorrow morning to Pyongyang, to sanitize the safe house, and then to go home.

Nothing else mattered to Veronika Martel.

5

The dented gray sedan carrying the four Campus operators and the body of ex – CIA officer Colin Hazelton pulled into the hangar of the fixed-base operator at the far east end of Tan Son Nhat airport just after one a.m.

The sole aircraft in the hangar, a sleek, white Gulfstream G550, had already been unplugged from its APU by the ground crew, who had conspicuously disappeared as the car approached the loading stairs.

As the men climbed out of the vehicle an attractive woman stepped out of the office of the fixed-base operator. Her blond hair was pulled into a neat bun, and her generic flight attendant's uniform was perfectly pressed.

Adara Sherman was officially the flight coordinator for the Campus G550, but this was just one of her many duties. She also provided security to the aircraft, organized every bit of travel for the operators in her organization, dealt with customs issues, and performed other duties as required.

Clark stepped up to Sherman as soon as he climbed out from behind the wheel. 'Good to see you again.'

'You, too, Mr Clark.'

'What's the situation?'

'We're fine. Customs is dealt with, the ground crew and office personnel are giving us some space.'

'I assume that cost a small fortune.'

'Discretion comes cheaper here than in some other places. Can I help with the body?'

'We'll handle him. Just let the flight crew know we needed to be out of the country an hour ago, so anything they can do to expedite will be appreciated.'

Sherman headed for the stairs.

Driscoll and Ryan carried the body of Colin Hazelton onto the plane while Clark and Chavez stood guard at the entrance to the hangar, making sure no personnel from the FBO or the airport made the mistake of taking a peek into the hangar during this critical moment of exposure.

Adara had already placed a body bag on the floor of the cabin. The presence of several ready-to-go body bags in the cargo hold of the G550 was a grim reminder to the operators of The Campus that the work they did was high stakes, but this was the first time one of the bags had been put to use. Hazelton's body was zipped inside, then he was placed into a hidden compartment built between the rear bulkhead and the cargo hold. It was specifically designed to hide a full-sized man, but it was just barely large enough for this role. Each of the operators had tested it out, and it had even been used operationally to hide one of the men during immigration and customs inspections.

All agreed that the person who customized the compartment had done so with no plans to put it to personal use.

Hazelton had no complaints, however.

When all were on board and the hatch sealed, the pilots began taxiing toward the tarmac. Slowly at first, but soon they began expediting their departure off the nearly empty runway, and they were airborne in minutes.

*

54

Shortly after leveling off, Adara served the men coffee, juice, and water. Clark sat alone up at the bulkhead, and here he called Gerry Hendley, the director of The Campus and the owner of the jet. While he drank coffee, Clark carefully filled him in on everything that had happened.

Soon the entire team converged around the teak table in the center of the aircraft, and together they inspected the note Colin Hazelton had scribbled seconds before succumbing to his wounds. Both Clark and Chavez wore reading glasses, but even with their corrected vision it was hard to make out the writing. It was clear there were only four words in total on the page, one word alone, and then below it, two more. Then, at the bottom, four more letters had been scribbled, badly, almost one on top of the other. The wide blood smear across the chicken scratch only added to the difficulty of discerning Hazelton's penmanship.

Chavez said, 'The first word is four letters, but it's completely obscured by the blood. Not a clue. Below it, there are two words. The first one looks like . . . is that "skata"?'

Clark said, 'That means "shit" in Greek.'

'You speak Greek?' Ryan asked, surprised.

'No, but I had Greeks working for me in Rainbow. Working for me causes a man to cuss, I guess. I heard that one a lot.'

Driscoll turned the sheet his way to look it over, and he leaned even closer. 'It's not "skata." I think it's "skala."'

After everyone looked again, Chavez and Ryan agreed with Driscoll, and Clark gave in to majority rule. 'Okay, "skala." Sounds like a proper name. Central European, maybe?'

Ryan was already at his laptop Googling the word while Adara Sherman refilled his bone-china coffee cup next to him. With excitement he said, 'Got it! It's a town in Poland.' Then, with a voice less enthusiastic, 'Wait. It's also a town in Bulgaria. Shit. There's one in Ukraine, too. Another in the Faroe Islands.'

Driscoll mumbled, 'Well, damn. That's not very helpful.'

Chavez said, 'It might be a person as well. I knew a Hungarian Army captain with that surname, back in CIA. He died in a helo crash fifteen years ago, though. Clark, you know anybody named Skala?'

Clark shook his head. He was concentrating on the next word now. 'What's that? Four letters? Looks like "IATA." All caps.'

Ryan Googled that as well. 'International Air Transport Association. Might just be a coincidence.'

Sherman was pouring orange juice for Chavez. She hadn't said a word during the conversation, because no one had asked her opinion. But she glanced at the page and said, 'Prague.'

The four men turned to look up at her, so she clarified. 'Sorry. It's the ICAO airport code. That's Václav Havel in Prague. Czech Republic.'

Ding said, 'I thought the Prague airport code was PRG.'

Sherman smiled. 'You are thinking of the IATA code that's used commercially, what you see on your ticket or when you book a flight. The ICAO is what pilots use.'

Ding looked at her doubtfully, but Clark buttressed her claim.

'Hazelton *was* a pilot. He was ex – Air Force and held a multi-engine private pilot's license.'

Ryan said, 'Skala could be a Czech name. Maybe if we go to Václav Havel Airport in Prague and start looking around for a guy named Skala, we will get lucky.'

Clark said, 'For now we are heading back to DC. The first item on our agenda after returning is to sit down with a certain someone and find out everything she knows about this. After that we'll decide how we are going to proceed.'

Clark held the note close to his face to look at the last scribble, down at the bottom of the page. After a few seconds he nodded, then tossed it on the table. 'Hazelton's last note tells us there is trouble ahead, boys.'

The others looked the note over. It was clear to all of them.

DPRK.

Sam took the words out of the others' mouths. 'I hate those guys.'

The Gulfstream flew northeast toward the dawn, the four men in back trying to catch as much sleep as possible because to a man they expected the events of the previous evening were merely the beginning, and more trouble lay ahead.

6

One year earlier

For as many of the twenty-eight years Choi Ji-hoon could remember, he had been surrounded by those who told him he would someday lead his nation. Most of those people were sycophants, though he'd never heard such a term. He knew these people only as unimportant. Still, he believed them. He believed them because his father, the only person who mattered, had told him the same thing. Choi Li-hung explained to his son, Choi Ji-hoon, that someday he would die, and when that happened, young Ji-hoon would replace him to become the Supreme Leader of North Korea.

Ji-hoon's father promised his son he would rule, but he did not reveal to his son that he had absolutely no faith in his ability to do so. Choi the father thought his son to be weak and lazy and not exceptionally smart, and he considered him the biggest sycophant of all. By the age of twenty-two, young Ji-hoon had become a party official, and his one duty involved traveling around North Korea commissioning works of art to commemorate historical events in the nation. Ji-hoon turned this job into a vehicle by which he could suck up to his father. Every single painting and statue Ji-hoon ordered created was of Choi Li-hung, a blatant way to curry favor and earn his succession.

But Choi the father felt he had no choice. He did not want to bequeath his nation to one of his brothers; they all had sons of their own and Li-hung refused to allow his nephews to lead the DPRK for the cynical reason that by doing so he would decrease his own legacy to future generations. His other children were all daughters, and it was out of the question a woman would lead North Korea.

This left succession to Choi Ji-hoon. The weak and lazy one was the only heir suitable to reign over the nation. He knew his son would not be a good steward of the DPRK, but in the end continuing the authority of the bloodline, and therefore his own immortality, was more important to Choi Li-hung than the lives of the twenty-five million citizens under his rule.

Choi Li-hung did little to prepare his country for his son's reign. His one nod to his son's incompetence was his insistence that Ji-hoon take power with six of Li-hung's advisers as his personal council. These men had been with Li-hung throughout his twenty-year rule; one of them, his foreign minister, was a brother. Li-hung knew putting remnants of his regime in his son's administration was no substitute for a competent Supreme Leader, but he thought it might save the nation from the utter destruction Ji-hoon might cause on his own.

And then it happened. When Choi Ji-hoon was twenty-seven years old his father died, and he became the Supreme Leader of North Korea. At first his six advisers effectively ruled while Ji-hoon reveled in his newfound power – power brought on not only by his job title, but by the fact his father was no longer around to scrutinize his every move. Ji-hoon spent money even more lavishly than he had before; new statues and paintings all bore his own face now, he commissioned parks and sports stadiums and monuments in his name, and he smuggled in luxury goods by the shipload, even while famine raged across the rural reaches of the DPRK.

But Choi Ji-hoon changed in the months after his ascendency. He grew less interested in debauchery and more consumed by a paranoia brought on by all the attention on him. On the one-year anniversary of his father's death, Choi Ji-hoon decided he needed to assert his own authority, to exert more control over all matters of state.

Nothing to him was more important than his relationship with the military, because they held the key to his survival. While his father had been called 'Dear Leader' by his subjects, Choi Ji-hoon demanded to be called Dae Wonsu, or grand marshal, signifying him as the commander of all armed forces in the nation. Although he'd spent no time in the military other than a four-week 'white-glove' program for the sons of party leaders, his biography was quickly rewritten, claiming him to be a bomber pilot who'd safely crash-landed a crippled aircraft on a highway to save his crew, and a Special Forces paratrooper who had led thirty-three covert missions into South Korea to rescue North Koreans kidnapped and sold into slavery in the South.

These exploits were taught in schools, songs were written about the events, and television and radio documentaries featured interviews with his supposed fellow soldiers and airmen.

That every bit of the Dae Wonsu's military history was bullshit was never uttered by anyone who knew the facts, because those who knew the facts also knew that the fiction was more im-portant than the facts, and maintaining the fiction would be done at the expense of the lives of anyone who disputed it.

Ji-hoon's father had been no dove – hardly. Li-hung had killed tens of thousands of his own countrymen through executions and imposed famine, and he brought the Korean Peninsula to the brink of war multiple times by firing artillery on South Korea. But Choi Ji-hoon distinguished himself by becoming even more hawkish. He pushed for the purchase and development of new weapons systems and he ordered provocative training operations on the border. He test-fired missiles that flew over the sovereign territory of his neighbors and his Korean Central Television station broadcast threats to South Korea, the United States, and Japan on a near-daily basis.

Ji-hoon's muscle flexing did not just take place on the world stage. As he grew into his role over time, he exerted more and more domestic power, and he took that power away from the six men his father had left behind. Any pushback by the six was seen as a direct menace to his reign, and Ji-hoon's growing paranoia about threats at home and abroad all but made it inevitable he would eliminate his council of advisers.

Within a month of this decision five of the council had been executed for myriad imagined crimes against the state. Getting rid of the sixth man, however, had proved more difficult. Choi Sang-u was Ji-hoon's uncle and a seventy-year-old diplomat who had served as his father's foreign minister. After his father's death Ji-hoon made

Sang-u ambassador to China, a step down from the nation's top diplomat but still an important posting, especially considering China's close relationship to North Korea. The two nations were allies, though less so now, because China had been frustrated by young Ji-hoon's saber rattling. The last thing China wanted or needed was a destabilized Korean Peninsula, after all, so China's relationship with its neighbor had cooled precipitously.

Other than some trade with China and a few other nations on a much smaller scale, the economy of North Korea was effectively closed. Ninety-five percent of all goods produced in the nation were created by state-owned firms.

Still, China was the North's largest trading partner, and China had no greater industrial influence than in the mining sector because it had long been known by the Chinese that North Korea's real value lay under its dirt.

Everything changed in the relationship between the two nations when a group of Chinese geologists working in North Korea revealed they had found deposits of valuable rare earth minerals in the mountains in the northwest of the nation. The North Koreans had hundreds of mining contracts with the Chinese, together they dug coal, iron, silver, and nickel, but this rare earth find was exceptional. The geologists dug test mines and their proclamations became more and more optimistic.

Finally it was decided by the Chinese that the world's largest find of rare earth minerals, some 213 tons in all, was likely buried near Chongju, under the rolling hills of Pyongan-bukto Province near the coastline of Korea Bay.

The Chinese state-owned mining company was given

rights to develop the deposits for twenty-five years, the paperwork was signed, and they began building up the infrastructure in the area necessary for the work.

And then, after one year of hard but productive work, Choi Ji-hoon ordered his uncle, the ambassador to China, home for consultations. He explained to his uncle that the newfound wealth the Chinese had promised was all very well and good, but the Chinese had something that was even more important to North Korea than wealth.

Ji-hoon's uncle was confused. 'What do they have, Dae Wonsu?'

'They have the technology we need.'

The uncle brightened. 'Yes. All the newest drilling equipment has been brought in already. The computers that maximize productivity are being installed as we speak. When the mine goes on line next year we will –'

'I am not talking about mining technology, Uncle. I am speaking of missile technology.'

'Missiles?'

'Of course. The Chinese have been reluctant to share with us their expertise for mid-range and long-range intercontinental ballistic missiles. I want the expertise. I want North Korea to develop its own domestic long-range rocket industry, and China is the key to this.'

Ji-hoon's uncle nodded slowly, looking off into space as if he were intrigued by his brilliant nephew's scheme. 'Are you saying we only continue the rare earth mining partnership if China supplies us with ICBMs?'

Choi Ji-hoon said, 'Exactly that, Uncle.'

The uncle had known his nephew for his entire life. That he had to couch his words carefully to him, just as he had his brother, was still odd, but he knew what was good for him. 'I think this is wise and shrewd diplomacy on your part, Dae Wonsu. I only wish the Chinese shared your brilliance. I am afraid that the Chinese diplomats are unrealistic, and they might jeopardize the lucrative mining operation if they refuse our reasonable request.'

Ji-hoon waved the comment away as if it were a trifling concern. 'You have excellent relations with the *gang-jae*.' It was a derogatory word for Chinese, akin to calling them Chinks. Ji-hoon's uncle fought back a wince. 'You must see that they do not refuse, Uncle.'

The negotiations happened in Pyongyang; several of China's top leaders came, hats in hand, ready to offer almost anything to continue the rare earth mining contract with North Korea.

Almost anything.

When Choi's negotiators explained the Chinese contract would be invalidated if they did not provide the DPRK with a ballistic missile manufacturing center, including the materials and the expertise to run it, the Chinese went home to Beijing, spoke with the Central Committee in secret, and returned. They offered more food, more money, *more* conventional weaponry, marine military technology on par with China's own Navy. They offered expanded trade rights, and better terms on China's processing of the rare earth minerals after extraction. They offered high-profile diplomatic official visits by the Chinese leader to increase North Korea's cachet on the world stage, and they extended invitations for Choi to come to China as a guest of the president.

But Choi had not been raised in a manner conducive to

producing a diplomat. He'd been given virtually everything he wanted since birth; those around him knew crossing him could be punishable by death. He was therefore a truly awful negotiator. He was intractable, inflexible, and impatient.

Choi rejected it all. He wanted the means to deliver a nuclear device to the United States. In his mind it was the only way to be safe from attack and assassination.

China refused to allow the DPRK access to the technology to create their own long-range ICBMS. It wasn't that China was trying to protect the United States, far from it. It was simply that China realized what North Korea would do once they had the most dangerous and most valuable bargaining chip in international affairs. They might or might not use the device, but the death of millions of Americans in nuclear fire was of lesser concern to the Chinese than the certainty that the ostracized pariah North Korea would exercise their newfound power on the world stage recklessly and threaten the region.

The destabilization of the Korean Peninsula was hardly in China's self-interest.

One month to the day after the negotiations for the Chongju mine began in Pyongyang, the Chinese were notified that every Chinese national at the mine had seventy-two hours to leave the country. The executives of Minmetals and Chinalco, China's state-owned mining operators, tried to reason with the North Koreans, but no North Korean official dared read any flexibility in Choi's demand where none existed. The Chinese at Chongju rushed out of the country, leaving much of their equipment behind, though the Chinese geologists and engineers had done a remarkable job getting as much of it out of the DPRK as possible.

The open-pit mine went dormant overnight despite Choi's demand to the director of the government's mining arm, Korea Natural Resources Trading Corporation, to keep the mine open and operational.

The truth was the North Koreans had neither the equipment nor the know-how to operate a rare earth mineral mine on their own. On top of that, the Chinese had taken their generators with them, and the power lines into Chongju were inadequate for the operation.

The director of the mining concern explained all this calmly and carefully to Choi Ji-hoon, and this candor benefitted him greatly.

He was only thrown into a labor camp. He wasn't executed.

There was one more piece of fallout from the Chinese rare earth mine negotiations. Choi had decided that his uncle, North Korea's ambassador to China, had not been an honest broker in the affair. He held him personally responsible for the breakdown in negotiations with the Chinese, although it was Ji-hoon's own uncompromising demands that had doomed the negotiations.

His uncle, his father's brother, a man who could have ruled the DPRK had the cards been dealt differently, was relieved of his position and thrown into the internment camp at Chongjin in the northeast of the nation.

7

Present day

President of the United States Jack Ryan stepped out of the Oval Office while slipping on his suit coat. He passed through his secretary's office and entered the adjacent cabinet room as he fixed his lapel and straightened his tie. In front of him he found a dozen men and women already waiting for his three p.m. meeting, and they stood as he appeared, but he waved them back to their seats quickly as he sat down at the head of the table and reached for a cup of coffee already positioned there for him.

His wife, Cathy, wasn't crazy about his afternoon cup, but his blood pressure had been so good during his last checkup he'd successfully negotiated five ounces of black Jamaican light roast five days a week.

And Ryan was especially proud of this diplomatic coup.

He looked around to confirm the attendance of the usual suspects for most meetings involving national security: Secretary of State Scott Adler, CIA director Jay Canfield, Director of National Intelligence Mary Pat Foley, National Security Adviser Joleen Robillio, and Secretary of Defense Bob Burgess all sat near Ryan at the northern end of the table and, farther away, more men and women of the military, intelligence community, and

Department of State sat with papers and tablet computers in front of them.

Also in attendance was Arnie Van Damm, Ryan's chief of staff. Arnie wasn't a national security official, but he, more than anyone else, had the President's ear, and he had the President's stopwatch. He had a lot of control over who got face time with Jack Ryan, and for this reason Ryan wanted him in important meetings of national security so Arnie could have an understanding of the stakes and give those involved in any crisis the access they needed to the Chief Executive. Ryan had heard of other Presidents being slaves to the agendas written up by lesser chiefs of staff, with the Girl Scout who sold the most cookies for the year getting more attention than an undersecretary of defense on a day when a world crisis loomed.

Ryan did his share of low-priority meet-and-greets, but he had no problem shooing away the Girl Scouts when he needed to give his attention to an impending catastrophe.

This meeting had been on the schedule for a few days; originally the topic had been a series of aggressive troop movements in Russian-held Eastern Ukraine, but Ryan had been given the heads-up this morning that the troubles in Central Europe would have to take a backseat today in favor of an even more pressing crisis. Ryan caught himself wishing the problems he faced on the world stage would all line up and approach in single file, but he'd been involved in government work for decades, and he knew emergencies preferred attacking simulta-neously along a wide and coordinated front.

Ryan had learned through experience that good leadership meant staying versatile, flexible, and ready to put out fires as they flared, and the last-minute changeup that had been called for in today's meeting was just one more example.

He'd also learned to do his homework; he wasn't walking into this meeting unprepared. He'd spent most of the last hour reading through National Intelligence Estimates and briefing books and even some raw intel on the crisis du jour.

Intelligence intercepts had determined days ago that North Korea was fueling a long-range rocket, a version of its most advanced ICBM, and moving it to its launch pad. They were clearly prepping to launch, likely for a test because their earlier launches of the device had all been unsuccessful. This new test had, quite understandably, caused concern at the White House, and Ryan had been boning up on the North Koreans' technology before the meeting.

As soon as Ryan sat down he said, 'I got word the agenda for today's meeting has been changed, so I guess that means the DPRK launched.'

SecDef Bob Burgess nodded. 'Yes, sir.'

Ryan sighed. 'Give me the details.'

'Colonel Richard Ward from DIA will brief us, Mr President.'

A tall, thin Army colonel in his forties stood up at the far end of the table. In his hand he held a laser pointer and in front of him was a folio with the seal of his organization, the Defense Intelligence Agency. Sitting next to Ward, a female DIA major controlled with her tablet computer the map and graphics on a large plasma screen on the far wall. The screen showed the entire Korean Peninsula at first, but quickly it zoomed in on the DPRK.

Ward said, 'Good afternoon, Mr President. At twenty-two hundred hours yesterday North Korean time, some six hours ago here in Washington, the DPRK launched an Unha-3, or Galaxy-3 rocket from their Dongchang-dong Launch Station in the northwestern part of the country. This facility is also known as Sohae Satellite Launching Station.'

The screen next showed the hundred-foot-long rocket. 'As you are aware, sir, the DPRK claims the Unha-3 is a space launch vehicle, and while this is technically accurate, it is merely an expendable carrier rocket and therefore virtually identical to the DPRK's most advanced but as yet unproven ICBM, the Taepodong-2.'

Ryan did know all of this. The colonel seemed a little eager and earnest, not intentionally patronizing his President but perhaps unaware of the fact Ryan made a point to know as much of this material as possible as part of his job.

Ryan waved a hand. 'Right. Any sat launch over there is just cover to test an ICBM. The Unha-3 is more than big enough to carry a nuke, and the range estimates say it could deliver a payload as far as Northern California.'

'That's correct, Mr President. *If* the North Koreans have successfully managed to miniaturize a nuclear device. We haven't been able to confirm they have perfected the tech-nology yet, but we suspect they have. The Unha-3 carries a hundred-kilo payload, and you can pack a lot of power into a hundred-kilo device if you have mastered the technology to miniaturize it.'

'Or if you have *stolen* the technology,' Ryan said.

The colonel nodded, though he looked a bit off balance by the comment, because it wasn't part of his briefing.

'Please continue, Colonel Ward,' the President said.

The screen now showed a graphic representation of the launch, and the separation of the first stage of the rocket/missile. 'We had a number of sensors in place to track the launch. Measurement and signature intelligence assets. From this we have put together what happened after the rocket cleared the launch pad. The first stage burned for approximately two minutes, burnout took place at one hundred twenty kilometers altitude over the east coastline of North Korea above the city of Tanchon, and there was good separation. The second-stage burnout occurred at three hundred fifty kilometers over the Sea of Japan. The rocket then apparently malfunctioned before third-stage separation, there was a catastrophic failure, and it crashed into the Sea of Japan, eighty miles west of Sapporo.'

Ryan was more than pleased by the failure, but he knew the diplomatic fallout from Japan would be near equal to the nuclear yield of the device if it had been armed.

Scott Adler was thinking the same thing. 'I'm sure Tokyo isn't too thrilled about the wreckage coming so close to their mainland.'

Jay Canfield replied, 'I'll bet they are pissed. As far as I'm concerned, though, that's better than it plowing into Seattle or San Fran.'

Ryan continued to address Ward. 'Any idea what went wrong?'

'MASINT, that's measurement and signature intelligence, detected an abnormal flare after second-stage burnout but before separation. We will be running tests for some time, but it looks like it was something we call a "staging failure." It is not uncommon, especially for the

DPRK. The last time they launched an Unha-3 they lost it at first-stage separation, so this time they got a little further.'

'What was the duration of the flare?' Ryan asked.

The colonel was obviously surprised by the question. He looked down to his sheet, then quickly began shuffling papers in front of him. The major sitting at her iPad scurried a bit as well, before finding what she was looking for. She pushed a page to Colonel Ward.

'Sorry for the delay, Mr President. The flare lasted approximately two seconds.'

Ryan made a face. 'That sounds a little short to be a staging failure, doesn't it? Normally with stage fail there will be a partial flameout before the explosion. This, to me, sounds like an instantaneous detonation. Maybe the ground control center saw the rocket wasn't going to make it into orbit for some other reason so they aborted. Just pushed a button and blew the ICBM up in flight. Does the Unha-3 have a flight termination system?'

Colonel Ward looked at some more papers. 'Uh . . . we actually do not know the answer to that, Mr President. Their mid-range ballistic missiles do not have flight termination systems, but this ICBM is much larger, so we think they might.'

'They *might*?' Ryan asked. This wasn't the kind of intelligence briefing he liked getting. And from the look on Ward's face, this wasn't the type of intelligence briefing the colonel liked giving.

'I'm sorry, sir. We don't have any hard intelligence that answers the question, one way or the other.'

'The Russians have flight term systems on their mid-range and larger ICBMs, and so do the Chinese. Right?'

'That is correct, Mr President.'

'Well . . . the North Koreans are basing their systems off of Russian and Chinese technology, so it should follow they have a similar setup.'

Ward did not reply.

'Yes or no, Colonel Ward?'

'Well . . . yes. But . . .'

'But *what*?'

'But the North Koreans have taken significant short-cuts with other aspects of the systems they copy. It's possible they did not put any flight termination systems on their Unha-3. We just cannot make a determination with the raw intel we have on the matter.'

Ryan was dissatisfied, but he changed gears. 'Okay. For some reason the missile failed. Let's talk about what happens next time, when it succeeds. Where are we on determining the efficiency of their nuclear weapons?'

Ward thought he was on firmer ground here. 'They have a stockpile of around fifty kilos of weapons-grade plutonium, most of which is disbursed in the existing weapons. They also have uranium enrichment facilities. They have one overt facility at Yongbyon, but we are virtually certain that is just a cover location to show their interest in uranium is for peaceful purposes. They have other clandestine facilities, but the location and efficiency of these are uncertain.' He frowned. 'Another function of our poor intelligence out of the country.'

Director of National Intelligence Mary Pat Foley chimed in. "The most recent nuclear test performed in North

Korea, we think, used uranium and not plutonium, and if this is, in fact, the case, it shows us they are expanding their capabilities.

'They've had three successful underground tests. They've got a plutonium bomb, that is not in doubt. We estimate they have between five and ten devices. The yield is in question, but suffice it to say they are big enough to pose a threat.'

When Foley finished, Ward picked back up. 'As I said before, DIA speculates the DPRK has reached the sophistication for miniaturization of their nuclear weapons to the degree they could, in theory, place a small plutonium-based warhead on one of their Rodong missiles, with a range of one thousand kilometers. If this is, in fact, the case, it isn't too far-fetched to think they could weaponize a longer, intermediate-range rocket.' Ward hastened to add, 'We do think the targeting of the missile would be inaccurate and the efficiency of the warhead to be low.'

Ryan asked, 'How low? What is the estimated accuracy of the Taepo-2?'

'Undetermined. There is a twenty-five percent probability of —'

Ryan interrupted. 'Are we talking accurate to within a few miles, tens of miles, hundreds of miles? Just a general idea.'

Ward looked back down to his page.

Ryan sighed. 'Colonel. You are being too careful. We're just two guys talking here. We didn't bring you in to read the damn paper in front of you, I can read it myself. I need to hear what you know, and what you *think*.'

Ward cleared his throat. 'Yes, sir. We think the Taepodong-2, if successfully deployed, would be accurate to within twenty-five to fifty miles.'

Secretary of State Adler broke in now. 'It doesn't have to be accurate. It's a terror weapon. An instrument of blackmail. Choi isn't after a tactical advantage. He's after money, power in his region. The world's worst nuclear bomb on top of the world's most inaccurate ICBM still scares the hell out of a lot of people.'

Ryan nodded. 'Me, for instance.'

'Me too,' Adler admitted. 'Still, it's important to remember what's going on here. The entire North Korean nuclear industry isn't some wacko plot to destroy the world, it's a wacko plot to earn the respect of the world.'

Ryan said, 'I agree with that, but I wouldn't characterize it as wacko. North Korea's GDP falls right between those of Kenya and Zambia. If we only had economic factors to consider and not military factors, we wouldn't be spending any more time concerning ourselves with Pyongyang than we would with Lusaka.'

Chief of Staff Arnie Van Damm glanced up from the papers in front of him with a look of confusion.

'Capital of Zambia, Arnie,' Ryan added.

Arnie nodded and looked back down.

Ryan said, 'The DPRK already gets more attention than they would warrant if they didn't have a nuke, but they want to be treated with all the deference of the other nuclear weapon – holding states. Frankly, once they have a working ICBM that can hit California, I will be forced to give them that respect.'

Ryan turned his attention back to Ward. 'So to recap, we know the rocket failed before third stage, we don't know why, but we're looking into it.'

Ward replied sheepishly, 'Yes, Mr President. Unfortunately, that's where we are.'

'Okay,' Ryan said. 'Thanks for your report.'

The two DIA employees looked to Mary Pat Foley, who nodded at them and then turned her gaze toward the door. Ward and the major packed up their briefcases and started heading out of the room.

Ryan called after them. 'Colonel? Major?'

They both spun on their heels. 'Sir?'

'You did the best with what you have. The fault wasn't the messengers. I just need more to the message.'

'Yes, sir,' the two DIA analysts said.

'And next time you come back, be ready for a discussion, not a presentation. You'll find I'm pretty easy to chat with when I'm engaged. You guys have the knowledge, and I'm just about the most curious son of a gun you'll ever meet.'

Another round of 'Yes, sir,' and the two left the room.

When they were gone Scott Adler smiled. 'That colonel looked like a recruit just off the bus. Did you see the deer-in-the-headlights look he gave you when you asked for the flare duration?'

Jack shrugged. 'I guess I went a little overboard. I've been reading a lot of our primary intelligence on the DPRK's systems. Frankly, I was hoping there was more intel than what was in the reports that make it to me. There are a hell of a lot of holes in our knowledge.'

CIA director Canfield said, 'You can't get too deep in

the trees, boss. You are the one everybody relies on to see the entire forest.'

'Yeah. I know.'

Canfield added, 'Mr President. It's important for you to understand why there are gaps in our knowledge of North Korea. Our SIGINT, ELINT, and MASINT are all fair to good. We have spaceborne platforms, airborne platforms, surface platforms, and even subsurface platforms, and they are all pointed at the Korean Peninsula. We have cyber-platforms too, of course. But our HUMINT is lacking. Most of the human intelligence we have comes from defectors to the south. They are usually of poor quality. Subsistence farmers, laborers, teenagers who make it over.'

Jack said, 'You are saying we are in the dark.'

'From a HUMINT perspective, we are nearly that. We have some low-level government officials in our pocket. But the ones in Pyongyang we do hold some influence over are not able to communicate with us regularly, if at all. We don't have a single, CIA-run government asset in the entire nation. Even at the absolute height of the Cold War, we always had agents in the Soviet Union. But these days we are dark in North Korea.'

'Okay,' Ryan said, then he drummed his fingers on the table. 'Getting back to this failed launch. I wish we could all celebrate, but the problem with North Korea' – he held a hand up quickly – '*one* of the problems with North Korea, is that bad news for them is not necessarily good news for us. We've all seen it before, right? They respond to an embarrassing failure with a flexing of their muscles. Saber rattling.'

Mary Pat agreed. 'Their long-range missile blows up during second-stage sep so they "test-fire" two dozen short-range missiles into the Sea of Japan.'

SecDef Burgess said, 'Or they shell islands, or send mini-subs south of the Thirty-eighth Parallel.'

Ryan added, 'The new Choi has been going out of his way to show us he is to be taken just as seriously as the old Choi.'

The national security adviser said, 'Mr President. May I be the voice of perspective here? Even with all this taken into account, the DPRK is not our main problem right now. Even if there is some new low-intensity conflict on the Korean Peninsula, there are other, more pressing issues going on in the world. I think we need to count our blessings they still can't hit California with a plutonium bomb, and then return our focus to Russia, NATO, China, the Middle East, and all the other more critical issues out there.'

Jack nodded and rubbed his eyes. 'Why can't all the assholes out there just take a number and threaten us one at a time?' There were stressed chuckles around the room. 'So . . . what do we do about this?'

Adler said, 'I suggest we go back to the Security Council, push for another vote condemning the DPRK.'

'The UN? Seriously? To what end?' Ryan asked. 'China will just veto. Russia, too.'

Adler shook his head now. 'China and North Korea aren't the allies they used to be. Now that Choi the son has taken over for Choi the father, his destabilizing is pissing them off in Beijing. Remember China and DPRK had that big blowup over mineral rights last year. We won't get a vote from China, but it's possible we'll get an abstention.'

National Security Adviser Robillio added, 'Russia will veto, but it creates another attempt to isolate Russia diplomatically. With a new resolution we can marginalize Russia and censor North Korea. Kill two birds with one stone.'

Ryan answered back, 'That's not killing two birds with one stone. That's yelling at two birds as they fly on by without a care. Russia will keep doing what they're doing, and Chairman Choi doesn't give a damn about condemnation in the Security Council. His focus is on holding and exerting power. Nothing more.'

Adler was unwavering. 'The UN might not have teeth, but the sanctions against the North are already as strict as we have any hope of making them without some dramatic new development. Diplomatically speaking, there is little we can do.' He looked across the table at SecDef Burgess. 'Unless you are going to send Bob to attack Pyongyang, Mr President, a UN resolution is about the only weapon we've got.'

Ryan dropped his elbows on the table. 'Even with the broad sanctions on their weapons development programs, conventional and nuclear weapons and ballistic missiles, they still manage to launch ICBMs and detonate nukes. The Chinese don't want them armed with nukes any more than we do, so we know they aren't supplying them. Russia is the one adding fuel to this fire.'

Canfield agreed. 'That's right. The Russians don't care if North Korea has a nuke. It's another headache for us to deal with, and the DPRK pays in cash. There are only two impediments to North Korea having a deployable ICBM.'

'And those are?' asked Ryan.

'One, the sanctions. Russia doesn't want to get caught sneaking banned items and technology into North Korea, because that hurts them diplomatically. They do it, but they do it carefully, and that means the technology comes in a slow trickle.'

'And the other?'

'The other, quite simply, is money. North Korea is a hopelessly poor regime, with very little hard currency in the West. If they suddenly found themselves flush with cash, they could up the ante with Russia and unscrupulous private defense contractors and command a lot better service. Russia will sell them anything at any time. If the DPRK ever starts waving around hundreds of millions instead of millions, you'll see the proliferation increase precipitously, and they *will* get an arsenal of ICBMs.'

Jack put it succinctly for the rest of his national security team. 'A poor DPRK is in US national interests. We can't go out and say it to the world, because we'll be accused of starving the citizens of North Korea, even though it is the government of North Korea that is starving its own people. But we have to do whatever we can to prevent Choi's government from flourishing financially.'

Mary Pat said, 'Violations of sanctions allow millions in wealth and goods to trickle in and out.'

Jack said, 'We've worked for two generations to bleed them dry so they would come to the bargaining table, and still they keep moving on. We need more intelligence out of the North.' He looked to Mary Pat and Jay. 'This is a critical need. I know you have a thousand other things to deal with, but after that DIA brief it is clear to me we aren't going to have a solid handle on DPRK's capabilities until they demonstrate their capability by dumping a payload onto San Francisco. At that point it will be too late to do anything about it. I want you to improve your HUMINT in the DPRK.'

The meeting broke up minutes later, and Mary Pat Foley stood from her chair, ready to return to her office at the Liberty Crossing complex in McLean, Virginia. Her President wasn't satisfied with the intelligence product he was getting, which meant she had a hell of a lot of work to do. She'd meet with CIA director Canfield and discuss it, because they were both feeling the same heat.

She had just left the cabinet room and collected her mobile phone from a wicker basket on the President's secretary's desk, when the device vibrated in her hand. She answered it without looking.

'Foley.'

'Mary Pat? It's Gerry Hendley here.'

Foley stepped into the West Wing hall. She could tell by Gerry's tone of voice something was wrong. 'What is it?'

'Are you where you can talk?'

Mary Pat looked around. Men and women walked all around her. 'I'll be back in my car in a few minutes. I'll call you then. Just tell me this. Is this about Colin Hazelton?'

'Yes.'

'Is he okay?'

Gerry sighed into the phone. 'No. No, he's not. I'm afraid he's dead.'

She stopped fully in the hall, her knees weakening in shock as she did so. *'Dead?'*

8

One year earlier

The office of the Supreme Leader of North Korea is the Ryongsong Residence, also called Residence No. 55. It is located on a small lake in the northern suburbs of Pyongyang, and it serves as one of ten private residences for the nation's ruler.

The compound is several miles square and surrounded with fencing and gates; the living facility is hardened for conventional and nuclear attack, and two brigades of elite troops reside on the property with the sole mission of protecting the Supreme Leader both from foreign armies and domestic insurrection.

A black limousine arrived at the compound's outer perimeter checkpoint at ten a.m.; armed guards checked the driver and the occupant in the back, a small, thin fifty-four-year-old bald man in a gray suit. Soon the limo drove north through the hills of Ryongsong, stopped at more checkpoints along the way, until finally the vehicle pulled up to the entrance of Residence No. 55 itself. The bald man climbed out and was led with his small entourage into the building, then he was brought into an ornate sitting area by three female assistants of the Dae Wonsu, and he sat down on a straight-back chair.

Tea was placed in front of him, and a second cup was

placed on the empty sofa on the other side of the table and left empty.

He sat nervously in the silence, concentrating with all his might on giving off an air of calm.

The man's name was Hwang Min-ho; he was the new director of the Korea Natural Resources Trading Corporation, the nation's state-owned mining concern. In his position for less than a week, he was here to meet Choi Ji-hoon; this would be his first face-to-face with the leader of his country, and the current occupant of the center of the personality cult to which Hwang had belonged every second of his life.

Both of Hwang's parents had been on the personal staff of a colonel who served as a deputy of the Workers' Party of Korea, his father a driver and his mother a nanny for the children, and they were both typically fervent believers of the propaganda upon which the entire society was based. Hwang was raised to revere not the party or the government but the leader of his nation, a benevolent god who created all and bestowed all his blessings upon his people. Choi Ji-hoon's grandfather, then his father, and now Ji-hoon himself, they had all been the epicenter of Hwang's universe.

Hwang never questioned the things he knew to be truth: His leader's perfection and omniscience were established facts as sure as the rising and the setting of the sun. That said, Hwang was worried about his new promotion.

Hwang saw what happened to his boss. He'd done his difficult job to the absolute best of his ability; the Dae Wonsu had demanded the impossible, and when the impossible was not delivered, Hwang's boss was taken from his home. The rumor at the state-run mining company was he'd been sent to Kyo-hwa-so No. 9, the notorious reeducation camp on the east coast of the country. The urbane sixty-year-old former director of mining was, if the rumors were true, now working on his hands and knees in a coal mine and subsisting on a cup of barley soup a day.

Hwang himself had been ordered to remove every single mention of the former director from Korea Natural Resources Trading Corporation literature. To erase the very existence of the man. He did as he was told unquestioningly, and he did not even doubt the Dae Wonsu's decision internally (as a boy, his mother had told him the leader of the nation could read his mind so to always project love and gratitude in his thoughts), but Hwang, though brainwashed, still was a sentient being, so when he was ordered to fill the former director's position, he could not help but recognize this great honor came with great danger.

Hwang thought of the danger now as he waited in the luxurious sitting room at Residence No. 55, especially when two armed men, both dressed in the olive-green uniforms of the Chosun Inmingun, the Korean People's Army, stepped into the room. They were armed with AK-47 rifles that hung over their shoulders, and they took up positions near the doorway. Four more men entered and stood behind the sofa in front of him. Hwang knew these men were members of Section Five of the Party Central Committee Guidance Department, and they were the Dae Wonsu's personal bodyguards. Still two more men, both wearing Mao suits, entered. These appeared to be personal secretaries of some form or another.

Soon Choi would enter, and Hwang knew the reason for the meeting. Choi would tell him his decision regarding foreign partnerships at the rare earth mineral mine at Chongju. Since the Chinese had been thrown off the project weeks before, there had been discussions to bring them back, if not as coequal partners in the project, at least as foreign contract employees. Hwang's staff had sent over all the relevant facts and figures about what was required at Chongju, and the information obviated the fact that the mining operation did not have a chance for success without outside help. He fully expected the Supreme Leader to come to the same conclusion.

A female secretary in the uniform of a Chosun Inmingun major entered with a transcription machine. She set up her operation on the chair next to the sofa opposite Hwang. When her machine was ready she bowed to Hwang, and he bowed to her.

Everyone greeted one another as *dongmu*. Comrade.

Everyone stood or sat silently and waited like this for more than thirty minutes. Hwang was ready to wait even longer, but when a beautiful female attendant entered through a side door and poured steaming tea into the cup across from him, he knew the Dae Wonsu was on his way.

No one would dare serve the leader of the nation tea that had grown cold.

Seconds later Choi Ji-hoon entered through the massive double doors into the residence, flanked by four older men in military uniforms. Hwang had seen his nation's leader numerous times before; as an elite of North Korea, Hwang often found himself at functions where the Supreme Leader appeared. As always, Hwang was taken by the man's young face and the wide cut of his impeccable black Mao suit.

As Hwang leapt to his feet, his placid face morphed into one of unbridled joy. He bowed over and over as Choi approached, but he did not speak. This was the way to greet the Dae Wonsu, and Hwang was damn well not going to mess it up.

The military men took positions against the wall; in their hands were notebooks and pens, and they smiled at Hwang, who bowed in their direction. He was careful to form his bows to appear gracious and subservient, but not as deep as those reserved for the Dae Wonsu.

Choi smiled back and sat down across from Hwang. He reached forward and took his tea and sipped it silently for a moment. He looked around the room with bright but furtive eyes, as if making sure everyone in his entourage was in place. After a few moments he looked to Hwang.

'*Dongmu* Hwang, someone said your father drove for Colonel Ahn.'

Hwang's heart leapt and his eyes fought back tears of joy. Both of his parents were still living, and he knew telling them the Dae Wonsu knew something of his father's life would bring them outrageous happiness. He bowed from his chair and struggled to keep his tone measured. 'Yes, Dae Wonsu, you are correct. You bring great honor to my family by speaking of him.'

But Choi had already moved on. 'The Chinese will not

be returning to Chongju. We will continue on without them.'

Hwang knew every relevant fact and figure on the subject. North Korea was abundant in many valuable natural resources, but due to acute shortages of electricity, it would be impossible to exploit the mine without help.

But if not the Chinese, then who?

Brazil had some joint mining ventures here in the North, but they didn't have the rare earth experience China did. Hwang knew Chongju would never have been discovered without China, and the exploitation of the find wouldn't happen in his lifetime without outside help.

Hwang did not say anything upon hearing his leader's decision. Choi cocked his head, as if noticing the delay in the response. If he took it as any sign of disrespect, Hwang knew, he would be executed. Dissent was punishable by death, and dissent was highly subjective in the DPRK, to say the least.

'You disagree with my decision?' Choi asked.

Hwang recovered quickly. He bowed. 'No, Dae Wonsu. Of course, I very much agree. I am only thinking of the difficulty with the mine at Chongju. We have been partnering with the Chinese at most all of our mineral extraction sites, but at Chongju we rely on them.'

'That reliance was a mistake by your predecessor. I told him it went against Juche. He has been punished for allowing China to outshine us technologically.' Juche was the North Korean philosophy of self-reliance. This and the worship of the Chois were the quasi-official religions in the nation.

Hwang said, 'Yes. Yes, of course, I agree.'

'Good.'

'But . . .'

'But?'

'We can extract the ore. Obviously our nation has the best mining capability in the world.' Hwang wouldn't have gotten anywhere in his career without calculated exaggeration, but this was an outright lie. 'But the actual processing of the rare earth minerals has always been done in China.'

'What do you mean, "processing"?'

Hwang was confused by the question. It had all been in his report. He said, 'The ore is mined at Chongju, then delivered by truck to China. The three minerals containing rare earths – bastnäsite, monazite, and xenotime – must be identified and put through a grinding process, and then different chemicals are applied to the powder so that the rare earth oxides will separate from the other minerals. This is a highly technical process that requires geologists, chemists, computers and computer experts, and others.'

Choi said nothing.

Hwang asked, 'Will we continue to ship our ore north to have it purified?'

'Of course not. We will do all this here. Not only do we have the largest reserves of minerals on the planet, we have the best scientists and the best technology with which to exploit these minerals.'

Hwang forced himself to nod. Not only did it seem as if Choi was ordering Hwang to create an industry where none had existed before, but he was also demanding he adopt a process no one in North Korea had even seen firsthand.

Choi looked up at the military men around him. Hwang did not know why, but he did not like the silence. To break it he said, 'We will develop the processing capability.' He added, 'We will lead the world.'

Choi smiled now, and Hwang thought the meeting was about to end. Instead, Choi said, 'Very well. I will give you my guidance to ensure everything goes smoothly. Now, you might wonder how long you have. This mine will generate great riches for our nation, and we need these riches to ensure our national security. Having said this, I do not want to rush things, because I know this will require some work on your part.' He looked up as if thinking, and said, 'I demand you to begin profitable mining at Chongju within . . .'

It looked to Hwang as if he was going to pick a time frame out of the air, though he didn't seem to be even remotely aware of the complexity of the endeavor, or even what rare earth mining and processing entailed. Hwang knew that other nations had taken decades to produce their rare earth mineral industries, but he doubted Choi would give him that long. He hoped to, at least, hear him say *ten to fifteen years*.

Instead, Choi said, 'Within eighteen months.'

The bald man's heart sank, but he managed to keep his visage the same other than a slight trembling of his lower lip. The task before him was impossible, but he knew there would be no discussion in the matter. The Dae Wonsu had spoken.

Hwang loved the Dae Wonsu. Both the state and his

parents had successfully brainwashed him into doing so, and he did not question his devotion to Choi. But even so, he knew Choi's words to be madness.

After only the slightest hesitation, Hwang Min-ho said, 'Yes. As the new director of Korea Natural Resources Trading Corporation, I promise you we will meet with great success in the endeavor.' He added, 'And we would be so honored for your continued advice.'

Choi nodded with a smile that made him look genuinely pleased with the talk, and then he stood.

Hwang stood quickly himself, and began a routine of beaming grins and bows, a show of utter subservience that was only enhanced by the fact he fully expected that the man in front of him would order him sent to a labor camp in exactly eighteen months.

9

Present day

Jack Ryan, Jr., awoke in the pitch dark, his eyes thick with sleep and his mind void of any clue of where the hell he was. He heard rain pounding on a window next to him, and he thought back, tried to remember the recent past.

This feels like jet lag. Where did you go this time, Jack?

It came to him slowly because he was so damn tired. Vietnam, Hazelton, the motorcycles, the plane ride home with the smell of death, halfway around the earth, the exhaustion after landing in Baltimore the previous evening.

Only then did it hit him. He realized where he was now.

He was home. His new place, a modern condominium overlooking the Potomac River in Old Town Alexandria, Virginia. He barely knew his own home, he'd been traveling so much, so it took him a while to get his bearings. Finally, he rolled out of bed and walked toward the kitchen, hoping he could remember the way in the dark.

Jack had bought this place on Oronoco Street six weeks earlier, but it still felt brand-new to him. He'd been undergoing a battery of advanced tradecraft and operations training that took him all over the world – until last week, that is, when he and most other members of his unit rushed off to Asia on special assignment. Ryan realized he'd spent only six or seven nights at his Alexandria address since moving in, so it came as no real surprise that he'd been disoriented rising early on the morning after an exhausting flight around the world.

To combat the cobwebs in his head now he threw a pod into his coffee machine, filled the reservoir with water, flipped the device on, and stuck a cup under the spout. As he stood there with his eyes closed, the machine began to spew the hot black liquid into the cup. Jack had become a bit of a coffee snob, and he knew 'pod' coffee couldn't compete with 'real' coffee in a taste contest, but in a speed race the pod won by a wide margin.

He stood in his dark kitchen and drank his coffee black and molten. It burned the back of his throat, but he needed the jolt because he could tell his brain was still somewhere back in Asia and he had to go to work today.

Thunder boomed on the street outside, and Ryan headed back upstairs to get in the shower.

Ryan had lived in Columbia, Maryland, for several years, but he moved here for the simple reason that his place of business had moved here. For years the offices of Hendley Associates had been north of DC, in West Odenton, Maryland, but that building had been shuttered months back, after Chinese op-eratives learned of the existence of The Campus. A unit of Chinese Special Forces raided the property, killing several employees, and even though the threat had been repelled, both the 'white side' Hendley Associates and the 'dark side' Campus had closed up shop to prevent any further compromise.

Gerry Hendley had spent most of the intervening months looking for a new space, until finally deciding on a building here in Old Town Alexandria. The new Hendley Associates property was on North Fairfax Street, in a four-story brick Federalist office building with views of the Potomac River and the distant DC skyline. The building turned out to be perfect for Hendley's needs. It had been built as the home of a government intelligence contractor run by a former US Army general, before he'd left it behind to move his offices to an address inside the District.

Ryan dressed for work in a charcoal-gray pin-striped suit and a red silk tie. His formal attire contrasted a little with his thick, dark beard and his slightly longer than collar-length brown hair, but the beard and the hair were more important to him now than the suit. His father was President of the United States, so Jack had made it a focus of his attention to do whatever he could to avoid notice and attention. And in this task he had enjoyed near mission success; in the past few months only two or three times had anyone stepped up to him to inform him of the fact he was Jack Ryan, Jr., son of the President.

After he checked his suit in the mirror for lint, he stepped over to his nightstand and hefted a black pistol in a black leather holster from its nightly resting place by his clock. He slipped it into the waistband of his pants on his right side, then slid a small leather pouch containing an extra magazine for the weapon on his left side.

The operators of The Campus appreciated the relocation to Virginia for a few reasons, but one of the main perks was that they could easily and legally carry firearms here, unlike in nearby DC and in Maryland, which were both much more restrictive. Jack's main carry weapon was the Austrian Glock 19, a squat, black, nearly feature-less automatic pistol that carried sixteen rounds of nine-millimeter hollow-point ammunition. It was a simple and effective weapon, without a lot of bells and whistles such as a manual external safety. If one kept the gun loaded – which one should if one carried it for defensive purposes – anytime the trigger was pulled, a round would fire. There were no extra levers, switches, or buttons to slow down the process.

Ryan considered himself much more of an intelligence analyst than a gunfighter, but he had entered into gun battles multiple times in his years with The Campus. It went with the job, so Ryan went armed as often as he could possibly get away with it.

Jack Junior popped open his umbrella on his covered back deck and he locked his back door, then he shouldered his backpack and exited his property through his rear garden gate. He walked past his black Mercedes E-Class in the driveway and continued down the street.

Ryan enjoyed walking to work; inside the Beltway it was the closest thing to paradise anyone had managed to find, and even in the rain it beat getting stuck in morning traffic.

Ten minutes later he shook out his umbrella at the entrance to Hendley Associates and stood in front of a bulletproof glass door until he was buzzed into the lobby by one of four guards inside.

A dozen armed men were employed as the security force of Hendley Associates. They were all ex-CIA para-military operations officers with top-secret security clearances who'd taken contracts as static security in the private sector. They knew the organization they protected was a sub rosa intelligence outfit, and they knew they weren't supposed to know more than that, save for one extra item of interest that was quite relevant to their positions. The son of the President of the United States was an analyst for the company. Jack Junior arrived each morning at eight a.m., unless of course he was out of town. No one could imagine he had any operational capacity for the company, but then again, none of the static security was aware of the true scope of the work done by the men on the top floor. The security force here just assumed that on occasion POTUS's kid had to go into the field to conduct some sort of financial analytics task for Gerry Hendley.

The director of security for Hendley Associates was a forty-seven-year-old ex – Army Ranger named Bryce Jennings. Jennings was no stranger to the world of clandestine security. After the Army he spent a decade in the CIA protecting secure facilities for the Agency. In his security career he'd been bombed in Baghdad, shot at in Kabul, he'd fought off an attempted overrun of a special mission compound in Sana'a and another outside Manila, and he'd once help save the US ambassador to Tunisia from an insider attack when a local police captain tried to kidnap him at gunpoint.

Jennings had seen a lot in his career, but he was happy to leave that behind now so that he could spend more time with his wife and young daughter back in the United States. He'd jumped at the chance to come back stateside to take this new position, but he solemnly guaranteed

Gerry Hendley he would treat his responsibilities here in the building in Alexandria, Virginia, as seriously as he would were they in Alexandria, Egypt.

Ryan was buzzed in after a moment and he entered the small lobby and then dropped off his umbrella in a rack.

Bryce was behind the desk by the elevator. 'Morning, Jack.' He'd tried calling him Mr Ryan the first half-dozen or so days he'd greeted him, but Ryan corrected him each time. Finally Jennings relented, so now it was just *Jack*.

'Hey, Bryce,' Ryan said. 'Nats and Phillies tonight if the rain moves out.'

'Damn right, I'll be there. Phillies have been hitting, but we've got Gonzalez on the mound. No problem.'

Ryan was an Orioles fan himself, but he knew Jennings lived and breathed the Washington Nationals, and took his six-year-old daughter to every game he could when he wasn't working.

As Ryan made his way to the elevator he said, 'Good luck tonight, but the Orioles will be down for a double-header Saturday. You'd better pray for rain then.'

Jennings's eyes narrowed, feigning seriousness. 'You really ought to root for the home team, you know. Your dad, too.'

Jack entered the elevator and turned around. 'Oh, we do. DC isn't home for either of us, Bryce.'

Jennings shook his head as the doors closed.

After the Chinese attack on The Campus the sub rosa intelligence organization had become a smaller, leaner outfit, and their offices reflected this. Fewer than seventy-five men and women worked in the building, and half of these worked exclusively in the white side. The first two floors of the building were devoted exclusively to the financial trading business. The third floor housed IT for both entities, as well as conference rooms and a small break room. The top floor was the location of Gerry Hendley's large executive office suite, as well as the offices of The Campus. An equipment locker and the company's mainframe computer, as well as an operations center for The Campus, were housed in the secure basement of the property.

Jack's elevator stopped on the second floor, and Gavin Biery stepped in and pushed the third-floor button. Gavin Biery was the IT director of The Campus, and as much as the operational side of the house hated to admit it, The Campus would not exist without him.

'Morning, Gav.'

'Welcome home, Ryan. You boys have a nice little vacay?'

Normally Biery supported Campus operations from his banks of computers here in Virginia, but the Vietnam op had come up quickly and Gavin hadn't been involved. Even so, Gavin Biery was cleared for anything that happened to the Campus operators, so Ryan knew he didn't need to keep quiet about the operation.

Jack said, 'Oh, it was a blast. Our subject got murdered right in front of me. Ding and Sam got shot at, and Clark flattened a dude with a rental car. How was *your* weekend?'

The elevator dinged as it stopped, and the doors opened on Gavin's floor. He stood there with his mouth half open, not sure if Ryan was serious.

Finally he said, 'Sure am sorry I missed that op.'

Gavin had gone out with the team a few times in his

career to provide computer support to their operations, and due to these limited forays into the field he considered himself something of a full-fledged spook. The rest of the team found this to be comical, although the computer geek had done an admirable job in the field.

'It's your floor, Gav,' Jack said.

'Right,' Gavin replied as he stepped out into the third-floor hall, still not sure if Ryan was pulling his leg about what had happened overseas or not.

Jack headed to his fourth-floor office to drop his bag on his way to the kitchen, but as he walked up the hall he saw someone sitting on the edge of his desk. As he got closer he realized it was his cousin, Dominic Caruso. Jack hadn't seen Dom in nearly three months. Dom was an operations officer here at The Campus, same as Jack, but the operators had all been off in different directions in specialized individual training, each on their own rotation around the world. Dom had stayed out on an evolution longer than the other men, and he and Jack hadn't spoken or e-mailed each other in weeks.

The two men embraced. 'Good to see you, cuz!' Caruso said.

After a post-embrace chest bump, a silly move they'd started doing as a joke, Ryan said, 'You, too. Damn, Dom. You've been training a long time. Me and the other guys have actually been out working while you've been rolling around on a cushy judo mat somewhere.'

Caruso cocked his head. 'Really? Gerry didn't tell you?'

Now Ryan cocked his own head. 'Tell me what?'

Caruso hesitated. Finally he said, 'Never mind. If Gerry didn't tell you, then you must not need to know.'

The truth was, Dom Caruso had been fighting his own battle in the past few weeks. A battle that had taken him from the Indian subcontinent to Central America and then to Europe, as he tried to stop a potentially devastating intelligence leak from falling into the hands of the Iranians. The rest of the team had been kept away from the situation, but Dom didn't know until now that the others had not even been informed he'd been in harm's way.

Hendley knew what Dom had been involved in, but apparently he'd kept the others in the dark. *Operational security.* He could already hear Hendley saying it as an explanation, and it did make sense, although it made Dom feel even more like he'd been swinging in the wind alone on his last operation.

Ryan said, 'Tell me about it. You get into anything inter-esting?'

'Later,' Dom replied, not sure if he would say anything about it at all now. 'I heard you guys were out on a job. Anything cool happen?'

Jack shrugged, then put his arm around Caruso's shoulders. 'Let's grab a cup of coffee and I'll fill you in.'

John Clark arrived in his fourth-floor office just after eight, and as soon as he put his briefcase down he picked up his phone and called Jack Ryan, Jr.'s office down the hall.

Jack answered on the second ring. 'Hey, John.'

'I'm guessing Dom is in there shooting the shit with you.'

Jack chuckled. 'We have a little catching up to do.'

'Right. Before you do that, send him down to me.'

'You got it.'

A minute later Caruso entered Clark's office and shut the door behind him. The two men shook hands.

Clark said, 'I meant to call you before you came in, but we had an in extremis situation come up last week.'

'Yeah, I heard. No details yet, but Jack was getting around to it. He doesn't seem to be aware of what I've been up to.'

'Gerry and I have decided to keep some of the work we do here compartmentalized. You were working your last job as a singleton. When an operator is in the field as a singleton, there is no need to know among the other operators.'

Dom said, 'I understand that.'

'Good.' The matter was settled, Caruso wouldn't talk about his operation to the rest of the team. 'How do you feel? Ready to get back to work?'

'Absolutely. I'm good to go.'

Clark said, 'I need to fill you in on what went down in Vietnam. We have a nine a.m. meeting where we might get further marching orders on the subject.'

Dom pulled up a chair. 'Let's hear it.'

10

One year earlier

A motorcade of five armored luxury vehicles rolled up to the same outer perimeter checkpoint that mining director Hwang passed an hour earlier. The lead car handed over some credentials to the uniformed guard and soon all five vehicles were moving again along the virtually empty blacktop road, much faster than the entourage from the Korea Natural Resources Trading Corporation. They sailed through the other checkpoints without even slowing down, rising through the wooded hills toward their destination.

The motorcade stopped at the entrance to Residence No. 55, and eighteen men in total disgorged from it, all wearing gray military uniforms signifying them as officers of the Korean People's Army. Their credos were checked here again by a large unit of armed guards, but only briefly, and soon the entourage had passed through the doors of the palace.

At the nucleus of this group was Lieutenant General Ri Tae-jin, a fit fifty-two-year-old who wore a chest full of medals and walked pridefully, chin first and shoulders back. His face was blank, void of emotion, though in the stony gaze a perceptive person might well notice an air of sadness.

Six of his staff remained in the entry hall; they were just along as escort, but they were not needed for today's meeting. And six more stopped off in an inner chamber for consultation with politburo members in concurrent talks at the residence. Five men followed Ri through another guarded doorway, heading for the personal residence of the Supreme Leader.

They ascended a flight of stairs and entered the long main gallery hall, and here Ri glanced at a clock on the wall and saw he was right on time for his meeting with the Dae Wonsu, which meant to him he would probably have to sit and wait for only an hour or so. Ji-hoon's father hadn't been punctual himself, really, but Ji-hoon seemed to take exceptional pleasure in making people wait for him.

Halfway down the main gallery hall Ri and his entourage encountered a smaller group of men in civilian dress approaching from the living quarters of the Supreme Leader. There were five men in this group, and they were led by one of the residence's beautiful young attendants. The lieutenant general identified one man in the group as the senior member because the attendant spoke to him, and the others walked behind. As he passed the man their eyes met, and Ri saw he was a small man with a bald head, a few years older than himself.

It bothered General Ri greatly that he did not recognize the man, because he'd obviously just left an audience with the Supreme Leader. If this bald-headed fellow had the ear of the Dae Wonsu and he wasn't, at least, a general, then he was most definitely an important person. And if he wasn't even in the military, Ri felt he had no excuse for not knowing the man's file backward and forward.

Ri was the nation's newly installed *foreign* intelligence chief, which meant there was no reason he would necessarily know every visitor to Residence No. 55 – that would be a job for the Ministry of State Security, the domestic arm of North Korean intelligence – but with every generalship in the Korean People's Army came the responsibility of deft political relationship-making. Ri knew the important people in this town, in this government.

But he didn't know this little man.

As he walked he tilted his head toward an aide, who spoke without being spoken to, because he knew what his general wanted.

Softly he said, 'Hwang Min-ho. Installed last week as the new director of Korea Natural Resources Trading.'

Ri nodded, as though he already knew this. He had heard the name, and he knew of the appointment. Ri had also heard of the order to have Hwang's boss snatched from his house in his bedclothes and helicoptered up to a reeducation camp, and he imagined that bastard would be dead inside six weeks.

Reeducation complete, he thought to himself as he walked on.

The general wondered about this Hwang. 'I want his file. Contact MSS. Generate a reason.' His voice echoed off the wooden flooring, and Hwang might have heard him had the footfalls of a dozen men and women not echoed along with it.

A few minutes later Ri had left the last vestiges of his entourage behind, and now he sat alone in a gilded office. He knew Choi had a dozen of these offices at a dozen palaces in the country, and he'd been to many meetings in this and other similar rooms, but never had he been left by himself in one.

This was strange.

He did not know why he had been summoned here today and then sequestered from his aides. Perhaps it was a formality, a way to welcome him into his new position at the Reconnaissance General Bureau, although that didn't seem plausible. If that had been the case, surely there would be attendants and transcriptionists and photographers galore ready to witness the event.

So this was something else. But what? Ri had served in the military intelligence field for more than a quarter-century already, and he was a brilliant man, but at the moment he couldn't come up with a scenario that made sense.

Although the man he would soon have an audience with held the power of life and death over every civilian in the nation, he wasn't worried about himself in the least. He knew that if Choi wanted him dead, he wouldn't be meeting with him personally.

Those things happened by proxy, as Ri Tae-jin was painfully well aware.

Lieutenant General Ri had received exactly two orders from the office of the Supreme Leader in the one week he had been in charge of the RGB. The first order was that Ri carry out the arrest of his predecessor. This he did reluctantly; he had worked with General Gang for more than a decade and quite liked the old man.

Gang's 'crime' was the recent failure of a long-range

ballistic missile test. ICBMs like the one that had exploded over the ocean were the responsibility of the Korean People's Army Missile Guidance Bureau, and General Gang's Reconnaissance General Bureau wasn't directly involved in making missiles fly. Several directors at MGB were arrested, but RGB was im-plicated as well, because a long-standing RGB plan to steal guidance software from a French aerospace company via a hacking operation had recently failed. Choi lumped that failure together with the unsuccessful missile test, and he ordered the directors of both the MGB and the RGB hauled out of their offices in disgrace.

The second message from Choi came down to Ri later that same day. It was a short, direct missive ordering Ri to put General Gang to death within twenty-four hours to pay for his disgrace.

At the bottom of the page, one additional word had been added to the order.

The word specified the manner of the execution.

Dogs.

Ri had sat alone in his office for fifteen minutes, stunned and sickened, with the order held loosely in his fingertips, until a ringing phone brought him back to life. It was a senior minister from Choi's office – his words carried the weight of the Dae Wonsu – asking if the order had been understood.

There was no problem there; Ri understood the order perfectly. His old mentor was to be fed to a pack of seven starving dogs that were maintained at Chongjin labor camp for just such a purpose. He confirmed to the minister the order would be followed with utmost haste.

But there was something else. The minister directed Ri himself to monitor the execution in order to ensure it was carried out to the letter of the instructions.

Ri said he understood and would comply, but he knew the real reason he would have to travel to Chongjin and watch his friend and mentor die a horrific death before his eyes. He was being forced to watch the event because as the new director, his cooperation was to be encouraged, and the best way for that, Choi and his ministers had decided, was by him learning in detail what would happen to him if he failed in his duties.

It took a tremendous amount of horror to impress the new director of the North Korean foreign intelligence service, but since the day of his director's death by the gnashing teeth of seven dogs a week earlier, Lieutenant General Ri Tae-jin had had a recurring nightmare of the event. In his dream he was never the one in the pit, although that could easily be the reality if Choi lost confidence in his ability to execute the duties of his office. Instead, he was a witness to the execution.

His nightmare was virtually the same as the actual event.

As he sat in the gilded ceremonial office Ri's mind drifted to the dog pit, and then it moved to one further horror. It became known at the RGB soon after Gang's death that his family had been executed as well. His wife, his three adult children, and their wives and even *their* small children had all been taken to Chongjin and shot in the dead of night. No criminal complaint had been read to them, no explanation at all for why they had to die.

Ri had trouble pushing his impure thoughts about his

society out of his head, but they cleared quickly when a group of transcriptionists, generals, bodyguards, and then finally the Dae Wonsu himself entered. Choi carried a snifter of Cognac in one hand and a handkerchief in the other. He wore his black Mao suit; Ri had seen him in nothing else save for a uniform he sometimes wore for purely military events. Ri also saw that Choi's eyes were typically active, flashing around the room, both on the general in front of him and at random objects. Choi looked at a clock, a container of water, a painting of his father on the wall.

Without preamble he said, 'You had no involvement over the failed operation to obtain the guidance software from France.'

Ri did not know if it was a question or a statement. He shook his head. 'None, Dae Wonsu. I was not involved in our cyber-operations at all.'

Choi seemed to know this already. 'General Gang's failures do not cast a shadow over you. You have my full confidence.'

Ri bowed four times and thanked his Supreme Leader, who seemed content to watch him bow. Then Choi said, 'Missile Guidance Bureau must do better, but General Gang had an opportunity to provide them with assistance, and he failed.'

Ri knew what was good for him. He agreed in a full-throated manner.

Choi then looked at his drink and said, 'My burden is this . . . like my father, and my grandfather, I am a keen expert on matters of history.'

'This is well known by all, Dae Wonsu.'

'Nothing has struck me more than what has happened in Ukraine, in Libya, in Iraq. When these nations parted with their most potent weapons, they were not rewarded with good relations. No, they became nonentities, lambs.'

'Yes,' Ri said. *Okay, so we are, in fact, going to talk about the problems at Missile Guidance Bureau.*

Choi sipped the Cognac. 'We must produce better rockets. Able to fly further and more reliably. We must develop, develop, develop!'

'I agree completely,' Ri said. Choi was used to hearing this, of course, no matter the topic. The last time Choi Ji-hoon had heard the words 'I disagree,' he was nine years old.

'The plutonium weapons are in our arsenal. Our uranium enrichment is progressing. We have miniaturized the bombs into warheads. Our nation has the power, but not the mechanism to deliver the power. We need a ballistic missile capable of delivering the warhead.'

Now Ri cocked his head in surprise. 'I am told the Rodong system performed flawlessly in its most recent test. My eyes have been focused outward at RGB. Have I been misinformed?'

Choi waved a hand. 'Rodong has a range of nine hundred kilometers. This makes it merely a defensive weapon. Yes, we can obliterate Seoul, but this will not protect us from America. They would gladly sacrifice South Korea in order to destroy us in North Korea. We need something with the range to reach the continental United States. The Taepodong-2 is not operational, and despite what I am being told by RGB, I don't think it soon will be.'

Ri assumed his nation's military leaders had received

an earful from their grand marshal. Fortunately for Ri, however, he and his department had not been given responsibility for the development of the ballistic systems.

Unfortunately for Ri, he feared this was about to change.

Choi leaned forward. 'Our military, our scientists, they have been unable to provide us with the technology we need. I want you to go out and get it.'

Ri thought of the nonproliferation sanctions. Of the naval blockade that checked shipping cargo in the Yellow Sea and the Sea of Japan. He thought of the tight controls on the manufacture and sale of items involved in the construction of all things rocket, including dual-use items that the West feared might be smuggled into North Korea.

In short, he thought of the dozens of barriers in front of him.

But he said the only thing he could say. 'Of course, Dae Wonsu. I will not fail.'

'You have three years.'

Now he thought of the seven dogs of Chongjin and he wondered if they were already hungry again after consuming General Gang.

'Three years? Three years for . . .'

'Three years to see that the Taepodong-2 is operational with our Missile Guidance Bureau.'

A purple vein on Ri's forehead pulsed a few times, but he made no overt reaction. 'That is not much time.'

'Three years is more time than I *should* give you. Does our nation have three years before our enemies attack?'

In a measured tone the general said, 'I confess I do not know.'

'No, you don't. The only thing that will stop an attack is the Taepodong-2. Operational and dependable. Our nuclear scientists have done their job. They have successfully miniaturized the device. But we have to be able to deliver it to the United States mainland.'

Choi held up three fingers. 'Three years. Three years until I find someone else.'

Ri knew what would happen to him if Choi decided to find someone else.

I I

Present day

Shortly before nine a.m. three large Chevy Suburbans rolled into the garage under the North Fairfax Street offices of Hendley Associates. The vehicles pulled up to an entrance, and out of view from the street all the doors on all the Suburbans opened as one, and a phalanx of young armed men stepped out. Soon a distinguished sixty-three-year-old woman climbed out of the center vehicle and moved purposefully to the entrance, where she was greeted by Gerry Hendley, ex – South Carolina senator and the director of both Hendley Associates and The Campus.

Gerry thought Director of National Intelligence Mary Pat Foley looked tired and worn. He knew she had been working hard since taking over the DNI job. She was the top intelligence official of the top intelligence community in the world, after all, so there was no surprise the position came with long hours and high stress. But even so, Gerry saw in Mary Pat a deep concern.

Together the two of them rode the elevator up to the fourth-floor conference room. On the way up Mary Pat said, 'I like the new place.' She tried a smile, but Gerry had known Mary Pat and her husband, Ed, for years, and he could tell she was just going through the motions of small talk.

He made it easy on her. 'Thanks very much. We were lucky to get the place. A private military contractor gave it up, and we moved in. It was stocked for our needs, we basically just switched out the locks and plugged in our computers.'

She nodded politely.

Gerry said, 'I'm very sorry about Colin Hazelton. You knew him well, did you?'

Mary Pat nodded again, but made no reply.

A minute later they entered the conference room. The five men sitting at the table stood and came forward. John Clark, Domingo Chavez, Dominic Caruso, Sam Driscoll, and Jack Ryan, Jr., all shook hands with the DNI before sitting back down.

Mary Pat was here this morning because The Campus had been sent to Vietnam on her personal request. As DNI, Mary Pat had every intelligence asset in the US government at her disposal, but she had reached out to Gerry Hendley and his team for help in the matter of Colin Hazelton because she wanted to keep the inquiry sensitive and below official channels.

Needless to say, she now felt that decision to have been a grave error.

John Clark began the meeting by running through everything that had happened between the time the Campus team arrived in Ho Chi Minh City and the moment their Gulfstream took off over the Gulf of Thailand with the body of Colin Hazelton hidden behind an access panel. He had the other members of the unit give their own perspective on specific events. Mary Pat sat quietly throughout the presentations, but she looked nearly overcome with emotion when Domingo relayed finding the wounded Hazelton in the street and his attempts to save him.

Ding had never seen Mary Pat like this, and he quickly toned down the level of detail in an attempt to spare her some discomfort.

Mary Pat seemed skeptical when she heard that Colin had written the letters DPRK in his last note, and she asked to look at the paper herself. Clark handed it over, and she had as much trouble deciphering the letters as the others.

When everyone was finished with the after-action report, Mary Pat took a moment to collect her thoughts. She said, 'I could have stopped this before it got out of hand. I didn't know the stakes,' she said. 'Had I known . . . Christ. I thought this was just a corporate intelligence issue. Shady, maybe. Crooked at worst. But not *this*.'

Clark replied softly, 'I wouldn't be surprised if *Hazelton* thought it was just a corporate intelligence issue as well. His threat posture didn't indicate he thought for a second he was in any physical danger.'

Mary Pat then said, 'I feel I know the answer, but I have to rule it out so I will ask anyway. Any chance at all this was just random street crime?'

Jack Junior took this one. 'None. I was the one watching when he was confronted. These guys were skilled, they locked on to Hazelton and trailed him for blocks. I don't know why he was targeted or killed, but I do know there wasn't anything random to it.'

Foley seemed satisfied by the answer, though she was still visibly upset.

Gerry said, 'Now, Mary Pat, it should come as no surprise we have questions for you. Why did you have us tail Hazelton? I assumed you suspected him of being involved in something illegal?'

She took a sip of water. "Colin, Ed, and I came up in CIA together. He'd been a pilot in the Air Force who'd moved into intelligence. He was a natural case officer. One of the good ones. After leaving the field, he worked for Ed for years on the seventh floor of the Agency, and became a trusted confidant to us both.

'When I moved out of CIA and began running the National Counterterrorism Center, I wanted to move Colin over with me. As always, a special personal security review was run on him, just a formality because he'd been in CIA for thirty years already. But the review turned up some problems.'

'Problems?' Gerry asked.

'Money problems. Colin had made some questionable investments. He put all of his savings in places where he thought the money would earn an especially high rate of return. High-risk Third World locations that others wouldn't touch. Colin felt like he knew the region.'

'What happened?'

Mary Pat's chest heaved. 'The Arab Spring. Tunisia flipped, Libya tanked, Egypt went one way, then the other, and then in another direction.'

Ryan whistled. 'Damn. Hazelton invested in *North Africa*?'

Mary Pat shrugged. "He'd made some good bets in the past. He grew overconfident in his ability to foresee events. And that proved his undoing. He borrowed some money, thinking he could earn it back. He lost that as well.

"When we found out about the investments they were still going strong. Nevertheless, we couldn't take him at NCTC, there was too much potential for compromise with all that money offshore. Then CIA found he had failed to report some of his accounts. He said it was just a screwup on his part, and I believe him. Colin was a good pilot and a first-rate intelligence officer, and he was a good executive from a big-picture standpoint, but he could be a bit disorganized when it came to paperwork. At that point in his CIA career he was no longer clandestine, he was a Seventh Floor administrator. Personally I thought he should have been allowed to retire. But the new head of CIA, Jay Canfield, is a by-the-book guy, so he drummed Hazelton out a year before eligibility for his pension. Shortly after that was the coup in Egypt. Colin lost everything. He was out of work and desperate. Ed and I tried to help him on a personal level, but he was too proud. He wouldn't return our calls.

'I'd gotten a tip from another old colleague that he'd started working for Duke Sharps in New York. I knew Duke before he left FBI's Counterintelligence Division. Since he's gone private sector he's only become an unscrupulous opportunist.'

John Clark said, 'That man is scum of the earth.'

Ding agreed with a nod, but the younger Campus operators all exchanged looks of surprise.

Mary Pat also agreed. 'Sharps Global Intelligence Partners employs hundreds of ex-spies, soldiers, and police detectives all over the planet, and Duke has his fingerprints on most every shady event happening anywhere. Still, there's one thing Duke has more of than morally questionable ex-spooks, and that's lawyers. His operation has stayed up and running even though the Justice Department has tried to shut him down.'

Gerry Hendley said, 'When you found out Hazelton worked for Sharps, what did you do?'

'At first I was just disappointed, but not terribly concerned. Some of Sharps's clients skirt the law, sure, but he also works with aboveboard corporate accounts on completely benign investigative issues. I didn't believe for an instant that Colin would do anything against the US Still, I put some resources into him, flagged his passport to ping if he went abroad, just in case. Then, the other day, he flew to Prague. I wanted him followed there, but he left the Czech Republic before we got anyone in place, and went to Vietnam. Our assets there were deployed on another matter, and I didn't want to alert the local authorities. So I called you, Gerry, and asked for help. John, you and your men tailed him in Ho Chi Minh City. I had no idea he was in any danger. I just wanted to know if he was involved in something illegal.'

Gerry could see that Mary Pat felt a sense of responsibility for what happened to Hazelton.

He said, 'You didn't get him killed. He met with some misfortune, yes, but a lot of it was self-inflicted.'

'I know that, Gerry. But if you work in the intelligence field long enough you really covet those few who've been with you all the way. He was a good man and a hell of an officer. If not so much in his later years, at least long ago. Ed and I both owed him a lot.'

It was quiet in the conference room for a moment, then Clark cleared his throat and said, 'Unfortunately, we weren't able to discern anything about the assassins. We had to leave the area before checking the body of the man I killed.'

Mary Pat replied, 'I'm just glad you guys got out of there alive.'

Ryan pulled out his iPad. 'Shortly before he was killed, however, Hazelton met with a woman. They had a short but apparently heated discussion. We didn't get audio, but she was after something he was carrying, or at least something she thought he was carrying. She didn't get it.'

Ryan pulled up the picture of the tall blonde sitting at the table with Hazelton and Mary Pat leaned forward and looked at it. 'I don't know her. E-mail it to me and I'll have NSA run facial recog on it.'

Jack said, 'We tried that. No luck.'

Mary Pat raised an eyebrow. 'Are you saying your facial-recognition software here at The Campus is as good or better than the US government's?'

In truth, it was the same system. IT director Gavin Biery had the ability to plug in to the NSA's database of images and use the same software the CIA was using. Mary Pat did not know this.

Gerry broke in quickly. 'We're not saying that at all. Jack will be happy to e-mail you the images of the young woman. Hopefully you'll get lucky.'

Mary Pat let the matter go, and she stood, indicating

the end to the meeting. 'Look, gentlemen. I am concerned about whatever Hazelton was working on, of course. Especially if it involved North Korea. But I put you guys on this operation because I was worried about an old friend, not because I wanted you in danger. And now that old friend is dead. I'll make in-quiries; I don't want you or your team risking your lives over this any longer. There are enough other problems on earth right now. I'm not going to push The Campus into the unknowns of some sort of corporate crime problem, even if there was an assumption by Hazelton that North Korea had some-thing to do with it. This is probably drugs, money laundering, even gun running. State will work with the local authorities to find out whatever they can. That will have to be good enough.'

Mary Pat Foley left a short time later, and then Gerry Hend-ley sat back down with his five operators to discuss their options.

Ding said, 'Don't know about you, Gerry, but I'm pretty damn curious about those dudes who almost punched our ticket in Vietnam.'

'Me, too,' admitted both Ryan and Driscoll.

Clark was more diplomatic. 'We're all just back to regu-lar operational duty. We aren't tasked on anything specific yet, so our workload is light enough at the moment to where maybe we can dig a little deeper.'

Hendley thought it over first, but soon enough he said, 'Don't worry. We're not dropping it. I think it's safe to operate under the assumption that whoever killed Colin Hazelton knew who he was. That means there is a bad actor out there with no qualms about killing ex – CIA executives. As far as I'm concerned, that warrants our attention, whether or not we have any official blessing from the DNI.'

Ding smiled. 'I was hoping you'd say that. Any idea what our next step is?'

Clark answered, 'I've got an idea, I just didn't want to burden Mary Pat with it.'

Gerry sighed. He knew, and he wasn't sure he liked it. 'Duke Sharps?'

'Yeah. But we're not about to start snooping on American citizens on the streets of New York. Not yet, anyway. For now we probe a little in open source to see what we can find out about Sharps and his operation. Anything too overt and he'll pick up on it. He and his employees are extremely good about their own security. Sharps Global Intelligence Partners will be a tough nut to crack.'

12

One year earlier

The offices of Korea Natural Resources Trading Corporation were in the Chung-guyok, or Central District, of Pyongyang, the nation's capital of two and a half million. It was a large building complex with a tower in the center and several smaller buildings also associated with the mining industry nearby. Mining was the largest sector of the North Korean economy, employing thousands just here at the administration offices in Pyongyang, and a million more around the nation.

And for the past two weeks, at the top of the entire hierarchy sat Hwang Min-ho, and this continued to amaze him each and every morning.

As the son of employees of a party elite, Hwang Min-ho was given opportunities not afforded to ninety-nine percent of his nation's children. Still, as with every citizen of North Korea, his future was ordained by the party. He was sent to study engineering at Beijing University, and then he was ordered to further his studies at Pyongyang University, where he earned the equivalent of a master's degree in public policy. He began his career as a Korean Workers' Party administrator in the Chagang Province. Chagang was one of the centers of the coal industry in the country, and Hwang's engineering background helped him in his dealings with the problems faced by the mines.

It was a natural thing for him to move from the Korean Workers' Party into the state-run mining entity, and by the age of thirty he was well ensconced in the administrative division of Korea Natural Resources Trading Corporation.

He met his first wife at a Workers' Party meeting when they were both still teenagers, but she had died on her twenty-second birthday while giving birth to a stillborn child. In that instant Hwang went from family man to bachelor, and it affected him greatly. He focused wholly on his career for the next twenty years, until finally meeting a young nurse at a copper mine in Ryanggang Province. Min-ho and So-ra were married a year later.

His intelligence, calm demeanor, and work ethic all made him a standout, and over the next two decades he rose through the ranks to the top echelon of the organization, finding himself the director of the coal and copper mining sectors of his company by age fifty.

When the rare earth mineral deposits were discovered at Chongju in Pyongan-bukto Province, many of the highest members of the company switched their focus to working with the Chinese on this new natural resource. Hwang, by contrast, remained focused on the nation's established mining operations, and by keeping his head down and concentrating on coal and copper, when the smoke cleared after the Chongju/China debacle, Hwang was virtually the only top-level executive in the organization left standing. He was ordered to take the reins of the organization when the director was imprisoned, and though it was the proudest moment in his life as well as the lives of his wife, children, and elderly parents, he would have much rather remained focused on coal and copper.

Nevertheless, now he was in charge, and he could no longer save himself by staying away from the rare earth mine. In fact, it had become eighty percent of his work. Since the Chinese were still partnering with North Korea at the copper mines and the zinc mines and the tungsten mine and the near-dormant gold mines, he felt certain no issue at any of those locations would get him thrown into Kangdong reeducation camp, so he knew his time was best spent concerning himself with the mining sector that, if not exploited in the next year and a half, would result in his being tossed into the back of an armored truck and rolled to Kangdong.

Hwang was father to a boy of nine and a girl of eight, and he considered himself a family man, but like all men in North Korea, his first allegiance was to the state and not his family, so this morning he rose before dawn and met his driver in front of his house in an elite neighborhood that overlooked the Taedong River. They drove silently together on the wide, empty boulevards. It was still dark, and in the capital city there were very few lighted streets, as electricity was in such short supply, but the large neon propaganda billboards on top of the tall apartment blocks and office buildings glowed dazzlingly, and bright spotlights ringed the large statues of Choi Ji-hoon that stood in the center of major intersections and traffic circles.

The drive took more than twenty minutes, and after

another ten minutes walking through darkened corridors and climbing seven flights of stairs, Hwang Min-ho was hunched over a laptop on his desk with the day's first cup of tea in his hand.

By the noon hour Hwang felt like this day would turn out like most every other – much work with little definite to show for it. Also like every other day he was getting nowhere in his attempts to advance the situation at Chongju. This morning he had suffered through a meeting with representatives of Korea General Machinery Trading Company, the state-owned manufacturer and importer of hydroelectric generators, and he had spent the better part of an hour both berating them for not fulfilling their promises from their last meeting and begging them to do a better job this time in their pledge to increase the electrical output to the mine. He'd received platitudes from the contingent, but little else.

Now he was prepping for an afternoon visit to Amroggang Development Banking Corporation a few blocks away. Hwang and his vice ministers were desperately trying to secure financing from abroad to purchase those few goods not enveloped by sanctions, and perhaps even find an overseas benefactor who would bankroll them outright. Hwang's resources in country were limited, thanks to both the nation's inefficiencies and the sanctions regime put upon them by the West, and he saw Amroggang Development as the thinnest and most fragile lifeline imaginable, but a lifeline nonetheless.

As he reached for the cup containing the dregs of his third tea of the day, his secretary's slightly agitated voice squawked over the intercom.

'Director Hwang. Apologies, but there is a General Ri here to see you.'

Hwang cocked his head. He had no idea who this man was. He knew dozens of men named Ri, many of whom were military officers, but he wasn't planning on talking to any of them today. 'Does he have an appointment?' Unannounced visits among government executives were unheard of. Even at the lowest levels preparations would need to be made, and Hwang was director of the state-owned company that ran the largest industrial sector in the nation, so any meeting should have been on the agenda for days.

There was a pause, then almost a shriek from his secretary. 'I am very sorry, sir, he is coming in!'

Hwang rose hurriedly as the door opened. There before him was a general in the green uniform of the Korean People's Army, with an impressive chest full of medals. Hwang thought he remembered seeing him the week before, during his visit to Residence No. 55.

Hwang's heart skipped a beat. He said, *'Jeoneun chepodoemnikka?'* Am I under arrest?

'Aniyo, dongmu.' No, comrade. 'Apologies for coming unannounced.' He stepped up to Hwang's desk and bowed. '-General Ri Tae-jin of the RGB.'

Hwang bowed. *'Foreign* intelligence? What can I do for you?' He shrugged. 'I've never even been out of the country.'

Ri smiled a little, but Hwang thought the man looked either tired or sad. 'I am not here to hire you on as an agent. May I sit down?'

'I will call for some tea.'

'No. Let us just talk.' Ri took the chair in front of the desk, and Hwang sat slowly in his own chair. This brash general with the sad face seemed to have taken charge here in Hwang's office. This was not the way meetings were held, and Hwang was utterly confused.

When both men were seated General Ri said, 'I congratulate you on your recent appointment. I, too, only took the reins at RGB two weeks ago.'

'I extend to you my congratulations and best wishes, comrade. May you bring honor to the Dae Wonsu.'

'I am aware of your predicament,' Ri said abruptly.

Hwang looked around the room. 'My *predicament*?'

'Yes. You have been given eighteen months to turn a slag pit in the mountains north of Chongju into the largest high-tech mineral mine in the world. The Chinese, the only business partner with the ability to make this happen, have been thrown out of the mine because the Dae Wonsu's demand that they provide us with ICBMs was rejected out of hand. You cannot work with Western businesses in this endeavor in any legal sense because the nations with the technology and expertise we need have restrictions imposed on business travel and high-tech exports, and there is great risk that the crippling sanctions against our nation will only squeeze you tighter.'

Hwang just looked back at the man. It was all true, but it was not the Juche way to complain or to even bring up the hardships.

Ri continued, 'You will not succeed, and you saw what happened to your predecessor, so you are aware of the ramifications of failure.'

Hwang puffed his chest out a little. 'I am working

diligently to ensure the mine reaches full output in the required time.'

'Work all you want. In fact, work up until the minute they drag you from behind that desk in chains. It will not happen without a lot of help.'

'What is it I can do for you, General?'

Somehow, the already stiff and stern-looking general managed to sit up even more erect. 'You and I have something in common, Hwang. We both have a countdown clock in our heads. I have been ordered to secure for the DPRK both the hardware and the know-how to produce a successful and working ICBM. I have been given three years, so . . . twice as long as you. I would feel lucky if my task were not even more difficult than yours.'

Hwang was both confused and nervous now. 'What you are telling me is not in my normal purview. There are security concerns in telling this to —'

'I don't care about that. You aren't going to violate security. I've read every word of your personnel and intelligence file. You are no risk to anyone.'

'Yes. Of course not. Go on, please, General Ri.'

'We have something else in common. A wife who is good, and two children who rely on us. If the only result of my failure would be my own demise, it would be a small worry.'

Hwang said, 'My own life is not important. I live to bring strength and prosperity to the Dae Wonsu.' It was official party doctrine. Communist ideology and personality cult.

And General Ri did not disagree with it, but he did deflect it. 'Well, Hwang, if we succeed, we will both bring strength and prosperity to the Dae Wonsu and save our families. Certainly you agree that would be a suitable outcome.'

Hwang just nodded.

'You have a year and a half to produce, process, and market rare earth metal. I have three years to acquire an operational ICBM.' He smiled thinly. 'As it stands now, we will both fail. Which means I will live exactly one and a half years longer than you.'

Hwang shrugged. 'If I fail, I fail. There are things worse than being shot by firing squad.'

Ri leapt to his feet, a wild look in his eyes. 'You are right about that! And I have seen those worse things. They fed my predecessor, General Gang, to starving dogs. It took him two minutes and forty seconds before he stopped resisting and they ripped out his throat. Which means that for two minutes and thirty-nine seconds he saw and felt and knew his fate. I have executed hundreds of men in my career. I will oversee an execution tomorrow morning, in fact. But what happened to General Gang was truly a horror no man should ever endure.'

Hwang's face blanched.

'And that's not all. His family paid for his failure with their lives.'

Hwang knew the families of traitors were often put to death. It wasn't a hidden practice. On the contrary, the military wanted it to be known that the ramifications for defying the state extended past the life of the culprit. It was a way to encourage families to inform on members who were a threat to the society as a whole.

Ri continued, 'Fail Choi as spectacularly as Gang did,

and you will suffer the same fate. I might even be ordered to witness your fate. And you should hope I am there, because while the dogs are ripping your flesh, you will have the small comfort of knowing I will be there in the pen eighteen months after you.'

'Are you just here to commiserate with me?'

'No. I am telling you all this so you know that the two of us need one another.'

'What are you proposing?'

Ri smiled at Hwang. 'I am proposing a partnership between our organizations. Between ourselves, in fact.'

'A partnership? I do not understand.'

'Your efforts are doomed to fail without outside help. I can get you that help. That which you need is all outside our borders, and I am the man who can go out and get it, and bring it back. You need foreign partnership. Not from China, but someone else. Someone who can acquire the goods and know-how and get them here, and someone who can take the metal and sell it quietly on the world market.'

'What do you want in return?'

'Twenty percent.'

'Twenty percent of what?'

'Twenty percent of everything. Direct into the coffers of the Ministry of Intelligence. Within one year this will triple my budget. With such monies I will be able to attain the technology we need.'

Hwang cracked a smile. 'The Chinese say the mine is worth twelve trillion US dollars. You think I have authority to divert twenty percent of twelve trillion dollars?'

'I think you can figure out a way if it keeps you out of

the labor camps and your children alive. I have access to a network of international bank accounts. I can help you divert payments. And twelve trillion will be over the life of the mine. I only need to use the promise of your mine to generate foreign investment, which I can use for my ICBM operation.'

'You are going to buy a missile?'

'No. I am going to buy a missile *industry*.'

The smile on Hwang's face returned. 'You don't lack for confidence.'

'It is not confidence. It is inspiration.' Ri leaned forward. 'Nothing so inspiring as watching your predecessor being eaten alive by hunger-crazed animals.'

Hwang cringed. Then said, 'Just tell me what you want, Ri.'

'No. You tell me what *you* want. And I will make it happen. I will use as much of my budget on this project as necessary, I'll shut down desks, departments, stations, and move resources, I will task foreign operatives, I will devote all my energies into this operation.'

'Operation? I'm sorry, Ri. I don't understand what you think you can do to help me mine and process rare earth minerals in Chongju.'

'Let me give you some examples of what I can do. I can bribe UN officials to loosen sanctions on banks and trade, I will hire armies of Western spies to infiltrate rare earth facilities all over the globe to learn that which you need to know. I will make deals with mining companies abroad to bring them on board in a clandestine fashion to help you with their expertise. I will offer secret employment contracts to chemists, geologists, engineers . . . you hand-pick the people you want and I will go out and get them, at gunpoint if necessary. I will organize deliveries of the goods you need and see that they make it past sanctions and embargo enforcement ships in the Yellow Sea. I will work with allies in Russia who can hack the computer systems of relevant industry to help you with blueprints. I will fund public relations initiatives around the world to make sure the market is accepting of your product once it's ready to export.'

Hwang had never heard anything like this in his life. Of course his office had made requests for information from foreign intelligence, but what Ri was offering was on a scale exponentially larger than anything he had ever considered. Ri was outlining just exactly all the things he needed to create a successful mining and processing operation at Chongju. 'Incredible,' he said. 'If you can do this, we have a chance.'

'So, you agree?'

What did he have to lose? 'I agree.'

Ri said, 'I need to establish partnerships outside of our nation, to create the conduits necessary to make this happen. If you had any suggestions for companies or personalities I should seek out to join us in our endeavor, I would like to hear them.'

Hwang nodded instantly. 'One name comes to mind. You get him involved as a benefactor, and you and I might just make this happen.'

The intelligence chief raised his eyebrows. 'Tell me.'

'Óscar Roblas de Mota.'

Ri nodded thoughtfully. He knew all about this man. 'Óscar Roblas. Why, yes. Of course.'

13

Present day

The small house on Jayhawk Street in Annandale, Virginia, showed its first signs of life most mornings at six. Forty-three-year-old Annette Brawley tapped the alarm clock, rolled up into a sitting position on her bed, and flipped on a light that shone through the curtains, out across the tiny yard and into the narrow street. She spent a few moments sitting on her bed, rubbing her eyes and dealing with the frustration that today was only Tuesday, and then she stood on tired legs.

As soon as she was up she made her bed. It was an old habit from her days in the Army, more than eight years removed now, and the process was especially quick and straightforward because no one slept with her, so she needed to remake only her side.

She then entered her kitchen and hit the button on the coffeepot, and grabbed a carton of eggs from the fridge. She pulled two cereal bowls out of the cupboard – this was about the time her head cleared enough for her to shut off her body's autopilot and actually think about what she was doing.

She fixed breakfast for two, then at six-fifteen on the nose she walked down the narrow hall to the back of the house, took a narrow flight of stairs up, and then knocked on the door at the top of the landing. After knocking she opened the door, because she knew knocking was only a formality and no one would answer, and she would therefore need to use more active measures to accomplish this daily task.

Stephanie Brawley was sixteen, and she liked getting up in the morning even less than her mom did. She also didn't like her mom very much, so she was doubly surly each and every time she awoke to a hoarse and tired female voice.

'Time to get up, Steph. I made you some eggs.'

'I hate you,' Stephanie croaked.

'I know, honey,' Annette calmly replied, wiping sleep from her eyes as she turned away. 'I made you some cereal, too.'

'Turn off the light!'

Annette left her daughter's room with the light on. She was subjected to a litany of insults as she retreated back downstairs to her coffee cup. Getting yelled at each morning had become part of her daily routine. She didn't like it, it saddened and depressed her, but she did her best to keep a bit of perspective. Annette herself had lived with her mom after her parents divorced, and she'd been no great joy to be around during her teenage years.

No, she'd probably been rough on her mother, and now as Stephanie berated her each morning, she tried to tell herself this phase was just the payback of karma and it would pass soon enough.

Annette had lived alone since her husband died in 2007. He was in the Pennsylvania National Guard, serving in

Afghanistan as a staff sergeant working as an intelligence analyst at his battalion headquarters in Nangarhar Province. He was far from any combat, and Annette thought he must have had one of the safer military jobs in the country, but his armored Humvee ran over an explosively formed projectile and he died instantly.

Annette was Army intelligence herself at the time, in active duty and serving just west of her husband in Kabul. Eight-year-old Stephanie had been home in Pittsburgh with Annette's mother, and it had been doubly hard on her that her own mother was not home at the time she heard about her father's death.

Yes, Stephanie's awful teenage-years behavior had an explanation, but Annette didn't let her use it as an excuse.

After the trials of her daily morning ordeal getting her daughter up and out the door to school, Annette actually enjoyed the short drive down to Springfield to work. She was no longer in the Army, but shortly before eight a.m., she pulled through the gates of Fort Belvoir. A few winding roads took her to her destination: the third-largest government building in the Washington area behind the Pentagon and the US Capitol, the National Geospatial-Intelligence Agency.

NGA is one of America's sixteen intelligence agencies under the Office of the Director of National Intelligence, and certainly one of the least well known. Formerly the National Imagery and Mapping Agency, NGA is dual-hatted as a combat support agency for the Department of Defense as well as being a member of the US intelligence community. The agency was only a few years old, but tremendous resources had been poured into this facility and another massive building in St Louis.

The organization received $5 billion a year in federal funds, and employed thousands of personnel, both military and civilian.

After showing her badge to a guard and then running it over a scanner she put her purse on a table for inspection and went through a metal detector. A long walk down a hallway with other employees – about a third of whom wore military uniforms – took her to a down escalator, above which ran the motto of the organization written out high on the wall:

KNOW THE EARTH . . . SHOW THE WAY . . . UNDERSTAND THE WORLD.

She passed into the massive atrium of the building – she'd read somewhere you could lay the Statue of Liberty on its side in here – and she scanned her badge at a reader in front of one of a half-dozen glass doorways in the center of the room that led to a bank of elevators. She took a ride to the fourth floor, then crossed the suspended hall over the atrium, made her way down another corridor, and scanned her badge a fourth time to get into her small office.

Annette was an imagery specialist for the NGA; she spent her days looking over all types of pictures using imagery manipulation and enhancement software, as well as compiling and analyzing other bits of data. Then she wrote interpretative reports of what she found, and these were delivered to the NGA's mission partners: policy makers, war fighters, and first responders.

Although she recognized her work wasn't going to

change the world, she found it interesting nonetheless, and she took solace in the fact she was damn good at it. Annette had spent her entire adult life focused on intelligence. After a full career in Army intel she had gotten hired here as a civilian analyst. She loved her work and her colleagues and the mission itself.

As fractured and stressful as her home life was – she was, after all, a widow with a teenage daughter with issues – Brawley took comfort in the fact she could come here every day, devote herself totally to the imagery and data points of a faraway place she would never visit personally, and build a coherent picture about what was going on there that just might help her country in some small way.

Her office was in the East Asia Department and her focus was North Korea, and while most of the others in her office spent their time on the 'sexy stuff,' fixated on either the opaque and mysterious government there or the nuclear and missile programs, Annette Brawley was in the economic section, and she concentrated almost exclusively on the DPRK's mining industry.

She'd become an expert on mining not out of any love for digging up rocks, but for the simple fact that she was tasked to North Korea's economic sector and that was their principal industry.

NGA geospatial technology was much more than looking at pictures and maps. The agency used all manner of data: spaceborne, airborne, seaborne, and landborne intelligence platforms at their disposal, as well as pulling the activity on cell-phone towers and even social media.

But much of that didn't apply in North Korea. NGA

had little to no visibility on cell-phone data inside the Hermit Kingdom, and social media there was banned. But there were other geospatial analysis tools at her disposal – satellite photos and videos ferried out of the country by smugglers and defectors; even government propaganda information could be gleaned to find hidden nuggets of information.

This morning she decided she'd take a look at some new images from one of the National Reconnaissance Office's KH-12 satellites. She pulled up the files on one of the three twenty-seven-inch monitors in front of her, and oriented herself with the global positioning information on the data screen next to it.

She spent a few minutes looking at a road project to a tungsten mine just outside Pyongyang, saw that nothing much had changed since she'd last looked in on the location a month earlier, and she noted it in her log.

Then she typed in the coordinates to the Chongju rare earth mineral mine.

A year earlier she had spent virtually all her time watching activities at the Chongju mineral mine. But that was when the Chinese were there, when there was real development going on. America's policy makers were interested back then, because rumors out of China said the deposit in the mountain there could have amounted to trillions of dollars for North Korea. This was something that worried the US government, so Annette had worked long hours tracking the progress on the site. She'd discovered small amounts of ore, just a few rail cars, traveling north from the open-pit mine to the Chinese border, presumably for processing at one of China's rare earth refineries.

When the Chinese were thrown out – Annette had received an intel briefing from the CIA that suggested they left because North Korean leader Choi invalidated their mining contract – interest in the mine quickly waned. Everyone concluded that the North Koreans wouldn't be able to do much more than continue to dig a small amount of ore out of the rocks and then ship it up to China for processing. Through her own work she determined the mine would reach only about four percent of its yearly production output capability without help from the Chinese.

When Chongju went on 'life support,' she refocused her attention on other mines in other parts of the DPRK, but she circled back every month or so to peek in on the sat images over Chongju. Each time she had done this over the past year she saw that the North Koreans were still trying to get something out of the site, but it was a shell of the operation it had been when they were partnered with those who knew what the hell they were doing.

Looking over the newest digital images from the KH-12 satellite, Brawley was happy to see there were no clouds over the site. The KH-12 sat had radar imagery capability, as well, but this wasn't the same as looking directly at the site through an optical lens.

She scanned the images the way she always did, slowly and methodically. First she ignored the buildings around the mine and focused directly on the open pit gouged out of the mountainside. The resolution of the KH-12 satellite cameras was fantastic. She could make out bulldozers and other earth-moving equipment; she even saw individual men, their shadows a further indication of what a clear day it was.

But nothing much was going on in the pit, so she began scanning to the south; the small city of Chongju was here, a few kilometers from the site itself, and she always liked to take a look at the train station and the freight storage lots nearby to see if it looked like there was any new industrial or commercial activity anywhere in the town that might relate to the mine.

This morning she saw something immediately. *That's odd,* she said to herself. Sixteen rectangles were lined up in a parking lot next to the one low and squat hotel near the train station. She never would have noticed the anomaly in the middle of the town if not for the fact she'd spent something in the neighborhood of two hundred hours looking at images of Chongju a year earlier, and her mind was programmed to burn images into it – she knew the layout of the town even now – certainly not every building, as there were hundreds, but the main clusters of development. These rectangles hadn't been there even last month. She would pull up the older images to double-check, but she was too sure of herself and too curious to do that now.

She knew what the rectangles were, because they were a common sight at mines and construction locations. They were portable buildings, like those used for temporary site offices or modular temp housing. Laid out as they were here, in neat rows lined up alongside the one hotel in the city and the train station, she knew this was housing brought in by the government for nonresident workers.

She could tell these were housing structures also because she saw a cluster of small outbuildings around an open-pit fire, and recognized it as a crude food-preparation facility.

Sixteen temporary buildings like these could house, Annette knew, a hundred fifty or more workers. But workers for *what*? There were a few factories in Chongju, but nothing that large. The only heavy industry around here was the mine.

She scanned back up to the mine. There was no major operation going on there, neither digging on the mine nor construction on other structures around it. She looked all over the city again, hunting for any signs that some new building or massive new statue of the Dae Wonsu was going up. When that turned up nothing, she scanned the roads around the town, and then the railroad tracks, trying her best to find any new project that would employ one hundred fifty workers.

It took her an hour to do this, but at the end of that hour, she had nothing to show for it.

But Annette Brawley had learned to be dogged and driven in the Army, and she had learned the nuances of her craft in intelligence school. She knew she was onto something, so she kept at it.

In a country like North Korea, where a lot of military activity takes place underground to stay hidden from satellites, she began to suspect she had uncovered something to do with the missile industry. The Sohae Satellite Launching Station was on a small peninsula jutting out into Korea Bay just twenty-five miles to the southwest; just maybe there was an underground secret project going on all the way over here.

It didn't track with anything she knew about how the

North Koreans operated, but she decided she'd talk to her colleagues in her analytical group who spent their days fixated on Sohae and get their take on it.

She was just about to break for lunch, a little frustrated that she felt like she'd wasted two hours on a futile hunt, when a thought occurred to her. There was a hydroelectric dam west of the Chongju mine, probably no more than ten minutes' drive on the paved roads in the area. It was an hour away from where the temp housing was located, but still she wondered if perhaps the guest workers were doing some refurbishing on the dam there.

She had to pull away from the enlarged image on her monitor to find the general area of the dam, and then she zoomed back in. She scanned along the dam, looked for any sign work was going on, but again she found nothing.

Shit. It was the last large structure in the area she could recall.

Without thinking she moved the image around to the left and the right, tracing around the banks of the reservoir created by the hydroelectric dam. There was a tiny village of square buildings on the north bank of the reservoir, and then she panned left to the west bank, on the far side of the water from the dam.

She stopped panning and leaned her face halfway to her monitor.

'What the *hell* is that?'

A series of long metal roofs ran on either side of some sort of raised track. On the eastern side of the roofs were a series of circular structures. Annette thought they looked like some sort of tanks. She counted twenty-six individual structures in the entire complex, and several vehicles were parked nearby.

'No . . . freakin' . . . way.'

She thought she knew what she was looking at, but to be certain she spun in her chair to the monitor on her right, typed something in a Google search, and then pulled up an image. This was the LAMP site in Malaysia. LAMP stood for Lynas Advanced Materials Plant; it was a rare earth mineral refinery owned by the Australian mining company Lynas.

She looked back to the location near the reservoir in the mountains of North Korea.

And then back to LAMP.

The two sites were virtually identical.

'What are you doing out there in the middle of nowhere?' she asked aloud.

She typed something on her keyboard and her third monitor displayed schematics of a typical rare earth refinery. Within a minute she had identified the round tanks as part of a rare earth oxide separation unit.

That confirmed it for her. North Korea was back in the rare earth mining game, and in a big way. They were cutting the Chinese out, even from the processing stage of the equation.

That would require high-tech equipment and massive amounts of expertise and skilled labor.

And Annette didn't think for one second that the North Koreans were doing this on their own.

Annette Brawley had worked through lunch, running down to one of the two cafeterias in the atrium only to grab a banana and a bag of animal crackers. She ate while she worked, compiling her astonishing findings and creating a quick but impactful PowerPoint presentation.

In Army intelligence her main weapon had been the PowerPoint slide show. It garnered a lot of insults from the soldiers devoted to combat operations, and rightly so, she admitted. She wasn't a shooter or a door kicker, she was an intel geek. But even though the door kickers she presented her slide shows to sometimes rolled their eyes, she took solace in the fact she'd done her best, and her best had helped the troops in harm's way.

Annette's superior at NGA was a Marine colonel named Mike Peters. He was younger than Annette by a few years and she found him roguishly handsome, and even though sometimes she felt he deferred unfairly to her colleagues in the armed services at the expense of his civilian employees, he did seem to appreciate Annette for her hard work and the lack of drama she brought to the workplace as compared with some of her younger colleagues, both in uniform and out.

She rapped on the door to his office at three-thirty in the afternoon. She'd checked his online agenda and saw he had a half-hour till his next appointment.

Peters looked up from his paperwork. 'Hey, Brawley. What's up?'

'I've got something good. You have ten minutes?'

'Got more than that. There's a meeting on five at sixteen hundred, but I'm yours till then.'

If only, she thought.

She pulled up her PowerPoint on his computer and sent it to a monitor on the far wall of his office. They went through it together over the next ten minutes; she showed her boss the temporary housing in Chongju near the hotel, new cars parked throughout the town, and then finally the processing plant near the dam north of Chongju.

When it was finished Colonel Peters turned away from the monitor and back to her. 'So the Chinese companies, Chinalco and Minmetals, are back at Chongju, and they are going to process their ore? Why would they need to do that?'

'They wouldn't. The Chinese have their own refineries over the border and the roads, rail, and bridges to get it there.'

'What's your conclusion?' he asked.

'The only conclusion I can come up with is that the Chinese are not involved.'

'Are you saying the DPRK domestic mining operation has developed to the extent they can extract rare earths?'

Brawley shook her head. She considered herself a pretty 'meat and potatoes' analyst. She didn't speculate wildly about anything, because that was a surefire way to make errors. Still, when she was sure of herself, she expressed herself with vehemence. 'Mike, I've been examining operations at this mine long enough to know this isn't DPRK doing this work alone. They are getting help.'

'Who is doing the work?'

'That's going to be impossible to tell from a satellite. CIA needs to get a man in there.'

Peters laughed. 'Have they been showing *Mission: Impossible* in the break room or something?'

Brawley laughed as well. 'Sorry, is that far-fetched? I

don't know HUMINT. I just look at roofs and heads. It's up to somebody else to get all the answers on the ground.'

Peters liked Brawley's work. She was careful, more careful than many of the twenty-somethings that worked at her level.

'This is good.'

'Thanks.'

'This might go all the way up to DNI. Who knows, it could make its way into the Presidential Daily Brief.'

Brawley's eyes widened. She had a smiling picture of President Jack Ryan on her desk. Even the fans of the President in her office teased her about it. 'Maybe I should work up another PowerPoint. More levels of distinction. More color.'

Peters shook his head. 'Everyone in the IC knows Jack Ryan likes to look at raw data for himself, but DNI Foley won't sit in the Oval with him and click through a Power-Point. Don't worry about your presentation. You've done great work, now get back to your office and produce something more.'

'Something more?'

'You aren't done, Annette.' He tapped the open-pit mine with the tip of his pen. 'As long as they keep digging, you keep digging.' Colonel Peters gave her a satisfied wink.

'Just thought that one up, Colonel Peters, or have you been saving that one for a while?'

'Just thought it up,' he said proudly. 'Though you can expect me to reuse it hundreds of times. It's pretty good, right?'

14

One year earlier

Mining director Hwang had met intelligence chief Ri just once, a week earlier when he showed up unannounced to his office, and at that time Ri had been wearing his military uniform. Hwang supposed the lieutenant general was always dressed as an officer in the Chosun Inmingun when he left his house, so Hwang found it surprising to see the fifty-two-year-old this morning wearing a light gray Western suit and a blue tie. Hwang had to admit that Ri was, if anything, even more impressive out of uniform. He obviously exercised regularly, unlike Hwang, who rarely seemed to find the time for evening walks with his family, and often got winded taking the stairs to his office of the Korea Natural Resources Trading Corporation.

The two men stood in front of each other in the business-class lounge at Pyongyang Sunan International Airport. Each man had his own small entourage with him; in Ri's case it was colonels as well as bodyguards, and in Hwang's case a single personal attendant as well as several assistant directors and high-level technical advisers. It was just five a.m., and the first commercial flight of the day wasn't leaving until eight-thirty, so the military and government men had the place all to themselves, although General Ri could have shut down the entire airport if he had any concern about eyes on him that might threaten today's operation.

Director Hwang Min-ho still could not believe he was leaving his country, even if it was just for twenty-four hours. Virtually no regular North Koreans ever set foot abroad, and even very few high-level government officials earned the opportunity. North Korea is as close to a closed society as exists in the world, and the government-imposed sheltering of its people from the outside world was a key component to the nation's ability to control the message to its citizens.

But Ri had orchestrated this trip; he'd arranged the travel for Hwang and himself and a total of nine of their translators and assistants, and he'd smoothed out the highly unusual situation with the Ministry of People's Security. A nation that regards unauthorized departure as an act of treason punishable by death clearly took foreign travel seriously, so Ri and his office had a lot of hoops to jump through to make this all happen. He forced his way through much of the bureaucracy by invoking the fact he was on an approved operation of the Dae Wonsu. He had, in fact, gone as high as Choi's office to get approval for the travel, and only after a few days of meetings with security men, meetings where General Ri and Director Hwang were asked personal questions to vet their commitment to the Supreme Leader, were they finally allowed the opportunity to go abroad, and only then in the presence of several domestic security agents posing as subordinates.

In Hwang's case it was a truly rare occurrence that such a high-ranking mineral executive would fly out of North

Korea without being part of some sort of organized delegation replete with state security officials sent along to watch over him, lest he either be kidnapped by the West or, and all knew this would be more likely, attempt defection.

And as uncommon as it was for Hwang to travel abroad, the fact that General Ri was outside North Korea at all was utterly unheard of.

But Ri made it happen. The men were supremely motivated by the threat to their own lives if this operation did not succeed; ergo, the men had torn up the rule book.

After a call came through the radio of an airport official, the entire group filed down a back stairwell of the terminal to ground level, then they took a rickety bus ride out to a Tu-134 twin-engine jet painted in the red, white, and blue markings of Air Koryo, North Korea's national carrier.

Hwang felt his legs shaking as he climbed the jet stairs. It was not from excitement – this was no thrill that he was getting to visit outside his country – this was real fear. He'd lived fifty-four years hearing stories about the outside world, all of them bad. There was a statue in his hometown showing American GIs spearing a screaming Korean baby with a bayonet – foreigners were evil – and the disease and rampant crime and moral and physical decay of South Korea and Japan were legendary.

He had spent the evening before holding his wife and children, fighting back tears, and telling them to be strong and have faith in the Dae Wonsu should he never return.

On board he had his choice of seats. The plane could accommodate up to eighty, and there were only sixteen on the flight. He strapped himself in next to Ri and sat silently, his hands trembling, thinking about the prospect of what he would face when they landed.

They took off toward the south and the aircraft climbed into the morning fog, and Hwang did little more than nod as Ri began discussing his strategy for the meeting later in the day.

Four hours later Hwang was deep into his work and past the terror of the unknowns of the trip. He barely looked up from his paperwork as the aircraft landed in Vientiane, Laos, to refuel and to obfuscate the origin of the flight. Within half an hour they were back in the air.

They landed a second time in Singapore during a mid-afternoon rain shower, and here they were met by local operatives of Ri's intelligence service and driven to the Mandarin Oriental hotel.

Hwang Min-ho could not believe his eyes when he saw the opulence and grandeur of the lobby. As one of a rare few of his countrymen who had actually seen the inner sanctum of Residence No. 55, he could say without reservation that this hotel was even more luxurious than the palace of the Dae Wonsu. As confused as he was by the riches on display, available, apparently, to regular businessmen and not just to government elite or royalty, he noticed Ri felt the same way. He could tell by the wide eyes and sideways glances of the general that he had never seen anything like this, either.

Neither man remarked on the amazing facility as they took an elevator up to the presidential suite. At their sides were domestic security agents, and both men knew they were being watched to see how they reacted.

In the hallway on the top floor of the hotel, four physically fit men in suits greeted the entourage from North Korea. The translator for the Hwang – Ri group, a middle-aged North Korean woman, spoke in English to the men, and then everyone stepped into the 2,500-square-foot presidential suite.

Hwang and Ri both smiled at the sight of the man they'd come all this way to meet. Óscar Roblas de Mota cut an impressive figure. Seventy-three years old and heavyset, he was nonetheless surprisingly fit and his hair dye, though fooling no one, at least gave him the appearance of vibrancy. He stood a head higher than Ri, and even taller than Hwang, and he wore a beautiful black three-piece suit from Savile Row. He stood at the floor-to-ceiling windows, but spun toward his guests and walked to them with an energetic spring in his step.

He spoke with an air of unbridled competence and power, introducing himself to both men as if they were fans in line for an autograph instead of two of the most important officers of a nuclear power.

But that was Roblas's way. Some successful men never do develop personalities fitting of their accomplishments, but Óscar Roblas was a winner, and he damn well knew it.

Roblas was the third-wealthiest man in Mexico and ranked number twenty-eight on the *Forbes* list, with personal and familial assets to the tune of $24 billion. He didn't start out with nothing, though the narrative his company propagated had pushed that history for the past thirty-five years. The truth was that his family made its money in copper mining going back three generations. The Roblas family company, Grupo Pacífico, still mined copper and zinc throughout the nation, but they'd made money in oil, leasing land for drilling across Mexico, and then Óscar Roblas had created exponential growth for himself by expanding to mineral mines around the world by using offshore companies and limited partnerships.

He owned or had owned dozens of mineral mines on all points on the globe: part of a titanium mine in Mozambique, diamond mines in Botswana and Sierra Leone. Gold, copper, zinc, and nickel mines in a dozen countries.

With his vast wealth he had the ability to create companies and even banking institutions out of thin air to keep the money trails of his endeavors hidden. Hwang knew of Roblas because Roblas had partnered on North Korean mines in the past, albeit on a scale a small fraction of what Hwang would propose at today's meeting.

The men all sat down at a large conference table brought up to the presidential suite just for the meeting, and after one of the North Korean state security men scanned the room for listening devices with a small apparatus, Roblas began the conversation with an uncomfortable question that was conveyed first in English, and then in Korean through the translator.

'And how is former director Kim?' Roblas asked. 'I enjoyed working with him in years past on the magnesite project in Daeheung. I found him to be a capable man. Mr Hwang, I understand you replaced him as director of Korea Natural Resources Trading due to ill health.'

Hwang paused for a moment, unsure as to what he should say. A state security minder sent along to watch the meeting sat on a sofa, away from the conference table, and stared stone-faced back at him.

'Yes,' Hwang replied to the translator, who converted his words effortlessly into English. 'He has taken ill, but he will recover. The rigors of the job, however, are too much for him now, so he will tend to his beautiful garden and enjoy his large and happy family.'

Roblas nodded without smiling. 'I understand.'

Hwang had a strong suspicion the Mexican did, in fact, understand quite well. He had been working on mining ventures in North Korea for decades. It would come as no surprise to him that a level of treachery such as that perpetrated by Director Kim would be dealt with quite harshly by the leadership.

With that matter settled, Director Hwang Min-ho spent the next hour laying out his proposal to restart the Chongju rare earth mineral mine without the partnership of the Chinese. He explained how General Ri would help him acquire some of the technology and information necessary, but that they would need an initial investment of hard currency and the support structure of a foreign partnership to obtain everything they needed to get the mine up and running.

Roblas listened politely, but with markedly little animation. Government mining ministers came to him asking for help on a regular basis. Only the month before, a Congolese minister approached him to partner on a new iron mine in his nation. Roblas declined. His own geologists doubted the size of the find, and he wasn't impressed with the returns at his other Congolese mines.

The North Koreans had talked him into coming all the

way to Asia to meet with them, assuring him they had an opportunity he would not want to pass up. Of course he knew this would involve the rare earth mine recently vacated by the Chinese, and of course he was interested. He had his finger on the pulse of the world mining community, so there was no way a find like Chongju would slip by him. He knew the Chinese had wanted to stay but Choi had forced them out, and Roblas was curious enough to fly to Singapore and sit with the little brainwashed fools from North Korea to see what they wanted to offer him.

He was ready to invest, to move mountains, both literally and figuratively, if and only if the North Koreans could show him that the value of the mine, and the terms of their contract offer, both made the deal worthwhile.

Hwang showed him the raw findings of the Chinese, all translated into English, and Óscar Roblas could not believe his eyes. He knew the North Koreans were sitting on a rare earth reserve large enough that the Chinese had been fighting to keep a partnership going despite Choi's actions, but the assertion that $12 trillion at today's value lay just beneath the rocks was nothing less than astounding to the Mexican.

He asked for clarification on various matters, but Hwang had been ready for this. He had the numbers from the tests and the CVs of the geologists who signed off on the find.

Roblas then said something that surprised both Hwang and Ri.

'I am interested. But as a businessman, I like to know what I am getting into. I haven't been to your country in over twenty years. If I am going to invest in this project of yours, I want to see it.'

Hwang was confused, at first. 'All of the findings of the Chinese are in the materials here. You may feel free to take your time in looking –'

The running translation was interrupted when Roblas said, 'No. I want to go to North Korea and see the merchandise. The mine. The location of the proposed processing plant. The infrastructure you have in place now. If I like what I see, if I agree the potential is there and the terms of our partnership are to my liking, then we will do business together.'

Hwang replied, 'Certainly. When would you like to come?'

'I suppose you have a plane at the airport now. I'd like to return with you tonight.'

'Tonight?'

'Yes. If I don't come now, if you make me wait a week or a month, then you will have time to put some window dressing up at the mine. To reroute electricity or to take generators out of Pyongyang and truck them to the mountains just for my visit. To move every skilled miner in the nation to Chongju, and to put them in a new uniform made just for my visit. I have been at this a long time, *amigos.* I know all the tricks.'

Hwang started to balk, but General Ri, who had been silent for the vast majority of the meeting, stood suddenly. With the air of a military man he said, 'Let us not delay.'

Even though the reception committee had less than twelve hours to put something together, in Pyongyang

Óscar Roblas was treated like a visiting head of state, although no cameras recorded his arrival. He met a cavalcade of senior officials at a private residence set up for visiting dignitaries, and they promised their full cooperation, should he enter into partnership on Chongju.

Roblas's other mining concern in North Korea had been a profitable exercise for him, and he found the North Koreans had held up their end of the bargain, so he was positively inclined to agree even before he headed up to Chongju.

The following morning they took off to the north in a long motorcade; Roblas sat with Ri and Hwang in a military SUV. They were silent on much of the journey. All that needed to be said had already been said, and there was little for the big Mexican to do but see for himself.

Roblas spent the day at the mine and the proposed location of the processing facility a few kilometers to the west of the pit itself. He walked the scoured earth, his patent leather shoes covered in mud and gravel. He knelt and held the dirt in his fingers.

Finally he smiled at Hwang and Ri. 'Not so different from the Sierra Madre.'

They smiled back.

Over the next two months Roblas sat in his Mexico City office and worked in secret with his senior staff, ironing out just what was necessary to assemble a rare earth mining operation from next to nothing. Everything from how much water would be brought in to the list of United Nations sanctions that would have to be skirted for the operation to be successful. He worked closely with Hwang and his senior staff, and he worked with Ri as well, directing the head of North Korea's foreign intelligence service in the drawing up of a battle plan of how to facilitate the successful mining operation.

The terms offered by Hwang were curious, but Roblas found them to be acceptable. There would be a huge capital outlay early on, of course, as Roblas deposited millions of dollars into North Korean offshore accounts. This was an initial cash buy-in that was a lot of money for the North Koreans, but nothing much for Roblas at all.

Then Roblas would use his own funds to move equipment and personnel into North Korea. This would cost, Roblas estimated, well north of $60 million. He'd been told about Choi's demand that production begin in a year and a half, and this was a tight timeline, but the $12 trillion buried under the dirt gave Roblas the incentive to get it up and running.

The third major outlay for Roblas would be the largest. The day production began at the mineral processing facility, he would owe the North Koreans a one-time cash payment of $500 million. A lot of money, to be sure, especially after his other expenses, but after this the contractual terms were firmly in Roblas's favor. He'd recoup his expenses in under five years, and he'd have so much pure profit after that his main concern would be on how to rake in and launder it all.

It was clear to the Mexican businessman that the North Koreans wanted the contract front-loaded to their advantage because they needed an infusion of cash. Roblas did not know why, nor did he ask. He knew theirs was a dirt-poor nation, and he hoped his money would go to improve the lives of the common people in North Korea, but he highly doubted this. He wondered if they would blow it all on luxury items and nuclear missiles, but he wondered this for only a moment, because he didn't really care all that much.

Roblas intended to keep his name out of the entire affair. It would appear to the world, if they found out about it at all, as if North Korea itself had played the world mining industry like a Stradivarius, orchestrating the movement of manpower, brainpower, machine and natural resources, bringing everything together. Many would assume the DPRK had outside help, but on this venture, just as in other operations Roblas had undertaken in less permissive parts of the world, he would conduct his part of the business in secret.

In the lists and charts and white papers created by his staff about the hardships of bringing this plan to life, nothing appeared as a more obvious problem than the processing of the ore. Roblas and Hwang could build the mine and extract the ore, and once the ore was refined, Roblas could assist the North Koreans in getting it onto the world market in a way to maximize its value, but the highly technical and intensive processing of the minerals was beyond even the scope of Roblas and his Grupo Pacífico. A few mines around the world did their own processing, but only in the United States, China, and Canada. Even the Australians sent their ore to an Australian operation based in Malaysia to be processed.

But that would not work for the North Koreans. They would have to do it themselves, right there at the mine.

This was yet another crucial matter that he'd have to bring up with Duke Sharps.

Roblas's Grupo Pacífico had relied on the work of Duke Sharps in New York City for much of its underhanded corporate espionage and investigations in the past decade, so it was a simple matter to contract with Sharps again.

The full scope of the North Korean operation was laid out to Sharps by Roblas himself at a luxury hotel in Saint Maarten. The American ex-spy agreed on the spot – as soon as Roblas agreed on a cost plus fee for the private intelligence firm.

Sharps charged an incredible amount of money for the work he did. Often the brash American infuriated Óscar Roblas by his near-extortionate fees and his occasional reluctance to get his hands *really* dirty. Sharps would spy, he would break some laws, and he would push some boundaries, but a man in Roblas's line of work occasionally needed extreme measures taken, and Sharps was too aboveboard to do the real dirty work.

But Sharps and his people had their place. They would help get foreign nationals into North Korea, they would help move material and steal proprietary software needed for the pro-duction facility, they would pressure elected officials and UN members to vote the way the North Koreans desired to keep the money and the material moving. In the final analysis, even though Duke charged too much and refused to assassinate, kidnap, or beat Roblas's enemies, the businessman in Óscar Roblas knew that Duke Sharps and his staff were worth every damn cent.

15

Present day

John Clark's mobile phone's alarm began chiming on his desk, and he looked away from the paperwork in front of him and turned it off. He sighed a little. It was ten a.m., time to do his daily exercises.

Damn, he thought to himself. *Ten o'clock comes around every day, doesn't it?*

He got up and shut the door to his office, then opened a drawer in his desk and removed a blue racquetball. He sat back down in his chair, took the ball in his right hand in front of him, and began squeezing with all his might.

Clark did all manner of other exercises in a small gym he'd built for himself in his Emmitsburg, Maryland, farmhouse, but the workout he did there he actually enjoyed. His hand therapy, on the other hand, was miserable.

Clark's hand had been smashed by torturers in Russia a couple of years back, and despite a half-dozen reconstructive surgeries in the intervening years the index finger on his right hand was still both stiff and weak. Arthritis and scar tissue around the small joints of the appendage were the root cause of the problem, and his surgeon had told him he'd done all he could to repair the damage. John asked the man what John himself could do to improve his situation, and the doctor had replied with a shrug.

'I'd say PT, every day, to strengthen the muscles and stretch the tissue. The only problem is the arthritis in the knuckles. Working out that hand is going to hurt. Every day, it will hurt.'

The doctor thought he was talking a senior citizen into just giving up on a full recovery and enjoying his retirement years in comfort, but the doctor didn't know John Clark. Clark had happily accepted that ten-second primer on what he needed to do to make the best of his horribly damaged hand, and since that day he'd put himself through an excruciating daily twenty-minute regimen of stretching and strengthening.

The doc had been correct. Yes, it hurt. A lot. Every day. And even with all the pain and suffering, Clark's trigger finger was still so noncompliant he'd taken to firing guns with his middle finger, resulting in the joke around The Campus that when Clark flipped you the bird, he *really* meant it. But his hand had improved markedly in the months he'd been putting himself through his daily ten a.m. torture session.

He squeezed down on the ball, and white-hot flame grew in the back of his hand and it shot up his index finger. He winced with pain.

And his office door flew open.

Clark quickly put the ball down and looked up at the doorway. Jack Ryan, Jr., stood there with a sheet of paper clutched in his hand. There was a wide grin on his face.

'Do you knock, kid?'

'Sorry, John,' Ryan said, but he looked too excited to mean it.

Clark blew out a long sigh. 'What do you have?'

'Skala.' When Clark did not react to this, Ryan said, 'Remember the name Hazelton wrote before he died?'

'Of course. Who is he?'

'Hazelton said he had something to do with Prague airport. It looked like a dead end, since we couldn't find anyone by that name associated with the airport. But finally I found a guy named Karel Skála, who is a low-rung consular official in the Ministry of Foreign Affairs in the Czech Republic who works in the bureaucracy of the European Union. He operates out of an office at the Ministry of Foreign Affairs building in Prague, so I didn't see a connection. But after some more digging, I see that by appointment he will meet traveling EU diplomats at the customs and immigration office at Václav Havel Airport.'

Clark was impressed. He said, 'Not too far of a stretch to speculate this guy gave something to Hazelton, and that was what the North Koreans were after. What might he have that interested them?'

Clark knew the answer to the question he had posed. He just wanted to see if Ryan would get it as well.

Ryan answered confidently. 'Probably travel documentation. That's foreign ministry territory. Issuing passports, entrance visas, or other EU documentation. Skála's particular job involves preparing travel documentation for Czech diplomatic employees. This guy knows what he gave Hazelton, which means he probably knows why someone killed Hazelton. I say we pay the man a visit.'

Clark stood. 'Let's grab the guys and then go talk to Gerry.'

Twenty minutes later Gerry sat in the conference room surrounded by all the Campus operators. He rubbed his temples. 'You want to go to the Czech Republic and find out what you can about this Skála character.'

'That's right,' said Ryan.

'Covertly or overtly?'

'Covertly, for sure.'

Gerry looked at Clark. 'What do you think, John?'

Clark said, 'I'm for it. We can send Ryan and Caruso to Prague. While they are there, the rest of us will go up to New York. I want to put some resources into learning a little more about what Sharps Global Intelligence Partners is up to.'

Sam said, 'John, you know Sharps, don't you?'

'I did.'

'You guys are old buddies?'

Clark gave Driscoll a sideways glance. 'I wouldn't piss on Duke Sharps if he was on fire.'

'You and Mary Pat seem to feel the same about the guy. What did he do?'

'Duke Sharps was working for FBI's Counterintelligence Division right after Nine-Eleven. He was based here, in Manhattan, and he was promoted to the top of the Manhattan Bureau. It was a time where we needed a lot of leadership in that job, but while everybody else saw it as their duty to stick around and work, Duke Sharps saw Nine-Eleven as an opportunity for personal enrichment. He quit FBI, then started his own consulting company. FBI needed his expertise, so they ended up paying him several times what they had been paying him.'

With a shrug Sam said, 'Sounds like capitalism.'

'It gets worse. Sharps Partners was set up to work exclusively with the federal government, but slowly, over the next few years, he started branching out into the private sector, creating new divisions and offices to assist corporations on intelligence and counterintelligence matters. His work here in New York was still first-rate, from what I've been told, so the government kept their hands off. But after a while it became clear his private-sector work wasn't as private-sector as everyone thought it was. He got caught working for the Saudis to identify Israeli Mossad officers in New York.'

Sam said, 'Holy shit. Why the hell is he not in prison for that?'

'Sharps claimed he thought he was doing work on behalf of a Gulf oil company, corporate intel against a rival company. He also pled ignorance that the men he was tailing were Mossad. He was hauled into hearings, but they were kept quiet for a lot of reasons.'

'I'll bet,' said Driscoll. 'A guy with Sharps's knowledge and clearances could raise a lot of issues in an open hearing.'

'Right. In the end, the government couldn't prove he was knowingly working for a foreign power. He lost all his federal contracts, President Ryan saw to that, and everyone thought Sharps Partners would dissolve without all those contracts coming in. But a funny thing happened . . .'

Sam shook his head in disbelief. 'He didn't need the US money anymore.'

'Nope. He had parlayed his high-profile FBI gig and US contracts into God knows how many foreign deals. He basically became the guy in the US the bad guys call when they want agents who talk and walk just like Americans, doing operations either on American soil or under the cover of the USA.'

'And no one has been able to prove anything?'

Clark shook his head. 'Not a goddamned thing. Sharps has foreign entities and they work with other foreign entities that are set up by whatever shady government or criminal group wants to hire him. It's a foolproof system, or at least it always has been.' Clark sneered. 'If I can find any proof that treasonous bastard is taking one single dime from some other state actor for the purpose of conducting intelligence, then I will nail his balls to the steps of the FBI building as a gift to all the hardworking men and women in government who didn't parlay their access and experience into a criminal career.'

Clark was ready to go. 'We'll need today to prep, to assemble equipment, to acquire transport and a safe house in theater. I'll go down and talk to IT about getting us some access to cameras outside of Sharps's office.'

Gerry said, 'Okay. I agree to both operations. Good luck, guys. Your work is cut out for you. Sharps and his people are good at what they do, and New York City is their turf. You do not tail them into subways, or through any choke points, because they *will* spot you.'

Clark said, 'You're right about that.'

Ryan understood why he got the foreign duty. With his

beard and other things he had done to alter his appearance in the past few years, he was almost never recognized, even on the streets of the US But in Prague he would garner even less attention. He hated that his semi-fame had to enter into the threat matrix for each operation, but he had no one to blame but himself. Not for his fame – the fact his dad was a household name around the world was at fault there – but Jack Junior himself had sought out a life of clandestine work, and celebrity and anonymity were polar opposites.

Ryan recognized his was an unusual life. It annoyed him sometimes, but he realized he wouldn't trade it for the world. He said, 'Thanks, Gerry. Maybe I shouldn't press my luck, but I'd like to request that Gavin comes with us on this.'

Gerry was surprised. 'To Prague? Why?'

'Whatever Skála's involvement in this matter, I'm thinking it likely he was doing it through back channels, and not in his official capacity in the government. It stands to reason. Sharps Global Intelligence Partners wasn't contracted with the Czech government, so I figure he was moonlighting if he was working with them. That might mean he used his personal phone or computer as a means of contact with someone else involved. I'm assuming we'll have to skim all the intel off of his electronic devices in order to figure out who he's been talking to. If we are to do this without him knowing we're there, then our infiltration might be time sensitive.'

'What if he's erased the data?'

Ryan didn't hesitate. 'Oh, I'm sure he has. But I've watched Gavin work. He's a bloodhound. If there is a trace of anything, even if it's something erased, Gavin will retrieve it.'

Gerry thought it over. He wasn't crazy about Biery running out into the field every time The Campus had a time-sensitive operation. Virtually all of their operations were time sensitive, and there was only one IT director.

Jack saw his employer's hesitancy, so he said, 'Of course, I guess I could just whack Karel Skála on the head and kidnap him.'

It was a joke, but Gerry just raised an annoyed eyebrow.

Ryan smiled. 'Sorry. Just kidding around. It's okay. We can go without Gavin. We'll make do.'

Gerry looked to Clark. He was the director of operations of The Campus, after all. 'If I send Gavin to Prague, is that going to negatively affect your operation in New York?'

Clark shook his head. 'We'll need schematics on Sharps's offices, employee lists, things of that sort. Might need some security measures disabled in his building if we decide to try a sneak-and-peek. Biery's staff is more than competent to handle all that.'

'Okay.' Gerry turned to Ryan and Caruso. 'You can take Gavin, but only if you promise to return him the way you found him.'

Jack and Dom laughed.

Gavin Biery was virtually the only employee of Hendley Associates who wasn't happy with the new building. Although his job title had not changed since the old place, here he had control of less than half the square footage as compared to the West Odenton campus, and to Gavin that felt like a kick in the pants.

Yes, The Campus was a leaner outfit now, he didn't need as much space, and Gerry had put in the money to ensure that the technology here was better than much of the equipment Gavin had used at their old address, but Gavin liked the feeling of control he had over the bigger operation. West Odenton had more computers and more personnel, and Gavin Biery had been master of it all.

Since the inception of The Campus many years earlier, the organization derived much of its raw intelligence by intercepting the satellite feeds beamed between the NSA building up in Fort Meade, Maryland, and the CIA building down in McLean, Virginia. To do this a huge array of dishes were necessary on the roof of the five-story West Odenton building.

The radio waves, in addition to being hard to access, were also encrypted, so that anyone who could pull them out of the air couldn't decipher the intel. Biery and his staff got around this with state-of-the-art decryption software and the massive amounts of high-tech hardware needed to run it.

But the technology had changed over the years, and now Gavin was able to access every bit of the Joint Worldwide Intelligence Communications System's intelligence networks, as well as other government networks, through a back door he developed through a virtual private network.

Gone now were the dishes, the miles of cabling running up and down a communications shaft, and the mainframes used just in the decoding and decrypting process. Biery did still have a mainframe here at the Alexandria building, but he was able to task it to other projects.

Gavin missed his sat dishes and his cabling. He had developed the virtual private network access to JWICS only out of necessity, after the Chinese assault on the West Odenton building meant The Campus no longer had the line-of-sight access necessary to intercept the radio traffic. Gavin lamented the loss of his massive computer and communications complex, but he was the architect of the new system, and objectively he did have to admit they were now in a newer, more secure, and better-connected location.

But there was another reason Biery missed the big Hendley Associates building in West Odenton. Up there, they had a nice cafeteria with excellent food. Here, by contrast, they had only a break room with snack machines. Of course there were restaurants nearby. Many of the employees walked the few blocks south down to King Street for lunch, but Gavin rarely took the time to go out for lunch. Usually he had pizza or sandwiches delivered from outside the building, but every mid-morning and mid-afternoon he liked a snack to keep him going, and for that he had to deal with the damn machines.

At ten-thirty a.m. Gavin was in the little break room, dropping quarters into a snack machine. He made his selection and then groaned in frustration as his fried blueberry pie got stuck between the plexiglass window and a bag of chips.

'Damn it,' he said. He banged on the glass a few times to no avail, and then started to fish through his pockets for more money, deciding this to be some omen telling him he really wanted the bag of chips as well.

While he was focused on his change, Jack Ryan and Dom Caruso came out of the stairwell into the break room.

Jack said, 'Your secretary said we'd find you here. Mid-morning munchies?'

'It takes a lot of fuel to power all this brain, Ryan.'

'Oh, I understand completely,' Jack said.

Dom said, 'Hey, Gav. We were just wondering if you felt like taking a little trip.'

Gavin couldn't contain his excitement. As he spun around in surprise, several quarters flew out of his hand and bounced across the tile floor. 'Hell, yes! Where and when?'

'Prague, and very soon. Like tonight.'

The fifty-six-year-old smiled broadly, and his chest heaved with excitement. 'Prague? Central European intrigue. Cobblestone streets. Gas lamps. Mist. The perfect town for real cloak-and-dagger work.'

Jack rolled his eyes a little. 'You've been reading too many spy novels. No cloak and dagger. More like sitting and watching, with you back at the hotel waiting for us to show up with a mobile phone or a laptop I'll need cracked.'

'I can do that.' Gavin shrugged. 'It's still pretty cool.'

He looked a little dejected, so Caruso added, 'If it will make you feel better, you can wear a cloak in your hotel room while you do it.'

Ryan laughed, and Biery played along. 'Better than nothing, I guess.'

Dom saw the stuck fruit pie. He punched the glass

window of the machine and the snack fell to the bottom. Pulling it out, Dom said, 'Come on, Gavin. This shit will kill you.'

Gavin snatched the fruit pie from Dom's hand. 'No, Dominic. Shooting it out with Iranians will kill you.'

Dom gave Biery a hard look that Ryan plainly saw. Biery realized he'd screwed up. Gavin cleared his throat uncomfortably. 'Okay. Well, I'd better go tell my staff they're going to have to read an instruction manual on computers, because I won't be here to hold their hands for a few days.' He took off toward the stairs.

Ryan looked at his cousin. 'What the hell is he talking about?'

'Nothing at all.'

'Tell me.'

'Clark says we have to be trained to go it alone from time to time. To keep our work compartmentalized for the good of the whole. Something happened. I dealt with it. Now it's time to move on.' Dom winked at his cousin and slapped him on the shoulder.

'But –'

'No *but*s.'

Ryan sighed. 'Okay.'

16

United Nations Resolution 1874 authorizes member states, in accordance with international law, to inspect cargo in transit to and from the Democratic People's Republic of Korea if a member state determines there are reasonable grounds to believe the cargo contains materials related to weapons of mass destruction.

As with all international law, there was much gray area with this resolution, including but not limited to the types of actions that constituted suspicious behavior. And *reasonable grounds* could mean different things to different nations at different times, and this meant the interdiction of cargo in transit could be applied unequally in different cases.

All that said, the actions of the *Emerald Endeavor*, a feedermax cargo ship flying the flag of Liberia and traveling in international waters due west of the city of Inchon, were without question highly suspicious, and anyone aware of UN1874 knew that this particular resolution certainly applied to this particular situation.

The *Emerald Endeavor*'s stated cargo was sugar from Cuba, and it did originate its voyage in Havana six and a half weeks earlier, but since then it had taken a strange route from the Caribbean. And one day out of the port of Batangas in the Philippines, the ship abruptly stopped transmitting its Automatic Identification System.

The AIS was required on all maritime traffic of more than 300 tons, the *Emerald Endeavor* was 2,300 tons, so its failure to broadcast was either the result of a serious mechanical problem or else it was a clear violation of international maritime law.

Further, attempts to raise the ship via radio over the past twenty-four hours had been unsuccessful. It was possible the *Emerald Endeavor*'s bridge communication system was down, but that would have been a huge problem for the captain, and the vessel steamed along in its shipping lane as if nothing were amiss, passing multiple ports of refuge as it headed north off the coast of South Korea.

Any UN member state had the authority to intercept the ship by UN rules, but not every UN member state had the ability to do so. If it was, indeed, carrying cargo in violation of international sanctions, then the crew might well resist interdiction, either by racing away at full speed or even by using weapons or other means to repel boarders, so a ship inclined to force compliance with UN1874 needed to have two things in sufficient quantities before attempting the interdiction.

Speed and guns.

It was well past midnight now, the *Emerald Endeavor* was just hours from entering the territorial waters of North Korea south of the port of Haeju, and it must have seemed to the North Korean captain of the ship that he was all but home free, until the moment the large blip on his radar representing a vessel outside the shipping lanes turned and began closing on him at forty-five knots, a speed impossible for a vessel of the size displayed on his screen.

Unless, of course, it was a modern warship.

Soon the captain learned who was after him because his radio did, in fact, work, and a Korean speaker announced, over and over, that the American naval ship USS *Freedom* planned on enforcing UN Resolution 1874, and the *Emerald Endeavor* should bring its engines to idle and prepare itself for boarding and inspection.

From then on the captain knew he would not make it to port in Haeju without a confrontation, but he did not acknowledge receipt of the message, and he did not slow.

The act of boarding and inspecting the noncompliant 2,300-ton cargo ship in transit fell to two groups of eight American men, all aged between twenty-three and forty. This was not a large number of men for such a daunting task, but this was Echo Platoon of SEAL Team 5, squads Alpha and Bravo, and these guys lived for this shit.

Thirty-seven-year-old Chief Daryl Ricks of Chico, California, was in charge of the eight-man Alpha squad. He and his seven special warfare operators rode in a rigged-hulled inflatable Zodiac boat that closed on the *Emerald Endeavor* from astern at thirty-eight knots.

Even though the RIB smashed plumes of spray as it bounced along on the black water and its motor roared, so far it had approached undetected because circling above the big cargo ship 350 yards off the RIB's bow were a pair of big and loud MH-60S Seahawk helicopters. The helos had been at it for a half-hour now, thumping low over the deck of the *Emerald Endeavor* in figure eights and swooping passes, shining spotlights on the crew on the weather deck and through the windows of the bridge.

The MH-60S helicopters had two functions this morning. The first was to make a lot of noise and flash a lot of lights in order to cover for the approach of the RIB at the ship's stern. And the other was to deposit the eight men of Bravo squad on the ship's deck as soon as Chief Ricks called for them.

The practice of hitting a ship at sea was called an 'underway boarding operation,' and it was about as good as it got for a Navy SEAL. Every one of these men had not only trained for events just like this, but had also dreamt of such events, prayed for them.

Their plan was straightforward. Alpha would use a grappling pole to board at the stern, and they would climb to the weather deck, then move in two four-man leap-frogging teams to the stairs of the superstructure. They would climb to the bridge while Bravo fast-roped from the helo to the bow, distracting those watching from the bridge deck and using a stack of containers as cover. This would put sixteen men on the ship, quickly and at multiple ingression points. 'Bottom up' Alpha would go for the wheelhouse, and 'top down' Bravo would go for the engine room. From here both teams could detain and isolate the crew from the cargo. When that was accomplished they would begin their own quick inspection of the cargo holds while Marines from the *Freedom* came over to help with the search.

If any hint of contraband was found a real inspection would take place after the ship had been towed to port in Inchon.

All sixteen Navy SEALs were armed with Colt M4A1 carbines outfitted with SOPMODs, special operations peculiar modification accessory kits, essentially allowing each operator to customize his weapons platform to his preference and mission.

Ricks's carbine was gadget-rich; it wore a flashlight and a thermal optic and an infrared illuminator and a suppressor and a foregrip, certainly not all the bells and whistles available with the SOPMOD, but an impressive array nonetheless. Other guys in the squad had grenade launchers and lasers and variable scopes latched onto their weapons, but the rifles themselves all fired the same 5.56 round, and any operator could pick up and employ any one of his teammates' guns in a firefight if it came down to it.

They wore night-vision goggles on their foreheads and black balaclava masks with the image of a white jawbone on their lower portion, fortifying the men with a particularly terrifying appearance.

At two hundred yards Ricks looked through the thermal scope of his rifle, scanning the aft decks. While he did so he spoke into his headset, yelling over the noise of the engine behind him. 'Bravo actual, Alpha actual! Two mikes!'

In his headset he heard Special Warfare Operator (One) Marty 'Bones' Hackworth reply from up in an MH-60S flying over the cargo ship, his own transmission delivered in a yell. 'Roger that, Chief! We're prepping ropes now!'

And then Ricks heard the man next to him in the boat, speaking with a noticeable Dutch accent. 'They know we're coming, Chief.'

Ricks knew Hendriks was right, and he knew this was

a problem, but he just said, 'Well, let's hope they're cool about it.'

Hendriks replied, 'I still don't see why we didn't just board covertly, take advantage of total surprise. Hell, we've been telling them we're on the way for the past four hours.'

Ricks did not take his eye out of his thermal scope. 'Rules and shit, Hendriks. We had to give them an opportunity to let us board.'

'We're giving them an opportunity to shoot back.'

Ricks wasn't going to argue. Hendriks liked to bitch, and normally that was okay, because if rounds *did* fly, Chief Ricks knew the big Dutchman with the heart of a lion would do more than his share. Ricks let him mumble and grumble a little, because it didn't affect his job, and sometimes it was pretty damn funny.

But not now. 'Stow it, Hendriks.'

'Yes, Chief.'

A special warfare operator called Greaser sat in the rear next to the Navy ensign steering the RIB. Greaser was a breaching specialist, but his job right now was to deploy the telescopic carbon-fiber 'hook on pole,' from which hung a Fibrelight II assault ladder, a double-rung polyester ladder reinforced with carbon-fiber poles that could take the weight of three operators laden for combat simultaneously.

Greaser extended the pole to six meters in length, just high enough to reach the railing at the stern of the *Emerald Endeavor*, and he lifted it, along with the ladder attached to it, and waited for the RIB to get into position.

The Zodiac closed the last fifty yards quickly, then

came along on the starboard side at the rear of the cargo ship. Greaser attached the pole hook to the railing high above, then looked down at a small computer monitor at the pole's base. It showed the view from the tiny fish-eye camera at the top of the hook, and through it he could see no one on the deck aft of the superstructure who might cause trouble for the men climbing the Fibrelight.

'Hook on and secure!'

'Go!' shouted Ricks, and one by one the eight men of Alpha squad began climbing the twenty feet up to the deck.

Parnell was first, then Elizondo and Jones. When they were up and over the railing they covered for the next three; Takenaka, Chief Ricks, and Hendriks. Finally Stovall and then Greaser brought up the rear.

Parnell fortified the pole hook with a carabineer locking system that kept it in place, the RIB below spun away and shot back into the darkness, and the eight men broke into their two fire teams and split up, heading toward the two staircases of the superstructure. Ricks led three men to the port side, and Takenaka led three more to the starboard stairs.

Eighty yards forward of their position, four fast ropes slapped onto the deck and black-clad operators with skull-face balaclavas began sliding down to the *Emerald Endeavor*.

'Chief, I've got movement.'

Ricks dropped to a knee on the metal landing between the main deck and the second deck, and he scanned forward, looking for any indication of the movement Greaser called out. Just fifty feet ahead of him, two men stood at the railing, looking forward at the bow. He could only see their backs at first, and he observed them as they watched the helicopter lift high into the air and peel away.

Ricks knew these men had overwatch on the SEALs of Bravo squad as they came up the main deck toward the superstructure. He needed to be certain neither man was armed.

One of the men turned a little to the side as he lifted his Kalashnikov rifle. Its stock was folded closed, but Ricks could see a magazine in the weapon. The man pointed it toward the deck in front of him, and held it away from his body awkwardly.

In the span of two heartbeats Chief Ricks knew the man was no soldier, and he was unsure of what he was doing, but he was a threat to the men on the deck below nonetheless.

Ricks thumbed off the safety of his M4 and fired two lightning-quick semiautomatic rounds. Both struck the man in the back of his head. Through his thermal Ricks saw the black-hot signature of exploding brain matter, and then the silhouette dropped to the deck.

The second man in his scope did not appear to be armed, but Ricks saw the AK had fallen right in front of him. The man looked down to it, and the moment he did so a short burst of suppressed fire came from the chief's right.

Greaser dropped the man within the weapon's reach with a trio of bullets into the back, center mass, and a second later the four-man fire team once again began climbing the stairs.

*

A minute later Ricks, Greaser, and Jones were in the dark but expansive bridge of the *Emerald Endeavor*. Elizondo was outside with Alpha's other fire team, they had detained eight men who all appeared to be Malaysian or perhaps Indonesian, and they were in the process of zip-tying their wrists and arms behind their backs.

Bravo team was belowdecks now, ferreting out crew members and securing them with ties.

But Chief Ricks and the two men with him still had work to do. In front of them were two senior crewmen – again, Ricks thought they might be Filipino or Malaysian – and one North Korean captain. The two crewmen were compliant, they stood with their back to the helm and their hands high, but the gray-haired captain was shouting wildly and swinging a rigging knife with a four-inch blade back and forth, waving it at the armed men in the skull masks in front of him.

Ricks had given the order to hold fire unless absolutely necessary. He knew they needed the captain's help to quickly inspect the cargo. Using the few Korean words he had learned he said, '*Nuo!*' – Lie down! – over and over, holding his carbine at the ready with one hand while making a downward gesture with his gloved left hand.

Ricks's attempt at breaching the vast cultural divide here on the bridge was getting nowhere. Out of desperation he pulled down his mask, smiled and said, '*Anneyong*' – Hello – because it was just about the only nice thing he'd learned to say in the language. Still, he kept the muzzle of his Colt M4 directed at the man's chest.

The captain continued swinging the knife around, and his panic remained.

'*Nuo,*' Ricks said again, imploring the man to lie down, but he could see it in the man's eyes. He wasn't going to lie down. He was psyching himself up for something.

Ricks kept his calm countenance going, but into his mike he said, 'He takes two steps our way and we drop him.'

'Roger that,' came the call back from Greaser and Jones.

The captain took two steps, but backward, not forward, then he brought the rigging knife over his throat.

Ricks shouted, '*Aniyo! Aniyo!*' No! No!

The little gray-haired man screamed, then dragged the shiny blade across his throat. Blood appeared instantly, along with the gurgling sound of the breach of his airway.

Ricks watched in fascinated horror as the captain finished his deep cut, then he seemed to look down at the spurting blood coming from him.

'Fuck!' shouted Greaser, just behind Ricks, and he started to move forward.

'Stand fast,' shouted the chief. 'Wait for him to –'

The knife fell from the captain's hands and he crumpled back onto the deck between the helm and the pilot chair.

'Secure that blade!' Chief Ricks ordered now, and Greaser leapt forward, kicked the knife out of reach, and then he pinned the wounded captain down to the deck. He rolled him over and pulled out a zip tie from his load-bearing vest to tie the captain's wrists.

Ricks turned to the medic of the squad, SO3 Joseph Jones. 'Joe-Joe, do what you can for him.' Ricks said this even though he knew without a blood transfusion and surgery the captain didn't have a prayer, and the chances of those happening here were zero.

The captain died quickly – even though the medic slid a tube into the wound to keep an airway going, there was no way to stop the blood loss in time to save the small man. Ricks stood over him the entire time, but his attention was split between the activity at his feet on the deck and the constant updates on his radio.

Bravo and fire team two of Alpha had rounded up the twelve surviving crew members on board. All of them had been searched and zipped, and put on the main deck just forward of the superstructure. They were all guarded by SEALs.

Jones covered the dead captain's body with a body bag out of his pack.

Greaser stood next to Ricks and looked down at the dead man. 'Chief, I'm going to go way out on a limb and say we've got ourselves some contraband on this ship.'

'Ya think?' Ricks replied. He called Takenaka, the radio man of the squad, and told him to get on the horn with the *Freedom* and tell them the ship was secure.

Hendriks, Elizondo, Parnell, and Stovall joined the others on the bridge, and they looked down at the body under the green plastic bag.

'You had to smoke him?' Hendriks asked.

Greaser answered for his chief. 'He smoked himself. Slit his own fuckin'' throat.'

'Holy shit. Why'd he do that?'

Ricks answered matter-of-factly, 'Because he didn't want to defect to the evil West, and slitting his own throat was better than going back home. For his failure he would have fared even worse there.'

Parnell said, 'There ain't a lot worse than gagging on your own blood.'

Ricks looked up at Parnell, then at the rest of his men. 'I read a thing a few months back. A DPRK major was suspected of giving intel to the South Koreans. He probably didn't do it, but he was suspected. The government took him out and executed him.'

The men waited for the punch line. They were all pretty sure it wasn't going to be funny.

Ricks said, 'With a goddamned flamethrower. They tossed that poor son of a bitch into a dirt pit and barbecued his ass. Took their time with it, too.'

'Jesus Christ,' mumbled Stovall.

Ricks said, 'On interdictions in these waters, we are engaging a uniquely motivated enemy. They are desperate men with their backs to the wall.'

Ricks fingered his skull-face balaclava and raised his Colt rifle. 'We think we're a bunch of terrifying motherfuckers, but don't forget. We don't scare anybody out here. They've seen worse.'

Two dozen Marines stationed on the USS *Freedom* arrived on the *Emerald Endeavor* within twenty minutes. Ricks figured these kids – their average age was about twenty – wished they'd had the chance to be involved in the raid, the shooting and scooting. In comparison, going through the cargo holds and containers of the big ship would be dull work, but at least it got them off the other boat for a few hours.

They found what they were looking for after ninety minutes. Cargo holds one through four all contained eighty-pound sacks of unrefined sugar with the markings of a Cuban agricultural entity. Hold seven contained the same thing. But holds five and six, just fore of the center of the ship, contained stacks of forty-foot containers. When the Marines broke open the doors of the locked containers, they saw they were piled high with various machine parts. The equipment looked like plumbing and air-conditioning equipment, and parts of an old boiler. It was all used and rusted and broken, certainly not equipment one would ship around the world. But after a half-hour of pulling out big hunks of metal equipment, the Marines came upon large aluminum tubes in fiberglass casing. There were no markings on the cases, but the tubes were some six and a half feet in diameter, and eighteen feet in length. The Marines found only two before the ship was brought into port in Inchon, but when inspected fully, a half-dozen precision aluminum tubes were found, along with sophisticated plastic crating containing precision-crafted O-rings and coupling bolts.

The young Marines had suspected it from the beginning, but the experts in South Korea confirmed the find. These were the hollow stages of an intercontinental ballistic missile, and they corresponded in diameter to the Taepodong-2, North Korea's still-unsuccessful longest-range nuclear-delivery vehicle.

Determining where all this equipment came from was the next order of business for the intelligence organizations of the West.

17

French intelligence operative Veronika Martel climbed out of a taxi on the corner of 88th and Columbus and began walking east in the rain. Her black umbrella protected her from the downpour, but it also helped her blend in with the other pedestrians, many of whom were under black umbrellas themselves.

Martel had no real reason to run a surveillance detection route here on the Upper West Side of New York City. It wasn't like she was in Tripoli or Bucharest or Dubrovnik; she wasn't even on the job at the moment. But SDRs were part of Martel's life. She'd learned to leave nothing to chance, to expect every opportunity to turn into a potential for danger, to concern herself with the minutiae of her tradecraft to keep herself safe.

The reasons for her concerns about everyone and everything all boiled down to a simple explanation: Veronika Martel did not trust the world.

Even though her SDR took her north, south, east, and west through the rainy mid-morning streets of one of the most congested metropolises on earth, she arrived at the offices of Sharps Global Intelligence Partners at ten a.m. Exactly on time. After a quick security check by a guard who met her in the ground-floor lobby of the building, the two of them took the elevator up five stories and the door opened on the marble foyer of the executive office of the nation's most successful corporate intelligence concern.

A guard force of six men manned the lobby; they all wore business suits and earpieces and salt-and-pepper hair over physiques that were still hardened from physical activity, making the men appear at once both distinguished and dangerous. Martel knew these guards were all ex-military, just like the force at her satellite office in Belgium, and just like the guard forces at all twenty-six sat offices around the globe. The men were polite and professional, but they all leered at her. Martel had come to expect this from men, and as always, it only stood to make her both uncomfortable and annoyed.

She didn't come to New York often and she had not seen Wayne Sharps since the day he hired her three years earlier; she was virtually always in the field and she liked it that way, but she'd been summoned by the director of her company and she knew the value of showing her face around the home office once in a while to remind the execs who she was.

She felt like she knew the reason behind her summons. The operation in Ho Chi Minh City two weeks earlier had been an odd one. The North Koreans' presence at the safe house, the Australians and their trepidation about what they had gotten themselves into, the American asset refusing to hand over the package. And the blood on the document, indicating it had been taken by force.

Veronika knew she had done everything correctly. Just as instructed. Nothing more, nothing less. She wasn't in any trouble. She thought they were just bringing her in for consultations, to make certain she was comfortable with everything, or at least comfortable enough to keep her mouth shut and her head down.

And Veronika had no problem with that at all.

She was escorted into Wayne Sharps's office by a secretary who Martel thought too young and attractive to have earned her position through merit alone, and once inside, she took in the view. The fifth-story corner office had floor-to-ceiling windows that looked out to Columbus Avenue and 77th, presenting a stellar vista of the American Museum of Natural History across the street. Sharps himself sat behind his large desk with his feet up. He was on the phone, speaking Arabic – and speaking it well, Martel noted.

She sat down on a modern sectional sofa in a sunken seating area across the large office. Tea and coffee were placed in front of her, but she instead just looked at the sofa. Duke Sharps was known as particularly lecherous, and Veronika wondered how many women the sixty-year-old man had taken right here in his office.

She pushed the thought out of her mind. If he tried anything on her she'd send him headfirst out the window and down into Columbus Avenue traffic.

Finally he hung up the phone and spun the chair around, a little too dramatically, as far as Veronika was concerned. He crossed the room as she stood from the sofa. He was burly but not unattractive, though his face had leathered noticeably in the three years since she'd last seen him in person.

'My dear Ms. Martel,' he said with a wide grin.

'Lovely to see you, Mr Sharps.'

'It's Duke to you,' he said.

It's Duke to everyone, she thought to herself.

'Veronika,' she replied, because she felt she had to, not because she liked the familiarity. She was European, after all, and normal Europeans rarely addressed business colleagues by their given names.

Moreover, Veronika Martel was not normal. She preferred keeping everyone at arm's length.

They sat down, and Sharps poured coffee for Veronika without asking, even though she would have preferred tea. He asked her about her trip over, about the office back in Belgium she was based out of, and about a job she had done in Paris recently involving a city administrator and a problem with his daughter.

It was a small-time operation. Nothing that would be brought to Duke's attention, since, at any one time, his company employed hundreds of operatives on dozens and dozens of missions. To Veronika it seemed as if he had just been brushing up on her file while she rode the elevator to his office.

After the small talk, Sharps got down to business. 'Veronika, I read the reports. You were stellar on that job in Vietnam. You are one of my bright lights here in the corporation. I expect you to go far.'

She smiled dryly. She didn't tell him about the blood on the passport. She didn't have a clue if he already knew about it, but she wouldn't bring it up, because she *was*, in fact, a bright light. She was an operative who did her job and kept her mouth shut.

She thought he would next show some contrition for the complications of the mission.

But instead Sharps said, 'I was lucky to steal you away from DGSE.'

Veronika paused to regroup, then she responded with typical coyness. 'You weren't lucky. You were wealthy. *That* stole me away. Plus the fact that I'd been fired from DGSE and had few other options.'

He hesitated with a slightly open mouth, trying to decide how to take her comment. Apparently he took it as a joke, because he laughed boisterously. 'Despite your problems in France, you didn't come cheap, that's for damn certain. But you are worth every last cent.'

'I do try to create value for myself.'

He nodded aggressively and repositioned himself on the sofa. Surprised by the movement, Veronika thought he was going to try and slide closer to her, but instead he just crossed his legs. She was uncertain if her surprised look had scared him off at the last second.

After a moment he said, 'I have a new assignment for you. I expect it to last a few weeks in duration, though it might run over just a tad.'

'That is fine.'

'It's a continuation of what you did in Vietnam.'

'Oh?'

'I'll give you the background you didn't have when you started this op. The North Koreans have discovered a huge deposit of rare earth minerals. I guess I should say the Chinese have discovered it, but that lunatic Choi has kicked out the Chinese, and now North Korea will continue operations on their own.'

Veronika said, 'A nation that can't feed their people or

keep their lights on is entering into the high-tech mining sector alone?'

'If they really could do it alone they wouldn't need us. No. They are not alone. Our client isn't North Korea. That would be illegal, of course. Our client is New World Metals LLC. A completely aboveboard mining consortium from Mexico via a dozen shell companies. They have a wholly legitimate contract to partner in the mining concern as a third party.'

Veronika was bored, and she let Sharps know. 'My assignment?'

'You are going to California.'

She sat up straighter on the sofa. That sounded nice. A hell of a lot better than Vietnam, anyway.

'The North Koreans don't trust the Chinese to process the ore once they dig it out of the mountains. This presents a serious problem, because the processing of rare earth materials is particularly complicated, and special equipment and know-how is required. New World Metals has purchased the computers for the processing equipment from Europe and they will fly them into North Korea via Bulgaria, but without proprietary software they are useless. They have asked us to send someone to Valley Floor, a NewCorp rare earth mine in California, and obtain the proprietary software they are using on the computers in their processing plant there.'

California, to Veronika Martel, meant Fisherman's Wharf in San Francisco or Rodeo Drive in Los Angeles. Wayne Sharps seemed to be describing a strip mine somewhere far away from these locations. Still, she was a dutiful employee.

'Okay, Duke. What specifically do you need me to do?'

'We need the software, every last bit of it. You will get it.'

'Of course.'

He moved again on the sofa, and this time there was no question – he was coming closer.

She stood up quickly.

He just smiled. It was clear to Veronika that he had expected her reaction and it didn't bother him at all. She took him for a man much more thrilled by the chase than the kill, and she knew she had just thrilled him greatly.

He did not miss a beat, continuing as if nothing had happened. He stood up as well. 'Your contact will be Edward Riley. Know him?'

She raised an eyebrow. 'The scandal in Italy?'

'Right. That's in his past. He's a good man. A Brit, but we won't hold it against him. He's running the entire New World Metals operation from stem to stern. We are positioning you as a quality-assurance officer from the Canadian company that manufactures some of the processing equipment. You will be there to run some diagnostics on the machines and to survey the operation. This will put you in contact with the software we need.'

'Fine,' she said.

Duke smiled at her. 'It was nice to see you. Until we meet again.'

He shook her hand, then held it. He hesitated, and she knew what was coming. Some sort of verbal attempt to hit on her, since his physical approach had failed. She expected it to be overt and charmless.

She was right.

'Your coldness only enhances your sex appeal. Has anyone ever said that?'

'Certainly not to my face, Duke.' She pulled her hand back with a smile, turned away, and left his office, aware of his eyes on her every step of the way.

18

President of the United States Jack Ryan would have normally called in his entire National Security Council to discuss a situation as important as the capture of the material for weapons of mass destruction on its way to North Korea, and he had intended to do just that. But when his chief of staff, Arnie Van Damm, contacted both Director of National Intelligence Mary Pat Foley and Director of the CIA Jay Canfield, he'd received requests from both to delay the meeting for a few hours while they worked on something that would be crucial to providing the President with a bigger and better picture of what was going on.

One does not normally tell POTUS 'No' when he asks for a meeting, but Van Damm knew Ryan would have no problem allowing his top intelligence community officials more time to do necessary work, so he pushed the meeting back until nine a.m. the next day. The only problem with this from a scheduling standpoint was that the President had to fly to London for a NATO conference on Russia first thing in the morning.

They could have conducted the meeting via video conference, as Air Force One had the secure telecom necessary to keep the President in touch with Washington wherever he flew, but Mary Pat made the last-minute decision to go to Andrews early in the morning and fly along to Europe with her President so she could present her material in person. Mary Pat had known Jack for more than thirty years, and more than any public figure she had ever worked with, she knew how much he enjoyed rolling up his sleeves and putting his hands on the intelligence itself.

She had an objective with today's meeting, and she knew she'd get a lot further with POTUS if he understood and agreed with all the intelligence she presented, and taking the flights to London and back would be a small price to pay for having his undivided attention for an hour or so.

Ryan agreed to the private conference with Mary Pat in the President's office on Air Force One. The full National Security Council meeting could wait – for now.

As the plane taxied to the runway, Ryan sat at his desk working on some early-morning paperwork. He heard a knock at the open door next to him, and he looked up to see Arnie Van Damm.

'Aren't you supposed to strap in for takeoff?' Ryan asked.

'Aren't you?' Ryan's desk chair had a seat belt, but it dangled off the side.

He said, 'I've been doing this so long, I have it down to a science. Right when I hear us go throttle up I buckle up and clear my desk.' He snatched his coffee cup with a smile. 'Then I grab my coffee so it doesn't spill.'

Van Damm entered the room and sat in the chair across from the desk. It, too, had a seat belt. 'For a guy who hates flying, I'd say you've got the hang of it.'

Ryan just chuckled and looked back down to his papers.

He could tell they were still taxiing, and would be for another few minutes. 'What's up?'

Arnie said, 'Secret Service wants to talk to you again about Mexico City.'

Ryan shook his head without looking up. 'We've talked. I'm not canceling. They need to drop it.'

Arnie was the only member of Ryan's staff who regularly argued with his boss. 'I think you should reconsider. We've got some outs, don't worry about that. Lots of problems in Asia and Ukraine that need attention. President Lopez will forgive you if you send regrets.'

Now Ryan did look up. '*No*, Arnie. I'm going. What's Secret Service's specific argument against the trip?'

'Well, I think they want to talk to you to make their case in person.'

'I'm asking *you*.'

'It's the Maldonado thing.'

The President waved it away. 'That was six months ago.'

'They are concerned that –'

Ryan called out to the hallway next to his office. 'Andrea, can you come in here a second?'

His lead protection agent, Andrea Price O'Day, was in the room in two seconds. 'Yes, sir?'

'I'd like to ask you to pistol-whip Arnie for me, but I bet you'll give me some song and dance about you having rules against that.'

Andrea laughed and looked to Van Damm. 'How about I just keep a close eye on him for now? He looks pretty harmless.'

Ryan said, 'What's this about you guys not wanting me to go to Mexico?'

Andrea replied, 'That's not me, Mr President. I understand our threats and assessment advance division had some concerns.'

Ryan shrugged. 'So as far as you're concerned, I should go?'

'Didn't say that, either. As far as *I'm* concerned, you'd never leave the White House. But it's not my call to make, Mr President.'

Ryan drummed his fingers on his desk for a moment. Then he said, 'I'm going. I don't duck and cover because some Mexican cartel psycho scumbag in the mountains goes on Twitter and threatens me. The office of the President is too important to show any reaction to a two-bit thug like that.'

Arnie said, 'But –'

Ryan cut him off. 'If Secret Service wants a meeting, I'll give it to them, but only out of respect. I have no plans of canceling that trip. Tell them that, maybe they can save us both some time.'

He looked at Andrea. She nodded. As far as she was concerned, the matter was settled. 'I'll be right there with you.'

'Then everything will be fine.' O'Day returned to her seat, and Ryan looked back to Arnie. 'We're about five seconds from throttle up. You'd better fasten your seat belt.' Both men reached for their seat belts just as the massive 747 began to vibrate.

Right after takeoff at seven-fifteen a.m. Ryan sent down for his intelligence chief, who was just finishing an apple bran muffin and a cup of coffee in the senior staff meeting room while she worked on her iPad. She climbed the steps to the President's office and found Ryan sitting behind his desk. He wore a dress shirt and a tie, but over that he wore his dark blue Air Force One flight jacket. He beckoned her over to a small rectangular conference table and grabbed a stack of papers from his desk. When he started to a chair opposite her, she reached out and pulled the chair around to her side of the table.

'Mind if we sit next to each other? I have to show you some things on my tablet.'

'As long as it doesn't get back to Ed,' he joked.

Mary Pat laughed and they both sat down. More coffee was poured for them while they got settled.

Ryan asked, 'Have you seen the reaction from the North Koreans about the interdiction of the *Emerald Endeavor*?'

Foley shook her head. 'I missed it. I haven't had a chance to turn on the TV.'

Ryan said, 'Any guesses as to the wording?'

'I don't know, something like "This illegal interdiction is an act of war perpetrated by America."'

Ryan looked down at this morning's Presidential Daily Brief, which contained an abbreviated transcript of the North Korean ambassador's remarks from the evening before. He read it silently, then said, 'Pretty good, Mary Pat.' He read from the transcript. '"We regard this unlawful interception by the US as an act of war."'

Mary Pat waved away Ryan's compliment. 'Easy guess. It's always the same with these guys.'

'So, what do we know about the material found? Definitely components to a missile?'

'Definitely. These tubes are the exact specs of a Dongfeng-3A. It is a Chinese single-stage medium-range nuclear ballistic missile.'

Ryan was confused. '*Chinese?* That doesn't make sense. The Chinese could truck them over the border. Why would they sail them out into international waters where they could be interdicted?'

Foley replied, 'The Chinese didn't make them or deliver them.'

'But you just said —'

'These are knockoffs.'

Jack cocked his head. 'Counterfeit?'

'Yes. They are exact reproductions of the tubes used for the fuselage of the DF-3A Chinese medium-range missiles. But these were made by a private aerospace company in France called Précision Aéro Toulouse.'

'That's interesting. Why?'

'The theory we have is this: We all know the North Koreans are having problems fielding a long-range ICBM because their Taepodong-2, the closest one they have to being ready, keeps failing, either between first and second stage or between second- and third-stage separation. That means something could be wrong with the second stage they are using.'

'Right. Go on.'

Mary Pat slid her iPad along the table to where Jack could see it and she began scrolling through several photos and diagrams of missiles. Each picture was labeled and time-stamped and captioned, and Ryan saw some of the photos were from open-source intel, and others were from top-secret sources.

'The second stage they are using now is taken from their Rodong medium-range ballistic missile. Basically they just slapped a single-stage rocket into the middle of their three-stage rocket, and it's not working out for them.'

'Imagine that.'

'Rocket science is tough,' Mary Pat said with a chuckle. 'But what we know is the Chinese are doing something similar with their long-range missiles. They use their Dongfeng-3A single-stage rocket as the second stage of their long-range ICBM.'

'And the North Koreans want to use the Dongfeng on their Taepodong-2?'

'It appears so. Back in the early nineties the Chinese gave the North Koreans one Dongfeng-3A missile. They never deployed it, they just took it apart to cobble pieces together in their own equipment. Now that China has refused to give Choi the ICBM technology that he wants, we think they are using this French aerospace firm to build replicas of the Dongfeng-3A.'

'Off Chinese plans?' Ryan asked.

'We don't think so. We think this company in France actually reengineered these missile components by using the tube of the one Dongfeng-3A in the North Koreans'' possession.'

Jack looked over the photos of the tubes pulled off the *Emerald Endeavor*. 'Wow.'

Mary Pat said, ' "Wow" is right. In order to reengineer these tubes, they would have had to have built proprietary tools and high-tech machines.'

Ryan said the obvious. 'And that didn't come cheap.'

'Not cheap at all. We've spent the past couple of days looking into this. Précision Aéro received a payment of seventeen million euros eight and a half months ago. That's nearly twenty-five million US dollars.'

Ryan sipped his coffee. 'Should it bother us North Korea has twenty-five million US to drop on a project as speculative as this?'

'It bothers *me*. We don't know what all they expected for that payment, or what all Précision Aéro has already shipped them.'

'We need to find out. Have we talked with the French government?'

'No, and there's a problem with doing that. We need to go carefully so they don't know we are looking into the bank accounts of one of their companies. Anyway, I know what they will say. The deal wasn't done with the North Koreans. It was with a shell company out of Luxembourg.'

Ryan sighed, looking again at the tubes taken from the *Emerald Endeavor*. 'This equipment *must* violate international nonproliferation treaties.'

'That's debatable.'

Ryan turned to Mary Pat, and she put her hands up quickly. '*I'm* not debating it. Of course the commerce in these kinds of "dual-use" parts should be banned by international treaty, but companies make the argument that as long as it is not overtly going to end users who are going to make ICBMs, then it should be fair game. There are enough private satellite companies on earth today to where firms like Précision Aéro can dip their toe into weapons proliferation with plausible deniability.'

Ryan rubbed his eyes under his glasses. 'I'll call the French president and let him know what we know. I'll play it like we got tipped off. He might not believe me, but he won't be able to challenge me.'

Foley said, 'The real issue here, Mr President, is not the material we found on board the *Emerald Endeavor*. It is the fact North Korea had the hard currency to buy this material on the world market in the first place.'

'I can tell by that look on your face you know something.'

'I do. CIA has been working on North Korean banking practices for a while now, and this fits right in with this new information. We traced the payment to Précision Aéro back to a bank account in Dubai. There was thirteen million in the account even after the purchase.'

'What is North Korea doing with that kind of cash?'

'We have a theory, and this is why Jay and I weren't able to meet with you yesterday. We've been working on this for three days solid, even before the *Emerald Endeavor*.'

Ryan leaned closer. 'Tell me.'

'Mr President, there is strong evidence North Korea has restarted production on their rare earth mineral mine at Chongju.'

Ryan just said, 'Shit.'

Mary Pat continued, 'Analysts at the National Geospatial-Intelligence Agency say there are indications that the rare earth mine in the northwest of the nation is up and running again. Further, they think it is happening without Chinese help.'

Ryan said, 'The Chinese were booted from that mine a few months back.'

'A year ago now, yes. Our contacts in China report no change in that relationship, so we find it curious the North Koreans are advancing with the program there. Especially because there is evidence they are actually building up the capacity to process the rare earth ore into refined materials. That's something light-years ahead of the current level of DPRK sophistication. Even the Chinese had planned on processing the ore at refineries in China.'

'Do the Chinese know the DPRK is going around them?'

'Virtually all of what we know about facts on the ground in North Korea comes from the Chinese, either intercepted communications, the odd HUMINT asset, or open sources. We see nothing about Chongju in any of these resources, so we feel the Chinese are in the dark on this, for now at least.'

Ryan asked, 'Do you have the NGA images?'

Mary Pat had learned long ago to expect Ryan to ask to see primary intelligence. She began flipping pages on her tablet, displaying a series of overhead shots of a cluster of buildings.

'What do you think?' Mary Pat asked after a moment.

'I think I'm glad we've got analysts at NGA to decipher this for us. I see the strip mine, obviously, but all the tanks and buildings look like they could belong to just about any sort of factory.'

Mary Pat reached to the tablet computer and brought up another page. On it were two images. One was captioned 'Chongju dam' and the other 'LAMP.'

'The one on the left is the ore-processing facility in

North Korea. We are calling it "Chongju dam" because that is the closest named structure, it's just north of Chongju and west of the mine. And the image here is of the LAMP rare earth – processing plant in Malaysia. Look at the oxidation tanks in both photos.'

Ryan looked them over and agreed the two installations were very similar.

Mary Pat said, 'We learned from Chinese intercepts last year that Chongju could bring North Korea as much as twelve trillion dollars in hard assets in the next two to three decades. With that kind of a potential haul, it's no big surprise they found someone new to help them build and run it.'

Ryan said, 'And that someone new is paying them in hard currency for the opportunity. And that connects this to the missile tubes on the *Emerald Endeavor*.'

Foley nodded. 'Right. The North Koreans are taking the offshore money they are getting for future mineral rights and they are using it to buy the ballistic missile technology they need to make their ICBMs operational, because the one thing they do not yet have is an ICBM that can reach the continental United States.'

Ryan almost mumbled to himself. 'A matter of time.'

'Yes. It is a cold fact of economics that if North Korea manages to earn just a fraction of the money we think they can earn from that rare earth mineral mine, then they will be able to buy the technology and expertise they need to threaten us.'

Ryan said, 'So often in diplomacy, there is a tendency to oversimplify things. Most situations are not the zero-sum games people make them out to be. But this is one such case. Success for North Korea means failure for us. We stop the mining and we stop the spigot of cash that's fueling their missile program.'

'Exactly. But as long as North Korea has access to banks where they can transact with shell companies for hard currency, we won't be able to stop them.'

Jack looked out the porthole next to him. They were just off the coast of Maine, heading northeast. The Atlantic looked impossibly blue below. 'We're not going to fire cruise missiles into North Korea to destroy a strip mine. We just have to find out who in the West is bankrolling them and how they are doing it.'

'The "how" is no problem. CIA has compiled a list of thirty banks in ten nations where we have found North Korean offshore accounts.'

'Where are they?'

She looked down at her iPad and found a file, then opened it and read aloud. 'Hong Kong, Vanuatu, Brunei, Singapore, Mexico, Switzerland, Malta, Belize, Nicaragua, and the Cayman Islands.'

'Not necessarily places we can apply direct pressure to get the assets frozen.'

'Not at all.'

Frustrated, Ryan said, 'What about identifying who is working with North Korea on the mine?'

'Easier said than done, Mr President. This transaction with Précision Aéro is a dead end. It won't lead back to the actual mining partners. It only leads to a shell company, which I'm sure was set up by the North Koreans to procure overseas equipment for their missile program.'

Jack turned and looked at his DNI with a grave face.

'Mary Pat, I do hate to sound like a broken record, but you know what I'm going to say.'

'You want me to get you more information.'

He nodded. 'However you can. A North Korea with an ICBM that can reach the US is a game changer. Not just in Asia, but in the entire planet. We can't punish the North for violating sanctions because we are already doing that. I might be able to push the UN for a new round of sanctions that will squeeze their accounts in those offshore banks, but that's a long shot, and it won't happen overnight. But if you can find out who is helping them with their rare earth mine, I will go after them with a vengeance, and that will, at least, slow down their new source of income.'

Mary Pat saw the task before her as nearly impossible, but she had her assignment from her superior. 'Yes, Mr President.'

19

Lieutenant General Ri Tae-jin flew via helicopter to the Kangdong Airport, just northeast of Pyongyang. With him were eight subordinates and a security detail of eight more, most of whom were flying in a follow-on helo.

The two Russian-made Mi-8s touched down at noon, and Ri stepped out moments later only to climb into the back of a waiting Mercedes limousine. The bulk of his entourage boarded military vehicles and they set off for their destination.

Kangdong was a suburb of sprawling Pyongyang, only thirty miles from Choi Li-hung Square, the center of the capital city, but Choi Ji-hoon had a second palatial residence here, and when he was at Kangdong-gun, anyone who was summoned had to make the two-hour drive on poor roads. Unless, of course, they were high-ranking government or military personnel, at which point they could simply fly.

The North Korean state had an official policy of Songun, which meant 'military first.' It was government doctrine that the Chosun Inmingun was fed first, fed best, housed and outfitted using the pick of the nation's resources. Most party officials reached their status via their military careers, and many high-ranking government department heads were still Chosun Inmingun.

High-ranking military personnel had access to helicopters, and when they drove on the roads they could order the roads blocked from ordinary civilians.

Songun made the military the elite social class of the nation.

Ri's flight was only ten minutes, and his limo ride was only twenty more, and this brought him through the checkpoints on the grounds of the luxury mansion and to the front door.

He was brought in to a small banquet hall by a half-dozen men of Section Five of the Party Central Committee Guidance Department. They were Choi's close protection detail, and they treated Ri with politeness, but no real deference. His body was wanded and he was seated at a small table and brought tea.

Here he waited one hour and twenty-three minutes.

He made no complaints, and displayed no show of frustration, because Section Five stood at parade rest around the room, and they kept their eyes on him.

Finally Choi walked in, and Ri immediately stood and fought off the natural desire to wince.

The Dae Wonsu's Mao jacket was half open, and his eyes were bloodshot. Choi's hair was cut too short to show dishevelment, but Ri could see creases on the young man's face that gave clues the man had been lying on a bed moments before. His fleshy cheeks were pinker than usual as well.

Ri realized almost instantly that the Dae Wonsu was drunk. He'd seen his nation's leader in various levels of inebriation before. Festive galas were thrown with some regularity, mostly at Ryongsong, and Ri was occasionally ordered to attend. Choi had the habit of arriving late, but always with a drink in his hand, and it was usually abundantly clear he had begun his revelry hours before. He'd never fallen over or passed out like many other officials during the festivities, but it was par for the course to see him slumped and sullen at his grand table while the party continued around him.

No, Ri wasn't surprised to see his leader drinking and affected by it, but he was disheartened, because he knew why he was here, and a drunk Dae Wonsu was only going to make this conversation more volatile.

The Americans had foiled his attempt to bring in precision-crafted second-stage tubes from France. Ri still had time to make it happen before the clock ran out on Choi's arbitrary timetable, and with more money coming in from Óscar Roblas than Ri knew what do to with he had other opportunities to get the tubes, but he worried Choi would lose confidence in him and sack him right here and now.

The lieutenant general knew good and well the Dae Wonsu wouldn't have to keep to his end of their three-year deal – he could change his mind on a whim and throw him to the dogs at any time.

Choi sat down at the table while giving Ri a distracted nod, and then, after the long protocol of deep and obligatory bows, Ri sat back down.

Choi swirled the dark brandy around in his glass for a moment; he seemed to be concentrating on the spiraling movement of the liquid. The general thought his leader would say something slurred and nonsensical, but when he spoke his voice was clear, and his words were lucid and biting.

'Another shipment has been interdicted, towed to port in Inchon. How far back does this put us?'

Ri kept his chin up. He'd been summoned to this meeting first thing this morning, which meant he'd had all day to prepare. 'It was unfortunate. The American warship USS *Freedom* is making things difficult for us in acquiring the larger items we need. Smaller equipment can travel by aircraft, and we have utilized this method with good results. It is only on the sea where we are still having problems.'

'The problem is America,' Choi said.

'Exactly correct, Dae Wonsu. The other nations in the UN are not pursuing interdiction. Even before the return of Jack Ryan to the White House, the former President, Ed Kealty, had not harassed our shipments nearly to the extent we are seeing now.'

'So the problem is Jack Ryan, specifically.'

'Again, this is true. But not to worry, we have ordered more rocket tubes, they are being built by another company in Russia. It will take six months for delivery, but we will have everything else in place by the time they arrive, and I feel sure the Taepodong-2 will be operational well within my window for success in the mission.'

In truth, the Russians would ship him nothing until he paid them, and he could not pay them until Roblas delivered his five hundred million. This wouldn't happen till Hwang's damn rare earth – processing plant went live.

Ri troubled Choi with none of these additional details.

Choi just asked, 'Won't the Americans capture the next ship like they did with this one?'

Ri smiled. His sad eyes did not brighten, but the smile

was there. 'The Russians have an aircraft, the An-225, that is large enough to transport the tubes by air. We won't have to worry about maritime interdiction.'

'You have less than two years.'

'Yes, Dae Wonsu. I am aware.'

'President Jack Ryan has two years left in his term.'

'I am aware of this as well, Dae Wonsu. If not for him, we would be operational much faster.'

'Your predecessor had many complaints about Jack Ryan as well.' Choi drank a long gulp of brandy. 'I called them excuses.'

Ri realized he needed to create distance between himself and his predecessor, so as to keep distance between himself and the kennels at Chongjin. 'I will not use them as excuses. Ryan is a problem, but we will succeed nonetheless.'

Choi looked across the table for a moment; his eyes were dull from the drink but they did not waver. 'What do you know about Rangoon?'

Ri knew Choi wasn't asking him what he knew about the capital of Myanmar, but instead about a particular event that happened there. When North Korean leadership spoke of Rangoon to the intelligence community, it could mean only one thing, because of the importance of the city to his nation's intelligence agency.

Ri answered with confidence. 'October ninth, 1983. I was a lieutenant in the Chosun Inmingun at the time. I will never forget learning of the bravery of our men who –'

Choi talked over him as if Ri were not speaking. 'October ninth, 1983. My grandfather sent three assassins to plant a bomb to kill the president of South Korea during his visit to the Martyrs'' Mausoleum in Burma. The bomb missed Choon Doo-hwan, lamentably, because his motorcade had been delayed by traffic.'

Ri knew all of this, of course. Twenty-one people had been killed, forty-six wounded. He did not know why Choi was bringing up this thirty-year-old event.

Choi said, 'As an expert on history, I cannot help but think about what might have been. If Rangoon had succeeded, South Korea would have been destabilized. Our army was better than theirs. America's will would have faltered. My grandfather would have taken the entire peninsula within one, perhaps two years, and we would have been in a position of incredible strength. Economic strength. Military strength. The problems of the famine during the 1990s would have never occurred, the United States would have realized the pressure and sanctions were futile. Just think where we would be today if there had been a little less traffic on the road that afternoon in Rangoon.' Choi smiled wistfully.

General Ri nodded. Undoubtedly, some of Choi's conclusions were sound. And undoubtedly those that were not sound would not be mentioned by Ri.

'You see what else would have happened?' Choi asked.

'I am sorry. I confess I do not.'

'My father would not have been killed by Jack Ryan.'

'Your father?'

'The Americans poisoned my father. How else to explain it? He was a healthy man. Hard of hearing, maybe, but his doctors say he would have lived another twenty to twenty-five years in good health.'

Ri didn't believe this was true for an instant, though he had no doubt believing the elder Choi's doctors would have made the claim he had been poisoned to deflect blame on themselves. Ri was the operations chief of RGB when Choi's father died, and he and his people were ordered to find evidence of an assas-sination. Ri found no such evidence, because no such evidence existed.

Choi went back to Rangoon. 'My grandfather's bravery in ordering this attack on the leader of the South was only matched by his forward thinking. Just consider it for a moment, Ri.'

Ri couldn't help but think the three assassins were the real brave ones, braver than the man who sent them down with orders to kill themselves after the attack. But of course he made no mention of this.

Choi finished his drink, and a beautiful young girl – Ri did not think she could have been more than seventeen – walked across the empty banquet room with a crystal flask and refilled Choi's snifter. Choi did not regard her; instead, he kept talking.

'If Rangoon had succeeded it would have changed the fate of our nation. Indeed, the fate of the world.'

Ri bowed. 'Yes.'

'If you were able to eliminate Jack Ryan, I feel certain this would have a similar outcome for our nation. Do you agree?'

Ri's heart sank. He was being given another impossible task. But he said, 'Yes. I agree wholeheartedly.'

Choi said, 'I know the difficult thing is to make it look like someone else is involved.' Choi leaned forward half-way across the table. Ri caught the unmistakable smell of brandy, not from the snifter in his hand, but from his skin. 'But that is your problem.'

An uncomfortable silence told General Ri that it was his turn to talk.

'Yes. Well . . . certainly there are many who would benefit from his death.'

'Of course. How would you do it?'

Ri blinked. He needed to say something to bolster Choi's confidence in him. He tried to show no doubt, no hesitation. He spoke off the top of his head, fighting for the words just as they came out of his mouth. 'I would find out his foreign travel schedule. I would use Middle Eastern bomb makers. I have access to them through our good relations with Syria and Iran. I would organize the affair through proxies.' He hastened to add, 'But I would be involved with every aspect of it, because there could be no failure. Jack Ryan is well protected now, but if there is a credible attempt on his life, the Americans can do so much more to keep away from assassins. There will be no second opportunity.'

Choi nodded thoughtfully.

Ri worried he was about to order him to proceed, so he spoke quickly, couching his words of warning in layer over layer of deference, lest he offend the Dae Wonsu. 'I am certain you are aware of this, because of your astute knowledge of world history, and I only bring this up to remind myself of the stakes of any such operation, but there is the need to remember how America reacts to insult, threat, and attack. Pearl Harbor is but one example. As the Japanese marshal admiral Isoroku Yamamoto said, they awoke a sleeping giant. America will look long and hard for the perpetrators of the act, and if they suspect for an instant we are the perpetrators, then they will seek revenge on our soil.'

Ri had hoped that would sink in for a moment, but Choi waved the threat away with his brandy snifter, sloshing some of the drink out of the bowl-shaped glass and onto the table.

'Your Middle Eastern bomber should not survive to talk.' Choi smiled as if he had solved all the problems and issues with one brilliant sentence.

Ri worked hard to match his leader's smile with one of his own. 'Yes, Dae Wonsu. That is an excellent idea.'

20

Londoner Edward Riley didn't much care for New York, as it was not his home. But since his home didn't much care for him, he'd relocated here to the States five years earlier, and he was bloody well determined to make the best of it.

Part and parcel of making the best of it included the vehicle in which Riley now drove as he motored down the West Side Highway through mid-morning traffic. It was a coal-black BMW i8 electric sports car. It shined as if he'd coated it with cooking spray before leaving his garage, and its lean, aerodynamic form turned heads and earned whistles and compliments even here in the sneering Upper West Side.

Edward Riley loved the attention, which was an odd thing, really, because Edward Riley was a spy.

Claiming fame is frowned upon for intelligence officers, but Edward Riley's claim to fame was undeniably impressive. He had been the youngest chief of station in the last thirty years at MI6, the foreign intelligence arm of the government of the United Kingdom. Now, at age thirty-six, he had the experience and the CV envied by men twice his age, and Riley played this up more like his own publicist than as a spook concerned with his own personal security.

As a young lad, short and sandy-haired Eddie had a love of language and culture. His parents traveled Europe as manufacturer representatives in the fitness-equipment industry, and he'd been to every country on the continent by age ten. Moreover, his grandparents on his mother's side were ardent travelers who 'borrowed' their grandson for summer hops to Africa and Asia and South America.

Eddie went into Eton with plans of following into his father's business so he could continue to see the world, and he studied French and Arabic and Russian as a means to that end.

He hadn't been a perfect candidate for intelligence work because although most spies have at least some level of loyalty to their own flag, Riley did not. It wasn't that he was unpatriotic, really, rather he just didn't give a toss about his own country or countrymen. But one of his professors at Eton was an unofficial recruiter for the Crown and he forwarded Eddie's name on a hunch, and soon Eddie was met after class by a middle-aged woman and asked if he'd be interested in taking the civil service exams.

'Not particularly,' was the honest answer.

But the woman was persuasive, and she hyped the travel and the study of culture and within seconds a light-bulb went off and Eddie Riley realized this was a recruitment attempt for the British secret services.

And that sounded interesting – there wasn't a James Bond film young Riley hadn't seen five times – so his 'not really' turned to 'why not?'

One does not apply to MI6. Instead, one applies for a position at the coordination staff for the Foreign and

Commonwealth Office – this is personnel code for foreign intelligence work. Riley did this and then he breezed through his training, and soon he was off into the world, beginning every young officer's saga of doing time at dusty outposts, learning the ropes the hard way.

Sana'a, Yemen. Windhoek, Namibia. Then a promotion to Montevideo, Uruguay.

After he had spent a year in South America the war in the Middle East had pulled enough more experienced intelligence officers into that region to leave some plum postings vacant for young officers who were both competent and easily mobile. He worked in Finland for a year, and then he did a longer stint in the British Virgin Islands. Riley made a name for himself and by age twenty-seven he was back in Europe, as assistant chief of station in Bulgaria, a rising star.

He'd been in that position for less than six months when his chief of station was recalled home due to a family illness. MI6 had plans to replace the senior spy with someone other than his young second-in-command, but a month as acting chief of station turned to three, and then by six someone decided he'd earned the position he'd fallen into, and the paperwork was completed to make it official.

Edward Riley of London became the twenty-seven-year-old SIS station chief of Bulgaria, making him the youngest in the service in more than thirty years.

But Riley did not stop there. He worked hard, which was important, and he had no qualms about using people and situations to his personal benefit. By his thirtieth birthday his skyrocketing career had landed him in Italy as station chief, a posting orders of magnitude more important than running the shop in nearby Bulgaria.

But in Rome it unraveled quickly. By violating orders and working with one group of local criminals he disrupted another local cell of Russian Mafia who were connected to the government in Moscow, as virtually all Russian criminals were. The criminals appealed to the SVR, Russian foreign intelligence, and the SVR developed an operation to get Riley out of the way.

The Russians identified Riley as the UK station chief, and then they targeted him, not for any lethal measures – that would have brought more trouble than the matter was worth – they just wanted him gone.

The Russians tricked him, though when it was over he had no one but himself to blame. A simple honey trap. Edward had a British wife and three small children, but one day he sat down next to a twenty-four-year-old Romanian model named Alina at a café he frequented on the Via Bergamo, and he started up a conversation.

She claimed to be an exchange student and she showed more interest in her textbook than in the handsome Briton chatting her up, but her beauty absolutely floored him, so he kept talking. He saw himself as the pursuer, so he didn't think for one moment he was being played. He asked for her number and she refused, but she showed up at the same café a few days later, and they went for a walk on the Via Piave and soon enough they had somehow wandered into the lobby of the Hotel Oxford on the Via Boncompagni. He had no idea how a credit card in one of his aliases just appeared from his wallet into his hand, and then into the hand of the desk clerk, and he couldn't for the life of him understand how he and young Alina found themselves in a fourth-floor suite on the bed.

A bloody mysterious thing all around, he told himself when it was over.

For her part Alina did not know she was working for the Russians. Instead, she thought she had been hired for this seduction by a British tabloid. She'd been paid well, and the tabloid, in fact, existed, but Alina had no idea it was owned, like much of the UK, by Russian concerns, and it went where Russian intelligence told it to go.

Even though the honey trap had been set and the paparazzi were in town to catch the young British spy in the act, it was really not quite so simple. Riley, like most adulterous spies, applied the tradecraft of his work to his pleasure. For a month he and his Romanian lover kept a clandestine relationship that would have made his MI6 training cadre proud. They used drop phones, they met in out-of-the-way cafés only after running surveillance detection routes, they varied their routines. Alina kept tipping off the cameramen as to where they would be and what they would be doing, but Riley kept the affair one step ahead of them, though wholly unaware anyone was on his trail.

On a moonlit beach in Sardinia the cameras finally caught him. Riley and Alina were nude, in flagrante delicto, and as the flashes flashed and the shutters clicked, thirty-one-year-old Edward Riley knew his career and his marriage were now items of the past.

The British tabloid was giddy with its reportage: photos

of the topless blonde, the dashing young spy, bare-chested, on top of her, staring into the lens with a deer-in-the-headlights look that solidified the sordid nature of the tryst.

'On Her Majesty's Sleazy Circus,' read the headline, and as Riley looked at the article the next morning he knew he'd been had, and he wished the rag had only the decency to admit what they'd done had been done for *fucking* Moscow by bylining the piece 'Written with help from Russia's Foreign Intelligence Service.'

Riley was recalled to London, of course. He was shamed out of the service after years of work and the paparazzi chased him and his family outside their flat in Knightsbridge.

Something snapped within Riley and he turned to self-preservation mode, not allowing himself the self-acuity to take responsibility for his action. He blamed England, his own country, for the debacle – certainly not himself.

He kept a stiff upper lip for a few months, but there's something about being the most publicly recognizable spy in your country that works against you, and Riley knew he'd have to do a runner and leave England behind.

And in swooped Duke Sharps. Riley had never met the man, he knew him only by his unscrupulous reputation. Duke had asked Edward to come over for a meeting, all expenses paid by Sharps Global Intelligence Partners, of course. Edward did so, he'd listened to the American's spiel about the work, and he'd agreed on the spot. Edward was ecstatic to be back in the intelligence game, even in a commercial capacity. He could do unscrupulous. He'd go into it for the money, eschew right and wrong and good and evil, and look out for himself now.

Of course, he'd been concerned that his new notoriety would make him completely ineffectual as an intelligence asset. But something happened that Edward Riley did not expect. He found his fame worked to his advantage. In this odd version of intelligence work at Sharps Partners, having a reputation served him well. He met the important people, he dined with potential clients and CEOs, and he appeared on television as a talking head, giving his view on UK intelligence issues from New York bureaus of the big news stations.

And he made a lot of money. Sharps paid its operatives more when their operations were successful, unlike MI6, where the bloke meeting an informant over a dinner of whale blubber in Iceland with six years of service earned the exact same amount as the bloke with six years of shooting it out with Russian Spetsnaz in a shit-stained basement in Chechnya.

Though he had some 'shine time' on TV, Riley wasn't a figurehead at Sharps. That was Sharps's job. No, the thirty-six-year-old Englishman worked surprisingly hard, built operations from the ground up, and put in the hours and the effort. He ran intelligence assets and demanded every bit of the same excellence he'd expected from his agents and officers when he was an MI6 station chief.

Sharps used Riley on the tough jobs, and Riley didn't care. He was in it for the money, full stop.

By the time the three-year anniversary of his fall from grace came around he took a thorough look at his life and he realized he bloody well loved his job and his life of amorality.

The Crown could bugger off.

Edward Riley pulled his BMW sports car up to the valet stand at the Mandarin Oriental near Columbus Circle; he climbed out and winked at the young Dominican valet as the man approached the vehicle with an appreciative grin.

'Staying with us, sir?' he said, nearly salivating at the prospect of folding himself into the luxurious sports car.

'Just a meeting over tea at Asiate.'

The valet turned away from the car. 'Perhaps with the woman who just arrived by taxi?'

'Tall, blond, legs for days?'

The Dominican smiled. He wanted Riley's life, and he did not hide the fact. 'That's the one, sir.'

The Englishman ate it up. 'Haven't yet met her in person, but I've heard reports she is quite something.'

'A beauty, sir. You enjoy your meeting, and I'll take great care of *this* beauty.'

Riley was a single man, if not on paper. His marriage had fallen apart in London, right after his fall from grace, and his wife – one of these days he'd go home and make it official, or she could bloody well come here with the papers to sign – had herself moved on. The thought of bedding this Frenchwoman was appealing, even though he hadn't even met her yet, but this operation was too damn important for him to mix business with pleasure.

He'd keep his hands to himself on this one.

He found Veronika Martel at a corner table in the rear of the nearly empty restaurant, sitting with her back to the wall. She rose and shook his hand, and he gazed into her eyes and found her every bit as beautiful as the rumors.

Riley was certain she would know all about him. Or she would know what Russian intelligence wanted the world to know. She would have too much class to say anything about it, but the fact this woman was aware about the scandal that wrecked his life hung over this meeting like a weight.

But Riley told himself he wouldn't let that threaten his authority. He chatted with the gorgeous blonde for a few minutes, a professional conversation about superficial matters. Her flight and her hotel and her impressions of the city and the United States. He found her to be intelligent but highly guarded.

Finally he got around to the subject of today's meeting. 'I know Duke talked to you about the Valley Floor assignment.'

'He did.'

'It's not a bad posting,' he said. "You'll be less than forty miles from Vegas, so you can commute in each morning. You'll have to, really, no other options in the area. We'll put you up in a nice hotel and take good care of you.

'The first week or so you're just there to establish yourself. You'll get the training on the diagnostic equipment here before heading over, so all you'll be doing is looking at readouts on machinery at the rare earth hydroseparation facility. Our Science and Tech department will give you a cell phone that has the ability to pull the software we want directly off the system servers, but you'll have to social engineer the password out of a systems administrator to obtain the access necessary.'

'I can manage that.'

'Undoubtedly,' Riley said. 'New World Metals has a shipment of ore-processing equipment heading to North Korea this month, and the computers will fly in from Europe, so we do have some time constraints. This is all machinery for the refinery. All of the mining machinery is already there.'

'Where did they get that?'

'The Chinese were tossed out in such a hurry they weren't able to take everything with them. They didn't leave enough equipment to operate the mine in any profitable capacity, but they do have some drilling going on. The processing equipment is crucial now because the ore is starting to back up.'

'Then I won't delay another moment to get started.'

'Excellent. I have a trainer flying into New York today. A woman from Brazil who works for Vale, a diversified metals mining concern there. She does just exactly the same thing you will be doing at the NewCorp facility. You'll have three days to work with her and make yourself legitimate. I trust you can pull that off.'

Veronika had been slipping into and then out of roles for her entire career. She'd been a hotel desk clerk and a software engineer and a fishmonger and a college professor and even a bikini model at a Le Mans race. Seventy-two hours of intense prep could turn her into just about anything as long as scrutiny by experts wasn't too high.

'I'll do my best,' she said.

Riley looked into his teacup for a moment. 'I'll ask you the question Duke won't ask. How does it make you feel to know your work will directly benefit North Korea?'

Martel was as calculating as Riley was off-the-cuff. 'I don't concern myself with that.'

"Good answer. Bloody lie, but I'll take a lie that says what I want to hear. I know you were face-to-face with the DPRK agents in Vietnam. That was a poorly handled mess, and not my doing. You won't see that level of unprofessionalism on this operation with me in charge, I can assure you of that.

'I also want you to understand what we are doing here. The end game is mining. Money for New World Metals, and some trickle-down for us at Sharps. We're not employees of the North Koreans. We're not doing anything we can't be proud of.'

Martel considered mentioning the American employee of Sharps's whose blood she'd wiped off of the passport. But she decided against it. Riley wanted to start fresh in this operation, and she felt the same way. There was no reason to reintroduce any ugly issues. She wanted him to understand he wouldn't have to worry about her morale on this job. It was just a job, like all the others.

'Mr Riley, I appreciate the gesture you seem to be making, but don't feel like you need to tend to my morale. I honestly don't give a damn what we are doing, who we are doing it for, or who we are doing it to. You have quite ably outlined my duties at Valley Floor, and I will comply to the best of my ability. You can rest assured I require no more special care than that.'

'I feel exactly the same way. We are men and women in a line of work where morality only gets in the way.'

'That's a good way of putting it, Mr Riley.'

Edward Riley's face slipped into an easy grin. 'You and I are going to get along perfectly, Ms. Martel.'

21

The conference room in the Situation Room below the West Wing began filling with principals before nine a.m. The President arrived soon after, and he waved the eleven men and women in front of him back to their seats.

The focus of today's discussion, as written on the agenda and left at each place setting, was almost comically simplistic.

'United Nations sanctions options in pursuit of solutions re North Korea.'

The United States and the United Nations had spent most of the past seventy years pursuing solutions re North Korea, and when Ryan noticed the heading on his briefing paper he let out a slight groan and mumbled that he sure hoped they'd have their solution figured out before lunch.

In front of him at the table was his national security staff, mostly, but also his secretary of commerce and the US ambassador to the United Nations, as well as his chief of staff, Arnie Van Damm.

The conference began with a discussion by Jay Canfield of the specific tactics the North Koreans were using to move money, from banks in the Cayman Islands and Singapore, where large deposits had been made, to smaller accounts in Brunei, Antigua, Mexico, Singapore, and other locations. It was clear several large payments had been made in the past few months, but the CIA did not have the access into the banking systems to know where the money had gone.

After a lot of detailed and often arcane explanations, Canfield wrapped up his presentation in plain speak. 'Suffice it to say, Mr President, that somebody is paying North Korea a hell of a lot of money, and North Korea, in turn, is wasting no time in blowing a hell of a lot of money. Who is paying them, and the full scope of what they are buying, is still unknown to us.'

Next the US ambassador to the United Nations, Danielle Rush, laid out her proposal, developed along with the sec-retaries of state, commerce, and treasury, to seek a UN resolution enhancing existing economic sanctions against the state of North Korea.

The President listened to the twenty-minute presentation in silence.

When it was over Ryan slid his fingers under his eyeglasses and rubbed his tired eyes. 'I get that we need to stop these transactions. I just don't see what the hell we will achieve by going to the United Nations for another round of economic sanctions on Korea. All this talk about what the United Nations is going to do. The UN can't do anything. It's not an enforcement body. It relies on its member nations to enforce sanctions. What makes you think all these countries that are making money off of North Korea will comply with the new sanctions?'

Secretary of State Scott Adler fielded this. 'We come out very strongly and say any nation who knowingly circumvents the sanctions will meet with unilateral sanctions from the US Commerce Department. We make a big noise about getting our European and Asian partners on board with this. Once we have the UN stamp on this action, we can add our own measures to make it more effective.'

There was a half-hour of back and forth after this, discussions of the tenor and the tone of the sanctions. Finally President Ryan was sold on the fact this was a necessary step. He nodded and said, 'Okay. You almost never hear me say this, but I agree the United Nations has an important role to play here. The US and Europe already sanction our banks against working with the North Koreans. But the banks we have identified as being involved in this are all in countries not saddled by their own domestic sanctions against North Korea.'

Ambassador Rush said, 'We need wording along the lines of a prohibition on commerce and banking ... restrictions to third-country persons, banks, and other commercial entities from facilitating trade with North Korea. We'll have to specify the thirty-eight accounts we've identified, all the go-betweens, all the countries involved.'

Ryan agreed. 'That's right. We have to shut down North Korea's access to hard currency. The best way in the short term to do that is to get a UN resolution sanctioning the banks abroad they are working with now.'

The UN ambassador said, 'If we, as a member of the UN Security Council, push for these new sanctions, the first step that will happen will be in the Security Council Sanctions Committee. They will have ten days to hold a rules vote to see if the measures requested meet the requirements of UN economic sanctions. This is a procedural vote, and it shouldn't be a major problem, but it is a definite hurdle. There is a lot of arcane wording in the charter, and the UN officials in the Sanctions Committee must themselves decide if the request is even valid.'

Ryan said, 'We can put pressure on the governments of the delegates.'

Ambassador Rush shook her head. 'Won't work. In the sanctions vote, sure, the ambassadors will vote in the interests of their own nations. But in this rules vote, the voters are employees of the UN. Simple bureaucrats. I'm not saying they are untouchable, but they are international law experts, and they pride themselves on reading the charter and ruling accordingly.'

Ryan nodded. 'Okay. Get started on drafting the sanctions immediately. I want something to sign as soon as possible so we can get the ball rolling. Every day North Korea has all this cash in all these bank accounts in all these offshore banks is another day closer to their acquisition of an ICBM.'

'Mr President,' Adler said. 'I want you to be perfectly clear on one thing. When you go forward with this push to get another round of sanctions passed, you will be outnumbered. There are a lot of countries, and a lot of very powerful companies who are aware that North Korea has potential in the rare earth mineral sector. The big technology firms want electromagnets for their computers, for example, and the nations who get tax dollars from these firms – the French and the Germans and the Japanese and the Taiwanese, for example – they will all be under a lot of pressure to kill these sanctions.'

Ryan chuckled. 'I've been outnumbered before. Hell,

I've spent the last hour and a half staring back at you guys arguing this over.'

The room broke into laughter.

Adler smiled but stayed on point. 'Diplomatically, politically, even ethically, we are going to look pretty awful if word gets out we are trying to inhibit an industry that has nothing to do with either weapons or human rights abuses. We will basically be saying to the world that we want to continue to starve a population of twenty-five million people in order to protect ourselves.'

Ryan said, 'You know that's bullshit. Nobody in North Korea who is starving now is going to get a bucket of Kentucky Fried Chicken when the government mineral mine starts producing.'

Arnie followed Adler's argument. 'But that's how it will play in the press if we push to cut off their access to manu-factured goods from abroad. Politically, Mr President, this is a dead end.'

Ryan heaved. 'I don't do politics anymore. I won my last election and I can't run again. You remember that, don't you?'

Van Damm rolled his eyes at the comment. "I'm not talking about you. Midterms are coming up, you've got a tenuous hold on Congress and a contested Senate. If you concentrate on issues that move the needle in our favor, you can write your own ticket for the last two years of your administration.

'The populace focuses on the shiny objects in front of them. The media is talking about domestic issues first, then the Russia – Ukraine problem, and lastly the conflagration in the Middle East. North Korea's craziness isn't even a blip on the radar to these people anymore, even with the missile test and the interdiction of the rocket tubes from France. That was barely a one-news-cycle story. The country doesn't care.'

'It's not my job to just focus on what's trending, Arnie. You know that. Just because this problem isn't as overt as some of the other world flash points, it doesn't mean I can just ignore it.'

'Fair enough,' Van Damm said. 'But be warned. You won't have a lot of friends on this issue.'

The Hendley Associates Gulfstream G550 flew overnight from Baltimore/Washington International Airport to Václav Havel Airport Prague. The aircraft had a range of well over 5,000 miles, so the 4,200-mile transoceanic flight was an easily makeable jaunt for the jet without any need to stop along the way to refuel.

On board the flight the needs of Jack Ryan, Dom Caruso, and Gavin Biery were attended to by Adara Sherman. She brought them drinks after takeoff, and the three passengers sat at the four-seat conference table in the center of the cabin so they could prep for the operation ahead.

The plan for the men during tonight's flight over was to use the time to acquaint themselves with the area they would be operating in in Prague. Karel Skála lived in the Žižkov district of the city, far to the east of the tourist traps of the Old Town and Hradčany. It was a large area of apartment buildings, working-class neighborhoods, and municipal parks, and the men knew if they were going to run any kind of a surveillance package on their target there they would need to know the area without having to walk around with their nose in a map.

The service they were using on their laptops tonight to acquaint them with the eastern neighborhoods of Prague was state-of-the-art. Gavin had recently briefed the operators of The Campus about the new application from the National Geospatial-Intelligence Agency that now ran on their computers. It was called Map of the World, and it was an incredibly detailed interactive mapping service that could show the team virtually any place on earth, and also give them an easy interface through which they could pull up all data on the area known by the US intelligence agency and the other members of the 'Five Eyes,' the English-speaking countries who shared intelligence product with the United States. Map of the World contained millions of pieces of information culled from open sources as well as the intelligence organizations from the United States, the UK, Canada, Australia, and New Zealand.

They spent time testing Map of the World by researching their target's apartment building. Through a few clicks they could see the façade, the parking area in the rear, photos of inner corridors, security camera angles and schematics, and even information on tenants of the building in the form of the computerized rental agreements kept on file by the property manager.

Map of the World was an incredible resource, like Google Earth on steroids, and Jack and Dom knew it would replace EagleView, the high-tech mapping program they had been using. EagleView was good, but it wasn't going to tell you what time a particular trash bin on a particular street corner was emptied. Map of the World could do that – provided someone in the US intelligence community had entered that bit of intel from any linked intelligence or open-source database.

Gavin Biery had loaded a mobile version of the service

onto Jack and Dominic's iPhones for quick reference while in the field, and he was even testing out a proprietary application he had created himself whereby the operators could speak commands into their phones and have answers computed for them using MOTW information, and then read aloud back to them.

As they ate their dinner and discussed the capabilities of the software, Gavin asked Jack to give it a try.

'What do I ask?'

'Whatever you want. Like I said, she's still in beta, so don't be too rough on her.'

Jack thought for a moment, then pushed the button on his mobile. 'MOTW,' he said, letting the computer know he was talking to the Map of the World app. 'Tell me which airport in Prague has the least police presence.'

All eyes in the cabin looked at the mobile. After just a few seconds, a female voice replied, 'I am sorry. I do not understand.'

Jack made a face at Gavin. 'Sorry, Gav, but I don't think this is quite ready for a field test.'

But Biery snatched the phone out of Jack's hand. He said, 'MOTW, how many police officers are at Václav Havel Airport in Prague?'

Another brief pause, and then, in a slightly computerized voice, the mobile replied, 'Exact answer unknown. There is a municipal police precinct at Václav Havel Airport, a federal police station at Václav Havel Airport, and an airport police office at Václav Havel Airport. Shall I give you terminal locations, phone numbers, or e-mail addresses?'

Jack and Dom both raised their eyebrows.

Gavin smiled. 'There are millions of bits of data at its disposal. You ask the right question in the right way, and it can be of use.'

Dom joked, 'Now that we've got this, what the hell do we need you for?'

Gavin rolled his eyes and went back to his dinner, and Adara refilled everyone's wineglass.

After dinner Adara cleared the table and offered coffee to the three men. Ryan and Biery never hesitated to thank Adara for her great service and even ask her if there was anything they could do to help out on the journey, but Caruso was the only passenger on tonight's flight who actually spent time up in the galley at the front of the cabin, helping with the dishes and the linens.

Neither Gavin nor Jack noticed it because they were engrossed in their work, but Caruso spent a lot of time on the flight over to Europe up front chatting with Sherman.

The G550 landed at nine a.m., and the three men of The Campus climbed into a black Mercedes E-Class sedan Sherman had arranged to be waiting for them at the hangar where they parked after clearing customs. They threw in several pieces of luggage, and then drove directly through morning traffic to Prague's 3rd district.

The workup Ryan had done on Skála over the past day gave the team some basic information about the man, but not much illumination into his habits and movements. Since Skála worked out of two different offices in two different locations, Ryan decided that in order to keep their operation simple they wouldn't try to surveil him at work.

That seemed like it would be a fifty-fifty prospect at best. Instead, they would watch the man at home, tail him as he left the house, and spend a couple days determining his habits and movements before proceeding, unless of course some great opportunity presented itself earlier.

The goal was to get a look inside whatever personal electronics he carried with him, in the hopes there were trackbacks to Hazelton and others that might give them an idea about who killed the American ex – CIA officer. Jack thought they might be able to lift Skála's mobile phone during his daily commute. He and Dominic had recently trained in pickpocketing under a master of the art in Las Vegas, so they had some confidence in their skills, and they thought they might be able to relieve Skála of his phone while he stood on the metro or at a stoplight. If they could do this, there would be no need to resort to heavier measures.

That said, heavier measures were not off the table. Ryan knew he might have to go overt on this trip – to confront Karel Skála and impress upon him the need for his cooperation, or else to simply mug him and steal his phone.

At this point there was no thought of breaking into his home because, Ryan reasoned, Skála wouldn't leave his laptop or his mobile phone there when he left the house. For now they would take their time, eye the target to find the best opportunity to close on him, and take it from there.

In most cases Campus operators in the field did not carry firearms, but it had been decided by Clark that, due to the surprising dangers that had presented themselves in Vietnam, both Dom and Jack would carry pistols during their operation in the Czech Republic.

Going armed internationally was problematic – getting into any country with guns would have been impossible if they hadn't been flying in their own jet. Even with the Gulfstream it was necessary to take measures to ensure the guns would stay hidden while customs and immigration looked the plane over after landing. This wasn't hard; special hidden compartments had been built into the G550 behind existing access panels in the cabin and cockpit, and once the inspection by customs and immigration was complete, Jack and Dom had simply retrieved their weapons from their hiding places and secreted them on their person.

Now both men wore subcompact Smith & Wesson M&P Shield nine-millimeter auto pistols in covert carry pouches under their pants. The holsters had the clever brand name of Thunderwear because the gun rode just above the wearer's crotch.

Back in the States Clark had made the operators train for hours with the Thunderwear and the small and thin handguns; Dom and Jack had each practiced drawing their weapons from inside their pants hundreds of times. Dom could complete his drawstroke and hit a target center mass at a range of seven yards in .85 seconds. Ryan got his time down to 1.01. Even with the difficulties of presenting a weapon from deep concealment, their times were faster than most police officers could pull their guns from their duty belts and fire them.

Gavin, in contrast to the younger men with him on this trip, did not have a gun, which bothered him considerably. As a consolation prize Caruso gave Gavin a less-than-lethal self-defense device for the trip. He took Gavin's iPhone and snapped on a new battery backup case for it. The case appeared to be thicker than normal and more robust than the model Gavin had been using, but Dom showed him how the device worked and he saw that it was no regular phone protector. Instead, by thumbing open a rubber cap on the side of the case and pressing a small red button under it, the case turned into a 7.8-million-volt stun device.

There was only enough juice to deliver one three-second jolt and, Dom explained to Gavin when he gave him the device, the power and efficacy of stun guns has been greatly ex-aggerated in movies and television. But it was a fair last-ditch defensive option in the right set of circumstances for a man with no other weapons and no hand-to-hand skills.

Both Ryan and Caruso had been offered similar stun devices from the Technology and Outfitting department at The Campus, but they turned them down. Both men decided they'd get better results punching a man in the nose than they would shocking him in the neck, and since they were expert martial artists, they had the training to accomplish this.

Skála lived alone in a two-bedroom unit on the fifth floor of a middle-class apartment building on Křišťanova Street, just a couple of blocks west of Olšany cemetery. Ryan had secured an overwatch nearby. He used a Campus front company registered in Luxembourg to arrange a three-month lease on a sixth-floor converted warehouse office space on nearby Baranova Street. The windows on the southern side of the office space gave the men a view of the entrance to Skála's building and the parking lot next to it, but they couldn't see into the windows of his condo without going up onto the roof and exposing themselves, so instead they placed a wireless camera and a long-range laser microphone on the roof, protected under a rubber container with holes cut to allow the devices a way to 'see' the windows across the intersection. The audio and video feeds would be picked up by Biery's computers, and it would give the men downstairs another set of eyes and ears on their target location.

They set up their three-man static surveillance operation in the corner of the office space, and hid the operation from the rest of the big room by stacking desks six feet high. Once they had their space, from a suitcase they pulled a pair of binoculars and mounted it onto a tripod. The lenses were centered and focused on the entrance to Skála's apartment building and the parking lot next to it. The men also pointed a second directional microphone out an open window, and they hung bedding in the windows so no one looking up from the street below would see any hint of the team.

They also laid two bedrolls, placed rubber doorstops at the entrances to the locked office to supplement the deadbolt lock, and they attached two large photos of Karel Skála to the curtain near the binoculars so they could study his face in their downtime.

Gavin placed one of his laptops on a desk, and the other he kept in a backpack by the door. Jack had explained that he would need to come along if they tailed the government official through the streets or metro of Prague, because if the operators were able to take possession of the man's mobile then they wanted Gavin close by and ready to hack the device and download all the data as quickly as possible. In an ideal scenario, they all agreed, they would get the phone back into Skála's pocket without him ever knowing anything was amiss.

Jack told Gavin he needed to be prepared for anything, however, because most scenarios don't come off the way the planners hope. Jack had been the planner of this mission, and he had the good sense to build some wiggle room into his operation wherever he could.

Jack, Dom, and Gavin were set up and in position by three p.m. The laser mike picked up no noise at all from inside Skála's apartment, so they were reasonably sure he wasn't home. This was no surprise. They assumed he'd return from work sometime after five, so they settled in to wait.

While they sat there Gavin did some research into Map of the World on his computer, and he used the basic data about Skála there to hack into his condo rental records. From this he saw their target owned a white VW Golf. The license plate was noted on the rental record, but Gavin couldn't find any information about whether or not Skála had a reserved parking space at his building on Křišťanova.

Caruso used the binoculars on the tripod to look for a car matching the description in the parking lot adjacent to the apartment building. He found the white Golf quickly, and although he couldn't see the tag number from his position, he thought it likely to be their target's vehicle.

This was odd, because this was a workday and they had assumed Skála to be at work right now.

Caruso said, 'Probably took the metro to work.'

That was a convenient theory, but by seven p.m., when they had seen no one who looked anything like their man coming in or leaving the apartment, they had their doubts.

And when midnight came and went without a single sighting of their target or any noise from inside the apartment, their concern grew.

The men passed the time speculating. It was the most common game to play on a stakeout. Any thoughts that their man might have stayed to work late in the office diminished with each passing hour. Skála wasn't married, so they wondered if he stayed over at a girlfriend's place.

Or a boyfriend – Ryan didn't know enough about his target to make any real assumptions about his life.

The team slept in shifts, one man up, two men down, two hours each, all through the night.

At nine the next morning Skála still had not shown himself, and the men braced themselves to wait through the workday for another chance to see the man they'd flown halfway around the world to target.

The lengthy surveillance was tougher on Gavin than it was on the younger men. Dom had well over a decade of experience on surveillance operations, both with the FBI and then in his career with The Campus. He'd gotten used to the boredom, the exhausting concentration necessary for the work, and the poor sleep and bad food that came along with the job when the target, not the watcher, was in control of the daily schedule and activities.

Ryan had spent considerably less time living this

arduous life, but in the past few years it seemed to him that a key component to his job involved sitting for hours in a parked vehicle, or days in a cramped and darkened room, eating takeout or cold food in plastic wrap and smelling the breath and sweat of one of his teammates.

He didn't much care for the downtime, but he very much did love the thrill of the chase and the payoff of succeeding in his mission, and that made all the downtime worthwhile.

Gavin had decades of experience with bad food and weird sleeping hours; this came from his life as a sedentary IT expert. But the frustrations inherent with having no idea when you needed to be awake, where you might need to go, and what you might need to do from minute to minute took a real toll on him, and sleeping in a thin blanket curled up on a hardwood floor made the fifty-six-year-old's back and neck cramp in protest.

When Skála didn't come home after twenty-four hours of surveillance, they realized their plan to follow him from his house wasn't going to work.

The bastard must have been out of town.

From the very beginning of the surveillance Jack and Dom had bandied around the idea of doing a quick entry on Skála's building, not to go to his apartment but instead to break into his mailbox, which, they knew from the images on Map of the World, would be down in the lobby. But they'd initially decided against it. Neither of them expected for a second that some letter relevant to the Hazelton situation would be sitting in the mailbox, so the probability of scoring anything useful would be low and, if something bad and unexpected happened on this op and things went loud, it would take only one nosy neighbor to remember the guy in the lobby who didn't belong. Both Jack and Dom had experienced plenty of Murphy's Law rearing its ugly head at the wrong time while on the job, so they made the decision to leave the mailbox alone.

But now it wasn't a question of discovering useful intel, it was simply a case of trying to find out where the hell Skála was. A look inside his box would certainly tell them if someone had been picking up his mail, and it would give them another piece of the puzzle.

Dom was chosen to do the walk-through. While both men had become excellent at lock picking in the past few years, Dom was slightly better at it. The tiny tumbler lock of the mailbox wouldn't be any challenge at all for him.

He made entry on the apartment building at one p.m. by holding the door for two movers delivering an antique wooden table and then following them inside. There were two people in the small and soulless lobby when the movers disappeared into the elevator, but Dom walked and acted like he belonged, and no one looked up at him.

He went directly to Skála's box, which had his name in handwritten block letters on the tab over the lock, and he picked it with one hand, as if the two-piece pick set were a single key. It took him twelve seconds, and when the box popped open he immediately shut it again and locked it back up without removing anything.

Ten minutes later he was a half-block away, back in the sixth-floor office space.

Ryan asked, 'What did you learn?'

'It was crammed full. He hasn't been here in a few days, at least.'

'Damn,' said Ryan. 'This has been an epic waste of time.'

'Not necessarily,' Caruso countered. 'That lobby was dead. We already know where the cameras are from Map of the World. How about we make something happen?'

Jack understood. 'You want to go take a peek at his place?'

Dom nodded. 'We go right now, before people get home from work.'

Gavin had been silent – he was out of his element here – but he was curious, so he asked, 'Why don't you do it late at night?'

Caruso replied, 'Why? Everybody is home then, sounds are amplified because there is less ambient noise, anyone sees us and they wonder what we're doing, whereas if we go now and act like we're supposed to be there, nobody will give us a second glance.'

Gavin understood, then said, 'If you want I can disable the security cameras.'

Ryan cocked his head. 'Really? How can you do that?'

'This apartment building is using one of the biggest alarm companies in Europe. We established a back door into their servers a couple years ago when we were doing an op in Paris. I can get in, turn the cams off, or just pan them out of the way so they don't see you when you come in.'

'That's awesome,' Ryan said. 'Let's shut them down while we are inside.'

Gavin slid to his laptop and let his fingers hover over

the keys. He looked up. 'What about me? You're not just going to leave me here by myself, are you?'

Dom rolled his eyes, but Jack said, 'You'll be fine, Gav. We need you to monitor the entrance to the building and listen to your headset. We'll remain in comms so you can let us know if Skála shows up while we're in his place.'

'What will you do if he *does* show up?'

Ryan answered, 'We'll improvise.'

Gavin didn't like this one bit, that was plain from the look on his face, but he grabbed his laptop off the table and took his seat at the tripod-mounted binoculars. Here with the computer in his lap he could see the view from the camera on the roof as well as through the binos, plus he could hear any noise on the laser mike and the directional boom mike, as well as listen in to all comms from Jack and Dominic.

The two men put hats on their heads and sunglasses over their eyes, and they headed for the door.

Before they left, Jack turned back to Gavin. 'If you see anything out of the ordinary, you let us know.'

'Got it,' Biery replied, with an intensity in his voice that sounded to the two operators as if Gavin himself was going to be the one to break into the target location.

23

Annette Brawley arrived at work early this morning. She'd left a sweet and apologetic note for her daughter on the kitchen table next to a box of Cheerios and a cereal bowl and a spoon. She even picked a Gerber daisy out of the flowerpot on the back patio and put it in a tiny vase to go with the table setting.

She knew, without a doubt, that Stephanie would ignore the flower and crumple up the sweet note and throw it in the trash. She probably would have done this anyway, but Annette suspected the focus for Stephanie's anger this morning would be the fact that her mother had left an alarm clock at the bottom of the stairs to her room, meaning when it went off she would have to get up and storm downstairs to turn it off.

It wasn't as sure a method for getting her daughter up for school as being there in person to annoy her, but Annette needed to get to the office early to look at a new set of sat images, so it was the best method available to her.

By seven a.m. Annette had been at it for an hour already. She had made it her personal mission to somehow identify the visiting workers at the new Chongju rare earth – processing plant just north of the mine. This was hard work – the resolution provided by the KH-12 satellite in orbit over North Korea was impressive; in just the right conditions she could make out a license plate, although it was extraordinarily rare that she'd been lucky enough to have the conditions in place when she needed a tag number. But determining the identity of a group of one hundred fifty or so men from outer space was no easy task.

She had a couple working assumptions going. For one, she decided these workers were not North Korean. There were definite security measures around the temporary housing compound near the hotel in Chongju. North Korea, of course, subjected its own citizens to positively Orwellian levels of scrutiny and security protocols, but this looked more like an armed camp inside a North Korean city. Annette decided if these were local workers they wouldn't have that number of guards, guns, and gates around them.

No, these were foreign workers, but foreign workers from *where*?

She wasn't able to identify any obvious Caucasians or blacks among the few people standing around the trailers. Everyone she saw looked Asian, but it was impossible to tell if these were North Korean minders or workers from another Asian country. Of course, if they were workers from another country, China would be the first assumption, if not for the fact North Korea had kicked out their Chinese partners more than a year earlier.

She kept hunting, using her three monitors to look at each trash bin, each vehicle, each piece of clothing as closely as possible.

At eight a.m. she thought she had something, and by

eight-fifteen the excitement of tangible results coursed through her like electric shocks.

Colonel Peters, Annette's boss, arrived at work at eight-thirty a.m. to find Annette Brawley standing by his locked door with a smile on her face and two fresh cups of coffee in her hands.

His smile in return was more perfunctory. 'Morning, Brawley. Any chance I can have a couple of minutes to myself before you waylay me with a PowerPoint?'

She replied like a schoolgirl. 'Pu-lease, I just need a few minutes.'

He sighed. 'Will I be impressed?'

'Positively floored.'

'Come on, then,' he said, and he opened the door to let Brawley in.

Peters had just set his briefcase down on his desk when Annette Brawley placed his coffee down, spun his computer to her, and began opening a PowerPoint loaded on the department server to put up on his wall screen. While doing so she said, 'I know who is working at the rare earth metal refinery.'

She put up a picture of the temporary housing in Chongju. She'd highlighted several guard posts on the outside with red circles. 'So first we see there are guards facing out and facing in, looks like two-way security. They don't want the locals meeting with these folks, which means they aren't locals.'

'I'll buy that,' Peters said.

She changed the slide; now it showed some sort of kitchen facility. Wood-burning stoves. Women walking with

246

pots. 'Here is the mess area for the guest workers. It's open-pit fires with grills on them, outdoor lean-to structures. Water tanks.'

'Right,' said Peters. 'No refrigeration. Nasty.'

'Yeah. For us, anyhow. But not for them. Much of the Third World doesn't refrigerate their meat. My daughter would gag if I told her that, but some of the things she eats make me want to puke.'

Another red circle was around a stack of square objects near the fire. 'What's that?' he asked. 'Are those chicken coops?'

'Nope,' she said, and she clicked again, enlarging the area.

Peters leaned forward. They were definitely cages, each one approximately two feet square, based on a woman standing next to them. The Marine colonel tried to look inside. After a few seconds he said, 'Wait. Are those . . . dogs?'

'Yes, they are,' she said. 'Twenty crates here, twenty dogs. This image is from twenty-four hours ago.' She clicked the mouse and the next picture came up. It was of the same area. 'And here is that mess facility just six and a half hours ago.'

Peters counted. 'Eight of the crates are gone.'

'The guest workers ate Fido and his friends for dinner.'

'So . . . the guest workers are Korean? Koreans eat dog sometimes, don't they?'

'They do. But so do some other Asian cultures. Vietnam, Indonesia, Taiwan, and China.'

'Well, we know they aren't Chinese.'

'No, sir. We know they aren't anyone else *but* Chinese. Only the Chinese have experience with rare earth processing. None of the other countries deal in this industry at all.'

Now Peters cocked his head. 'But ... China was kicked out.'

Brawley smiled broadly. 'The Chinese state-owned metal mining corporations, Chinalco and Minmetals, were kicked out, but what I have determined is that these guest workers are Chinese gangster miners.'

'*Gangster* miners?'

'Yes. There are illegal mining companies working all over the country.'

'How do you know?'

She clicked to the next slide. 'This is a rare earth mine in Mongolia. It's a gangster mine, run by an illegal outfit out of Shanghai. This image is from last August.' The mine was full of people. Cars, trucks, earth-moving equipment. 'This mine has been underproducing for a few years, but they kept it open, digging out what they could. Three hundred fifty or so workers, based on the housing.'

She switched to the next slide, and the next, and the next. They all showed the same mine and surrounding buildings; the only difference was the date in the upper left corner changed. October, December, February.

She clicked to bring up the next image, from April. Peters looked at it for a moment and said, 'I'll be damned.'

Annette grinned. 'Where did everyone go, boss?'

'To North Korea? To Chongju?'

'Damn right,' she said. 'The gangster miners must have

been hired in secret by the North Korean state-run mining industry because they didn't have the expertise to operate the mine themselves. Same with the processing facility. The only difference there is the Chinese will need to somehow get some workers with experience in that. The existing gangster mines don't process their own ore.'

Peters stood up from his desk. He had not even taken a sip of his coffee. 'We need to run this up to the fifth floor. Even though it's a little early to present the director with stories about dog meat, they'll need to see this right away.'

'*We?*' she said. 'I look like crap.'

'You look tired, Brawley. Like you've been working your ass off. That's a good thing. I might have to rumple myself up a little before we go so you don't make me look bad.' He said it with a smile.

'You couldn't if you tried, boss.'

24

The breach of Karel Skála's apartment building on Kišt'anova Street in Prague took place at two p.m. It went smoothly; an old man exited the building just as Ryan and Caruso walked up the steps and they caught the door before it closed. Once inside, they moved to the right, sticking close to the wall, and then they stepped into the stairwell without anyone noticing them.

The stairs were empty at this time of the afternoon, so they came out onto the fifth floor, still undetected. They made their way down to Karel Skála's door, and Ryan knocked while Dom sized up the lock.

After a second and third knock, Ryan nodded to Dom and stepped out of the way. While Dom dropped to his knees and began working on the lock, Ryan watched up the hallway, keeping his eyes trained on the stairwell. The elevator bank was closer than the stairs, but Jack knew he'd hear anyone coming via elevator long before the doors slid open. No, their main concern now was the possibility of a neighbor coming out of one of the five other apartments on this floor, or else the stairwell on the far end of the hallway flying open.

No words were exchanged between the two men. Ryan wanted to tell his cousin to hurry the fuck up, but he fought the urge. He knew Dom would defeat the lock faster than he could, so he forced himself to be patient.

Finally, Jack heard the click of the latch opening, and then he followed his cousin through the door.

The small entryway was dark and unremarkable, and this led to an equally dark hallway about twenty feet long. Halfway down on the right was an archway, and they found this led to a well-appointed living room. There was not a single light on in the small apartment, so Jack flipped on a lamp by a sofa so they could look around. Everything was neat and undisturbed.

Both men sniffed the air, trying to decide if anyone might be in the apartment, but neither man detected any particular smell.

They split up and did a quick but careful walk-through to make sure the place was unoccupied, then they met in the living room.

Dom spoke softly. 'An office in back. No computer. Guest bedroom is empty as well.'

Jack said, 'Master bedroom off the right here. Lot of junk lying around, it will take a little while to search this place. Let's snoop around. I'll start in the office. You start in the bedroom.' He then called Gavin. 'Gavin, everything okay?'

Gavin Biery replied from his overwatch position: 'All's well outside.'

Jack reentered the master bedroom and looked for anything interesting out in the open, but that didn't take long. Skála looked like he lived the life of a regular educated European male in his late twenties. There were clothes lying around, books and magazines on his bed, some cheap art on the wall. The guy obviously liked to play squash; there were racquets and other gear lying on a shelf, and a picture of Skála posing on a squash court and holding a trophy rested on his dresser, next to the small trophy itself.

Jack stepped into the master bathroom and went through the medicine cabinets, noted the man had what appeared to be a prescription to combat male pattern baldness, and a large bottle of over-the-counter medicine to treat an upset stomach.

On the other side of the apartment Dom combed through the office. He didn't speak or read Czech so he couldn't identify any of the papers or notes on Skála's little desk, but nothing looked terribly interesting. He felt around under the desk, pulled out the drawers and looked for false compartments, and he searched behind the bookshelves of the small office. When he came up empty in this room he went into a guest room and checked under the bed, then stepped into the bathroom and started searching there.

In Skála's bedroom Jack opened the closet and saw Skála had an impressive array of suits on one side, and on the far side, in the back of the closet, a long row of winter coats were pressed together tightly. Jack decided this would be a great place to hide a safe or anything else Skála wanted to keep hidden, so he began feeling around through the coats. While he searched for any sort of a safe or hidden door, Dom called from the kitchen.

'We can plant a bug in here, but we'll just have to come back and get it if he doesn't show up before we leave.'

Jack felt play in a board in the back wall of the closet. He yanked a few coats off the rod and dropped them to the floor to reveal a loose piece of wallboard a foot and a half wide and several feet tall. He started to pull on it, and while doing so, he said, 'Hey, cuz. Check this out. I might have a –'

The large board peeled back easily, and behind it knelt a pale white man in his underwear. His eyes were red but wide, and he held a large metal object in his hand.

The man screamed and raised the metal object.

'What the –' Jack leapt back in surprise, which worked to his advantage, because the man jumped out from his hiding place swinging.

Jack rolled backward across the bed, ended up on his feet against the shelf with the squash equipment on it. The attacker came forward, leapt up on the bed, and raised the weapon high to swing it down. It was a brass lamp, big and heavy, and the man wielded it like a two-handed sword.

'Wait!' Ryan shouted, but the man swung again as he jumped off the bed. Ryan spun out of the way and felt the breeze as the brass lamp whipped by his face.

Ryan heard his cousin shout from the kitchen. 'Jack?'

Ryan didn't have time to answer. He stumbled back over the dresser as the man closed quickly, chasing Jack with the heavy blunt object. He swung again, but Jack managed to fall backward out of the bedroom and into the hall before the lamp connected.

He rolled to the left and shouted at the man again. This time he said, 'Skála, wait!'

Dom Caruso turned into the hallway from the kitchen, his pistol already out of its Thunderwear holster. Skála swung at the gun before Caruso could fire, and the brass lamp in Skála's hand clanged against the steel and poly-mer weapon, knocking it out of Caruso's hand.

Caruso leapt back to avoid a second swing, but then he moved in quickly, got between the attacker and his weapon, and he slammed the man hard up against the wall of the hallway. The brass lamp clanged to the hardwood floor and Dom shoved the man again. The back of his head made violent contact with the wall. He slid down to the floor, dazed, and Dom stepped over him, fists balled and ready to break his jaw with a right cross.

Jack shouted, 'No! Don't hurt him. It's Skála.'

Dom looked at the man's face for a second, then he relaxed his hands, turned, and went to retrieve his pistol.

Jack stood up and looked down at the dazed man in his underwear. 'You speak English?'

The Czech man was only twenty-eight, but his blond hair was wispy thin. His eyes were impossibly bloodshot, and he smelled like sweat and urine. Jack's first impression was the man was some sort of a drug addict.

Skála nodded slowly. 'Yes.'

'What the fuck were you doing in your closet?' Jack asked.

He coughed a few times. His throat sounded as dry as paper. 'Hiding from you bastards.'

'How did you know we were here?'

This confused the man, it was plain to see. He rubbed his eyes. 'You . . . Aren't you with the North Koreans?'

Caruso holstered his pistol. He was pissed at losing his weapon in a fight with a man with more luck than train-ing, and his anger was reflected in his voice. He snapped back, 'Do we fucking *look* like we're with the North Koreans?'

Jack added, 'We're American.'

Skála said, 'So? The last American I talked to was working with the North Koreans.'

Hazelton, Jack thought, but he did not say it. Instead, he said, 'We're not with the North Koreans. Are they after you?'

Skála just nodded. He was still coming out of his daze, and he was plainly afraid.

Jack said, 'We're going to sit down in the living room and talk a minute. We have a man outside and we are in communication with him. He'll tell us if anybody else shows up.'

This seemed to relax Skála a little. 'I would very much like to have a beer,' he said.

While Dom went to the kitchen to get Skála a beer from the refrigerator, Jack went into the bedroom and looked at the little spider hole in the back of the closet. It was two feet wide and five feet tall and only a foot and a half deep, smaller than a casket and certainly just as dark.

The North Koreans had this guy spooked enough to virtually bury himself alive in his own home, and this realization chilled Ryan.

Inside the hole Ryan found Skála's mobile phone and a laptop. There was a battery charger plugged into both devices. Jack took it all out and headed back for the living room. Here he found Dom standing with a beer in his hand. Skála was in the bathroom urinating, but Dom made him leave the door open so he could be sure he wasn't trying to escape through the little window high in the wall.

When Skála finished in the bathroom, he came out and sat on his couch across from an archway that led to the hallway to the front door. Dom gave him his beer, then sat next to him. Jack sat in the chair on Skála's left.

Jack asked, 'How long have you been in your wall?'

The man looked down at his watch for a second, then he said. 'Almost two and a half days. I came out at night for a few minutes to walk around and use the toilet.'

'Who are you hiding from?'

He didn't answer the question. Instead, he asked, 'Who are *you*?'

'A friend of ours met you at the airport. He wanted us to look you up.'

'What friend?'

'Colin Hazelton?'

Skála didn't react to the name at all. Jack said, 'Big American. Early sixties.'

'Yes,' he said with a nod. 'So . . . if you are friends with him – you are working with –'

Dom interrupted. 'We told you we're not with anybody. Somebody killed Hazelton. We think it might have been the North Koreans. We are here to find out why.'

'They killed him,' Skála said softly. He didn't seem surprised, but the weight of the words affected him. He chugged a third of the bottle of beer. His terror was greater even than his exhaustion, and his hands trembled.

Jack said, 'You gave Hazelton some documents.'

Skála nodded. 'Yes. Five sets of papers. EU diplomatic passports and Czech travel authorizations.'

'You still have copies of them?'

'No. I deleted everything.' He shrugged. 'Of course I did. I didn't want to get caught with it.'

Jack winced in frustration. 'Who were the people?'

'I don't know. I was given photographs. I made everything else up.'

'Where were they from?'

'I don't have any idea. I guess they are Americans, because the American was the one who paid me and picked up the documents.'

Jack shrugged. He wasn't so sure. He asked, 'And where were they going?'

Skála cocked his head. 'North Korea. Of course. I created paperwork claiming them to be Czech diplomats traveling to the mission in Pyongyang.'

Jack said, 'Somebody killed Hazelton in Vietnam and took the documents, but I don't know who, and I don't know why. I don't even know if they made it to North Korea.'

Skála surprised Ryan by saying, 'They made it.'

'How do you know that?'

'Because the North Koreans themselves came here, last week. They said they needed paperwork to get more people into North Korea. They offered big money. Said over time there would be dozens traveling. I tried to explain to them how dangerous it was for me. I almost got caught with the last batch of five I created. There was no way I would be able to pull off forging that many. But they wouldn't listen. They got threatening.

They were animals. I had no idea anything like this would happen.'

Dom snorted. 'So when you agreed to work with the North Koreans you never imagined you might be working with the North Koreans?'

He shrugged. 'Sometimes I work for an organization in the US that needs forged EU passports.'

'Sharps Global Intelligence Partners?' Jack asked.

Skála nodded. 'Yes. They are the ones who came to me. I thought this would be the same as ever, but the man wanted the North Korean letters as well. I was surprised. I thought it was just for some cover story, I didn't think they actually would be traveling there. The American paid me twice my normal rate, so I agreed.'

'This was Hazelton?'

'No. Another man. An Englishman. Thirties. Very polite. A pleasure to work with.'

'Then what happened?'

"The day before I had them ready he called me. He'd taken ill, something he ate, he said, so another man from his company would meet me at the airport to collect them. I was told to package them up in a way he could not see the contents. This man was your friend. The big American. He took the documents and left.

'I thought that was the end of it. Then North Koreans from the embassy here came, and they told me if I didn't agree to work with them they would kill me. I agreed, but said I needed to wait a day before getting access to the passport-printing equipment. I used that day to hide.'

'Why didn't you run away? Why stay here?'

'I wanted to run. Of course. But I couldn't think of any place I could go without using friends for help. I was afraid of involving anyone else. They would have learned about the forgery. Anyway, I thought the North Koreans would give up after a day or two.'

'But they didn't, did they?'

'They came back, two nights ago. I was in my hiding place. I know it was them, I heard their voices. Of course I don't speak their language, but they sounded like the same men. They were here for a long time, but they didn't find me.'

Ryan looked around the room. 'Wait. They were in your apartment?'

'Yes, all over.'

He and Dom exchanged a look.

Skála saw the look. 'What?'

Dom just said, 'Shit.'

'What's wrong?'

Jack stood back up. 'They might have left a listening device. Something that would let them know if you came back.' He turned away from Skála and called Biery. 'Gav. We still okay out there?'

Biery replied confidently. 'Quiet as a tomb.'

'Okay,' Ryan replied. 'We'll be moving in five minutes. Eyes peeled.'

'Roger.'

Seconds later, in the office building on nearby Baranova Street, Gavin Biery launched out of his chair. A knock at the door to the office made him jump up and spin around.

He didn't answer at first. He sat back down and willed whoever it was to go away, because he had a job to do and didn't want to let the guys down.

Another knock.

He started to call Jack and Dom back, but he stopped himself. He would just ignore the knocking. He had wanted to be involved in fieldwork, after all; he couldn't let Dom and Jack know he spooked every time someone rapped on the door.

Another set of knocks came, but he focused his attention through the binoculars at the street below Skála's apartment to make sure nothing was going on.

He heard the rattling of keys now, and a key sliding into the lock of the door. He figured it was just the superintendent of the building, a woman named Gretta. She'd come by once before, and shaken her keys like that. He leapt to his feet and ran to the door. Even though Jack had placed a rubber door stopper to keep the door closed, Gavin figured if Gretta couldn't get in she'd immediately start making problems. On his way through the kitchen, though, he picked up a steak knife, just in case, and slid it under the cuff of his shirt.

Just as he did so the door opened and he saw Gretta entering alone. She was an older woman, she'd walked the men through the property when they arrived the day before, and he knew she was no threat. Under her arm he saw a square air filter.

The woman didn't speak English, but she was nice enough. With hand gestures and smiles she indicated what she wanted to do, and Gavin followed her through the large open office. When she wasn't looking he pulled the knife from the cuff of his shirt and placed it on a desk, then he quickly caught up with her.

The space in the corner of the big room where the Campus men had set up their surveillance was hidden from the rest of the room by stacked desks, but the heavy-set American also positioned his body between his hide site and the woman while she opened the heating unit in a back utility closet.

Soon she was finished and she headed for the kitchen and the exit with Gavin carefully walking alongside her. As she walked she looked around with some curiosity, Gavin noticed, but he imagined she was just wondering what the hell the Americans were doing here in the space. There was nothing on any of the desks, and other than a few water bottles and groceries in the kitchen and the one tenant walking oddly close to her, there was no sign of any activity in the unit.

At the door, Gretta turned to try to communicate with Gavin. Normally he would have been helpful and done his part to bridge the language gap, but he knew he had to get back to his overwatch, so he just stood there, silent and more than a little annoyed-looking.

Eventually, she gave up. With a frustrated smile she said, 'Everything okay?'

'Yes. Okay, Gretta. Everything is very okay. Good-bye.'

'Good-bye,' she said, and Gavin closed the door inches from her smiling face. He turned and ran through the warehouse office, made it back around the desks and to his overwatch and looked into the binoculars mounted on the tripod.

Thankfully, he saw no movement at the front of the

apartment on Křišt'anova. He blew out a long sigh that was interrupted two-thirds of the way through when he gasped.

Wait.

A gray van was parked in the parking lot next to the apartment. Gavin had been looking at this same area for most of the past day. That van *definitely* had not been there before. He squinted into the binos and through the windshield of the van he could see a lone man behind the wheel.

This didn't look good.

He connected with Ryan by hitting his PTT button in his pocket.

'Ryan?'

He heard someone push their own transmit button, but immediately he heard a shout in his headset. It was the unmistakable voice of Jack Ryan, Jr. 'Gun!'

The muffled thump of a gunshot followed a heartbeat later.

25

The team that hit Skála's house weren't tier-one operators, but they were well motivated, and as far as Jack Ryan was concerned, there sure were a *goddamned* lot of them. The Czech Republic's diplomatic relations with the DPRK meant North Korea had an embassy in Prague, although it was just a small, squat redbrick building way out west of the city in the suburban 6th district. But even though it was small and spare, it was staffed at any one time with more than a dozen members of Ri Tae-jin's Reconnaissance General Bureau's spies, and another dozen military security forces who did any work for RGB that was required.

That meant twenty-four men were available for Ri's mission in country, and one of those missions meant hunting for one Karel Skála, a Czech consular official with the ability to create travel documents to get scientists out of the West and into North Korea in furtherance of the DPRK's fledgling rare earth minerals industry. Skála had gone into hiding. Most of the RGB officers at the embassy thought he'd fled the country, but when they paid a visit to his home two nights earlier they left a hidden microphone behind his television set, and twenty minutes ago when English-speaking voices were heard by the embassy RGB communications staff the order came for a team of six North Korean security agents to race to the building to see what was happening.

While they were on the way they received a second call from their superior. This one notified them that Skála himself was in the building – he was talking to the Americans, discussing his relationship with North Korea, and suddenly their job changed from a capture mission to a kill mission.

Only five of the men were armed – they carried CZ pistols, nine-millimeter weapons of a local manufacturer. The other man was the driver; he, like the others, had military martial-arts training and basic surveillance skills given to him by his nation's spy services before he moved into the foreign posting.

And more than firepower, the main weapon the North Koreans had was incentive. Failing their mission right now would be failing the Dae Wonsu, and all of these men knew the penalty for this could be their lives or the lives of their families. They would go up to that fifth-floor apartment and rip the three men there apart limb from limb if necessary, but they were determined not to go back to the embassy without getting the job done.

Caruso had stepped back into the master bedroom of Skála's apartment to grab the young man a set of clothes. He and Ryan wanted the Czech man dressed and out of the building quickly in case the North Koreans had bugged the place, but Skála himself was still dazed from exhaustion and the blow to the head, and Dom decided it would take Skála longer to get himself together than either he or Jack wanted to wait, so Dom just randomly grabbed pants and shoes and a shirt, and then threw toiletries along with other odds and ends into a bag he found on a shelf.

Ryan stood watch over Skála next to the entryway to the hall. The Czech consular official sat on his sofa facing the archway next to Ryan, which meant he was in the right position to have seen the men filing into the apartment first if he had only been looking in the right direction. Instead, his attention had been focused on the floor in front of him and the dizziness in his head. He did look up just in time to see two men in the archway; they were plainly Korean, and they were just two meters or so from the bearded American leaning against the wall, although they had not seen him yet.

Skála blinked hard at the image, then he started to stand.

Ryan was in the process of taking a call from Gavin Biery when he saw the movement and the astonished expression on Skála's face, and he turned to see what had him so terrified. Jack saw only the tip of a handgun as it aimed through the archway on his left. He leapt toward it instinctively, tried to grab it or knock it away from its target.

'Gun!' he shouted. The weapon fired, Ryan folded his right hand over the hot barrel, and his left arm swung in a wide haymaker. He connected with the side of a man's head – he hadn't even focused his eyes on the assailant because his attention was still on the pistol.

A second gunshot cracked in the hallway of the apartment a few feet to his left. Ryan sensed rather than saw a large group of men bursting through the doorway there, and to keep himself out of the line of fire from their weapons he swung his now unconscious victim around so the man's limp body would be positioned between himself and the attackers. Another shot came from less than ten feet away, and Ryan immediately felt the small man in his arms jolt – he'd been shot in the back.

Ryan wanted to get his gun out of its Thunderwear holster and into the fight; he knew he could do it in one second in optimal conditions, but he was standing at one end of a hallway that was full of gunmen at the other end, protected only by a wounded or dead man held up in his arms. One second was an eternity in this situation – dropping his cover to jam his hand down the front of his pants to pull out his Smith & Wesson would certainly just result in him getting gunned down with his hand stuck down the front of his pants.

Shouting men filed up the hall and a third booming handgun report sounded in the small space. The man in Ryan's arms jerked again and Jack crouched tighter. He decided he'd have to at least try for his gun. But just as he let the man in his arms go to do this, out of the corner of his left eye he saw Dominic Caruso running into the living room from the back bedroom, his small black pistol high in a combat grip and pointed to the wall, behind which it looked like at least four or five North Koreans stood engaging Ryan, unaware of the man on their right.

Dominic couldn't see any targets, but he *could* see his cousin crouched low with a spasming, bleeding man in his arms, and he heard the direction the last gunshot came from. He aimed his weapon to a point waist-high on the wall between himself and the hallway, and he pressed the trigger once, twice, three times, moving his aim laterally to the left toward the doorway while he moved his body laterally right toward his cousin and a better view of what was in the hall.

Ejected cartridges from his pistol arced through the air and bounced on the floor of the living room while he moved.

After five rounds he saw puffs of masonry and wall-board above his point of aim, and this told him the shooters there realized they were under fire from an unseen assailant on the other side of the wall and they had begun shooting back. Dom crouched lower and kept moving across the living room. He crossed in front of the crumpled body of Karel Skála on the floor in front of the sofa.

He fired nine rounds just as he stepped into the hall-way, his weapon locked open as he pulled the trigger on the back of a North Korean fleeing through the door out of the apartment and in to the hall that ran down the spine of the building. It appeared more than one assailant had retreated into the main hall, but there were two bodies lying still on the floor by the door, plus the dead man at Ryan's feet.

Dom stepped in front of Ryan, who was now down on one knee and drawing his weapon. Dom's gun was empty, so he started to draw his one spare magazine from his Thunderwear holster. While doing so, however, he saw a North Korean lean back around into view from the main hallway, his pistol rising in front of him.

'Down!' Dom heard from behind, and he dropped flat on his chest.

Jack Ryan rose from his crouch over his cousin, his Smith & Wesson M&P Shield barking in his hand. The North Korean caught a nine-millimeter hollow-point round right in the forehead, an inch left of center, and he tumbled back, his pistol spinning through the air and bouncing into the hallway.

After the gun settled and Jack's hot brass finished spinning on the floor, it was eerily quiet in the apartment. The smell of gun smoke was pervasive and a heavy blue tinge hung in the air, the result of twenty or so rounds being fired from multiple weapons in such a small enclosed space.

One of the men lying in front of Jack moved. His head lifted a little, and he reached out for a pistol lying on the legs of a dead man next to him.

Jack fired once, hitting the man in the back of the neck. Blood sprayed down the hall with the impact of the round.

Jack kept his gun trained on the open doorway. He said, 'I count four down. How many more?'

Caruso reloaded quickly. 'How the fuck should I know? I just got here.'

Jack looked over to Skála now. His eyes were open and rolled back. 'Damn it. Target's dead.'

Dom had his gun back in the fight and pointed toward the doorway. 'Yep.'

Jack connected with Biery. 'Gavin? Are you still with us?'

There was no reply.

'Gavin, do you copy?'

Nothing.

Jack shouted now. 'If you can hear me, we've got squirt-ers coming your way! Do *not* come in this building!' He climbed to his feet. Shouting to his cousin he said, 'Get Skála's laptop!' and then took off, leaping over the dead bodies in front of him on his way out the door.

Gavin was stuck in a slow-moving elevator in the office building on Baranova Street, and he realized he'd lost his mobile connection with the guys right at the worst pos-sible time. It occurred to him, too late, that he should have taken the stairs; as well as being a mobile phone dead zone, the elevator descended at a glacial pace.

'Shit, shit, shit!' he shouted at himself.

When he finally got down to street level he ran outside, then down the sidewalk toward Skála's Křišťanova Street apartment building. While he ran he looked down at his phone and redialed into the conference call to reestablish his connection with Jack and Dom.

If they were still alive, that was. The gunfire he'd heard through his earpiece before he lost comms had been extraordinary, it sounded like a war was being fought in the building across the street.

As soon as he heard the call answered, he looked up and saw an Asian man running out of Skála's building, directly across the street from him. Gavin stopped in his tracks and watched him; the Asian shielded a pistol inside his coat. Several other people ran out of the building all around the armed man, unaware this was one of the people responsible for all the gunfire that had them run-ning for their lives.

Gavin said, 'Jack? Dom?'

Jack's breathless response caused Gavin to blow out a sigh of relief. 'We're here. Do *not* approach the building, there is at least one squirter heading down toward the lobby.'

'Is a squirter a bad guy running away?'

'Yes.'

'I'm watching him now. He is getting into a gray van with a man behind the wheel. They are leaving the scene.'

'Just let them go. We'll be down in thirty seconds. You need to get us packed up and ready to get the fuck out of here.'

Gavin spun around, began running back to the office building. 'I'm on it.'

The team had their hide site broken down, packed up, and loaded into the Mercedes in ten minutes flat. While Jack pulled the vehicle out of the underground parking garage, doing his best to keep from burning rubber to get out of the neighborhood, Dom called Adara from the backseat. She answered on the first ring. 'Yes?'

Dom knew the encryption on his phone was good, so he had no worries about watching what he said. 'You aren't going to believe this.'

'You need another in extremis departure?'

'It's becoming a thing, isn't it?'

'Any wounded?'

'Negative. We're okay, but we've got to get out of here.'

'What's the opposition?'

'North Korean. I don't know anything more than that,

and I doubt they know who we are, but the local police are going to be looking for two guys matching the description of Jack and I as soon as they start taking statements at the crime scene.'

'Crime scene?' Adara asked.

'One dead local. Our target. Four dead foreign nationals. North Koreans.'

'Jesus, Dom.'

'Shit got crazy.'

'Just get here and I'll get you out of the country.'

'Roger that.'

Dom ended the call and slipped the phone back in his poc-k-et. Ryan called out from behind the wheel. 'What did Sherman say?'

'She said she'll be ready.'

Gavin spoke up for the first time. 'Guys, I'm so sorry.' He explained what happened with the arrival of the building superintendent. Dom wasn't in the mood to listen, he just closed his eyes and leaned his head back, but Jack paid attention.

When Biery had explained himself, Jack said, 'If you had let us know you were leaving your overwatch we could have been ready, Gavin. You see that, don't you?'

Gavin said, 'Yeah. I see. It happened so fast. I . . . didn't want to alarm you.'

Dom kept his eyes closed and his head back, but he said, 'You know what *really* alarmed me? The half-dozen bastards shooting at me.'

'I'm sorry,' Gavin repeated.

The remainder of the drive to the airport passed in silence.

26

The flight from Chicago O'Hare to Reagan National was only ninety minutes in duration, but thirty-five-year-old CIA officer Adam Yao climbed up the jetway looking like he'd traveled halfway around the planet. And with good reason. This flight to DC was the end of nearly twenty-four hours of commercial air travel for Yao that began on the other side of the world and had left his body clock utterly confused. Although it was mid-morning now, Adam's brain thought it was somewhere around midnight. After sleeping poorly in coach as well as traveling across nearly half the world's time zones he struggled with the task of putting one foot in front of the other, and he noticed he was leaning onto his carry-on as he walked for balance.

Adam Yao's flight from Singapore to DC was a three-legged odyssey that took him through Tokyo and Chicago before depositing him bleary-eyed and achy here at Reagan National. It was just nine-thirty a.m.; he'd love nothing more than to check into a hotel for a few hours' rest before making an appearance at work, but his instructions were to get himself to McLean, Virginia, as soon as possible.

He planned on renting a car, but as soon as he turned his phone on after touchdown he received word a driver was outside in the arrivals area. He had no checked luggage – rare for a man flying halfway around the globe – so he stepped out into the bright morning and found a black Lincoln Navigator waiting for him.

Adam was an operations officer with the Central Intelligence Agency, but he was no desk-riding embassy spook with diplomatic cover. He'd spent a good portion of his young career working in Hong Kong under non-official cover, meaning he worked out in the shadows. After Hong Kong he was transferred back to Langley for several months of desk work, but the very week he was cleared to return to NOC status he was wheels up for Singapore, desperate to leave the boring bureaucracy of federal government employment behind and get back to what he loved to do.

Work in the shadows.

While the home office of Yao's employer, the Central Intelligence Agency, was here in McLean, CIA was not his desti-nation this morning. Instead, he was driven to Liberty Crossing, a gated government building complex not far away from Langley HQ.

There are two main buildings at the Liberty Crossing property off Lewinsville Road; they are virtually identical, and they are referred to by those in government as LX1 and LX2. LX1 houses the National Counterterrorism Center, and LX2 is the home of ODNI, the Office of the Director of National Intelligence.

Though the CIA was Yao's employer, ODNI was the umbrella organization over all sixteen US intelligence agencies, and this made ODNI Yao's masters as well.

His identification was checked at the front gate, he was brought into the building and checked again, his phone was placed in a tiny locker, he was scanned and wanded, and after all these measures, measures that he had endured countless times in his decade with a top-secret clearance, he was ushered into an office on the third floor of the building.

He waited alone for a moment. There was coffee in front of him, but he'd had so much this morning already on the flight over from Chicago that his stomach burned, so he didn't touch it.

Adam did not have a clue why he had been recalled to the United States, and he certainly did not know why he was here at LX2 instead of the CIA building just a ten-minute drive away. He was pretty good at guessing when things like this happened, but at the moment he was more tired than curious, so he just sat there.

Until a side door to the conference room opened.

When it did Adam glanced up, then he immediately launched to his feet. Entering the room alone was Brian Calhoun, the CIA's director of National Clandestine Service. Calhoun was the head spy at the Agency, nearly at the top of the pecking order and so many rungs above Adam Yao he'd need a pen and a sheet of paper to figure out just how many positions separated them.

He'd never met Calhoun, outside a brief handshake during a debrief last year, but Yao was a fan, and now he wished he'd bothered to check the knot of his tie in the bathroom. He imagined he looked like hell, and Adam Yao was a young man who liked to make a good impression with his appearance.

Adam chanced a look behind the director of NCS as he entered, thinking for sure Calhoun would be followed by a gaggle of underlings, but instead Calhoun shut the side door himself and crossed the conference room with a smile.

'Son, that flight was a bitch, wasn't it?'

'Oh, I'm fine, sir.'

'Then you're a better man than me. Singapore to DC always kicks my ass. Australia's worse, but not much.'

Adam said, 'I managed some sleep along the way. I'm good to go, sir.' It wasn't true, but he assumed Calhoun wasn't here to listen to him complain about air travel.

'Take a seat.'

Both men sat down at the large table.

'I talked to your control officers on the fifth floor. I've read pretty much every report you've filed for the last nine months. You are doing a hell of a job.'

'Thank you, sir.' Adam couldn't help it. His mind was spinning, trying to figure out what this was all about. A promotion? That would have surprised him. He had not been at his new assignment for long at all. Unless someone above him he didn't know had moved on, it didn't seem likely they'd pull Adam out of NOC work to move him back to Langley. And unless he was being promoted to station chief, a half-dozen steps above his level now, then Brian Calhoun wouldn't be involved in the promotion.

That meant, to Adam, that Calhoun must be here because of a new operation. A good NOC, no matter how deep he is in his cover and no matter what it is he is doing, knew he could be moved at any time. But again, Adam thought to himself, the damn head of the service shouldn't be the guy doling out the op orders.

'Your work in Singapore is going nicely, so far. And what you did in Hong Kong was nothing short of magnificent.'

'Thank you very much,' Adam said.

'But we rushed you back home like this because we have a new opportunity, and we think you might be just the man for the job.'

'A new operation?'

'Potentially, yes.'

'Okay,' Adam said, a hint of confusion bleeding through into his voice.

Calhoun cocked his head. 'Something wrong?'

Adam smiled apologetically and said, 'You can understand my confusion, sir. Normally my control officer, or maybe a section head, would brief me. I find it more than surprising that someone like yourself is talking to me about a new assignment.'

Now it was Calhoun's turn to smile. 'Yao, you ain't seen nothing yet.'

As if on cue, the same side door opened and Mary Pat Foley, the director of national intelligence, entered the room. Adam rose to his feet quickly, and Calhoun did the same.

Yao never saw top-level IC execs without three or four attendants and subordinates. It was confusing to him to see both Calhoun and Foley unaccompanied.

'Good morning, Adam.'

'Madame Director.'

'I heard you flew in from Singapore.'

'Yes, ma'am.'

'And then we rushed you here without a shower?'

Adam reddened with embarrassment. 'Is it that obvious?'

Mary Pat smiled without responding, then she, Calhoun, and Yao sat at the conference table. 'How far did we get?' she asked Calhoun.

'He's still in the "what the hell is going on?" phase.'

Foley laughed. 'Unfortunately, Adam, some government servants spend their entire career in that phase. Not you, though. I'll explain everything. First, I assume Brian already gave you the whole obligatory "we love your work" spiel?'

'Uh . . . yes, ma'am.'

'Then I will cut to the chase. Adam, what do you know about the mining sector in China?'

Adam raised his eyebrows, surprised by the question for a few reasons, but at least, as far as the topic was concerned, he found himself on firm ground. 'Quite a bit. When I was working undercover in Hong Kong as a corporate investigations consultant I had a lot of issues with two of China's six state-owned mining concerns. Chinalco and Minmetals. They were stealing technology from Western firms, and I worked to bring these transgressions to light.'

'And what about rare earth element mining in particular?'

He was still off kilter because he was in an ODNI conference room with the top intelligence official in the US government, but now he was more intrigued by this mysterious operation than he was by the manner it was being presented to him. 'That's huge over in China. They are *the* player in the industry, controlling over ninety percent of the world's extraction and supply.'

'Go on,' Mary Pat said.

Adam smiled. If this was a test, he was about to nail it. "There are seventeen rare earth minerals, and they all occur together, so while a rare earth deposit might have a higher relative proportion of one of the minerals as opposed to another, a rare earth mine extracts all of the minerals together as ore, and then sends it off to be processed.

"Rare earths are divided into two categories: light and heavy.

"China extracts the majority of the world's rare earth minerals for a number of reasons: Low labor costs and negligible en-vironment standards for a process that is very hard on the environment allow them to price the goods cheaply. But the main reason for China's supply-side dominance is the discovery of massive mineral deposits. They simply have more of the stuff than anyone else. Having said that, they also use more of it than anyone else. China ran into trouble due to its explosive growth. Its manufacturing sector began using more of the rare earths just as its demand for other commodities increased, and this left less available to export, increasing the cost of the commodity.

'Australia has been increasing its mining in the past few years, as has the US, but they are whistling in the wind in this industry.'

'Why do you say that?'

'China will always be at a competitive advantage with the West. They have absurdly low labor costs, their mines operate on government land without paying for the privilege, there are virtually no environmental regs for them there. We have some rare earth mining in the West, but we pay a lot more to get the commodity out of the ground and processed than the Chinese ever will.'

Calhoun slapped Yao on his back, startling him. He looked to Mary Pat. 'I told you Yao would know his stuff.'

Adam clarified, 'I know a good bit about the Chinese rare earth operations, the major players and the regions where they mine the ore. And I understand the technique of the mining and the ore processing in a general sense, but I sure couldn't operate a gas scrubber at a rare earth mine or anything like that.'

Mary Pat said, 'We don't need you with a pick down in a shaft, but we were hoping you would already possess some knowledge about the industry.'

'That I do,' Adam said. He was humble about a lot of things, but he had been sitting in China, Hong Kong and then Singapore for the past few years totally engrossed in the Chinese economy. He had all the confidence in the world about his deep knowledge of it.

Mary Pat then asked, 'And what about the *illegal* rare earth mining industry in China?'

'Sure,' he said, a little less confidently. 'Gangster mines. Illegal private corporations run by Chinese organized crime have big REM mines in Inner Mongolia as well as other places. They are successful because local and regional governments benefit from them. The gangsters pay bribes and such.' He chuckled. 'And if you think the government-run mines fall short of environmental stand-ards, the gangster miners are a whole lot worse.'

Foley turned to Calhoun and nodded. Adam realized

he'd passed some sort of a test, but he wasn't sure what that had earned him. Calhoun leaned forward on his elbows. 'We have one hell of a problem, and we have one hell of an opportunity.'

'You want to put me into a Chinese mine?' Adam knew the Chinese government had tried to kill him once, in Hong Kong. They got close, so close it was clear an intelligence breach had occurred that gave them information about Yao and his actions. He wasn't crazy about working in China, and he felt awkward about the fact it looked like he'd have to remind these two in front of him of his unique situation.

But Calhoun shook his head and said, 'No. We'd need you to go into China for a very short time to establish your cover, but we are confident we have a way to make that happen. Your ultimate destination would, instead, be somewhere else.'

Adam relaxed a little, but he was careful not to show it. 'Okay, where do you need me to go?'

Mary Pat took over. 'Your file says you speak Korean.'

'Just fair. I spent a semester in high school as an exchange student in Seoul, then I returned for a semester of college. Studied the language in school, and took a night class while doing NOC work in HK.'

The two intelligence executives nodded at the young officer. They knew all this already.

Adam asked the next question with some concern. 'We are talking about me going into *South* Korea. Correct?'

When the answer did not immediately come from either Foley or Calhoun, Adam just muttered, 'You've got to be kidding.'

Mary Pat answered now. 'What would you say if I told you we have a way to get you into North Korea?'

'I would respectfully ask you to provide a little more in-formation.'

The room was tense, but Foley laughed. 'That is understandable. Nearly two years ago Chinese geologists and miners working in the DPRK found deposits in the mountains of the Chongju region near their northern border with China. They dug test shafts and confirmed the find, then began establishing the infrastructure for extraction.'

Adam had heard something about this, but it had never been on his radar enough to look into it more closely.

Mary Pat said, 'Then, about a year ago, Choi Ji-hoon threw the Chinese mining concern out of his country.'

'Why?'

'We don't know. Some contractual issue, perhaps? What we do know is his new minister of mining, a man named Hwang, has recently allowed a group of illegal Chinese mining industry personnel into Chongju to work at the mine. Clearly he's smart enough to know DPRK can't extract the rare earths without expert help. The gangster miners are crucial to his operation.'

'Sounds prudent.'

'This gangster mining company is very experienced and well organized, but they have specialized in extraction, not processing. The North Koreans have to process the ore themselves now, they can't very well hand it off to the Chinese after canceling the Chinese contract, so the illegal operation has established a front company in Shanghai for the sole purpose of obtaining processing technology and brainpower from abroad.' She paused. 'Are you with me so far?'

Yao just nodded, urging her on.

"This company has been in contact with a Chinese national working at a rare earth mineral mine in California. We only found out about it because we've had a surveillance package on the man for some time. Initially we thought the man was working for Chinese intelligence. He is not. Quite the opposite, actually. He is a gangster miner himself who managed to get hired in the US to headhunt talent at NewCorp, the American mining concern.

'We have the ability to intercept communications between the gangster mining company and their agent in California. We know what the Chongju rare earth – processing plant needs as far as specialized labor. They are rushing to find the right people for the jobs, because in just two weeks they will be sending another group into North Korea to work at the mine and the processing plant. Our plan is to notify the gangster miners that he has recruited a Chinese American with knowledge of a critical piece of technology used in rare earth ore processing. That man, our man, will then fly to Shanghai to join the gangster miners, and from there go into Pyongyang along with the rest of the Chinese. He will go to Chongju under DPRK government control and work at the mine.'

Yao was astonished. This was a *massive* operation. 'And report back to the US some way?'

Calhoun answered this one. 'That's right. Science and Technology has some communications equipment that can go into DPRK. They say it is undetectable.'

Adam kept an impassive face, but he couldn't help but think the eggheads at S&T wouldn't be stood in front of a wall and shot if their 'undetectable' device was somehow detected in the DPRK. If Adam went into North Korea, that fate would fall to him.

He muttered an unenergetic 'Great.'

Mary Pat picked up on his doubt. 'The North Koreans aren't just allowing miners and processors into the country, they are also trying to get equipment in. The communications system will not travel with our asset. It will be embedded in a computer that our asset will have access to at the mine. We've learned a shipment of computers will be sent from Bulgaria to North Korea next week. We'll have one of the machines altered with the hidden communications equipment. As long as our asset isn't caught communicating with the device red-handed, our asset will be free and clear on this operation.'

'Yes, ma'am. I understand.' He noted that Mary Pat was speaking in general terms, still referring to the person going into North Korea as 'our asset.' Clearly she wanted him to agree to go, but she wasn't assuming anything yet, and this Adam appreciated.

He asked, 'What specific intelligence are you trying to get from an asset in the Chongju mine?'

Mary Pat replied, 'Satellites aren't telling us what we need to know. Is there equipment in the mine in violation of sanctions? Are there personnel from other countries there? Experts? Specialists? How soon till that mine is generating revenue for the DPRK?'

'May I ask how many other CIA officers are operating inside North Korea?'

Mary Pat shook her head. 'I can't give you that information. I can only tell you that you will be working without a network in country.'

Adam assumed as much. If he went into the DPRK, he would be on his own. But this wasn't the only thing bothering him. 'I have to ask. Is this really that big an issue, considering all the other problems we have with North Korea? I mean, they are involved in illegal mining in violation of sanctions . . . but if you can get me in the country, shouldn't I be trying to get a look at something more important than mining?'

Mary Pat said, 'If possible, yes, you should. We see it as an incredible coincidence, and hopefully one we can capitalize on, that in a nation some forty-six thousand square miles in size, the Chongju mine happens to be located only twenty-four miles away from Sohae Satellite Launching Station. Sohae is where they launch their ICBMs.'

'That is a coincidence that probably seems a bit easier to capitalize on while we're sitting here in Virginia. In country twenty-four miles might seem like a long way.'

She smiled. 'Very true. And we're not sending you there because of Sohae.'

Mary Pat shook her head. 'President Ryan has dictated that this mine at Chongju represents a critical intelligence need of the United States.'

That sounded, to Adam, like hyperbole. He didn't know Mary Pat Foley personally, but he knew that her reputation was of a supremely levelheaded individual. 'What makes it a critical need?'

'Because estimates put the capacity under those

mountains at two hundred thirteen million tons of heavy rare earth minerals. A value approaching, depending on market conditions, twelve trillion dollars.'

Adam reached out with both hands and took hold of the conference table. 'Twelve *trillion*? That can't be possible, can it?'

'It can. Is your imagination big enough to consider what all Pyongyang could buy with twelve trillion?'

Adam nodded slowly. 'They could buy nukes, ballistic missiles, every bit of armament made by the Russians or the Chinese. They could buy technology and intellectual capital.'

Mary Pat leaned over the table. 'They can buy all that, but they can also buy something more important. *Friends*.'

'Friends?'

'Votes in the UN. States that would go against official sanctions. Trading partners they can't even dream of now. With that much money on the table, many nations who seem so perfectly resolute now in their insistence they won't work with a rogue regime would suddenly find some flexibility in the issue.'

'Right.'

Mary Pat added, 'And someone outside of North Korea is already paying them for the right to extract minerals there. A lot of money. These hard currency payments are being converted into an expansion of North Korea's missile program. The rocket tubes captured off the coast of North Korea last week were purchased with this money, and we assume there is a lot more money, and a lot more proliferation, going on out there that we don't know about.'

Calhoun said, 'You see why this Chongju mine represents a clear and present danger to the United States, don't you?'

Adam's answer was barely audible. He was still in awe. 'I get it,' he said. 'North Korea with hard currency is a bad thing.'

Mary Pat nodded and said, 'Now. Back to you. If you accept this operation, you need to understand something. This is not going to be a career maker for you, simply because you don't need it. What you did in HK last year was more than enough to make your career. Your trip to North Korea is going to be one hundred percent risk for not much reward.'

Adam shrugged. 'Maybe everybody says this, Director Foley, but I'm not looking for advancement. I'm looking for a challenge.'

She eyed him for a moment. Then looked away. 'My husband and I loved what we did. There are a thousand frustrations and a million levels of bullshit with this job, but at its core, it can be one hell of a thrill, can't it?'

Adam grinned. 'Nothing like it.'

Calhoun nodded silently.

Mary Pat said, 'We think our plan to get you in, established, and reporting back is solid. I just need to know if you will volunteer to go. So?'

Adam didn't hesitate. 'So . . . let's do this.'

Mary Pat said, 'Good. But remember, they don't call it gangster mining without reason. You will be in danger from the people you are around the moment you get off the airplane in Shanghai.'

'I understand.'

'Time is critical, so we'll need to get you up to speed very quickly. After a few days here you will go to California to learn the skills you need to backstop your legend. You have today to rest up and we'll start tomorrow prepping you.'

The adrenaline coursing through Adam Yao dictated the next words out of his mouth. 'I can start right now.'

Mary Pat shook her head. 'Nope. Your national intelligence director is directing you to a hotel to sleep and take a shower. You'll thank me in the morning. We'll have someone drive you and then bring you some food, toiletries, and a change of gear. Tomorrow morning CIA will pick you up and begin a quick workup of your legend before you're off to California.'

'Yes, ma'am,' he said.

27

By the time Ryan, Caruso, and Biery returned to Alexandria, Virginia, from their mission in the Czech Republic, the rest of the Campus operational staff had relocated to New York City to begin looking into the operation of Duke Sharps.

Dom and Jack would have loved to have joined their cohorts in Manhattan, not just so they could get to the bottom of the operation that had nearly cost them their lives, but also to avoid going back into their office and facing Gerry Hendley.

They had briefed Gerry over the sat phone during the long flight back to the States, and to say he was displeased was an understatement. Gerry wasn't a field operative himself, so normally he demurred and left the 'hot wash' aspects of the after-action reports to John Clark, but when he learned IT director Gavin Biery had been given an overwatch role during a covert breach, and Biery's failure to warn the team about an approaching threat had resulted in the near death of two of his operators, the death of the target, and the deaths of somewhere to the tune of a half-dozen North Korean aggressors, all in the middle of a major European city, Gerry had told his two operators that as soon as their plane landed they needed to get themselves down from Baltimore and into Hendley Associates, and by then they better have some sort of an explanation.

Dom didn't feel like he and Jack were at fault. As far as he was concerned Gavin was the one who screwed up, and Gavin should have taken most of the heat that was now focused on him and his cousin. But Jack understood Gavin couldn't be blamed for not being a trained field operative. Just as Dom wouldn't get grief from Hendley for failing to hack into an opposition computer server, Biery got a pass for his inability to execute his forced role in a covert entry.

But Gavin had not excused himself, far from it. He was nearly beside himself with shame for his mistake. By the end of the flight Dom had gotten to the point where he was no longer furious with the IT director, and Jack had told Gavin all along that the blame lay at his own feet, not Gavin's, but the big man remained inconsolable.

This morning, while Dom and Jack were in Gerry's office trying to explain what the hell had happened in Prague, Gavin sat sullenly at his desk, though he was working. He'd taken Karel Skála's laptop, retrieved in Prague by Dom and Jack, and he did a deep search of deleted files on the hard drive. It didn't take him long to find what he was looking for: five images sent to Skála three weeks earlier, just one week before Colin Hazelton died in Vietnam. There was no question that these were the five pictures used for the documents; they were typical passport pictures of four men and one woman, and they'd arrived at the right time. So Gavin uploaded the images into his facial-recognition application, and now the software ran on the machine in front of him.

While Gavin sat and sulked, the images were in the process of being measured hundreds of ways, from the width, height, depth, and shape of the periocular region of the face to the precise spatial relationship between the nose and the upper lip. The tabulated scores of each of the measurements were added together to create a numerical value for each face, which was then compared with millions of images of faces culled from virtually every source on the Internet, as well as the databases of the 'Five Eyes' intelligence agencies of the United States, Canada, the United Kingdom, New Zealand, and Australia. Any image with a significantly different numerical value from the unknown images was instantly discarded by the computer, but those close in value were then compared more carefully.

The computer checked through the individual measurements for additional matches. If the ears were the same distance from the nose, the computer went on to the periocular depth. If that was similar to the unknown image, then the score measuring shape of the jawline was compared. If that panned out, then the computer moved on to the shape of the lips.

In this fashion, millions of images were compared with the unknown image. The process took some time, of course. Although all faces are different – even identical twins have differing measurements when evaluated as precisely as the facial-recognition software did – many faces of people who do not appear to the naked eye to be that similar actually have value scores that are nearly alike.

Gavin expected it would be another few hours before he knew if he would be able to put names to any of the five faces from Skála's computer.

While Gavin's monitor spun images faster than a slot

machine, he leaned forward with his face between his elbows. He felt like shit. There was no getting around the mistake he made in Prague. Jack Junior, to his credit, had tried to tell Gavin it wasn't his fault, but Gavin knew he'd blown it. His own actions, or inactions, had led to the death of an important witness and nearly caused the death of his two friends and colleagues.

Gavin Biery had no idea how he would ever redeem himself for his error.

Just then a computerized female voice startled him.

'Match found.'

Gavin lifted his head and stared at his machine in astonishment. He couldn't believe an identity had been determined so quickly.

It was the woman, the redhead who looked to be in her mid-forties. The monitor displayed the image used in her passport photo in the Czech Republic on one side of the screen, and on the other was another picture of her. Here she stood at a lectern; apparently she was speaking to an audience. Several other photos, all identified by the facial-recog software as the same woman, were tiled under this photo.

Gavin saw why the software identified the redhead so quickly. She was apparently quite prominent in her field, and there were a lot of images of her on the Internet.

He worked another few minutes to double-check the woman's name and biography with his own Internet search, then snatched up his phone's receiver and dialed Gerry's extension.

He supposed this could wait until Gerry's meeting with Dom and Jack broke up, but Gavin thought it possible this bit of good news just might help the two cousins out of their predicament.

Hendley answered on the first ring. 'Yeah, Gavin?' He sounded annoyed, and Gavin read that to mean he was annoyed not just at the two young men sitting in front of him, but also at the man on the other end of the line.

Gavin said, 'Sorry to bother you, Gerry. But we have a match on a face we got from Karel Skála.'

Hendley sighed. 'Okay. You'd better come up.'

Gavin swallowed. He wanted to take some of the heat off the cousins, but he didn't want to go up there and sit with them while they got yelled at.

'Um . . . sure. I'm on the way.'

A few minutes later Gavin entered Hendley's office and found Dom and Jack sitting quietly in front of the ex-senator's desk. Hendley sat in his chair behind the desk, but unusual for him, he did not stand when Gavin came in.

An empty chair sat next to Jack.

Gerry said, 'Come in, shut the door, and tell us what you've got.'

Gavin sat down. 'I have an ID on the redheaded woman. The software is still trying to identify the other four images.'

Gerry Hendley waited for a moment, then he sighed. A little irritated. 'Well, who is she?'

'Oh, sorry. Her name is Dr. Helen Powers. She is Australian. A geologist.'

Jack and Dom stared at each other. *A geologist?* They had been expecting the five mystery travelers to be nuclear engineers or rocket scientists.

Gavin said, 'She's a big deal in Australian geology, apparently, lots of pictures of her at conferences and such. She's involved in the search for rare earth mineral deposits, mostly in the Australian outback.'

Dom said the thing the others were thinking. 'Why the hell are all these people getting killed over geology?'

Gavin left a minute later, and Gerry turned his attention back to the two men in front of him. "Jack, Dominic. Prague was a disaster. You are lucky to have survived, and any chance that that target of yours might have been able to pass on more intelligence about whatever the North Koreans are planning was lost when he was killed.

'The fact that the last two men that The Campus has gone into the field to watch over have both turned up dead within hours of our arrival makes me wonder if we need to reevaluate what the hell we are doing.'

Jack and Dom just nodded. They'd been doing a lot of that over the past hour. Now wasn't the time to argue with the director of The Campus. But even taking that into consideration, Jack felt like he needed to get Gerry on another topic.

Jack said, 'I guess this is not the time to ask. But I was wondering if there was any chance we could go up and support Clark's operation in New York. He's thin up there with just three guys.'

Gerry turned to Caruso. 'Dom, I want you up there by this evening.'

Dominic sat up, surprised. Gerry said, 'You are John Clark's subordinate, don't go thinking for yourself on this one. Let John use you for surveillance.'

Dom was too happy to be offended. He had pictured

himself sitting at his desk for the next few months while Clark and the others got to delve into this mystery in the Big Apple, so he was thrilled to get the chance to go.

He said, 'You've got it, Gerry.'

Jack raised an eyebrow. Was he going to be punished with desk duty?

Gerry said, "And as for you, Jack. That was your operation in Prague, there was a poor result, so you take the brunt of the heat.

'Let's put you at your desk to remember what it's like to do straight analytical work for a while. Go to work on Dr. Helen Powers. Find out what the hell is going on involving mines that is getting people murdered on multiple continents.'

'Okay, Gerry,' Jack said. He and his cousin stood to leave soon after.

Out in the hallway Dom put his hand on Jack's shoulder. 'Not fair, cuz. I pushed you to do the sneak-and-peek on Skála's place.'

Ryan shrugged. 'Gerry's putting both of us where we need to go right now. You go up there and get some dirt on Sharps. I'll stay here and figure out what the next piece to this puzzle is.'

28

Lieutenant General Ri Tae-jin of the Reconnaissance General Bureau was surprised with the incredible speed at which his plan was taking shape. Normally when a scheme formed at anything more than a snail's pace he was satisfied, so hard was the intelligence game when it came to real-world application. But his new operation – the computer had chosen the code name Fire Axe – might have been progressing too fast for its own good. Fire Axe, if successful, would culminate with the assassination of the President of the United States, and the general had more concerns than good feelings about its prospects – he wondered if he was rushing into a maelstrom of his own making.

He hoped the quick development of Fire Axe was simply fortune intervening, and that his good fortune would continue. And as each step of the operation came and went with a positive outcome, he became . . . if not more confident, at least less quick to dismiss the entire prospect of the affair.

Ri had lost full confidence in Choi Ji-hoon, but he did have to admit, the Dae Wonsu was absolutely right in his analysis. Killing Jack Ryan would almost unquestionably lead to success in his other quest, that to obtain a working mid-range ICBM.

He allowed himself to entertain thoughts of the

post-Ryan world, where North Korea had the ability to strike the United States or Western Europe with a plutonium missile. He didn't consider actually seeing the ICBM put to use in this task. No, that would mean the certain death of everyone in North Korea when the USA retaliated. But if North Korea possessed the missile and threatened to use it, the fortunes of his nation would be starkly and unquestioningly improved.

And this was part of the fuel that spurred him forward. The other part, the larger part, was the same fuel that propelled his quest for the ICBM. His own self-preservation. He did not have the luxury to shelve Fire Axe if it did not pan out perfectly, because he knew his next meeting with Choi, were he to balk at the assassination attempt, would only lead to his own death.

The evening after his meeting with Choi at his Kangdong-gun property he had organized an emergency conference with his top lieutenants and he tasked them to work on the plan. Almost immediately there was a framework – in truth, the assassination of world leaders was a constant theoretical, and occasional real-world, exercise at RGB, and several proposals were drawn up every month, so the infrastructure was already in place.

And there were few state actors on earth more experienced in international crime than North Korea.

Even though North Korea was known as being a nation cut off from the rest of the world, its intelligence was, in fact, uniquely well positioned for a conspiracy on a global scale. Ri personally worked with top agents of many regimes, either buying or selling weapons and sending his officers and agents into other nations to train their officers and agents in the art of enhanced interrogation techniques.

And the RGB was also deeply involved with most all of the major criminal syndicates in the world. They made millions of dollars every year in the drug trade producing and selling methamphetamine, mostly to European crime families or Mexican drug cartels. They printed and trafficked counterfeit hard currency, and bought and sold illegal weapons of all classification.

Ri and his staff knew the players who could make Fire Axe a reality, there was no question that he could put an assassin with a network in the same place as the American President. But to do it with no comebacks on North Korea was another matter entirely.

Ri and his officers looked at all Ryan's scheduled foreign travel over the next few months. He'd be in Europe on two separate trips. Once in Berlin at a trade conference, and once in Poland for another meeting of NATO leadership.

He would also be in Mexico City in two and a half weeks' time for a two-day official visit, and later he would fly to Buenos Aires for two more days of meetings and travel.

Europe was an enticing possibility for the simple matter that relations between the United States and Russia were terrible at the moment. Ri knew the Russian president, Valeri Volodin, wanted Jack Ryan dead, and more important, he knew the Americans knew it. But fingering Russia would be all but impossible. Yes, he had contacts in Moscow, but mostly with small computer hacking organizations or with Rosoboronexport, the nation's state-owned arms trader. He'd dealt in drugs with a

Russian *bratva*, but he didn't have the influence over them he needed to perpetrate such a crime.

Ri liked Mexico more. The timeline was short, but the atmospherics were perfect. Six months earlier one of the larger and more violent Mexican drug cartels lost its leader, Antonio Maldonado, in a shootout with Federal Police in Acapulco. The Guerrero-based Maldonado cartel had been reeling ever since, and now that the leader's younger brother, Santiago Maldonado, had been put in charge they had shown themselves to be even more volatile, more reactionary, than before. It had been rumored at the time of the killing that the Mexican authorities had found Antonio Maldonado only through the technical help they received from a group of American military communications specialists. The unit, known informally as the Activity, had been instrumental in locating Colombian drug lord Pablo Escobar more than twenty years earlier, and they had been in and out of South America ever since pinch-hitting for friendly nations in the war on drugs. Neither the US nor Mexico had acknowledged the fact American military advisers were on the ground in Acapulco when Antonio Maldonado was cut down in a fusillade of carbine fire, but his brother, the mercurial Santiago, had vowed revenge.

Ri contacted his non-official cover officers in Mexico who worked with the Maldonado cartel, and they confirmed they thought it likely he could be persuaded to support an assas-sination attempt on the American President. Santiago was a drug-addled, nihilistic maniac, according to Ri's officers, and if Santiago harbored any concerns for his own self-preservation he didn't show them. Moreover, he would have absolutely no qualms about sending his own cultlike followers to a slaughter if there was the chance to exact retribution for the man responsible for his brother's death.

But the North Koreans quickly realized that although Maldonado had men and guns, his force was unskilled, and he had no way to assassinate the President of the United States.

General Ri decided that the Mexican cartel could, however, still play a crucial role in the operation, because Ri knew where to find the killer.

He looked to another piece of the puzzle after he fleshed out the idea he had relayed to the Dae Wonsu. The general himself spoke with a close confidant who formerly was the head of Syria's General Security Directorate, but had gone into hiding in North Africa during the war. Ri let the man know he was looking for someone who could work independently and be involved in a high-level assassination. The Syrian did not ask about the target, since he knew Ri would not tell him. Instead, he accepted a finder's fee to give Ri the contact information for a single bomb maker, a man who, so said the Syrian, was both abundantly talented and looking for a way out of his present circumstance.

Ri was surprised to see the contact was not Syrian himself. He was Iranian, but he worked independently of Tehran; in fact, he'd freelanced as a bomb maker for the last few years. Ri contacted the Syrian government and asked for the opportunity to hire the man for some training in North Korea. They were open to the idea, and they arranged a meeting.

Adel Zarif lived in a Syrian intelligence safe house in Damascus, the city in which the Iranian had been living for more than three years. There was a price on his head by both Hezbollah and the Free Syrian Army rebels, and rumors were he was on an American presidential kill list as well.

Hezbollah wanted him dead for leaving their fold and turning freelance, the FSA wanted him dead for killing hundreds of their fighters in the civil war, and American drones combed the world for him because of the years he spent in Iraq, training insurgents in his specialty.

The improvised explosive device.

Zarif disagreed with the term; to him there was nothing improvised about his explosive devices. He had studied electrical engineering in Tehran before becoming a Hezbollah operative; in the nineties he'd wired bombs for Hezbollah and built bomb vests for Palestinian terrorists in southern Lebanon. When the war came to Iraq he was already in the country, already working with the Shiite militias, and Hezbollah pulled him back home for further training and study of tactics to defeat American armor. He came up with ingenious low-tech ways to build and employ explosively formed penetrator weapons, a normally high-tech device that shapes metal projectiles by the blast of the explosive, sending them through steel like a knife through butter.

He destroyed his first American tank in 2005, and by 2007, a year in which 33,900 IED attacks took place against coalition forces in Iraq, Zarif had trained hundreds of bomb makers in his tactics.

He was moved to Afghanistan in 2011 by Hezbollah,

and there he built his largest IED. He wired a two-thousand-pound bomb to a detonator and placed it in the back of a water truck. A martyr then drove it into Kandahar, and made it to within one hundred yards of a British base before he was shot dead by a sniper's bullet. He then let go of the dead man's switch, detonating the device and killing seventy-six, all but five of them local.

By the time of the Arab Spring and the civil wars throughout the region Zarif was in his late forties, and he was old enough to see he was being used as a tool by different sects, beliefs, tribes, and factions. He decided his only true allegiance was to himself, and he went freelance.

The Syrian government snatched him up, both to help their forces build booby traps in the cities they fled in order to escape the FSA and to take him off the market so that he did not fight against them. The relationship was transactional, he didn't care for the Assad regime any more than he cared for the people he blew to bits with his IEDs. But soon he was with Assad's 17th Division, wiring entire buildings to blow on trip wires and lining roads behind the division's retreat with car bombs.

His reputation grew in Syria, and the world's intelligence organizations located him through his actions. Soon it became clear he could not leave Damascus because of all the parties who wanted him dead.

Ri's agents met him at his safe house, and they revealed they weren't there to talk about a training trip to North Korea. Instead, they proposed the plan to transport him to Mexico City, link him up with agents of a local group there, and to provide him with all the intelligence and material he needed to kill the US President. After he succeeded, he would then be secreted out of the country by North Korean agents and taken either back to Syria if he wanted or, better yet, to North Korea, where he would live all of the rest of his days feeling the warmth of a grateful nation. The agents showed him pictures on their tablet computer of his future home, a palace on the beaches near the city of Hamhŭng, along with photos of beautiful young girls, any of which he could choose as his own to be his wife.

Zarif wanted out of Syria, and he saw this Mexico City operation as his best bet. But he did not agree to it outright. He knew his only chance to make it to the beautiful beaches and live like a king in a palace was success in his mission and the absolute deniability that either he or North Korea had any involvement. He peppered the agents with technical questions and he demanded to go to North Korea to meet with the leadership there.

Ri did not like this, but he saw no choice.

Although the Syrian government had all but held their best bomb maker like a prisoner for the past few years, North Korean intelligence officers persuaded Zarif's handlers to give him travel documents to leave the country. The North Koreans said they wanted to bring Zarif to Pyongyang to train their direct-action forces in how to make explosively formed penetrator bombs, and while there, North Koreans would in turn give him access to recently acquired high-tech South Korean communications equipment. This knowledge would help him keep up with advances in remote detonators. Working in Syria, he'd had little access to new equipment, and the DPRK convinced the Syrian government that a short trip for Zarif would be in Syria's best interests.

The ruse was a lie, of course. Zarif would travel to Mexico, he would kill the President of the United States, and he would then retire to the ocean side in North Korea.

Or so Zarif had been led to believe.

Zarif was transported to Pyongyang the next day, where he met with Ri and others, and when he showed reluctance to agree to the plan – he was unsure of the efficiency of the Mexicans and the credibility of their intelligence – he was flown to Hamhŭng and shown his future home.

The palace existed, it was stately and impressive, and the beautiful girls were lined up at the entryway to meet him. Adel Zarif was sold.

In truth, the mansion was one of many properties for use by the Supreme Leader, and General Ri had no plans to call the Dae Wonsu and tell him he was offering up his home to a foreign Muslim assassin.

No. As Adel Zarif smiled and shook Ri's hand on the tarmac in Pyongyang, anxious to leave North Korea to head to Mexico to begin preparations for the biggest operation of his career, the sad, hangdog eyes of General Ri brightened for a moment, and he smiled back. The man before him would die during the execution of Operation Fire Axe, and no one in the world would know Zarif had ever been here.

29

Edward Riley left his BMW i8 parked in a garage on 23rd Street and walked the last six blocks to his destination. It was raining this afternoon in Manhattan, but this was good news for Riley, because it gave him an excuse to wear his raincoat. He would have worn it anyway for operational reasons, but it would have looked odd in the sun.

He'd received a call five minutes earlier letting him know his trap had been sprung. He wasn't sure exactly how long he should wait before showing up at the trap, but he knew his best chance for success was to catch his victim at the exact moment of maximum distress, so he did not delay.

On 29th near Lexington he turned off of the sidewalk and walked down a few steps to a basement entrance below a five-story apartment building. He rapped on the metal door a few times and then closed his umbrella, leaving it against a small table sitting there by the door.

The door was opened from the inside a moment later. Riley stepped into a poorly lit narrow hallway, and he nodded to the middle-aged Asian woman standing there.

'Room four,' she said, her gravelly voice barely above a whisper.

Riley headed up the hall, taking care to avoid touching anything. Not the walls or the doorknobs of the doors he passed. He even made sure his pants leg below his rain-coat didn't brush against the curtains covering an alcove on his right.

It wasn't that he was trying to avoid leaving finger-prints or DNA at the scene. Instead, he kept his hands tight at his sides and his slacks away from any surface at ankle height because Riley felt this place was utterly filthy. It was a massage parlor, a house of prostitution, and it was in heavy use from what Riley had been told.

Riley's men had followed a man to this establishment twice in three days. It was clear that his target had a habit, so Riley stopped in to talk to the proprietor, then flashed a badge, a smile, and some cash. He showed the Japanese *'mamasan'* in charge a picture of his target, then asked her to tip him off the next time the man showed up. Riley explained how he would conduct a raid, and he told her she'd make two thousand dollars to reimburse her for the disturbance to her business, and he assured her that her cooperation would mean the New York Police Depart-ment would show its gratitude by not interfering with her operation afterward.

His promises were only half bullshit.

The two grand Riley could come up with, but he couldn't do a damn thing about the NYPD.

At the door marked 4 he used his elbow, enshrouded in his raincoat, and with it he banged just once. This door, like the other, was opened from the inside, but this time he was greeted by an American. A black man in his thir-ties, big and strong, with a badge around his neck proclaiming him to be a detective from the NYPD.

Riley knew Bridgeforth wasn't a detective. He was an

employee of Sharps Partners, and a subordinate of Riley's, but the badge went along with today's ruse.

Riley reached into his raincoat, around his neck, and he pulled out a similar-looking badge of his own.

There was one more person here in room 4 with Riley and Bridgeforth, and the badges were for his benefit. Seated on a wooden massage table was a thin, middle-aged European-looking male wearing nothing but his underwear.

Riley nodded to Bridgeforth and the African American left the room, shutting the door behind him. He ignored the one chair in the room. Instead, he stood in front of the door, his raincoat thin protection against the trillions of microbes he pictured swarming in the air around him.

The thin man looked at him with panic-stricken eyes.

Good, Riley thought.

The Englishman could do a spot-on New York accent; he'd practiced it for hundreds of hours in the past year, even going days 'in character' around the city, to the point he never saw any hint of doubt from anyone he came in contact with.

He slipped into his character with ease. In his booming Brooklyn voice he said, 'Detective Rich Kincaid, NYPD.' And then, 'Vice.'

The man before him just nodded, then he spoke with a pronounced Austrian accent. 'As I mentioned to your colleague, Detective, I have diplomatic immunity from prosecution.'

Riley shrugged, his hands wide, a gesture in keeping with his character. 'Who's prosecuting?'

'You are required to –'

'You are required to sit there and shut the fuck up!'

The Austrian recoiled in surprise.

'Now, let's figure out where we stand here. You are Hans Tischer. You are with the Austrian delegation to the UN. That means, even though my partner has pictures of you bumping uglies with some teenage hooker right in the middle of America's greatest city, I have to let you go.'

The man on the massage table did not hide his expression of relief.

'But I can hold you here till my friend the photog from the *New York Post* shows up outside and gets into position.'

Tischer gasped now. '*Nein!* No. Please, you must not do this.'

'Of course, you could always shoot out the back. Yeah ... might work.' He affected another half-shrug. 'Although I already told my pal from the *Daily News* that you might try that, so I don't really recommend it.'

'*Mein Gott.* Why are you doing this to me?'

Riley took a step closer. 'When your ugly mug is on the front page of the paper, are you gonna tell your family that little girl said she was eighteen? Will they believe you? She's in an ambulance outside, and she don't look eighteen to me, Hans.'

Tischer covered his face with his hands.

'I've gotta cut you loose, but I don't gotta like it, and there's no law that says I've gotta do it without walkin'' you by the press. You know what I'm sayin''?'

Tischer sobbed softly.

Riley leaned in now, closer and softer. 'Or I can make it all go away. No name, no picture. No problem.'

Tischer looked up, eyes wide in disbelief. 'Yes? How?'

Even softer, Riley said, 'This is where it gets interesting, Hans.' He looked back over his shoulder to make sure the door was closed. 'Three days from now your committee has a procedural vote.' Just as Riley expected, the emotions displayed on the face of the man in front of him ran the gamut. From confusion to outrage to a new concern.

After a few moments he said, 'What *is* this?'

Riley shrugged, still in character. 'It's one guy needin'' a favor, that's you. And another guy needin'' a favor. That's me.'

'Who are you? You aren't a policeman.'

'I'm the guy with the pictures of you in the act, I'm the guy with the friends in the press outside, and I'm the guy who will fucking burn you if you don't vote against the sanctions hearing.'

'Why?'

Riley just said, 'Why? Why does anyone do what they do? Why do you pull your pants down in nasty-ass places like this?' It wasn't an answer to the question, but it had the effect of shutting down Tischer's line of questioning.

The Austrian man looked down at the floor for a long time. 'It won't matter. If I vote the way you want me to, it won't matter. There are nine of us. We took a straw poll yesterday, and the majority are in favor of the Security Council sanctions hearing. The vote on Friday is just a formality.'

Riley smiled. 'You might just find others have changed their position since the last straw poll. The world is coming to its senses on the matter.'

Tischer realized what this man was saying. He'd gotten to others on the committee. The middle-aged Austrian did not doubt this for a second.

He said, 'I tell you I will vote no, and you will let me go without anyone seeing me?'

'Yes. I go out and tell my buddy from the *Post* I was wrong, you weren't here. He and I hit the road. Five minutes later you walk on out and go back to your life like nothing happened. You vote no on Friday and you'll get an envelope with the disk with all the images my colleague took. You destroy that, and this whole little escapade is behind you.'

Tischer said, 'You can't possibly work for North Korea. Can you?'

'Of course not. I'm NYPD. Along with this, let's just say I moonlight for an interested party. We'll leave it there.'

Tischer nodded slowly. 'Okay. Let us leave it there.'

Riley smiled.

30

John Clark, Ding Chavez, and Sam Driscoll had been in the city for five days before they managed to tail Sharps employee Edward Riley to the massage parlor on 29th Street. Driscoll had the eye when Riley went in, but then he continued on, walking under his umbrella up the street a few hundred yards, bought a gyro from a vendor on 3rd Avenue, and then stepped inside a covered bus stop to shield himself from the rain while he ate it. He was just within sight of the building Riley had entered, but he'd be useful only if he pulled his camera and its zoom lens from his backpack.

For now, however, he enjoyed his gyro, because he'd handed the eye off to Chavez.

Domingo Chavez approached from the other direction. He wore a suit and tie and talked into a mobile phone. He stopped inside a Duane Reade drugstore across the street from Riley's destination, and he began looking at umbrellas at a stand. From his vantage point here he had a perfect view of the entrance to the building less than thirty yards away.

His conversation into his phone continued; it was Clark at the other end and he was back at the safe house, sitting in front of a computer and watching his men's movements on a com-puterized map. Their banter was inane cover material about the perfect weather 'back home' in L. A. as compared with here in New York. When Ding stopped in the pharmacy, Clark saw this on his map, and when Ding said – in a hushed voice – 'across the street from my poz, basement entrance,' Clark began scanning the area on Map of the World for information.

It took just seconds to realize the location was a massage parlor. There were links to a webpage with a phone number and an offer of 'Asian massage' that, without coming right out and offering sex for money, certainly implied as much by filling the webpage full of young Asian women in lingerie.

Clark was pretty sure this wasn't the kind of place you got a referral from your doc to visit if you needed help treating a chronic sports injury.

He relayed his findings to Ding, who by then had begun browsing through other parts of the pharmacy. Ding made no reply; he just continued talking about the weather and glancing through the glass at the front of the room.

Riley left the building after just ten minutes, and on a hunch Sam stuck around while Ding trailed the target back in the direction of his car.

Five minutes after this, a nervous-looking middle-aged man in dress slacks and an open-collared dress shirt came up the steps from the exit of the building. Sam finished his gyro and reached into his backpack, from where he retrieved a Nikon with a 300-millimeter lens, and even as he snapped off a dozen pictures of the man's face he had a feeling he knew who he was.

The man stood in the rain as if he were unaware of it

while he hailed a taxi. Sam slipped his camera into his bag and headed back to the safe house.

Sharps Global Intelligence Partners' corporate HQ was on the Upper West Side, so The Campus had secured a safe house nearby, in a sixteenth-floor condo on West 79th Street.

It was a simple three-bedroom, two-thousand-square-foot property, and the safe house itself gave the team no direct overwatch of any part of Sharps's operation, but this wasn't a normal surveillance. Their intentions had been simply to find any of Sharps's operatives in the field, and track their movements and their contacts.

Their mission to prove Sharps was working with North Korea had taken on even more significance when Gerry called the team the day before and had them assemble for a conference call.

Gerry had started the conference by saying, "I'm sure you all have seen the news that there is going to be a procedural vote in the UN Security Council Sanctions Committee next week on the North Korean situation. Nine UN bureaucrats will decide if the request from the Ryan White House meets the arcane conditions to go before a full Security Council vote.

'Needless to say, the US government needs this procedural vote to pass. Without it, the conduits to North Korea's trade remain in place and they get closer and closer to buying the material and expertise they need to build the missiles they want.'

Clark asked, 'If it's just a pro forma – type vote, what's the concern?'

'Wayne Duke Sharps is the concern. Mary Pat has heard rumors that employees from Sharps Global Intelligence Partners have been walking the halls in the United Nations, trying to get meetings between Sharps and the nine members of the Sanctions Committee.'

'Influence peddling?'

'No question about it. Foley can keep Sharps himself away from the UN people, at least during their official duties. But Sharps Partners has agents all over Manhattan. She is concerned Sharps will find a way to get to these men and women, and either buy their votes or affect the outcome in some way.'

Ding said, 'So . . . this damn well indicates Sharps is working for the North Koreans, right?'

'Just like in Vietnam, his organization clearly is working in the *interests* of the North Koreans, but there is no evidence he is working for them directly. It is crucial you find exactly what Sharps and his minions are up to. But there is something more important than that. If we can find out he is working for North Korea, in any direct way whatsoever, we can have him shut down ASAP. It is treasonous to work for a foreign power.'

Sam Driscoll said, 'Why doesn't Foley just contact the FBI? They could watch over them.'

Gerry said, 'The problem with Sharps's operation always has been that they have their fingers so far in the cookie jar at FBI and CIA, they are stocked with former employees and people who are still in contact with those in the government, that there is no way the FBI can get close enough to Sharps's operation to catch him red-handed. They've only got a week and a half before the vote, so they will be running around going after the committee members. They'll have to take risks to get this done, and this creates an opportunity for you.'

After that call, Clark refined his hunt for Sharps's operators, and within hours they were tracking Edward Riley through New York as he met with United Nations Sanctions Committee leadership. It didn't take them any time at all to realize what was going on.

Sam's photos of the man leaving the massage parlor in the rain were brought up on the computer. No facial-recognition software was required. There were only nine people, seven men and two women, on the Sanctions Committee, and this photo was clearly Hans Tischer, a forty-one-year-old Austrian and career UN employee at One Dag Hammarskjöld Plaza in Manhattan's Turtle Bay.

Clark said, 'Edward Riley is Sharps's second-in-command, and he seems to be spearheading things as a director of operations. The rules vote next week is their objective. They are trying to affect the delegates on board, to get them to vote no on drafting another round of economic sanctions.'

Sam said, 'We can nip this in the bud. Just let it slip to the press what Sharps is up to. That gets out and he'll have to stop.'

Clark said, "I considered that, but the problem is, Sharps is the devil we know. There are other unscrupulous private intelligence firms in the US, plus there are similar companies in other countries who could operate here and stay below our radar. And above all, interested nations could do the same thing. I have no doubt the DPRK is running agents here in the city. They could be tasked with targeting the Sanctions Committee membership, and we'll have no insight to what's going on.

'No. We can't tip our hand. If Sharps finds out his op is under surveillance, we will lose all the potential leverage we have in finding out how big this goes. We won't blow Sharps unless we can prove he's working for the North Koreans. That would put him in prison for treason.' Clark gave a sly smile. 'And *that* couldn't happen to a nicer guy.'

Ding said, 'So we keep following him. If he meets with North Koreans we hit the jackpot, but if we know who he's compromised, like this Austrian guy he just busted in the massage parlor, we can push back on them quietly, to try and pressure their vote.'

Sam had kicked off his shoes, and now he rubbed his calves. He'd been on nearly constant foot-follow surveillance for several days. 'I guess we'd better get back out there. He's in his office now, but he usually leaves around four.'

Clark stood. 'No, Sam. You and Domingo stay here. It's my turn at bat. Good news, though, Dom will be here in a couple hours to give us another pair of eyes in the hunt.'

31

Lieutenant General Ri was not one to micromanage his operations. At present he had more than one hundred different schemes and plans in motion around the globe, and they were most all being run effectively – some more effectively than others – by his subordinates.

Counterfeiting operations, drug-smuggling operations, weap-ons transfers to Syria and Iraq and East Africa, and weapons purchases from Iran and Pakistan. Kidnappings in Japan and in South Korea.

And Fire Axe, the assassination of the President of the United States, in Mexico.

He couldn't involve himself any more in Fire Axe, for the sake of deniability, but of all the other operations, the New World Metals operation was different, and therefore it required his full attention and scrutiny. As far as Ri was concerned, the Dae Wonsu himself had gone so far as to threaten him with violent death if he did not attain the ICBM, he had two years left to do so, and Ri saw no possible way this would happen without the success of New World Metals and the Chongju mine.

So he kept an eye on every last aspect of the mission. Even though Ri and his RGB did not hire Duke Sharps directly, the North Korean lieutenant general knew all about the American man and his part in the plan. He knew the importance of the procedural vote in the United

Nations, and he had been watching Sharps work via reports he received from Óscar Roblas.

Ri felt Sharps was doing an excellent job with his coercion operation, and under any other circumstances he would have simply allowed his American proxy force in New York City to continue on, but he knew how utterly important the success of Sharps and his operation was to Ri's own personal fortune.

And two days earlier something had happened in Prague which further affected the equation. A team of RGB men had been looking for a low-ranking consular affairs officer who had helped them with some documentation they had needed to get foreign expertise into Chongju. Ri had not been micromanaging this situation, but he was, of course, aware of the 'underground railroad' of scientists coming in to work at Chongju from nations that would not have permitted their travel. Ri had not even been aware the Czech consular official had disappeared, but, according to the report he read this morning, the man turned up back at his apartment in Prague, along with two Americans. The North Koreans moved in, a rush decision to eliminate the consular official was made because he was in the process of revealing aspects of the North Korean operation, and according to the surviving agents, the Americans had been ready to repel force with force of their own.

Four North Koreans, three from Ri's own RGB, had died in a gunfight.

Lieutenant General Ri had been deeply distressed by this incident because he did not know who the Americans were, what they knew about his operation or his plans, or what they would do next. He immediately thought of Sharps in New York City and how incredibly crucial a good result in the United Nations would be to New World Metals' continued transfer of the money he needed.

Ri would not sit back and hope for the best from Duke Sharps. He would send his own operators to monitor the situation and, if necessary, employ stronger measures. He'd sanction his men to kill on the streets of America, if necessary, because the stakes were high enough to warrant it.

That wasn't Sharps's game – this Ri had been informed by his US-based RGB staff. The American ex – FBI agent skirted the laws in his home country, but he wouldn't run crews of armed direct-action forces, so Ri had to look into other avenues for this.

The North Korean permanent mission to the United Nations is on the thirteenth floor of an office building on the corner of 2nd Avenue and 44th Street, a block away from the entrance to the United Nations building. The comings and goings of the personnel associated with the mission are carefully watched by FBI Counterintelligence Division special agents, as well as many other US government entities. General Ri knew he could not easily call his New York office and simply order up agents to fan into the area to protect Duke Sharps and his employees as they worked on Ri's behalf.

But Ri had other resources at his disposal in the city. There are more than two hundred thousand Koreans or Korean Americans living in New York, and Ri had influence over hundreds of North Korean agents or expatriates residing in the area, and some of these were covert employees of the Reconnaissance General Bureau. There were even direct-action agents in the city, there for the purpose of targeting North Korean dissidents or South Korean troublemakers. After a meeting and a phone call in his Pyongyang office, Ri had secured the use of a unit of twelve highly trained North Korean sleepers in Manhattan and notified their control of his desire that they watch over Sharps and report back.

Within twenty-four hours of his order, the North Koreans in Manhattan had begun shadowing Sharps Global Intelligence Partners employees while they worked their operations within the city. They were tasked with making sure the Americans succeeded in their efforts to affect the procedural vote, and they had been given the green light to use any measures and resources necessary to see that the mission was a success.

32

President of the United States Jack Ryan was officially off duty, or as off duty as a President ever gets. All his official responsibilities were done for the day, and this was one of those too-few evenings where the agenda didn't have him meeting anyone after hours, or going anywhere but back to the residence.

After leaving the Oval around six, he had dinner with Cathy, Kyle, and Katie in the Family Dining Room, and there they made plans to watch a Discovery Channel show about snow leopards. Katie had announced to her family recently that she was destined to be a veterinarian, and although Kyle had mocked her because he walked the family dog around the Rose Garden more than she did, her parents were thrilled with her young ambition and they ramped up their intake of nature documentaries.

Katie loved learning about animals, and Kyle enjoyed it as well, although his sights were set firmly on a career as a pro-fessional stuntman, and he thought it unfair that his mom and dad didn't support him by allowing him to build the scaffold on the back lawn with the mattresses below it, because without this how was he going to ever learn how to fall off buildings like the real stuntmen in the movies do?

Jack and Cathy put their foot down with Kyle, did their

best to steer him toward something else – *anything* else – but as for Katie, the nine-year-old who didn't like to operate the pooper scooper in the backyard was, in her parents' eyes at least, well on her way to becoming a world-renowned zoologist or an exotic-animal vet.

Jack started heading back to his room to change to watch TV, but a steward let him know Mary Pat Foley was on the phone wishing to speak with him.

He took the call in his study. 'Hey, Mary Pat. Anything wrong?'

'No, Mr President, everything is fine. Sorry to disturb you like this.'

'Not at all. What's up?'

Mary Pat said, 'Mr President, I think there is an opportunity here to get a human source inside North Korea, into the Chongju mine and refinery operations, to give us much better elucidation on the situation there. It won't be easy, the officer will obviously be in great danger.'

'Wait. You said "officer," not "agent." You are talking about an employee of one of our intel agencies?'

'Yes, Mr President. CIA. He's a Chinese American, first-generation.' She offered the President no more information.

Ryan loosened his tie and leaned back. 'You want a "go, no-go," from me. Is that it?'

'Yes, Mr President.'

'The operation . . . how long in duration?'

'Open-ended. We don't think it will be more than a couple months once our man is in country.'

'You are satisfied the backstopping of the officer's legend is good? The infiltration plan is solid? You are convinced he has the best resources you can give him, and a clear understanding of the objectives?'

'Yes to all.'

'What about fail-safes if he gets in trouble?'

Mary Pat paused. 'I could tell you about the training he has and the exfiltration options available to him if he is compromised, but I will be honest with you. If he is compromised while on the ground in North Korea, he will likely be captured and then killed, or else killed outright.'

'Is there a plan to coordinate with US military in case of emergency? We have special operations troops near the South Korean border, of course. And the USS *Freedom* is in the Yellow Sea. SEALs on board the *Freedom* were the ones who found the launch tubes on that cargo ship.'

'We are going to play our cards very close to the vest on this operation, for purposes of OPSEC. If our man is compromised from over here it will be ruinous to him and to any future efforts we might have. But I will notify JSOC that a personnel recovery mission is a possibility.' Mary Pat knew JSOC would just ask for more information, and although she couldn't blame them for that, she wouldn't give any more information unless Yao was on the run in North Korea.

The very thought of this made her blood run cold.

Ryan was thinking, too. He pictured this unknown officer as a man standing at a precipice and facing a tightrope that led to the other side. There was no net below. And Jack Ryan was the one who had to tell him either to turn around and go home . . . or to start walking.

But he also pictured the future. A future where the West Coast of the United States was in range of North Korean ICBMs.

His deliberation was brief.

'Send him,' Ryan said. He wasn't as sure as he made himself sound. It was his job to appear resolute, even to Mary Pat. If he vacillated it would add unnecessary uncertainty into her oversight of the operation. She needed to know she had his full support and backing, and even though the prospect of having a man on the ground in North Korea would probably lead him to redevelop his stomach ulcers in the next few weeks, his belief in the importance of this mission was without question.

Mary Pat said, 'Thank you, Mr President. Know we have our best people working on this, and I'll meet with them daily.'

'I know you will, Mary Pat. You and I both know what's at stake. For him, and for the US. Get the intelligence product we need, and then get his ass out of there.'

'Yes, Mr President.'

Jack hung up the phone and went into the bedroom to change. Cathy was already there; she'd thrown on a jogging suit she liked to wear when lounging in the media room. She looked up at her husband and instantly asked, 'What is it? What's wrong?'

Jack faked a smile. 'Nothing.' He sat down on the edge of the bed, suddenly very tired.

Cathy sat next to him. 'Jack?'

'It was Mary Pat. She wanted my approval for an operation that will put a young officer in harm's way.' He paused. 'I gave that approval.'

Cathy hugged him. 'It's Mary Pat, Jack. She knows what she's doing.'

He shrugged. 'It feels like bullshit sometimes. I have to make decisions based on less information than the people who seek my approval. I know a fiftieth of what she knows, and I told her to go ahead. Maybe I should have spent a couple days looking at the operation.'

Cathy said, 'You know, Jack, there are a lot of people who are paid to read all that raw data and put it into an easily digestible form for you. You are upsetting the natural order when you try and micromanage.'

Jack smiled, the lines around his eyes pronounced with his lack of sleep. 'I know. And I trust the people we have working for us. I just feel like I should have as much information as I can get to make decisions as important as this.'

'You can't know everything.'

'True. But I can always know more.' He sighed a long sigh and let his shoulders slump in a fashion that only Cathy had ever seen. 'Two more years of this. Jesus. What was I thinking when I ran this last time?'

Cathy brushed her hand across the well-worn worry lines on his forehead, around his eyes. 'You'll miss this when it's over. But when it's over . . . we'll have a lot more time to relax.'

He smiled now, took her hand in his. 'Yeah.' He felt better. Just a little, but it was enough to get him off his ass. He stood and went to change out of his presidential uniform and into his dad uniform.

It was the best part of his day.

33

Having Dom Caruso up in New York, thereby giving Clark four sets of eyes instead of just three, had made a huge difference in the Campus operation to gain intelligence in the actions of Sharps Partners.

The other change to their operation that was proving helpful was that now they were primarily tracking the movements of Edward Riley. There was no question that he was in charge of the operation to influence the committee vote, and after the honey trap in the sleazy massage parlor the previous day, Clark and his men wondered if he'd managed to line up at least one vote in North Korea's favor.

Tonight Riley took a cab to Chinatown at nine, so Sam, Domingo, and Dom followed him down. While Riley sat in a nearly empty dim sum restaurant on Mott Street, Sam took the eye in a nondescript charcoal-gray sedan. He had to circle the block four times to catch an open spot on the curb, but he found a place on Bayard near the corner that gave him a great backward view into the restaurant, as well as a fair angle of view to both the north and south on Mott. Once he parked, he pulled his camera from its bag and put it down between his feet.

Dom was on foot – he'd arrived by subway, then walked across Canal Street – and he remained two blocks up on Mott and out of direct view of the dim sum restaurant.

He wore a black polo shirt and khakis and he sat alone at a fast-food restaurant on the corner of Mott and Canal, but he had earpiece comms with the team and was ready to move closer if Sam had to bug out for some reason, or if Riley left the restaurant with his contact on foot.

Ding was dressed in warm-up pants and a light sweat-shirt, and he jogged at a leisurely pace south and west of the dim sum restaurant. While he listened in his headset to Sam call out news from his static surveillance up the street, he circled over to Columbus Park and made his way through pedestrians, all the while ready to head back and take the eye if Sam ran into any problems.

With only three men in the team there wasn't a lot of room for error, but Clark was back at the safe house on the Upper West Side, both monitoring the team's movements on the computer and working directly with the analysts in Alexandria on developing a better target picture on the UN bureaucrats involved in the Sanctions Committee vote.

Just after nine-thirty p.m. a woman wearing a beige rain-coat walked past Dom's position on the corner of Canal and Mott, and then she turned to head south. She was one of a hundred pedestrians he'd tracked in the past ten minutes, so she barely stood out and he hadn't gotten a close look at her face, but two minutes later when Sam described a woman entering the dim sum restaurant alone, Dom recognized her as a person who'd passed his static point.

And when Sam confirmed that the woman had sat down at Edward Riley's table, Dom said, 'She came on foot from the west on Canal. She either parked up there somewhere or else she came up out of the subway.'

'Roger,' said Ding. 'Sam, we need her ID'd as soon as possible.'

'Working on it,' replied Sam. His digital Nikon had a 500-millimeter lens. With this equipment and at this range he knew he should be able to catch her through the window and get a good headshot. Unfortunately, however, the conditions on the street were less than ideal. All the neon signs around were reflecting off the glass, so Sam couldn't get a perfect sightline of her face. So far he could just tell she had dark brown or auburn hair, it was pulled back in a bun, and she appeared to be in her forties. He said, 'Only two females on the committee.' He opened a small notebook on the passenger side of the car and thumbed through the images.

He found the first female profile. 'This is definitely not Noreen Paige from the USA . . .' He turned two pages and found the other. 'But this could well be Marleni Allende from Chile. Can't be sure yet, though. I'll have to wait for her to move to get a better line of sight.'

As soon as he said this he saw movement at the table; he'd been looking for any exchange of property between them, but this wasn't that. Instead, the woman was speaking with her hands, and Riley was lolling his head back, clearly in some frustration.

Sam spoke for the benefit of the rest of the detail. 'Our boy looks pissed. This should be fun.'

Ten minutes into his meeting with the UN official from Chile, Edward Riley finally began to accept her words at face value. This was no bluff.

The bloody bitch had changed her mind.

Riley had brought the twenty-five thousand US dollars with him. They'd agreed on this amount in an early conversation, that one while making the harbor crossing on the Staten Island Ferry several days earlier. She'd come up with an excuse to cancel the first meet for the exchange, two days after that, but she'd agreed on tonight without hesitation. Now Riley realized he should have been more concerned that the lady was getting cold feet about taking money for her vote.

He'd always known this could happen. So far he'd managed to bribe two of the nine officials, and he'd coerced an agreement out of two more by threatening them with scandalous revelations, but he had thought he had Marleni Allende in the bag already.

Allende had a problem with money. She was a middle-class woman back home, an international law professor who, through merit alone, worked her way into a respectable but not terribly high-paying job in New York City, and here she was surrounded by men and women who made more money and lived better for it. Over time her resistance to running up her credit cards had weakened; it was easy to spend lavishly here in New York, and she'd put herself twenty thousand dollars in debt.

As soon as Riley and the rest of Sharps Partners identified her as a target they snooped around her bank accounts, and in minutes he had his attack vector sorted. He approached her, shocking her greatly, but she certainly seemed excited by the prospect of a financial lifeline.

But now it looked like he'd overestimated her concern for her financial problems, or else he'd underestimated her dedication to her organization.

And this led him to a new problem. He needed her no vote, but more than that, he needed her discretion. If she revealed the scheme to bribe UN officials, Riley himself would be the one facing the threat of a scandal.

He sipped his Tsingtao beer, taking a minute to regroup. Then he spoke, sticking with his Kincaid legend, the NYPD detective. With a Brooklyn accent he said, 'Look, Marleni, you came here tonight on foot, you wanted to meet me in this out-of-the-way hole-in-the-wall. You're dressed like you're in a frickin'' Sam Spade novel, for cryin'' out loud. You don't look to me like a woman who doesn't want to go along with the plan. Just tell me what it is you want and I'll do my best to make it happen.'

Allende shook her head. 'Nothing. I want nothing. I came like this because I am ashamed to be meeting with you again. If someone I know sees me ... I *want* the money, of course, but I am no criminal. I have a duty to my organization. I cannot do this. I *will* not.'

Riley gave her a challenging look. 'How are you going to feel when the vote fails anyway because many of your colleagues don't share your bright and shining sense of mission? You are going to be the only one who doesn't benefit.'

'I know you have approached others. I can see it on their faces around the office. They all want to know if others in the committee know about their secret. I am sure they hope everyone knows, so everyone will go along quietly.'

Riley raised an eyebrow, but Marleni Allende lifted a hand quickly; on her face she had an expression of worry.

'I will go quietly, don't doubt this. I will not say a word about anything that has happened. It is not my place to hurt my friends and coworkers. But I will not join in this . . . corruption.'

She stood. 'I am sorry, Mr Kincaid. Good night.'

Without another word she turned and headed for the door.

Allende was still in the restaurant when Driscoll noticed the new arrival to the neighborhood. A small black SUV with its lights off pulled up to the curb some twenty-five yards north of his position on the corner of Bayard and Mott. He could just see one person behind the wheel, but he wasn't sure with all the reflecting neon from the Chinese character signs running up and down both sides of the street.

Marleni Allende – Sam had confirmed her identity when he got a perfect shot of her face during her meeting with Riley – stepped out of the dim sum place and began walking up Mott Street, in the direction of the black SUV.

Sam had not seen anything passed between Riley and the UN woman, and now, watching the way she had spun away and marched off, he read it as a show of resolution. He got the distinct impression she was turning her back on Riley, figuratively as well as literally.

Sam said, 'Listen up. The woman is not going to play ball with Riley, and she is on the move, heading northbound on foot. A suspicious vehicle just pulled up on the corner.'

Ding called back. 'I'm en route from the south.'

Dom said, 'I'm in position if she comes all the way to Canal Street.'

Sam just sat in his dark car. As much as he wanted to tail the woman leaving on foot immediately, he wouldn't reveal himself by firing up his engine right now. Instead, he sat and watched while she crossed the street. While she did so the SUV started to move forward, directly facing her. But a passing Audi sedan honked its horn and swerved to avoid a collision with the SUV, then it turned right onto Mott.

The black SUV, all its lights still off, stopped and let the passing traffic by.

Sam said, 'Be advised, we might have aggressors. This SUV is thinking about either following her or running her over. Can't tell which yet.'

Dom said, 'You've got to be kidding. In Manhattan?'

Sam said, 'I just call 'em like I see 'em. Wait one –'

The SUV pulled into traffic behind the Audi and went straight on Bayard, passing behind the Chilean UN official, who was now back on the sidewalk and heading north toward Dom on the corner of Canal and Mott. The vehicle turned on its lights as it took off up the street.

Quickly Sam looked back toward the dim sum restaurant. Edward Riley was leaving through the front door, heading off to the south, in the opposite direction of the activity. He was talking on his phone, but he did not seem overly excited or concerned.

Sam said, 'The SUV has moved on, but they might be handing off the tail to another team, or else they're trying to get ahead of her. Can't explain it, but I have a feeling they aren't bugging out.'

Ding Chavez said, 'Then we go on your intuition. I'll stay parallel of you to the west, you stay in traffic, get up to Canal, and Dom will take the eye in the foot-follow when the target passes.'

Everyone agreed, and the three men all began the orchestrated ballet that is a coordinated mobile surveillance operation.

Ding was in condition yellow as he moved, his eyes open for any countersurveillance. But he had no way of seeing the seventy-year-old Korean woman sitting back from the window in the second-floor apartment over a bodega, the dirty curtains parted just enough for the lens of a video camera. She took twelve seconds of video as Ding passed below her.

A minute later she had sent the video to her local contact, an RGB officer. In a subsequent phone call she told the man that the Hispanic-looking fellow in the video was, unquestionably, near the British man she had been ordered to watch over tonight.

She was just a watcher. There were other RGB men here in the area, and they had used her for intelligence about the activities in the dim sum restaurant, but she had never seen her contact face-to-face, nor did she know a thing about the mission.

She had been working on this job for the past several days. Once each day she would get a call from her contact, and she would go to the address listed, either a restaurant or a laundromat or a food court or a parking lot or, in this evening's case, an empty and unlocked but obviously lived-in apartment on Mott Street in Chinatown.

She would then keep an eye out for anything out of the ordinary around her. By her second day she recognized the one constant to each scene was the white man with the dark hair. She was not told his name, but when she pointed him out she was directed to keep watch for anyone else interested in him.

And now that she'd been at this for five days, she finally had success.

The Hispanic man she had identified tonight had not done anything wrong. He had not gotten too close to his subject, nor had he acted in any way different from any other random passerby on the street – any of the three times she had seen him.

That was what compromised him. The old lady had a memory like a trap. Three mornings earlier on 3rd Avenue the short, dark-haired man in his forties had been walking with another man, deep in conversation and with a cup of coffee in his hands. They were across the street and some seventy-five yards from where Edward Riley was having coffee with a contact at a Starbucks. The Korean lady had been stationed in a Hallmark shop, looking out the window and simply noting passersby.

Two days later, in the mid-afternoon, a construction worker in denim pants and a T-shirt sat on a residential stoop in Chelsea, a block and a half from where Riley and one of his agents had gone into a brownstone.

The Korean woman had been browsing in a luggage store on the corner, she'd been far from the construction worker, but she thought he might have been the suited Hispanic from two days earlier. If she'd had binoculars she could have made the connection with certainty, but her cover was more important to her than his cover, so she let it go.

But tonight she saw the same man again, running in the dark, dressed like he was just out for a jog. He was either a businessman – construction worker – jogger, or he was a member of the opposition.

She doubted seriously he was working alone, but she'd not managed to identify any confederates.

She neither knew nor cared about the reasons he was following Edward Riley, no more than she knew or cared about what Edward Riley was up to. But her grown son and daughter lived in North Korea, and her occasional work here in New York for RGB always brought good news from them. The last time she worked an operation here in the city for North Korean intelligence her son sent a letter a few months later telling her he had received a new bicycle and his sister a new radio. They did not know the reason why, but they thanked the Dae Wonsu and professed their everlasting love and affection for him.

The elderly Korean Manhattanite was pleased her work here in America brought her family happiness back home, even if she would have loved to be able to have them come here to live with her.

The three Campus operators continued their coordinated leapfrogging movements through Chinatown, and it was still something of a ballet, but by now the complexity of the cho-reography had increased because the black SUV had turned up again, this time shadowing the woman on Canal Street. Marleni Allende continued walking unaware, her beige raincoat contrasting with the T-shirts of many of the other pedestrians here shopping for cheap knock-off goods in the rows of sidewalk stalls. Behind her, carefully tracking her, the Ford Escape moved normally through traffic, turning onto perpendicular streets and then pulling back onto Canal moments later.

Caruso still had the eye; he was one hundred feet directly behind the target, which meant at times he was moving right along with the black Ford. He spoke softly, but his earbud picked up his words with no problem. 'This is starting to feel like that deal in Vietnam. I count four in the Ford. They aren't closing on her, but there are a lot of civilians around here.'

Sam had pushed ahead through traffic, and now he raced to the nearest subway stop on Canal. During Allende's meeting in the restaurant, he'd called Clark and asked for information on the woman. Clark read aloud everything the Campus analysts had given him, and from this Sam knew she lived alone in an apartment in Midtown.

She wasn't walking home, that was for sure. Unless the Chilean woman hailed a taxi, it was a fair bet she was going to go down into the subway.

He knew there was no way in hell he'd find a place to park to go on foot, but at least he'd be able to identify any threats on the woman when she passed by.

Dom had no concerns the UN woman was going to see him; she walked with her head down and her shoulders rolled forward. If she started to look back over her shoulder, Dom had the training to recognize the telltale body

335

movements that would come before her eyes actually put her in position to compromise him.

But the men in the Ford were a concern. They were alternately behind him, next to him, and facing him as they went up one street and down the other, and he assumed whoever these guys were, they had the training to be on the lookout for countersurveillance.

So Dom stopped now and then to look at cheap T-shirts and tacky wallets for sale in the stalls, and he just made occasional spot checks on Allende to confirm the other team on her tail hadn't yet closed distance on her.

As he walked he saw the Ford Escape leave the tail completely and move up the street. He called it out to his teammates, and they all surmised the Escape was heading to the subway station as well.

Sam asked over the net, 'What are we doing, guys?'

Clark had been monitoring the progression of the tail. 'You two have to call it. I'm not there and Ding doesn't have the eye. Dom, I don't want you guys in the subway if I can avoid it, but if you think this woman is in peril, I'll approve you going down and watching over her. Dom? Sam? Talk to me.'

Sam watched the Ford stop at the entrance to the subway. Two Asian men climbed out of the back and hurried down the stairs.

Before Dom had a chance to respond to Clark's query, Sam said, 'I've got two potential North Korean FAMs descending into the Canal Street station. Both wearing light-colored button-downs under black business suits.'

FAMs meant the same thing to all four men on the

net. 'Fighting-aged males.' They could be spooks, military, or any other bad actor. Of course, they could also be insurance salesmen, on their way home from work. .

But Clark was betting against the latter. 'Sam, you stay in the vehicle. Ding, you catch up to Dom.'

'He's in view ahead of me,' Ding said. It was evident he was still jogging, keeping his cover going as well as closing the distance between himself and the surveillance target.

Clark finished with, 'Ding and Dom, follow Allende tight. Go overt if you have to, let the DPRK assholes know you're there, but keep her out of danger. No unnecessary risks. You *will* lose comms with Sam and I up here, so reestablish contact as soon as you're able. Good luck.'

In front of Dom, the Chilean woman in the raincoat descended into the station, unaware men were watching her at this moment, and equally unaware others were waiting for her below.

34

Canal Street station was surprisingly quiet, even for ten-fifteen on a weeknight, but a light stream of foot traffic on the stairs headed toward the track. Marleni Allende walked along with the others, all but unaware of her surroundings because her mind was still on her worries.

She passed through the turnstile on her way to the northbound N train, her mind still unable to free itself of the stress of the past few days. She told herself she'd done the right thing, no amount of money would assuage the guilt she would feel for the rest of her life if she succumbed to corruption. She considered herself a good Catholic, and though here in New York she had made many mistakes, finding herself unable to resist running up her credit cards and blowing through her life savings, she at least had the backbone to know that accepting a bribe from shadowy men obviously working for the interests of an evil regime was no way to dig herself out of her troubles.

She wasn't paying attention at first, so she didn't notice when, directly in front of her, two young Asian men walked on the platform against the flow of pedestrians heading toward the train. And she became only obliquely aware of them a moment later and took a step to the right because she sensed them in her path and approaching her direction.

When she noticed the two men adjusting their gait to move again in her path, now just fifteen feet away, she looked up. Both men eyed her without reservation and they kept moving toward her.

She slowed her walk in surprise. She didn't have the training to be instantly fearful, but she thought they were perhaps walking up to her to say something.

At eight feet she sensed rather than saw both men reach inside their jackets.

As her eyes began moving down to see what they were retrieving from inside their coats, her heart lurched in her chest.

Oh, God! They are police and they know.

Just then she felt hands touch her from behind, grasping her at her elbows, and two men formed at her sides and began leading her gently but surely along the platform diagonally, out of the path of the men in front of her.

As she looked up at them, certain she was under arrest, one of them, smiling, spoke in a friendly voice.

'*¿Marleni?*' he said. '*¡No lo creo! ¿Como te vas, amiga?*' Marleni? I can't believe it! How are you doing, friend?

She glanced up and saw the Asian men standing on the platform, their hands still in their coats. Confusion on their faces. The men leading her to the subway didn't seem to notice them.

'*¿Todo bien, chica?*' the smaller of the two said. He was on her left, and he continued to guide her toward the track's edge. He acted like he knew her, and was happy to see her, but it was clearly an act.

'*¿Quién es usted?*' she asked. Who are you? The man on her right was a little taller, just as dark but bearded, and he

339

shielded her from the two Asian men who were now behind her. A few more people came forward on the platform as the train came to a stop.

The Latino with his hand on her back — from his accent, Marleni had identified him as Mexican — spoke softly now, still in Spanish. 'Get on the train with us. It's okay, we're friends.'

She did as she was told, not because she understood or trusted him, but only because there were two of them and they moved her forward with gentle but unmistakable force.

When the doors closed, Chavez turned around to look for the two North Koreans, but he couldn't see through the crowd of people leaving the train and heading for the exit. He thought it possible they had boarded another car, but he hoped the sudden appearance of him and Dom gave them enough pause to slow them down.

Chavez helped the woman to a seat; she was compliant but scared.

He said, 'Ms. Allende. I don't want to alarm you, I am a friend.'

'Who are you?' She clutched her bag. Ding was a forty-seven-year-old Hispanic male in warm-up pants and a gray sweatshirt. While he didn't look threatening, his approach like this was jarring enough to make Allende wonder if perhaps she was about to be robbed.

'Those men have been following you since you met with Riley. We think it's possible they were going to hurt you in some way. We can't let that happen.'

'I don't know any Riley.'

'He may have given you another name. I am talking about the man you met with at the restaurant on Mott Street twenty minutes ago.'

Allende's face reddened. 'I don't know –'

'It doesn't matter what is going on. We just want to make sure you are safe. Please let us escort you back someplace where we can talk.'

'I don't know what this is all about. Really. I demand to be allowed to call my embassy immediately.'

Chavez said, 'You aren't safe in the subway. We can get you out at the next stop and meet friends at street level who can help us.'

Allende stood suddenly. Her confusion was subsiding quickly, and now she had acquired a sense of authority, even outrage. 'I told you. I demand to speak to my embassy.'

The train slowed at the Prince Street station. Dominic moved for the door, his hand hovering at his waist, ready to draw his weapon if any North Korean operatives entered the car.

Ding said, 'Okay. You can call whoever you want, but we've got to go up to the street, right?'

'I refuse to talk to –'

Dom spun away from the door, moved over to the Chilean UN official, and reached for his wallet. 'Pay attention, lady.' He opened his wallet and displayed his Bureau credentials. 'I'm FBI. You are coming with us.'

'I have diplomatic immunity.'

'And I don't give a shit. You are not being arrested, you are being escorted to safety. You need to appreciate what is happening. We're leaving right now.'

She started to move, but it took her too long.

At the stop a thick crowd of some fifteen people, the majority obviously tourists, were already boarding at the door nearest to Allende before she made it close enough to get off. An equal amount boarded at the door at the front of the car. By the time Chavez and Caruso had her moved through the group, the doors had closed again.

The train began moving.

Ding looked at Dom. 'Stand her by the door and keep your head on a swivel. At the next stop we are moving.'

'Roger that.'

If not for the large group of straphangers standing in the middle of the car, Ding and Dom would have seen the two Asian men board from the door between their car and the car forward of them. But the men entered the car and began moving through the crowd, looking for their targets. When they did see the woman and her two mysterious protectors, they were only ten feet away, close to the rear side door. Instantly the North Korean operatives reached inside their coats to the small of their backs.

Caruso and Chavez saw the men right as the guns came out.

The North Koreans drew pistols, pushed a middle-aged woman and her grown daughter out of the way, and the guns rose in the middle of the group of stunned passengers.

The two Campus operatives went into their pants for their own weapons. Dom pulled a Smith & Wesson M&P Shield .40-caliber from inside his waistband under his shirt, and Chavez snatched a Glock 26 nine-millimeter from a Thunderwear holster. As Chavez drew, he stepped in front of Marleni Allende and shielded her with his body.

The North Koreans got the jump on the Americans, but the Americans executed their drawstrokes faster, so the race to get sights on targets was a four-way tie.

The screams and yells of thirty people came last of all.

Within one and a half seconds of the two teams seeing each other in the same train car, the four men had one another at gunpoint, each with two hands on his pistol in a combat grip. Their extended arms and gun barrels meant their muzzles were within eighteen inches of one another.

Men and women all around them dropped to the floor or recoiled out of the way in all directions, but the four professionals stood still as stones in the middle of the train car.

It was clear to Chavez these were North Koreans; he guessed they were members of their foreign intelligence service. He was surprised they were operating in the city with firearms, but, Chavez told himself, a gun was a decent tool for an assassin, so it stood to reason these guys were packing.

Caruso was on Chavez's right, and as it happened, he had his gun on the man directly in front of Chavez, while Chavez himself was targeting the man just six feet in front of Caruso. The North Koreans had crossed their aim as well. The four weapons formed a near-perfect X that rocked and rolled with the rhythm of the moving train, and Chavez couldn't help but think about the fact that he and the other three men would catch simultaneous point-blank rounds to the head if anybody on this train car so much as even sneezed.

He pictured what that would look like to the captive audience here. One extra-loud bang and four armed assholes dropping dead to the floor in a massive pool of blood.

That would be one hell of a vacation memory for all the tourists on the train.

No one said anything for the first few seconds, so Chavez took the role of master of ceremonies. 'English? Either of you boys speak English?'

Sweat covered the brow of the man at the end of Chavez's notch-and-post gunsight. Chavez didn't look at the man in front of him, because that was Dom's responsibility, and he knew Dom would have that guy covered.

Chavez's man, dripping with sweat, had eyes that were wide and alert, but he did not seem panicked. He said, 'I speak English.'

Chavez nodded. 'That's good.' He smiled a little, trying to bring even the slightest bit of calm to the scene. 'This is a mess, huh?'

The North Korean didn't reply.

Chavez continued, 'I bet you and your partner want to go home tonight just like me and my partner. Am I right?'

The North Korean did speak now, but it was low and guttural and in Korean. He was talking to his partner, and while Chavez thought he might have just been translating for his partner's benefit, it didn't sound good at all.

The guns wavered a little as the train began a bumpy curve to the left, but still four muzzles were pointed at four faces, and four trigger fingers took up the slack in four triggers.

A female tourist in her thirties started to say something, but Caruso just hushed her without looking.

Chavez said, 'Why don't you two lower your weapons and you walk out of here at the next stop? We'll let you do it. Matter of fact . . . we'd *love* for you to do it.'

The leader of the two shook his head no. Sweat drained down his temples.

The train began to slow for the 8th Street stop. In a voice that was demonstrative but cautious, because he didn't want to startle the dude with the gun in his face, Dom said, 'Everybody relax. I'm a federal officer. Nobody move until we're stopped, but as soon as the doors open I want everyone to leave the train in a quiet and orderly fashion.'

The North Korean said, 'No! No! No one leaves!'

Chavez said, 'If either of you take your guns off of us to point them at these civilians, we will shoot you dead.' That sank in for a moment, then Chavez added, 'Tell your buddy if he doesn't understand.'

A college-age man sitting on the bench behind Dom said, 'Sir, do you want me to –'

Caruso said, 'I want you to do exactly what I just said. Nothing else.'

The subway car was quiet other than the rattling of the movement over the tracks, but when Caruso heard sounds behind him, a slight shuffling of clothing or a purse, he said, 'Anybody who pulls out a camera phone will probably get themselves killed, but if you don't, I'm gonna throw your ass in prison. Stay still!'

The sound behind ceased instantly.

It was a jolting stop at 8th Street; all four men stumbled a little, but the guns were back up and in their X in an instant. The men and women on the train – fortunately, it was late enough at night that no children had been on board – behaved even better than Dom had expected, and in seconds the train was clear.

Marleni Allende was one of the first off. Caruso and Chavez noticed that the North Koreans, though obviously on a life-or-death mission, had the good sense to not try to stop her. They were focused on their difficult predicament.

Caruso expected the train to stay at 8th Street. Surely someone would tell the motorman that there was an armed standoff on his train, and he'd sound the alarm and stay right there. But the doors closed and it began moving again.

He realized they were in the second-to-last car, and perhaps the people who'd scrambled off had been more concerned about getting the hell out of the line of fire and going to the exits and less concerned about running all the way up the platform to the front of the train.

Of course, everyone would be on their mobiles once they got to street level, or else they would tell the first transit cop they came across, so both Caruso and Chavez knew the train wouldn't make it past Union Square, the next stop.

Chavez tried his hand at dialogue again. 'The woman is gone. We can shoot it out over nothing, or we can just call it a night.'

The North Korean said, 'We have diplomatic immunity.'

Caruso replied, 'Who doesn't, really, at this point?'

Chavez latched on to this. 'Then drop your guns. You haven't done anything that will get you more than an expulsion. It doesn't have to end bad.'

The sweat on the Korean's face made him blink, over and over.

His partner said something in Korean, and the two men started some sort of argument that got heated.

While they shouted at each other, getting more volatile by the second, Caruso spoke softly to Chavez. 'They're losing it.'

Chavez said, 'Talking over the consequences of failure.'

Dom took in a slow breath. 'Dead-enders.'

Chavez knew what he meant. These guys were coming to the realization they had nothing to lose, and this meant, to both of the Campus operators, they were in the same predicament.

There was going to be a point-blank shootout in a minute, and Chavez and Caruso had nothing to lose at this point, either.

The North Koreans had stopped their arguing, and both Americans took that to mean they had reached a conclusion. The train began to slow at the Union Square station, and all four men softened their knees to absorb the inevitable shift in momentum that came along with pulling into the stop. Although they couldn't communicate it to each other, the Campus men both felt certain the North Koreans were going to fire right as the train made its final jolt before the doors opened. That was their best opportunity for success, and their best opportunity for escape.

Chavez said, 'You trust me, Dom?'

It took Caruso a moment, but soon enough he thought he understood. 'I trust you.'

'What are you saying?' shouted the English-speaking North Korean.

'I'm saying I give up,' answered Chavez.

He took his left hand off his gun slowly, and held it up in front of him, like he was telling the man with the gun on him he was going to surrender. Slowly he turned his pistol barrel away, changing his grip on the Glock so the gun rolled forward on his trigger finger. It hung upside down in his hand, the grip facing away from him. He turned away from the man he had been aiming at, and toward the man directly in front of him. 'Here. Take it.'

As he said this, the man in front of Chavez, the one with the gun pointed at Caruso, took his eyes off his sights for an instant to look up at the man offering his gun to him. A change in the dynamic caused him a half-second of surprise as he reevaluated the situation.

As soon as his eyes shifted, Dominic Caruso swiveled his body to the right and shot the other North Korean, the man with the gun on Chavez, in the forehead.

The man with the gun pointed at Caruso startled at the movement, and his eyes flicked back toward his gunsight. He recognized he'd been caught off guard, looking at one man and aiming at another, but he was still on target, and he jerked his finger against the taut trigger of his semiautomatic.

But he never got a shot off.

Chavez flicked his pistol around in his hand so the grip was in his palm and his pinkie finger was inside the trigger guard. Though the weapon was upside down, the barrel pointed at the aggressor in front of him. He pulled his pinkie back and fired the pistol upside down. The round hit the North Korean in the upper chest and knocked him backward. He stumbled back, and his gun fired once into the ceiling of the train.

Dom Caruso swiveled his Smith & Wesson to the falling man and shot him twice more before he hit the floor.

The train lurched to a stop. Out the windows on the platform the two Campus operators saw a sea of dark blue uniforms running down the staircase twenty-five yards away. The police weren't sure which car they were going for, so there was confusion at the bottom of the stairs.

Chavez turned toward the back of the train, away from the police, and started running. 'We're going for the tunnel!'

They leapt down to the tracks in the gap between the last two cars. Careful to avoid going anywhere near the third rail, they took off to the south.

Two cars behind them, the transit police held their weapons on all the cars. It would be thirty seconds before they boarded and another minute and a half before they suspected someone had left the train to run through the tunnel.

By then Caruso and Chavez were halfway back to 8th Street.

By the time they got to the 8th Street station, Caruso and Chavez had moved to the southbound side of the tracks. Since all the witnesses had climbed out of the subway car onto the northbound platform, the two Campus men expected there would be a police presence at the scene there, and they were right. A dozen or more police in light blue and dark blue uniforms, some carrying carbines or submachine guns, stood around with witnesses and other passersby.

But Chavez and Caruso climbed up on the southbound platform, fifty yards away from the gaggle of cops across the station, and they made it up to street level with no one noticing them.

Sam picked them up a few minutes later and they were back in the 79th Street safe house shortly after that.

By the time Domingo and Dominic sat down with a bottle of water and a gun-cleaning kit, Campus IT staffers had already reviewed all the relevant NYPD and Metropolitan Transportation Authority camera footage in the area, and they saw nothing that identified their two operatives. There was always a chance some kid on the train had gotten his phone out, but this wasn't an event likely to have been recorded, for the simple fact that everyone on that train was in immediate mortal peril and knew reaching for a phone or raising a hand to point a camera might have earned them a bullet to the head.

After spending hours on an after-action hot wash of the event with Clark in the living room of the safe house, they determined they had somehow managed to avoid compromise during the incident. No one had any idea just why the North Koreans were so hell-bent on killing a single member of the Sanctions Committee, but Sam's assertion that Allende and Riley had not managed to come to terms on whatever it was they were meeting about made them all think it likely Riley had notified the North Koreans that the woman knew about the operation to coerce committee members, and the North Koreans decided to silence her before she could talk.

There was a lot of guessing necessary to come to this conclusion, but the facts all seemed to lead in this direction.

Clark said, 'Just like in Vietnam, the North Koreans are playing for absolute keeps on this. In situations where some other bad actor might just pull up stakes and bug out, or else threaten a noncompliant party, the North Koreans are using lethal means. This is an ugly game they are playing, and we cannot make assumptions about how they will act without taking that into consideration.'

35

Adam Yao sat in a glass-walled conference room on the third floor of the Office of the Director of National Intelligence. A window faced southwest and he looked out over a green forested hillside that obstructed the view of anyone driving by on the Capital Beltway. Adam was sure the hill had been built with security in mind, but it was nice to veg out for a minute and gaze at the greenery. But not for long. After a moment he looked down to the reams of books, notes, and briefing papers laid out on the table in front of him.

Time to get back to work.

He had spent a full week of sixteen-hour days prepping for Operation Acrid Herald, the attempt to place a CIA asset into a rare earth mineral mining operation in northwestern North Korea. He would be leaving for the West Coast in the morning, heading to the Valley Floor rare earth mineral mine in California, for more specific training and legend building, before heading to China, where the real work would begin.

Acrid Herald was a code-word operation; only a select few in the US intelligence agency had any inkling what was happening. For purposes of operational security, no one at CIA Station Seoul would be informed, and certainly no personnel from any South Korean intelligence agency would be read in on the plan, because of the likelihood North Korea had a penetration agent high up in the South Korean spy services.

Even most at Langley HQ would be kept away. The op was, instead, run out of an office suite converted into a special operations center at the ODNI's Liberty Crossing complex.

A portion of Adam's week had been spent committing to memory all the code words, call signs, radio frequencies, and other information he would need in his weeks in the danger zone. His code name was Avalanche; this moniker had been computer-generated for him, and Adam liked the sound of it, especially because he'd been told a recent code name generated by the computer for a male agent had been Sunflower.

Adam felt bad for Sunflower, whoever he was, and hoped his mission went off without a hitch. Having to call control to request a quick-reaction-force extract for Agent Sunflower didn't sound like something Adam would much enjoy doing.

He'd take Avalanche any damn day over that. This operation might have been an incredibly difficult and dangerous mission, but, Adam told himself, at least they'd outfitted him with a badass call sign before he left.

While the plan was for Adam Yao to go to Valley Floor to learn the computer system he would be operating in Chongju, he knew he would already need to know his cover legend back-to-front when he got out to California, so he spent the afternoon of his last day here at LX2 digging deeper into his legend. This type of work was familiar to him, learning the life story of a fictional character, and he actually enjoyed the study. He felt like an actor preparing for a role, and although all the lines he would use on the stage would be improvisational, the better he knew his character's upbringing, circumstances, education, and life experiences, the better able he would be to bring his character to life.

According to his legend, Adam was Shan Xin, a thirty-five-year-old mechanical engineer and Chinese national from Nanchang who moved to the US to go to the University of Chicago, but then overstayed his student visa by fourteen years. The gangster miners in Shanghai would be told that he then took a job in the mining sector, where he became an expert in ore-processing machinery, specifically the computers used to operate a hydraulic cone crusher, a massive grinding device that turned the ore into precisely sized smaller bits so that the rare earth minerals contained within could be removed through a series of treatments and processes, depending on the minerals themselves. The CIA had learned through its access to the Chinese gangster mining operation that the North Koreans already had the huge crushing machines, as well as the hydraulic system to operate them, all thanks to the Chinalco operation that had pulled out a year before, but the Chinese had taken their computers with them when Choi threw them out of his country.

A new computer was on the way from France via Bulgaria, and the CIA had already intercepted it at the warehouse of a shipping agent and implanted the hardware that would allow Adam to use the device as something of a direct-line telephone back to his command and control here at ODNI.

The fact Adam, or Shan Xin, had lived and worked in

the US for the past eighteen years would account for both his knowledge of the equipment and the fact no one in the illegal mining company had ever heard of him. As with all undercover work, of course, there was always the chance Adam would run into someone who had been to the places Adam claimed to have visited or knew the people Adam claimed to have known, so it was crucial he got his legend information down cold to pull this off.

Like every good non-official cover officer, Adam was an expert at the ability to fold his own life experiences into his backstory; this always helped with a cover story, because the more truth involved, the less the chance to be caught in a deception.

And he would hide the fact that he spoke Korean. He and his control officers on Acrid Herald were working under the assumption the North Koreans might speak more freely around the Chinese workers than they would if they knew one of their number could understand them. The relationship between the North Korean minders and the illegal Chinese workers was sure to be unforthcoming, and the CIA knew they wanted to hear as much as possible from the Koreans that was not filtered through channels going to the Chinese.

Adam's Korean wasn't great, but he was trying to 'crash-course' his skill level up a notch with intensive language study on top of all the other work he was doing. This morning he'd worked on his language skills with a native Korean speaker, a translator and trainer at CIA. Additionally, he had listened to recordings in the evening for the past few nights, and this had retuned his brain to the language somewhat, but today they focused on vocabulary specific to the mining industry.

Adam's study wouldn't end when he left Virginia for California. Instead, he would travel to Valley Floor with his instructor, Myun, and she would play the role of his wife so they could spend the evenings studying together.

He expected to be in Valley Floor no more than a week and a half, but another ten days of language study might just make the difference between success and failure on the operation.

And it didn't bother Adam Yao at all that Myun was an attractive woman. Unfortunately for him, she was married, and her husband, a blond-haired, blue-eyed CIA analyst from Boston, had popped in on them in the language lab a couple times. He seemed to Yao to be a nice enough guy, and although he didn't know the nature of Yao's operation or where Yao and his wife would be heading, overall he projected an air of support.

It was going to be weird to live in an apartment for a week and a half with a married woman, but Adam knew this wasn't the weirdest thing he'd done working as a spy.

Normal rules did not apply in this life.

It was late afternoon now; he closed up one briefing book and reached for another. Just as he started to settle into some reading on ore processing, Mary Pat Foley knocked on the glass door to the conference room.

Adam waved her in and stood.

'Sorry to bother you, Adam.'

'Not at all,' Adam said. 'It's nice to see you again.'

She paused for a moment, then said, 'Acrid Herald is a go. You leave in the morning.'

'Outstanding.'

She and Yao both sat down.

'They're working you hard?'

'I've got the legend memorized. I've got the codes and commo tech down cold. I've boned up on the processing of ore and the mechanics of the crushing systems in place there, but I'll learn the actual computer software in California. I'll keep working on my language.' He nodded. 'I'll do my part in Acrid Herald.'

Mary Pat said, 'And I'll do mine, and see that others do theirs. I won't micromanage this op, but I'll be getting twice-daily updates from your control officers. I recognize the risks. I know I won't be in the field with you . . . but –'

'Madame Director, I know you've spent a good part of your career in the field. Trust me, the fact you know what it's like is very much appreciated at a time like this.'

Foley smiled.

Adam gave her a moment to reply, but when he realized she was holding back, he added, 'And although I appreciate you coming to see me off, I am wondering if there is something specific you wanted to tell me.'

She looked out the window and over the trees. 'I lost a good friend recently. An operative, not too unlike yourself, although much older. He was one hell of a foot soldier during the Cold War and even beyond.'

Adam cleared his throat uncomfortably. 'You *lost* him?'

'Murdered,' she acknowledged. 'He was out of the Agency, but he did die in the field. We don't know for sure, but it's quite possible North Korean assets killed him.'

'I'm a little curious as to why I didn't hear anything about this in my workup for the op.'

'He wasn't on official Agency work. He freelanced for a corporate intelligence firm. There is no known relationship between him and what is going on here. Not yet, anyway.'

Yao said nothing.

'In my job it doesn't pay to be sentimental, but I look at it like this. The moment I become something other than a human being, I need to get out of this line of work.'

'Understandable.'

'I know about everything that happened in China last year.'

'Yes, ma'am,' he said.

She leaned forward a little. 'And I know about Jack Junior.'

Yao had met the son of the President of the United States in Hong Kong. Ryan had claimed to be working for a private investment company at the time, but soon enough Yao figured out that was a cover story for an intelligence mission Ryan was working. POTUS's kid wasn't CIA, that much was clear, but it was also clear that Ryan Junior was in direct comms with Director of National Intelligence Mary Pat Foley. Yao had thought it almost comically surreal at the time when he and the President's son snuck over the border and onto the Chinese mainland, but the joke ended quickly when the shooting war started.

Yao and Ryan had accomplished their mission, and Ryan had kept quiet about who, exactly, he was working for. Yao had been told once, upon his return to the States, to keep Jack Ryan, Jr., out of his reports. No other mention had been made of the President's son, and Yao had certainly told no one.

He knew that Mary Pat was aware of Ryan's involvement in the Chinese operation, but he certainly did not expect her to talk to him about it, so this moment was a little awkward.

'Yes, ma'am,' he said.

'That's a complicated issue, and one that does not affect your work on this operation, but I do make mention of it to say I know you are going into harm's way with some specific knowledge that must not fall into enemy hands.'

Yao wondered if Foley was going to give him a cyanide pill. *Holy shit, that happens only in the movies, right?*

'Yes, ma'am,' he said again. With a nervous chuckle he said, 'I certainly won't mention it.' He worried that comment sounded sarcastic, so he was pleased to see Foley shrug, as if the matter was put to bed.

She then said, 'I am sure your control talked to you about in extremis extraction options.' She was talking about his ability to escape in an emergency.

'You mean the lack thereof?'

Foley nodded. 'Yes. Your best bet is to head for the Chinese border if compromised. It's guarded and patrolled, but the natural impediments to getting across, mountains and rivers and such, are relied on by both sides to some degree. It would be hard to get into China, but in an emergency, attempting it is your best course of action.'

'Yes, I've been briefed and I've memorized the routes.'

She added, 'It's also important you realize that even if you do make it over the border, you are not safe. We could get you back if you are picked up by the Chinese, but North Korean agents also patrol inside the Chinese border, looking for defectors and spies. If they catch you they will pull you back over the Yalu River and into the DPRK.'

Adam blew out a sigh. He knew this, but it was hard to take. 'Right. That does complicate an extraction via China.' He and his control officers had considered sewing forged papers into his clothing to help him in the event of an overland escape into China. They went as far as creating an identity card that claimed him to be a resident of Liaoning Province, which bordered North Korea.

But ultimately they decided against it. As much as Yao would have liked to know he had a way out of North Korea in the case of emergency, the possibility the North Koreans would find the ID card and identify him as a spy had been too great. So in the end, he decided to go in 'naked.'

If he was caught in China by the Chinese, he would be thrown into prison. If he was caught on either side of the border by the DPRK, he would be executed.

Foley said, 'There is another option to get you out of the country. It would be in a worst-case scenario.'

Adam hadn't been told of other options. 'I'm all ears.'

'Actually, this is something from a code-word access program that you don't need to know about.' She paused. 'Unless, of course, you do. I'm asking you to trust me on this one. Trust me that we will do our best to get to you if something unforeseen happens.'

Adam had no idea what she was talking about, or why she'd even mentioned it, but he thanked her anyway.

After a time Mary Pat stood, shook Adam's hand, and said, 'Good luck, Avalanche. Remember, we need that intelligence, but we need men like you even more. Err on the side of personal safety.'

'Thank you, Madame Director,' said Yao.

'I look forward to welcoming you home when you are done.'

Yao smiled. 'I look forward to *coming* home when I'm done.'

36

They had run out of coffee in the safe house, and John Clark found this wholly unacceptable. After the shootout, Sam, Ding, and Dom were all out this morning tailing a Sharps employee named Bridgeforth, and Clark decided he had time to run out to a coffee shop to grab a cup. As far as he was concerned, he would have just gone into the first 7-Eleven, or whatever the little bodegas around here were called – he didn't need anything more fancy than a hot jolt of caffeine – but the closest place to him was actually right next door to his condo building down at street level, so he stepped in there.

Within ten seconds he turned to step back out, the place was too damn crowded, but there were already four college-age kids behind him in a line that blocked the exit, so with a sigh he decided to stick it out and wait his turn.

The crowd was heavy, even at nine forty-five in the morning when most of these young people should have been, at least as far as Clark was concerned, at work. The establishment was far too trendy for Clark's taste; he was the oldest patron in sight by at least a quarter-century, and when he scanned the large menu handwritten in chalk on a board on the wall, he saw this roaster – the joint was even too pretentious to call itself a coffee shop – served every imaginable permutation of beans and teas and soy and foam. He rolled his eyes at the seemingly never-ending options of syrups and caramels and cookie bits and protein powders that could be added to the drink.

As he waited in line he had every intention of asking the waifish pixie behind the counter with the pin through her septum if he could, by any slim chance, purchase a regular *goddamned* cup of coffee, but fortunately for all involved, he had time to kill, and he spent the time rereading the choices of sixty or seventy drinks on the board. To his relief, on his second scan of the menu he finally saw that the establishment would be able to accommodate his outlandish request for a simple cup of black joe.

His transaction went smoothly, he even calmed a bit and bought himself a multigrain bagel, and he sat down at a small bistro table in the back. There was a *New York Times* on the seat next to him, so he picked it up and began looking at the front page.

President Ryan was taking heat from the *Times* for his stance on North Korea. Clark didn't have to turn to the editorial section to see this; the invective came through in a front-page above-the-fold 'straight news' piece. The procedural vote next week was going to be tight, and the *Times* reported on North Korea's promises to use its bank accounts to help its citizenry. The North Koreans said any restriction on their ability to do this would starve innocent civilians.

The *Times* was pushing a 'trust but verify' line, giving the DPRK the room it needed to handle its banking affairs so it could spend the hard currency in its overseas bank accounts, with the caveat that Western accounting inspectors spot-check more financial transactions to make sure the DPRK wasn't earning offshore monies via drugs or counterfeiting or illegal weapons sales.

Clark rolled his eyes. He was no accountant himself, but he sure knew assholes, and this made him an expert on Choi. He knew without reservation the lunatic kid running North Korea couldn't be trusted to open his accounting ledgers to inspectors.

If the UN Sanctions Committee vote failed, then Choi would keep his worldwide criminal enterprises operating; and either he would give the UN cooked books to look through or else he would rope-a-dope them with obfuscations and delays, and it would be half a decade before the UN would pronounce him in violation of the agreement and do anything about it.

And in five years Choi could have the ICBM he was after, and when that happened, the UN wouldn't do a damn thing to stop him ever again.

Clark tossed the paper on the table in frustration, and then looked up quickly when he realized a man was seating himself right in front of him at his little two-top.

The man had wavy blond hair streaked with gray, a ruddy complexion, and a big grin on his face.

Well, shit, Clark said to himself.

It was Duke Sharps.

Clark showed no surprise, and he said nothing, he just gazed at the man in front of him with eyes that were too cold to read.

Sharps kept his smile wide. Clark was pretty sure he was looking at veneers, and the man's blue double-breasted blazer and striped shirt made him look to John like he should have been sitting on a yacht in Palm Beach instead of in a hipster coffee shop in Manhattan.

Duke said, 'John Clark. It has been one hell of a long while. How are you, brother?' He extended a hand and Clark reluctantly shook it.

He was waiting for the man's pitch or threat, whichever way Sharps was going to play it. Sharps, however, was in no rush.

'When and where was the last time we ran into one another? It was after I left the Bureau. You were at Rainbow. Was it over in the UK?'

'What can I do for you, Sharps?'

'Right to the chase? Not going to waste my time, I see. I respect that.' Sharps picked up the copy of the *Times* and pointed to the article Clark had just been reading. 'A blind squirrel finds a nut once in a while. No big fan of the *Times*, but they are right on this one. North Korea isn't the bad guy here. They have as much right to interact in the marketplace as any other country. As long as they are not proliferating weapons, how dare Jack *fucking* Ryan tell them where they can put their money and how they can spend it?'

Clark snorted a little. 'When did you become a card-carrying member of the Fair Play for the DPRK Committee?' Clark's reference was to Lee Harvey Oswald. He had worked for the Fair Play for Cuba Committee, an organization that protested the US government's heavy-handed tactics over the communist island.

Sharps chuckled. After a moment he said, 'I'm in the right on this one, Clark, but my high school debate team days are long behind me. I'm not going to try to convince you.' He leaned forward on his elbows. His smile dissipated. 'An associate of mine mentioned he happened to notice a known colleague of yours down in Turtle Bay yesterday. I guess it could have been a coincidence, but it got me thinking. You're an old fox like I am, and you know there is no such thing as a chance encounter. I snooped into your colleague, which led me to you. My man was on the job, and this leads me to believe you are on the job in some capacity as well. You aren't with the Agency anymore, not even as a training cadre, so I'm guessing you're doing contract work for someone.'

Sharps leaned closer. 'Maybe some people are still scared of you. You're an old snake eater, after all. But as far as I'm concerned, the operative word is "old."'

Clark was not a snake eater, old or otherwise. That was an archaic term used for Green Berets, US Army Special Forces, and Clark had been a Navy SEAL. He didn't expect Sharps to know the difference, and he didn't bother to correct him.

The sixty-year-old Sharps said, 'I sit before you as a pro-fessional courtesy. I am here to kindly ask you to pack up your op and take your gang of washed-up boys down to Penn Station and put them, along with yourself, back on a train for DC You're out of your element here. My guys and your guys keep bumping into one another . . . and somebody is going to get themselves hurt.'

Clark's jaw tensed, clamping down tight to keep from saying what he wanted to say. He knew he had to take whatever Sharps dished out as a short-term tactical defeat. Sharps had somehow compromised his operation, and this was a terrible blow, but Clark identified something quickly. Sharps had misidentified what Clark's operation was all about. He clearly thought Clark was working some sort of counterintelligence contract job for one of the foreign embassies or UN delegations. This would have been highly illegal, but Sharps wasn't objecting on moral or legal grounds. No, his quarrel with Clark was that he thought Clark was trying to protect one of the delegates Sharps and Riley had been targeting.

If Clark pushed back at this moment, it would just up Sharps's level of curiosity. Much better, Clark realized, for him to make Sharps think he'd won, that it was all over.

Clark, for the first time in this conversation and for one of the first times in his life, demurred.

With a long, slow nod he said, 'You can't get good help these days. My crew blew it. Fucking Keystone Kops.'

He saw the glint in Sharps's eye, the look of a man full of his own power and worth. A winner, glorious in his victory but forcing a magnanimous comment. He said, 'It happens, friend. Maybe my crew just got lucky.'

Clark pulled his phone out of his pocket and dialed Ding. When he answered, Clark said, 'Go back to the place, break it all down. Get yourself and the others to Penn Station in ninety minutes.' A pause. 'Just do it. I'll see you there.' Clark hung up and slipped the phone back in his jeans.

The glint in Sharps's eye remained.

Clark shrugged like a man who knew he was busted, but a man acting like it was no big deal. 'What the hell, the money wasn't what we thought it was going to be, anyway. Shitty per diem. You'd think they had us working in Port-au-Prince for what they were giving us for food and booze.'

Sharps smiled. 'Ouch.' With a nonchalance that Clark read as bullshit he said, 'Since it doesn't matter anymore, maybe you'll tell me. Which delegation were you working for? My guess is Chile, or Denmark, but I'm prepared for you to surprise me.'

Clark put up an apologetic hand and gave his shoulders another huge shrug. 'C'mon, Duke. We're running home with our tails between our legs on this one. Allow me to retain a modicum of self-respect by not having me completely lose my professional decorum and reveal my client's identity.'

Sharps said, 'You had a lot of glory days in your career. One hell of a good run. Everybody gets old. Everybody loses their touch.' He smiled, a look that seemed like he felt sorry for the old man in front of him. 'Just as there was honor in being the best, there is also honor in knowing when it's over.'

Clark took three slow breaths, forced his blood pressure back down a notch, then stood and extended his hand. 'Thanks, Duke. I owe you.'

Duke Sharps shook Clark's hand, but he did not get up.

Clark pushed his way through a crowd of hipsters, left the coffee shop, and walked back to the safe house. He assumed he was being watched, but Sharps had known he was in the 79th Street coffee shop, which surely meant he knew Clark's operation was set up at the building next door.

*

Five minutes later, Clark entered the safe house.

Sam and Dom were hurriedly packing up equipment, but Ding was standing in the middle of the room with a Glock pistol on his hip and a worried look on his face. 'You okay?'

'I'll be better after I vomit.'

'What happened?'

'Sharps compromised us. I don't know how he did it, but he did.'

Sam said, 'So we're all leaving?'

'No,' Clark said. 'Sam, you are staying here. You'll get an apartment or a hotel room with eyes on the front of Sharps's building, and you will lock yourself in and stay out of sight. You'll keep watch on who comes and goes into that entire building. It will be a shitty job, but you'll have facial recog and video equipment to help you.'

'No problem,' Sam said.

'As for the rest of us, we're going home, but we'll be back.'

'What about the UN vote?' asked Caruso.

'My guess is the rules vote will end up "no," and the Sanctions Committee will not hear the petition to extend the economic sanctions on North Korea.'

Caruso couldn't believe it. 'So Sharps wins? Just like that?'

'He wins a battle, but only that. I'm going to take down that son of a bitch, and nothing I've ever done will give me greater pleasure.'

37

Iranian bomb maker Adel Zarif arrived in Mexico City using his Syrian papers after flying from Pyongyang to Havana, where he had to wait a day for his connection. Even in Cuba he'd been watched over by North Korean RGB minders, who allowed him freedom of action but little freedom of movement.

On touchdown at Mexico City's Benito Juárez International Airport he expected to be met by RGB, but instead a single Maldonado cartel member was waiting in the arrivals section for him. He gave his name as Emilio, and he spoke English. Zarif had learned English in Lebanon, and although his knowledge of the language was not as good as Emilio's, they were able to communicate without any problems.

Together they drove to a building on a congested intersection in the downtown Tepito section of the city. Zarif was taken to a second-floor safe house that was guarded by three other men, all of whom seemed to be in their early twenties.

He was given his own small apartment in a back corner of the safe house, and a stocked refrigerator full of Pacífico beer that he would not drink and foreign food he would not eat, and he had Emilio at his beck and call, which meant sending him out to get meat and salad and bread and bottled water.

And a laptop computer. Zarif had a lot of work to do to pull off this Mexico operation, and he did not want to spend his time sitting around in some apartment waiting for something to happen.

At the end of the first day Emilio delivered Zarif a clean cell phone and a used laptop, and once he leeched onto the Wi-Fi signal from an Internet café downstairs, he was able to begin his research and start his operation.

He had been told that Maldonado had men working in the Federal Police, and they would meet with him five days before the American President's arrival to go over the motorcade route. In the meantime, however, Zarif spent virtually all his time on YouTube, pulling up clips of previous presidential visits to the city.

From the beginning he knew the President's arrival was the best time for him to act. Even if he had a perfect itinerary for the official visit to go on, there would be so many unknown variables at each location that his chances of success would be low.

But two absolutes, he knew already, were that the President would land at Benito Juárez airport, and then he would go via motorcade to the Palacio Nacional in the center of the city, where he would meet with President Lopez of Mexico.

With two fixed points to work with, he then had only to observe previous motorcades' movements through the city to get a feeling for the route. Yes, Zarif knew the US Secret Service would do what they could to change the route from other visits, but there almost always existed unavoidable repetitions, usually nearest to the beginning and ending of the route, where the President's vehicle would necessarily have to pass.

He watched video after video, official films, documentaries in Spanish and English and even Chinese, as well as dozens upon dozens of jerky and blurry camera-phone street-level clips, and he pored over every frame, doing his best to match locations in the videos to places he could pinpoint on Google Maps. Using the Street View feature, he'd made his own maps, and it was a slow and laborious process, but from time to time he would ask for Emilio's help in identifying a street or a building in the videos. From this Zarif managed to trace his best estimate of the route taken by every official motorcade coming from the airport on record.

After working for two days on little else, he had identified four locations where every official motorcade from Benito Juárez to the Palacio Nacional passed.

This was progress, but he knew he was doing this backward. He had no access to explosives himself; those had to be provided to him. Furthermore, he had no idea what he would be given to work with. Without this information, he found it impossible to pinpoint an exact location for his action. The conditions on the street would normally determine what kind of weapon he chose, but in this instance, the weaponry he was given access to would determine where he would place it.

On the third day Zarif met with two Maldonado men who were also members of the Federal District police force. These men knew details of the upcoming presidential visit, and they confirmed Zarif's assumption about the general route of the motorcade.

He showed them four locations he'd circled on a map, and he asked them to drive him to each so he could take a look. Along with Emilio, the men immediately piled into a new Cadillac Escalade driven by yet another Maldonado member, and the five took off into the city.

Zarif had spent the last few years in Syria, and there, even in government-held Damascus, he never went anywhere without a small team of armed and trained men who were always on the lookout for attackers. But here in Mexico City, despite what he'd heard about how dangerous the place was, he felt incredibly safe.

A few blocks from his Tepito safe house they stopped at a streetlight. On the sidewalk next to him he saw two blond-haired young women. The driver of his car rolled his window down and whistled, and one of the women laughed and spoke back in English.

The Mexican driver turned to Zarif in the backseat. 'American girls.' He smiled and Zarif turned and stared at them.

He was going to change their world when he killed their President, and they didn't even know it.

The first location on the agenda was near the airport, on Oriente 172. Zarif saw in the open-source videos that every motorcade passed by here after leaving a VIP airport gate. Immediately he disregarded this as a potential attack point. On Street View he had not noticed any obvious problems with the surroundings, but in person he saw there was a police checkpoint just up the street. No matter what kind of bomb he would plant, he wouldn't just be placing a backpack on the ground and walking away. Zarif's kind of high-yield bombs required hours at the location to construct and secure them, and of course he needed to do this with utmost care. He couldn't be worrying about the cops two blocks away while he was laboring over his device.

The second location was on a wide road in a warehouse district near the airport. He'd been told the area was quiet at night, and that sounded good, but Zarif thought the sidewalks on either side of the street were too empty. He could set the bomb here with no problem, but no matter how well he hid it he felt it was likely it would be discovered before the event.

Zarif knew all about how the US Secret Service would comb the motorcade route on the day before the action – his bomb needed to be invisible for this operation to have any chance for success.

The third location was at the other end of the route, much closer to the President's destination, the Palacio Nacional in the Centro Histórico. This was a wide north-south street running through Tepito called Vidal Alcocer, with low buildings and construction on one side of the street and parking lots on the other.

From the outset Zarif felt like the intersection had potential. There was a market on the two-lane street that entered the intersection from the east and west, and this meant a lot of traffic, especially now at four in the afternoon. In the evening, on the other hand, he felt the area might have been quieter, as there were no residential buildings for several blocks.

He looked at the construction site on the corner, then he turned to his contact. 'Is there a way we could arrange a visit to that unfinished building?'

Emilio looked at him, somewhat perplexed, then he just climbed out of the Cadillac and began walking across the street. Zarif followed after a moment. Emilio walked right up to the orange plastic tarp barrier, ducked down, and lifted it up for the bomber.

Zarif crawled in and began looking around. The construction site was obviously dormant. It appeared nothing had happened here in weeks or months, although the smell of concrete and plaster and dust was prevalent.

From the shape of the floors and the poured-concrete ramp it seemed to Zarif that this place was going to be a parking garage of some sort. The northern and western walls already were poured, there was a framed staircase that was built up three stories in the center of the property, but the southern and eastern sides of the building stood open, save for some areas where metal beams and an open rebar grid had been set.

There were walls going up here, or at least there had been before the project shut down. Now it was just a twelve-foot-tall net of thick iron and steel, waiting for tons and tons of poured concrete.

Zarif walked over to the rebar on the eastern side, and he put his hands inside the latticework of hot metal.

Here. Here exactly. Ten feet off the ground and facing out, he would build his bomb and he would fill in the concrete around it. If he put a steel plate in back to direct the force toward the street, and if he covered it all uniformly, it would appear to be a new wall, nothing more.

Of course, Zarif did have one problem. He couldn't very well just take over construction of a downtown parking lot on his own.

'Emilio,' he said, 'I need a construction team, and some way we can work in here without anyone stopping us.'

'*No hay problema.*' No problem.

Zarif smiled. He still didn't know anything about the bomb he would be using in this operation, and this was a problem, but he had no complaints about the level of service he was getting from his local contacts. The Maldonado people moved around and acted with all the authority of the Syrian Army back in Damascus.

38

Gavin had spent the first couple days after the debacle in Prague absolutely useless to anyone. He was so downtrodden he'd barely shown up for work, he'd done little more than sit at his desk, and other than making excuses about a cold he'd picked up during all the international running around he'd done a few days earlier, he barely spoke to his coworkers.

But by the end of his third day something clicked in him. He needed to make himself useful here in the office, because he had proven to be utterly useless in the field.

His subordinates in the IT department here at Hendley Associates, assisted by the analytical staff in the building, had been overseeing the Clark operation up in New York City. He'd heard earlier in the day that the operation had folded, and the men were on their way back to the DC area.

Just as his staff were shutting down their machines to go home for the evening, Gavin stepped out of his office and asked his chief analytical systems engineer to fill him in on the operation. He led Gavin through a forty-five-minute primer on the steps he had taken to provide intelligence to Clark and his team in New York.

Needless to say, Biery's team of first-rate hackers had, at first, tried to find a way to hack into the Sharps computer network. But they'd been unable to crack the secure infrastructure, so they moved on to digging into the personalities working for the company. At this task they'd had great success. All this information had helped Clark and his team locate Riley and his subordinates during the operation, and they'd photographed them meeting with United Nations personnel, but they were unable to find a smoking gun that could have proven Sharps Partners was either actively interfering with the Sanctions Committee vote or working with the North Korean state.

Gavin knew what The Campus needed right now. They needed some access into the Sharps network, so he went back into his office. The small amount of staff still in the IT department all grabbed their briefcases and headed for the doors, and they assumed Gavin would do the same, but instead he sat at his desk and started his work.

He told himself he was going to find a way into the network of Sharps Global Intelligence Partners.

Six hours later it was midnight, and he'd gotten nowhere. Sharps's system was ironclad. But unfortunately for Sharps, Gavin was not one to give up easily, so he ate a candy bar, changed his attack vector, and went back to work.

Jack Ryan, Jr., knocked his cell phone off the night table in his attempt to pick it up with a sleeping hand. Before he crawled off his bed to find the ringing phone on the floor, he looked at the clock at his bedside and saw it was three forty-eight a.m. A wave of panic nearly overcame him; he always thought about his dad when the phone rang at night. He knew his father was at once one of the most loved and most hated people in the world, depending on one's point of view, and he knew there was always someone out there planning harm to him.

As he snatched up the phone to look at the caller ID he told himself there was a more likely explanation for the late call. It could be Gavin. Gavin worked all hours of the night, and he didn't think twice about calling Jack when the mood arose. Jack had complained about it before, but Gavin kept on, and by now Jack had given up the fight.

The caller ID read 'Biery.'

Ryan was relieved it wasn't the White House calling, but he wasn't thrilled about the early wake-up call.

'*Damn it*, Gav.'

'Careful what you say, Ryan, you're just going to have to take it all back when I tell you what I've got to tell you.'

Jack was sitting on the floor next to his bed now, his body half wrapped in the sheets. With a yawn he said, 'What's up?'

'Been working the last nine hours and forty-three minutes trying to get into Duke Sharps's network. Gotta tell ya, his IT personnel are top-notch. The infrastructure is about as solid as I've ever –'

'I'm warning you, man. Tell me something I care about in five seconds or I'm hanging up.'

Gavin said, 'The blonde you saw in Vietnam, the one you've probably been dreaming about for the past few weeks? She is in the USA right now, operating under the alias of Élise Legrande, working at a rare earth mineral – processing plant in California near the Nevada border.'

Jack rolled up to his knees and turned on the light next to the bed.

Gavin said, 'Got your attention, didn't I?'

'Yeah, you did. Your facial recog came up blank on her. But you found her in Sharps's network?'

'Not exactly. I ran facial recog on people coming and

going at Sharps's building. From that I managed to ID a woman who works for a small boutique graphic-arts and printing company in Greenwich Village. I looked into the woman and saw she'd done time for forgery, and I researched her company and saw some of the equipment they owned. All top-of-the-line badge-making and Auto-CAD stuff. I thought that seemed interesting, wondered if maybe Sharps farmed out some of their credential-making work, either for alias travel or fake employment badges for covers. I spent a couple hours hacking into the printer's networks, haven't gotten too deep yet but was able to break into files stored on a cloud server for them. Did some digging there and found a full set of credentials for your dream girl. Definitely the same woman.'

'And she's working at a rare earth refinery?'

'Yes. She has a Canadian passport, a temp worker visa, and employment credentials at a rare earth consulting company in Ottawa called TRU Alloy. The worker visa gave me the idea that she would be working at a rare earth facility here in the States, and since there is only one major location, I did some open-source poking around on the NewCorp Valley Floor website. There is a note on an online bulletin board that one Élise Legrande from TRU Alloy arrived on Thursday, and she'll be there for the next few days monitoring the use of some new equipment.'

'I'll be damned, Gavin. That's good work.'

'I know.' He paused. 'I also know this doesn't get me off the hook for Prague.'

'Prague was my mistake, not yours, Gavin. You can't keep beating yourself up over it. You are too important to this or-ganization. You accomplished more last night than all of us in the operations staff managed to accomplish in Prague and New York.'

Gavin brightened a little. 'Thanks, Ryan. So, you think Gerry will let you go to Valley Floor?'

'I hope so. He was pissed about Prague, but now that the New York op has run into problems, we don't have much left to go on. If this woman is working for Sharps, she might just be the link we need to tie them to North Korea.'

Mary Pat Foley made her second visit to the offices of Hendley Associates on a stormy afternoon, and she found the mood in the building wasn't much better than the weather outside.

The UN Sanctions Committee procedural rules vote had taken place days ago and the Ryan administration had come out the loser. The vote failed; at least for the next 180 days, there could be no hearing on further economic sanctions against North Korea.

Everyone in the fourth-floor conference room at Hendley Associates knew the reason for the poor result. Several Sanctions Committee personnel had been influenced by Sharps Global Intelligence Partners. This could not be proven without a major Justice Department investigation, and as much as Mary Pat and the members of The Campus all wanted to shut Sharps down cold, none of them wanted to spin up the Justice Department on a process that would undoubtedly take longer than it would for the DPRK to acquire an arsenal of nuclear-tipped ICBMs.

No, Mary Pat was confident that The Campus could take the lead in monitoring the work of Sharps and his operational commander in the North Korea situation,

Edward Riley. Even though The Campus had been compromised in New York, they had the talent and the resources to keep at it, and they didn't have nearly the potential for compromise a federal bureaucracy like the Justice Department would have, where Sharps had feelers, informants, and access into virtually every corridor.

The discovery of a Sharps infiltrator at Valley Floor had been a huge revelation, and it gave her renewed confidence in The Campus. When Jack Ryan, Jr., revealed this to her, and outlined his plan to go to the facility himself, Mary Pat made a silent mental note to inform the handlers of Operation Acrid Herald. She saw no reason to believe her officer in place at Valley Floor, Adam Yao, was in any danger because of the Sharps woman – they worked in wholly different facilities at the large complex – but it was one more moving piece that needed to be monitored nonetheless.

For her part, Mary Pat did not mention a word of Acrid Herald to the men of The Campus, but she did pass on some information helpful to their operation. She informed them about construction of a mineral-processing facility near the city of Chongju in northwestern DPRK. She also revealed the existence of an unknown foreign benefactor who was providing the North Koreans with, at a minimum, tens of millions of dollars that they were in turn using to procure updated missile technology.

The Campus would keep digging into the Sharps operation, which they all thought to be merely a tiny piece of the larger North Korean scheme, but the fact that Sharps Partners had managed to influence a critical vote in the United Nations made it obvious it was a damn important piece.

39

Jack Ryan, Jr., flew to Las Vegas along with Domingo Chavez and John Clark in the Hendley Associates jet, and the three men took separate rooms in the Mandarin Oriental on the Strip. They checked into their rooms and then met to coordinate their plan of action.

Ryan would be going into the NewCorp Valley Floor facility the next morning. His visit had been arranged beforehand, and he felt ready.

He would be using an unusual cover on this operation – none at all. By the time they found out about the woman's work there – they were calling her Élise because they did not know her true identity – they knew there wasn't much time to build an ironclad and backstopped legend for one of the Campus men, and then put him in place as part of a large-scale operation to find out what was going on. And by the time they got him up and running at Valley Floor, Élise might well have concluded her operation and moved on.

Instead, Gerry Hendley himself said he could simply make a couple phone calls, establish his interest in an investment, and have Ryan on his way in twenty-four hours using the 'white side' of the house as a perfect excuse to obtain access to the facility.

When Ryan arrived, no one doubted him at NewCorp. Ryan was a financial analyst for Hendley Associates, and he had come to Valley Floor because his firm was considering buying shares in NewCorp in general and this facility in particular. The US had been ramping up its rare earth industry over the past few years, as China began to have trouble meeting demand for its own needs in the commodity, and it was quite common for NewCorp executives to indulge accountants and financial analysts from investment firms who wanted to come for the tour and an examination of the processes and financials.

Of course, Ryan was aware of the fact a massive new deposit of rare earth minerals had been discovered, and this might have the effect of making the NewCorp shares all but worthless, if not for the fact the deposit had been found in an area where easy extraction was nearly impossible.

Jack certainly had no plans to discuss North Korea with the Valley Floor officials here. He had to show real interest in investing, and for that to look legit, he couldn't be running around talking about a deposit somewhere else exponentially larger than what was under his feet right now.

Jack's one objective at the facility was to make contact with Élise Legrande, or whatever the real name of the agent was. He needed to find out what she was doing at Valley Floor, to connect her mission, through Sharps, back to North Korea. If he could do this, he could stop Sharps and his operation, and he might be able to thwart whatever high-level industrial espionage she had in store.

The corporate announcement of Legrande's visit to the facility mentioned the department she'd be working in,

Hydrometallurgy Quality Control. Needless to say, Ryan planned on getting a tour of this area of the complex as soon as possible, in hope of running into the Sharps employee operating under the Canadian cover.

Jack didn't even know if she was really Canadian. He doubted it. If he had to guess, the Canadian legend was an easy cover for her because she was actually French. He made this determination because Canada's intelligence agencies worked relatively closely with their American counterparts, and so far they'd been able to find no identification for the woman. The French played their spooks closer to the vest, keeping them out of sight from the US much more than the Canadians did.

Ryan knew at some point he'd have to meet her to be able to get close enough to skim her electronic devices. Clark had warned him to be especially careful with his 'bump,' the process of making contact with someone in a way that is meant to appear accidental. Sharps did not hire junior intelligence officers, after all, so she would be on the lookout for an enemy approach that appeared casual.

His first opportunity for the bump came much faster than he'd anticipated.

In the late afternoon of his first day in the offices of Valley Floor, Ryan walked alone from his temporary office up a hallway on his way to a meeting with one of the company's accountants. He was a little lost, but that was no big surprise. Valley Floor was a big complex, with more than a dozen buildings in all; this Ryan learned during a two-hour facility tour he took earlier in the day.

He'd been taken out to the open mine, the water-treatment complex, and the ore-processing facility, as well as the R&D buildings and even the motor pool, where he got a look at the impressive massive earthmoving equipment.

Now, as he looked at a small map in his hand to make sure he was going in the right direction, he was glad his meeting was in the same building as his office. He knew he'd really get himself lost on the other end of the facility. He'd made it halfway up the hall when a door opened just ahead of him on his left, and the woman he'd last seen on a busy street in Ho Chi Minh City stepped out.

Jack had been moving quickly to his meeting, but he slowed as the blonde turned to shut the door behind her. She wouldn't have seen the change in his gait, and he needed a second to come up with a spur-of-the-moment introduction.

She looked at him and he smiled, but before he could form a greeting he heard someone call out from behind. 'Élise? There you are. We were supposed to meet in the second-floor lab. That's where the server is.'

She looked away from Ryan and toward a man behind him. With a soft French-Canadian accent she said, 'Yes, I am sorry, Ralph.' She laughed self-deprecatingly. 'I'm still getting lost around here.'

Jack walked on. He was pretty certain she'd almost been caught in the act of lurking around the building, but he was just as sure that she'd managed to wiggle her way out of it without raising the suspicions of whomever she was talking to.

As he turned at the end of the hall he looked back over his shoulder and saw the woman walking away with the man who had been speaking to her. Jack recognized the man from the tour of the plant he'd taken earlier in the day. He was Ralph Baggett, the NewCorp Valley Floor IT director.

Immediately Ryan tried to determine if there was any significance to this. Could she be in the process of ingratiating herself to him as part of her mission here?

With nothing else to go on, Ryan decided he'd gin up a reason to meet with Ralph Baggett tomorrow, to see what he could find.

During his long drive back to his Las Vegas Strip hotel, Ryan called Gavin Biery in Alexandria to see if he could shed some light on what the woman might be up to. He filled Gavin in on how he had seen her around the IT guy, and snooping around the systems themselves, and from that he had determined the IT department was her particular focus.

'As it should be. That's where the action is,' Biery said, making a joke Ryan didn't have time for.

'Seriously. What's her objective? Any guesses?'

Gavin didn't have to think. 'A password. Credentials to get into the system.'

'What could she do with that?'

Biery sighed, as if it was self-evident. 'Ryan, I've held your hand through this stuff before.'

'Indulge me.'

'Keys to the kingdom. She logs on as him and she can insert viruses if she wants, or erase drives or commit untold damage to the physical system of the place by running equipment improperly. Several years ago we blew up some turbines in an Iranian nuclear reactor by uploading some malware.'

Jack thought that over. 'No. If the North Koreans get the rare earth – processing facility set up, they will be at such a competitive advantage as compared to this place that there will be no competition. NewCorp has to pay US wages to extract and process, the North Koreans will pay their people chicken feed. She's not here to hurt Valley Floor, she's here to take something that the North Koreans need.'

Gavin thought for a long while. Finally he said, 'You got me there, Ryan. Unless she wants instructions on how to work machinery, or some sort of in-house database of experts, I can't really say.'

Jack knew he'd have to figure this out for himself.

Biery then said, 'If you think she's trying to get info from them, she'll have to put it somewhere.'

Jack said, 'Like on a drive or something?'

'Yeah, but you don't really need a dedicated piece of equipment. A better bet would be to make it part of something she carries all the time. My guess would be her mobile phone.'

'So . . . I should just snatch her phone? Like what we didn't pull off in Prague?'

'Yeah. I'll FedEx you a dummy phone that you can carry. If you get hold of hers, just link them up with a little connector built into the side, and it will copy everything on her device.'

'What if it's encrypted?'

'Oh, it will be encrypted for sure. But the copy will still be made. We get it back here and we go to work on cracking it.' Biery's confident voice returned. 'I'm pretty good at that sort of thing, in case you haven't noticed.'

'I noticed.'

'The only problem is getting your hands on her device. We'll have to see if you have the skills to make that happen.'

'I'll do my best, Gav. Send me that phone.'

40

The official presidential visit to Mexico City had been on the books for months, which meant members of the Secret Service had been devoting attention to it virtually just as long.

Now, just five days before his arrival, the advance team had already been on the ground in the city for days. They had a temporary operations center at the aptly named InterContinental Presidente hotel, and they'd met with Secret Service personnel stationed here in the city as well as with other law enforcement and intelligence partners at the US embassy on the beautiful Paseo de la Reforma.

The lead advance agent for the trip was a twenty-year veteran of the service named Dale Herbers. Herbers was a road warrior for the Secret Service; he had arrived in Mexico City on a direct flight from London after working the President's recent trip to the United Kingdom.

The UK trip, like every international POTUS trip he'd led in his career, had gone off flawlessly, but Herbers knew Mexico City would be the most difficult operation he'd run as lead advance agent. There was a confluence of credible threats, access to weapons, and well-developed criminal infrastructure in the area that meant Herbers would have to bring his A game to his preparations.

The public image of the Secret Service is the square-jawed linebacker-looking man in sunglasses and a suit who moves close enough to the President of the United States to catch a bullet for him, and these men did exist, but the truth of the service is more mundane. For every close protection agent caught on camera at Jack Ryan's shoulder, there were a hundred or more other men and women working to ensure the safety of all protectees. And for every second a Secret Service agent is responding to a threat to the life of his protectee, there are literally years' worth of meetings to make certain that those threats never materialize.

Today in a conference room at his suite in the Inter-Continental, Dale Herbers had convened one of those meetings. It was a breakfast gathering of high-ranking local law enforcement officials as well as the department heads of several US agencies based at the embassy. The point of today's confab was to run down, again, the list of known potential threats in the area, and to make sure all organizations had the same level of confidence that the threats were at a manageable level.

From the outset, the Secret Service knew that Mexico was going to be a security challenge. There had been credible threats from the Maldonado cartel after their leader, Antonio Maldonado, was gunned down six months earlier, and while virtually all analysts in DC agreed there was little chance his brother Santiago Maldonado would be able to execute an attack on the President in Mexico City, the analysts weren't able to say with confidence that someone affiliated with the organization wouldn't try *something* against SWORDSMAN – the Secret Service's code name for President Ryan.

Herbers kicked off the meeting after introductions.

"Okay. Since Antonio Maldonado was killed, his brother Santiago has been blaming the US Whether or not the US was involved in the raid in Acapulco doesn't really matter. What matters is that Santiago is telling his minions that we were involved, and his minions have weapons. It's been our assessment in DC that the threats we've gotten are more aspirational in nature than credible in nature, and we've been in touch with your various agencies and departments over the past few weeks to make sure you all agree.

"Now we're five days out from the visit, and I wanted to get one final chance for us to all sit down and talk about any concerns we may have about this threat and any other out there.

'So . . . do we expect an attack by followers of the Maldonados?'

He turned to a sixty-five-year-old Mexican with a thick mustache and thicker eyeglasses. He was the head of the División de Inteligencia de la Policía Federal. The Federal Police's Department of Intelligence.

The man shook his head without reservation. 'No. They control large parts of Guerrero state, but that is far away from the capital. The other cartels keep them out of the Distrito Federal for the most part.' He shrugged. 'Sure, we've arrested known Maldonado men in the capital, but that was before the shootout in Acapulco. Once Antonio Maldonado was taken off of the chessboard, the group has become much more violent, but very much less organized.'

Herbers took this all in. It tracked, more or less, with what others had been saying about the organization previously, but he wanted to make sure nothing new had happened.

The local director of the Drug Enforcement Administration was seated across the table from Herbers. 'Raúl? What say you?'

The silver-haired Hispanic American nodded. 'I agree. Once Antonio died, Maldonado members posted dozens of threats against SWORDSMAN on social media sites. Federal Police, along with us, raided a safe house in Iguala about two months after the Acapulco shootout, and found a DVD. On it was a video of men with RPGs saying they would kill Jack Ryan when he came to Mexico. We assume it was going to be uploaded to YouTube or something. Still, that was months back. Nothing like that recently.'

Herbers had seen the video. Things like that never failed to get the attention of the Secret Service.

Herbers said, 'One thing bothers me, though. These guys used to be all over Twitter screaming threats about SWORDSMAN, making videos and such. But now as the date of his arrival nears, we aren't hearing the same amount of chatter. Does that concern anyone?'

The director of the Secret Service office here in Mexico City said, 'I considered that. Wondered if maybe they were going radio silent because they had something cooking. But ultimately I determined it's just like the others say. These guys are in such disarray right now, they couldn't put together a real threat. Obviously I'm all for fortifying the motorcade and SWORDSMAN's appearances to condition-red levels, but I don't see Maldonado's people orchestrating an attack.'

Herbers gave the matter one last prod. He turned to the embassy FBI agent-in-charge. 'Any chance they could be coordinating with another group? Russians? Cubans, North Koreans? Any other bad actor who's got POTUS in their sights?'

The AIC didn't discount the possibility out of hand, but he clearly doubted it. 'We have seen transactional relationships between all sorts of different groups and Maldonado. He gets guns from Russia, meth from North Korea, he sells to organized crime in the States. But something on a scale of a presidential assassination? I think that's a bridge too far.'

'Fair enough,' said Herbers. He had a dozen more items on his agenda, and every one of them seemed just as important at the time.

41

Adel Zarif had been pestering his Mexican contacts for days about the bomb-making materials he needed, but Emilio and the others had just pled ignorance, claiming some men would arrive from the West and talk to him soon enough.

With five days before the President's arrival in Mexico, the Iranian had reached the point where he was considering contacting the North Koreans directly to complain about the situation. He had a contact number for a team of RGB men here in Mexico, with instructions to call as soon as the operation was complete, but he thought he might have to call it to raise his concerns about the lack of activity.

Things were getting dire, but Emilio's continued promises had persuaded Zarif to wait.

Finally, with just four days left, Emilio sat Zarif down on the couch in the living room of his tiny safe-house apartment.

He said, 'I've been asked to get a list of everything you want.'

Zarif cocked his head. 'I don't know what is available to me.'

'Everything.'

'What does that mean?'

'We have access to Base Aérea Militar Numero Siete.

It's an Army facility in the state of Guerrero. We can obtain anything that they have in their weapons stores. If what you need is small enough to fit in the trunk of a car, we can have it for you by tomorrow.'

Zarif was astonished. He was worried he'd have to make his weapon out of fertilizer and gasoline. At the very high end he'd hoped they would have access to some TNT. But Emilio was promising him ready-made military ordnance.

It didn't get any better than that.

Zarif thought it over, trying to determine what would work best for the task at hand. The President would be traveling in his limousine, and the limo used by the US President was legendary, and that was a problem for Zarif for two reasons. One, if it was as good as the legend, then it would take a massive charge, or else an extremely well-made device, to penetrate it.

And two, the legend was just that, a legend. There were very few specific details known about the vehicle itself. The weight, the thickness of the steel, the types of other materials used, and the locations of the most and least vulnerable parts – it was all officially unknown. Zarif was an engineer, he could do a lot with good data, but in his research on the vehicle itself he had discovered little more than conjecture, rumor, hyperbole, and wild guesses.

Legend.

The way to combat this unknown was to build the bomb as large and as precise as he could reasonably make it.

He thought about what the base would have. Instantly he decided he would construct the weapon out of artillery

396

shells. As far as Zarif knew, every modern military had a 105-millimeter howitzer in its arsenal. Their shells made incredibly effective IEDs; he'd used them hundreds of times in Iraq, Afghanistan, Lebanon, and Syria.

One high-explosive or armor-piercing shell, if exploded into the side of the presidential limousine, would surely destroy it and all inside.

But there were other considerations. The President always traveled with two limousines that drove one in front of the other. This way, if there was any problem with one car, the President could be slipped into the other. Two shells would be necessary to target both vehicles, because he wouldn't know which limo the President would be in at the moment they reached the target zone.

Zarif thought for a moment more. He was somewhat concerned about overkill. A bunch of dead civilians might anger his Mexican associates, but he was more concerned about failure. If he did not kill Jack Ryan the North Koreans would not fulfill their end of the bargain. He fought the urge to request four high-explosive howitzer shells, settled for three, and then handed over another list of items that he had already written down, all of which could be purchased at a hardware store and an electronics hobbyist shop.

Emilio looked it all over without comment, then with a nod he said, 'The 105s will come from Guerrero, as I said. And I will have the rest of the pieces purchased far from here, so they will not cause any suspicion.'

Zarif said, 'Very good. How long?'

'Twenty-four hours, and then you can begin your work.'

42

On his third day at Valley Floor, Jack Ryan, Jr., knew he had to make something happen. The day before he had spent virtually every moment in meetings that he had to attend in order to solidify his cover, and all day today he'd tried and failed to bump into Élise Legrande again, even making two visits to the Hydrometallurgy Quality Control department. It seemed she'd been spending time in the IT area, so he'd finagled a reason to drop in on Ralph Baggett, only to find out the IT director had to run to an important meeting somewhere else at the facility.

Jack started back toward his temporary office, but on the way there he decided to head to the cafeteria to grab a late lunch and to think over his next step. While he walked he considered his predicament. He'd managed to piece together very little of what Élise Legrande was up to, other than the fact she was ostensibly running diagnostics on some hydroseparation equipment that was used to pull the minerals out of the ore. More important, she was also clearly trying to get close to the IT director of the facility, and she seemed to be succeeding in this mission.

In the cafeteria Ryan ran into a couple of execs he'd met the day before, and he sat with them and chatted over lunch. After a few minutes the execs stood to head off to yet another meeting, and just as they did so, the woman posing as Élise Legrande entered together with Ralph

Baggett. Jack stayed behind, dawdling over his turkey sandwich.

A few minutes later Jack was alone at his table, and Ralph and Élise were sitting a few tables away. Jack had hoped Ralph would, on his own, make the introductions, but apparently Ralph didn't want to share his tablemate's attention with anyone else. Watching him eat his lunch with the beautiful blonde, Ryan determined the frumpy IT director was happy to keep the woman all to himself.

But even though Baggett and Legrande had not paid any attention to him, another person in the cafeteria, a middle-aged woman wearing a lab coat and a badge that identified her as an R&D research technician, had been openly staring at Jack. He used to get a lot more of this treatment before he'd grown a beard, and even though it was exceedingly rare he was recognized now, he still knew exactly what was going on.

Jack did his best to ignore the R&D lady, and he tried to think of a casual way to introduce himself to Élise, but while he was mulling it over, Baggett's secretary paged him on the overhead intercom. The IT director apologized to Élise and stood to return to his office. As Baggett walked off, Jack noticed the man run his hand across Legrande's back, an awkwardly affectionate touch that looked like something Jack *might* have tried out once or twice in sixth grade.

Élise showed no outward acknowledgment of the gesture.

Jack was just about to get up and make his way over to her table when he saw that the lady from R&D was now standing at his table with a smile on her face.

'I'm sorry to interrupt your lunch.'

Jack stood himself. 'No, not at all.'

'I just want to say I'm a strong supporter of your father.'

Jack smiled. 'That's great. I know he appreciates it.'

The woman gushed for another minute, then she ripped a sheet of paper out of a notebook and asked Ryan to sign it for her. When he had done so, she thanked him, and left the cafeteria seconds later.

Jack knew the beautiful blonde sitting across the room would not have been able to hear any of the conversation, but she had certainly seen the entire exchange. He glanced over in her direction and saw her staring intently back at him. He gave her a tiny smile, but she did not return it, nor did she shy away from his eyes.

Jack decided this was as good an opportunity as any to make an introduction. But just when he was about to start walking over to her, she stood and headed in his direction.

Okay, he thought. *I can work with this.*

'Hello,' he said with a friendly smile.

She did not smile back. Instead, she looked at him with unabashed curiosity. 'I asked Ralph who you were. He said you were an accountant with an investment company.'

'Sort of, yes,' Jack replied. He found himself taken in by her strong but feminine voice.

'Then obviously I must ask the question. What accountant gives autographs to swooning women?'

Ryan had prepped for a lot of different ways to bump the French agent, though discussing his own notoriety hadn't made his list.

But he came up with something quickly. 'Your accent. French, I take it?'

'French-Canadian.'

Bullshit, Ryan thought, but did not say. 'Very nice. What department do you work in?'

'I'm with an outside vendor.' He felt like her smoky eyes were burrowing into him. He knew what it felt like to be running an op and then find yourself curious about another person's presence. She must have been wondering if this was some sort of a play, although she had been the one to initiate the conversation.

Jack reached out and shook her hand. 'Jack,' he said.

'Élise,' she replied, but while she spoke she eyed his visitor's badge. *Jack* was in large letters, but below it were smaller letters. She read them aloud.

'Ryan.'

She looked up quizzically, and then she rolled her eyes. 'Oh, I see. That woman thinks you are the President of the United States.'

'Actually, she thinks I'm one of his kids.'

Another eye roll. And then the woman's eyes widened as she caught up with what he was saying. 'Oh . . . Is she correct?'

'At your service, Miss Legrande. Or Mrs?'

Veronika Martel did not answer the question; she was still working this through in her head. She remembered hearing about President Ryan's family. He had a daughter who was close to Veronika's age, and he had two young kids. She knew something about another son, but she couldn't remember many details about him. She had only a vague recollection of seeing the entire family in a magazine spread many years ago.

She asked, 'Are you the one they used to call "Junior"?'

'That's right. I'm surprised anyone in Canada has ever heard of me.'

Élise just nodded slowly. 'I am vaguely aware, yes.'

Ryan saw the mistrust and concern in the woman's eyes. Spies learn quickly to be suspicious of chance encounters. This must have looked like a coincidental meeting, and she had to have been deeply confused about how it could have been anything else. She also must have been mulling over how a relative of the American chief executive could possibly threaten her or her mission.

'How fascinating,' she said now.

A minute later Jack realized he and Élise were sitting down. She asked him what he was doing here at Valley Floor.

'I'm a financial analyst. Not really an accountant. My company is buying into the mine. Or at least we are considering it. I am here looking things over, meeting with the CFO and others. If the numbers crunch the way we want them to, I'm sure we will purchase an interest.'

The woman seemed to be taking it all in. Jack actually enjoyed watching her think about what this all meant to her operation.

He asked, 'How about you? What brings you here to California?'

She said, 'I've been in the mining industry for some time. In Canada.'

It wasn't an answer, but it was supposed to have been

enough. Jack assumed she was going to try to deflect the conversation back on him, but he wasn't going to let her get away with it. He just nodded and said, 'Go on.'

'Oh, yes. Well, we've developed some exciting new techniques for solvent extraction processes, and New-Corp has adapted their machinery to the new changes we've come up with. I'm simply watching how the new ideas are executed in a real-world setting.'

Ryan nodded appreciatively. She was good. No, she was great. She almost had him buying it. He decided he needed to play his part, so he asked her a few questions about the research, he even took some notes about the study she referred to, ostensibly so he could research it as part of his due diligence into the investment opportunity here.

'This is terrific,' he said finally. 'I wonder if I could see some of the work in practice.'

She nodded. 'You should contact Hydrometallurgy Quality Control. I'm sure they could show you the chemical dissolution equipment.'

'I'll do that. Will you be there?'

Élise hesitated. Jack felt sure she was still sizing up the situation, trying to determine if she was in any danger with him being here. It was so utterly random and odd that he knew there was no way she wouldn't be very confused and even wary.

She said, 'If you come tomorrow I'll be there all day. After that, no. I head home the day after tomorrow.'

'Great. I'll see you then.'

The two of them headed out of the cafeteria and down the hall to the elevator bank. He'd wanted to ask her out to dinner, but he fought the urge for two reasons. For one, he didn't want to overload her brain's synapses trying to determine if this was some sort of a play. If he worked it too hard it would tip her off there was nothing coincidental about his being here. Only by backing away from her now could he possibly convince her their meeting was happenstance.

And the second reason he would disengage now: he knew Chavez and Clark would be apoplectic. From an operational standpoint, Ryan getting even closer to the woman made no sense and only subjected the President's son to compromise.

At the elevators Jack pushed the up arrow to return to his office, and Élise the down arrow to head downstairs and then back to her building. They shook hands and went their separate ways.

Just as the door to Jack's elevator started to close, he heard someone running up the hall.

'Can you hold it, please?' a man shouted.

Jack held open the door, a little annoyed because it was a long drive back to the hotel and he knew he had to talk to Clark and Ding about Élise Legrande before they could break for dinner.

A young, fit Asian man in jeans and a polo shirt stepped quickly into the elevator. He held a backpack over his shoulder, and at first he faced away from Ryan.

'Appreciate it,' he said as he turned and looked forward.

Jack let the door go, pushed the button for his floor, then glanced up. 'Not a prob –'

Jack cocked his head. The one other person on the elevator did the same.

'Yao?'

'Ryan?'

They shook hands, both men keeping the confused looks on their faces. Ryan said, 'Fancy seeing you here.'

'Uh, yeah. Likewise.'

'Can I ask what brings you to Valley Floor?' Ryan asked.

Yao replied, 'Only if I can.'

Neither man spoke for the rest of the ride up to Ryan's floor. They just faced each other, each man trying to simulta-neously figure out the relevance of seeing the other here.

Finally, shortly before the elevator doors closed on the two silent men, Jack said, 'You want to grab a beer?'

Adam reached out and held the doors open. 'I've got to go by Personnel, then I'm free. Meet in the lobby in twenty?'

Ryan nodded. 'Looking forward to it.'

The closest bar to the NewCorp complex was just over the border in Nevada on Interstate 15. Several low-end but enterprising casinos had sprung up within sight of California, hoping to catch the first Angelenos heading east to gamble in Nevada. It was another thirty miles or so to Vegas, but this desert oasis of hotels, strip malls, gambling halls, and fast-food joints served as a way station for those without the time, gas, or inclination to drive all the way to the Strip.

Jack Ryan and Adam Yao sat at a table in the back of an utterly nondescript bar at Whiskey Pete's Hotel & Casino. Both men had beers in front of them – a Sam Adams for Ryan and a Shiner Bock for Yao.

There was little talk those first few minutes beyond idle conversation about the casino and the drive. Each man was sizing the other up. They weren't unfriendly; these guys had a history together and they liked and respected each other. But that was then, this was now, and they were each curious about what the other was up to.

'You look different,' Yao said.

'The beard?'

'Yeah. That, and you've put on some muscle.'

'Got tired of being recognized.'

'I guess so. Can't be too helpful in your occupation.'

'What occupation?' Ryan asked.

'Never mind,' Adam said over the rim of his glass before taking a sip. 'I ran into a friend of yours.'

'Really? Who's that?'

'Mary Pat Foley.'

'Great lady. Where did you see her?'

A pause. 'You know. Just a work function.'

'Right.'

'So . . . who was the girl?' Yao asked.

'Élise Legrande? She's with an outside vendor. Here at NewCorp for a couple of weeks. Down from Canada, she says.'

'Nice.'

'Yeah.'

Another long pause.

This conversation was going nowhere.

'Look,' Yao said, 'it's good to see you, but I guess neither of us has much to talk about.'

Ryan replied, 'The beer is okay.'

Yao chuckled, surprised by the comment. 'It is, isn't it?

I guess we could play craps or something, but you know I *can't* talk, and I doubt you *will* talk.'

Jack Ryan shook his head now. He'd been thinking it over, and even though he didn't know what Yao was up to, he decided the guy could probably use a little intel. 'Not true. I need to tell you something. Hope you'll take the info as a favor and not ask a lot of questions.'

'I've done good so far, haven't I?'

Jack said, 'The blonde?'

'Yeah? What about her?'

'She's a spook.'

Yao made no outward reaction, but he lifted his beer and took a long drink. When he put it back down he just said, 'You don't say.'

'She's not here for you. I mean . . . I don't think so. She is supposed to be Canadian, but I think she might be French. Ex-DGSE would be my guess. Now she's working for a private company. NYC-based.'

'How do you know this?'

'I'm with some guys looking into her outfit.'

'Some guys?'

'Yep.'

Adam shrugged. He let it go. 'You know what she's doing here?'

'Our guess is that she's here to steal intel for a company working with North Korea on a rare earth mineral mine they are developing.'

Ryan stared at Yao's face, searching for a reaction.

But Adam didn't blink.

*

Adam Yao was a pro. Although he and Ryan had worked together in China, Ryan wasn't read in on Acrid Herald, or at least Yao hadn't been told Ryan had been read in on it. Things were getting weirder by the day on this op, however, so the CIA officer couldn't be sure. But he wasn't about to start offering up intel, even to the son of the President of the United States.

That would be even weirder.

'Interesting,' Yao said. 'Unrelated to me, but interesting. If you'd like, I could make a call and have her checked out by the authorities.'

Ryan knew Yao was pulling his chain. He was here on the job, and it *had* to be related to the North Korean mine.

'Not necessary. Just letting you know in case her being here compromises you in some way.'

'Not at all,' he said. 'But I appreciate your concern.' He glanced at the waitress as she passed. 'I'll take a check.'

The two men walked out into the windblown parking lot. Ryan said, 'Good seeing you, Adam. Take care of yourself.'

'You do the same, Ryan. Thanks again.'

They parted with a handshake, each man climbing back into his car and taking off for Vegas.

Ryan had no idea what Yao was up to, but he was damn curious. Yao also didn't have a clue what Ryan was doing here, but in contrast to Ryan, he didn't really want to know. He would alert Mary Pat to what Ryan had told him, but for all he knew, she was already aware.

Yao was less concerned about what was going on in California and more concerned about where he was heading next. He would fly out the next morning, and he couldn't go into this with any doubt in his mind he could pull it off.

43

Veronika Martel returned to her nineteenth-floor hotel room at the Palazzo on the Las Vegas Strip, threw her purse on her bed, and sat down at her open laptop. She clicked open a program; then she slipped a connector into the base of her mobile phone and the other end into the laptop. She hit a key, and instantly the contents of the phone, or at least the contents of the phone that were the application files stolen from NewCorp's servers, began to upload to a cloud file-sharing service. There they would be picked up by Edward Riley and forwarded on to whoever at New World Metals LLC was going to give them to the North Koreans.

She didn't know how that end of the chain worked, and she didn't care. All she knew was her job, and the fact she had done her job perfectly today.

It had not been an easy task. It had been an ordeal to spend the last two weeks working in an industry she knew little about while simultaneously feigning rapt fascination with Ralph Baggett, the slovenly IT director at Valley Floor. This certainly didn't make the top ten worst assignments she had faced in her career, but she would have much rather spent her time doing most anything other than this.

Nevertheless, she'd done it. She'd not gleaned the password to the server from Baggett as she had planned, but she had been able to download the files from his terminal, after he'd put in the password himself and left the machine unattended, and that was just as good.

The fact she'd pulled it off with a minimal amount of heavy petting and no actual sex with Baggett was a bonus for her, but she had been prepared to go to whatever lengths were necessary to achieve her goal.

And now, with her operation complete, Veronika had only to return to Valley Floor mine tomorrow for her last day of her two-week stint and then endure an evening bon voyage party with several people she'd been working with in Hydrometallurgy Quality Control, as well as Baggett, who'd managed to get himself invited along.

Veronika thought it idiotic that these people she'd worked with for only two weeks were throwing a going-away party for her. In France she could have worked in an office ten years and not even known the first names of her colleagues, but this was America, and it was the American way to be silly like this.

If she had her choice she'd fly home tonight and never see any of them again.

No. Actually, this was not true. There was someone she wouldn't mind seeing again.

Veronika found it ironic that on the day she had executed her mission, she found the actual execution of the mission to be the second most interesting thing that had happened to her.

On that note, Veronika lifted her phone to make a call. Now that she had downloaded the NewCorp files, it was time for her to call Riley and report a contact.

Among the first things an intelligence officer learns as part of his or her training in both OPSEC and PERSEC is to report all contacts with strangers up the chain of command. An idle conversation about the weather with an unfamiliar person at the taxi queue might be relevant to someone with knowledge of the larger scheme of the operation, no matter how random it feels to the operator on the ground.

Meeting the son of the US President while in the act of obtaining access to the plant application server could not possibly have any sort of relevance to her New World Metals operation, but letting her boss know was SOP. Operational security on any mission dictated that an agent in the field notify his or her control officer at the first sight of anything out of the ordinary, and if anything ever qualified as out of the ordinary it would be exactly this situation.

But as she prepared to dial Riley's New York mobile number, Veronika stopped herself.

Wait. Could this be useful?

She put the phone down and thought for a moment, and when she was finished thinking she chastised herself for taking all afternoon to come to the obvious conclusion. She'd been in the corporate intel world so long she'd forgotten how to see past her small, narrow, and mundane marching orders and take a look at the larger picture.

The larger opportunity in front of her.

No, now was not the time to dutifully consider Sharps Global Intelligence Partners' best practices.

Now was the time to look out for herself.

The US President's son. *Yes,* Veronika thought. *I can use this.*

Veronika had lived like a rudderless ship for the past few years working in corporate intel, but the one thing that guided her was the hope – she wondered if it was fantasy – that someday she would get back to French intelligence. She'd left on bad terms three years earlier, and she'd wanted back in almost from the start.

Her old colleagues had told her to forget about it. She wasn't ever getting back in the good graces of the executives at DGSE.

Then *today* happened. Today she bumped Jack Ryan, Jr. There was no question that, if exploited carefully and slowly, he could prove to be an incredible access point for French intelligence. They could learn details about the American President that they wouldn't otherwise be able to obtain.

And they could only do it through Veronika. They'd *have* to take her back.

Of course, Martel would need to start a relationship with the handsome and eligible young bachelor, but that problem looked like it was sorting itself out nicely. Jack had proven to be just like so many other men in this world. He would close the distance between the two of them without her having to lift a finger.

Yes. She would begin a relationship with Ryan, she would contact DGSE, and she would tell them she was coming home with a prize.

French intelligence would welcome her back with open arms.

She wasn't going to breathe a word of this to Riley, of

course. Instead, she would mention her going-away party to Ryan the next day when he came to her department, and she would spend the evening ignoring Baggett and cultivating Ryan as an asset.

She smiled to herself, satisfied to be finishing one job and overlapping into a job that had the potential to reap incredible rewards.

44

Adam flew from Las Vegas to Los Angeles, and from there to Shanghai on an Airbus A330 flown by China Eastern. He sat in the back of coach and spent his time listening to Korean-language audio files on his mobile phone.

He erased the files two hours before touchdown in China so there would be no record of his study of the language anywhere on his person.

Shortly after landing, Adam entered the immigrations area of Shanghai Pudong International Airport, waited his turn, and then stepped up to the immigration control officer sitting behind a desk. The man took Adam's US passport – it claimed his name was Shan Xin – and then looked through it. He stopped on the Chinese visa, affixed to one of the pages.

In Mandarin he asked, 'You are Chinese?'

'Yes. I left China eighteen years ago to go to school in US'

'You haven't been back here?'

'No, sir.'

'Married an American?' The immigration officer didn't know this, but he assumed as much.

'That is correct. I am home to visit family.'

'Where is your Chinese passport?'

'I lost it long ago. The embassy said I could travel on

my US passport and obtain a new Chinese passport while I am here if I provide my birth records. All that information is here with my mother.'

The officer eyed Yao carefully, then began thumbing through his passport slowly. He checked the few stamps that were there, and then he put the passport under a tabletop magnifier and examined the binding.

If Adam hadn't known what was going on he would have been nervous, but he was aware they always did this at Chinese immigration control. The man was looking for evidence a page or pages had been removed with a razor in an attempt to get rid of entrance stamps. Foreigners traveling to China are not admitted if they have any Nepal entrance stamps.

The control officer found nothing amiss, and four minutes after stepping up to the desk, Adam Yao took his passport back, hefted his luggage off the floor, and began walking toward the arrivals area of the airport. He was now, according to his legend, Shan Xin, a Chinese national.

Three hours after arriving in Shanghai, Adam Yao entered a plain building in Shanghai's Kunshan suburb. Inside he took an elevator to the second floor and then knocked on an unmarked metal door. He saw the peephole darken for a moment, and then an intercom next to the door crackled.

In Mandarin, he heard: 'Name?'

'Shan Xin. I have an appointment with Mr Hu.'

The door clicked open. Two men looked at his passport and then they frisked him carefully, removing his wallet, his mobile phone, and even a watch. One of them said, 'Listening devices. Everyone must be searched.'

Adam had brought nothing incriminating into China, so he remained relaxed, and soon they led him into an office where a dour-looking older man sat behind a desk. This was Hu; Adam knew because he had videoconferenced with the man from Virginia via Skype in order to get the job. At the time, Hu had explained the job would be at one of the gangster miner operations in Mongolia, and he'd stressed that he needed Adam – or Shan Xin, as he knew him – to come to Shanghai as soon as possible for further vetting and processing.

As in the Skype teleconference, in person Hu was all business. He questioned Adam on his background, and on his knowledge of the computer system used to operate the hydraulic cone crushers. Adam could tell from the outset this wasn't some sort of security check to confirm Yao's identity. Instead, Hu was just making sure that Shan Xin possessed the qualifications for the job. Adam had passed all this in their Skype interview two weeks earlier, but it was clear to Yao that Hu was a careful man.

Perhaps not careful enough to recognize a CIA plant, but more than careful enough not to hire an unqualified employee.

Finally the older Chinese man was satisfied, and he pulled out some paperwork. 'As we are not state-owned, we have a more informal approach.'

Adam thought Hu's understatement was funny. Not only was the company not state-owned, it was wholly illegal. He kept his face blank.

'You will work on an eight-week contract, and you can be let go at any time.'

'Yes.'

'After eight weeks you can get one week off, or you can keep working if you want.'

Adam wanted to look eager. 'I came here to work. Not for vacation.'

Hu looked him over and then nodded. He said, 'You will tell no one that you have been in America. Ever. Certainly you will keep quiet that you have an American passport. I will keep it here. It is procedure.'

Yao knew why, but he pretended like he didn't. 'The people at the mine don't like Americans?'

Hu lit a cigarette and leaned back. He spoke matter-of-factly. 'This processing plant you are going to is not in Mongolia like we said. I wasn't allowed to mention it before you came here, and when I tell you where you will be working you will understand why.'

Yao was a good actor, and reveled in the portrayal of a man genuinely confused. 'I don't understand. Where will I be working?'

'Later today you and forty-three other men and women will travel in a bus to the airport and you will board a plane to Pyongyang. The mine is in the north of the DPRK, not very far from the border with China.'

Yao's eyes went wide. Before he spoke, Hu said, 'It is all arranged at the highest levels of their state-owned mining corporation. Once you are in the air to Pyongyang, a North Korean government official will give you the documentation you need to get into the country.'

'What about the Chinese government?'

'To the government here, you never left China.'

Adam raised no complaints, and he signed all the papers using the name Shan Xin.

Hu finished the meeting with a warning. 'We already have sent over one hundred fifty workers to the mining operation in North Korea. They are paid well, so they do not complain, but they report difficult conditions.'

'I understand.'

'Remember, you will be working in a facility under guard at all times. Don't do anything to raise any suspicion with the authorities in North Korea. Do your work. Don't ask questions, don't look around, don't complain, and don't give them any reason to mistrust you. You do this and you will make a lot of money. If you don't do this . . . there is nothing anyone here can do for you.'

Adam nodded calmly, as if blowing off the warning. But the truth was different. He felt an unmistakable feeling of dread about where he was going.

The flight from Shanghai to Pyongyang was in an Airbus A319 flown by Deer Jet, a Chinese charter company based in Beijing. On board the aircraft Adam met a few of the others heading to Chongju. Most if not all seemed bewildered by the fact they were heading into North Korea.

It was clear all these men and women were educated professionals. They didn't look like miners any more than Adam did. He knew that in order to staff the processing facility Hu and his gangster mining company needed to recruit qualified systems engineers, computer technicians, and other high-tech industry professionals, and few if any of these people would have experience with the criminal underworld. Adam hoped to use this to his advantage. He'd fit in better where he was going if he behaved just like the rest of them. A little wide-eyed about the whole thing, but dedicated to his one specific role.

They landed at seven in the evening and deplaned within minutes. Adam had the feeling this was the only aircraft flying into the airport at the moment, because the terminal was empty except for two long rows of young soldiers in green parade dress uniforms, who virtually lined the walkway from the gate to the immigration control area.

Adam walked between the soldiers, following in the middle of the pack of tired Chinese, doing his best to keep his head down. He stole a couple of furtive glances, though, and he saw the soldiers were both male and female, they seemed to have programmed scowls on their faces, and they held their locally made Kalashnikov-style rifles across their chests at the ready. Adam could plainly see the weapons' fire selectors were switched off the standard safe setting and set to fire semiautomatically at the press of the trigger.

Christ, the American thought.

His trip through immigration control was like none he'd ever experienced in his life. The Chinese technicians were each sent to their own table in a large open area in the middle of the terminal. Here, five armed and scowling immigration officers stood at the ready. Adam was led to his table, and in the poor Mandarin spoken by a female soldier standing behind him he was told to put his bag up on the table and unzip it. He did so, and two officers began taking everything out and going through it. He then was ordered to hand over his wallet, his employment contract, and his passport to a white-haired man. While this man looked through every page of his documents, a fourth official began frisking Adam from head to toe. He was ordered to strip down to his underwear – this he did in the view of not only the female North Korean officers but also the female Chinese technicians, who were stripping down themselves.

Every shred of their clothing was inspected, and then each person was wanded with a handheld metal detector.

All in all, Adam spent more than twenty minutes in his underwear. He was a fit and confident young man, but standing in front of two young females with guns in their hands and 'Fuck you' stares on their faces was as uncomfortable an experience as he'd ever felt.

Right in the middle of the lengthy process Yao heard a disturbance at another table. A man raised his voice, speaking in Korean.

'What is this? What did I find here? What do you have to say for yourself?'

Adam turned to the action. A thirtyish female Chinese woman Adam had met on the flight over stood in her bra and panties, looking at what an immigration officer held out in his hand. She didn't understand his words, so she waited for a translation. A North Korean minder who spoke Chinese came over and looked at the alleged contraband, then turned to the woman. 'This is a Korean dictionary. Why do you have this?'

In Chinese the woman replied with genuine confusion. '*Why*? Are you kidding? I don't speak Korean. I bought it in the airport. I thought it would be helpful to know a few words.'

'Helpful to your espionage?'

'*What?* Of course not.'

The woman was led away by the arm, still in her underwear and openly weeping. Her luggage remained open and unattended on the table, with her clothes scattered across the table and the floor.

Adam did not say a word. He hoped like hell she'd be expelled for this; he couldn't imagine a better outcome for the lady. In fact, he didn't know if he should feel sorry for her or envy her.

North Korea sucked already.

He chastised himself for this thought. Silently, he said, *What the hell did you expect, Adam?*

After the lengthy immigration process and the loss of one of their number, Adam and the forty-two remaining Chinese technicians were put on a bus and taken through the dark and nearly empty streets of Pyongyang to the Yanggakdo International Hotel.

Adam knew all about this place. The rumors were there was only one floor in operation: the twenty-sixth. The rest of the place was closed and shuttered because, despite the impression the North Koreans wanted to make with the massive business-class hotel, there were so few foreign businessmen in the city they needed only a couple dozen rooms at any one time.

Of course, with the arrival of the technicians, Adam assumed he'd be going to some previously mothballed floor.

In the lobby they were told to line up, and one of the impeccably dressed minders said, 'I will pass out your keys. Four people to a room. Everyone will be staying on the twenty-sixth floor.'

Wow, Adam thought. He and his cohorts were probably the only people in the hotel, and virtually the only foreign travelers in the huge city.

A small reception for the Chinese technicians began at nine p.m. in a banquet room in the basement. To get there, Adam had to line up with the others on the twenty-sixth floor and wait for a group of minders to come up and then ferry everyone down in groups in the elevator.

Adam knew he should have been made uneasy by the tight control; it was probably like being in a maximum-security prison, after all. But to Adam it felt more like his memories of grammar school. Grown-ups making the children line up and wait, and constantly checking their every move.

The banquet room was almost comically ornate, and five times too large for the quantity of Chinese technicians. A dozen waitresses worked the room, none of whom spoke a word of Chinese. Adam chatted with his new colleagues, but most of them were too nervous to enjoy themselves, so the conversation was stilted. One of the waitresses turned a radio on and held a PA microphone up to the little speaker, broadcasting thin and scratchy revolutionary music throughout the banquet hall. Adam would have enjoyed the spectacle of the scene, and he could have stayed for hours, but he stopped drinking after two beers. He figured he would need fifty to calm his nerves, considering his predicament, and he was very aware of the fact good intelligence officers did not become *better* intelligence officers the drunker they got, so he just held his mostly empty bottle, grinned stupidly, and bobbed his head with the music.

He tipped well, but not enough to draw attention to himself, and then he went to the door, where a minder met him to escort him back to his room.

On his way back up to the twenty-sixth floor, he remembered something else about this hotel. To confirm the rumor, he leaned around his minder at the front of the car and looked at the floor numbers.

Yes. Just like he'd been told, Adam saw that the fifth floor did not exist. He assumed that was where the watchers and listeners associated with North Korean counterintelligence all worked. He knew that here in the Yanggakdo International Hotel, every last thing he did and said would be recorded and videoed. Yao wasn't terribly concerned by this. He'd lived in China, after all, so he was accustomed to draconian intelligence measures.

But when it came to paranoid security protocols, the DPRK was starting to make the Chinese look like rank amateurs.

45

Things were going according to plan for Veronika Martel. Her goal of getting close to Jack Ryan, Jr., was moving along even quicker and more easily than she'd anticipated, and she caught herself already thinking about her life back in Paris once she returned to French intelligence with him as a recruited asset.

He had come into her department just after nine this morning and spent most of an hour making notes about the equipment and the processes. Then he returned to her temporary office and talked to her a little more about solvent extraction. He'd thanked her for her time and exchanged business cards, and then, after allowing herself a reasonable time so as not to show a level of interest that had the tendency to drive confident men away, she'd brought up the evening soiree that her colleagues were putting on and, in as offhand a way as possible, she suggested Ryan might drop by. Ryan took the bait easily, and said he would love to attend. Luckily for Veronika, the woman in QC in charge of arranging the after-work event had yet to settle on a meeting place, so Veronika had gotten Ryan's mobile number, with plans to text him when all was decided upon.

He'd gone back to his office for a few hours, but at the end of the day she told him everyone was getting together at eight o'clock in the trendy V Bar in the Venetian hotel.

Veronika had not doubted for a minute that he would show up. He entered the bar at eight-fifteen, looking admittedly handsome in a lightweight tan sport coat and jeans, and although he'd sat farther away than the ever-present and always annoying Ralph Baggett, Ryan had soon slipped down a few seats to position himself directly across from her.

Baggett, as he had been for the past two weeks, was doing his best to monopolize Martel's time, but the French spy handled him deftly. She included Ryan in her conversations and did it in a way that she was certain felt natural to both Baggett and Ryan.

Things were going according to plan for Jack Ryan, Jr. His goal of getting close to Élise Legrand was progressing even quicker and more easily than he'd anticipated. He'd entered her department this morning, spent just the right amount of time with her to show casual interest, and garnered himself an invitation to her going-away party that evening.

As soon as he learned he'd see her again he relaxed, because he knew his objective would be easier to fulfill in a crowd than alone in her office. It was crucial that he get his hands on her phone, since Gavin Biery had decided it to be the most likely device she would employ to remove anything from the NewCorp servers. Jack had been trained in pickpocketing and other sleight-of-hand techniques, so he liked his chances if he could get close enough to the woman in a social environment where others were around.

He and the rest of the team had spent the early evening

working out a plan to take a peek at her digital data. Ryan had the phone Gavin had sent him from Alexandria, and to extract the data from her phone and put it on Gavin's he needed to have her device in his possession for only two to three minutes. He was certain he could do this at some point during the party, but the guys also bandied around other possibilities. Could he actually social-engineer more information out of her? Details on where she was going next, information about her client's identity – the bene-factor paying millions of dollars to the North Koreans? The Campus operatives knew there was likely as much or more crucial data in the head of Élise Legrande as there was on her phone, and the question remained how they could get that data out.

Clark was against Ryan pursuing some sort of physical relationship with the woman. Even when Jack suggested he ask her for an innocuous drink after the party so he could dig a little deeper into her psyche to see if there was an opening there, Clark was less than enthusiastic.

'One question for you, Ryan.'

'Shoot.'

'What happened to the last son of a bitch we watched having a drink with that woman? Have you forgotten about Vietnam?'

Dom had been sitting quietly, listening to the conver-sation, but he said, 'Ouch.'

Ryan shook his head. 'I've got you guys watching my back.'

'We were watching Hazelton's back, too,' Clark growled. 'Damn lot of good *that* did him.'

This sank in for a moment. Ultimately, however, a

426

compromise was made in the form of another device Biery had FedExed over from Alexandria. It was a tiny clear earpiece with a half-inch-long dangling battery pack; it looked just like a small hearing aid, but it could attach via Bluetooth like a regular earpiece headset and transmit as well as receive. Unlike the other units the men wore, this one had an external microphone that picked up sounds around the person wearing it. Ryan tested it out, his hair just long enough to cover most of it in his ear, and with it in place the rest of the team could hear him and the conversations of those around him. And more important to Clark, Ryan would be able to hear transmissions and take direction.

Clark gave Ryan the green light to go to the party and do his best to access the Frenchwoman's phone, and he gave him the yellow light to proceed carefully after that to garner more intel if feasible. That said, Clark was going to be listening in on the entire evening, and he even went along to the Venetian hotel and found a bench in the lobby's shopping galleria, where he would be just a few seconds away if Ryan ran into trouble. He made it very clear to Ryan he would not hesitate to give the younger man the hook and put the kibosh on the operation if he didn't think things were working out.

The party, like most after-work company get-togethers, started with work-related chatter, but by the time the second round of drinks had been polished off, the participants loosened up. Except for Élise Legrande. Ryan noted her great skill in deflecting personal conversation, and the almost hawklike way she watched the other people

427

at the table, usually silently. She eyed Ryan most of all, and this was not lost on him. He'd caught her eye a number of times, which wasn't difficult as they were seated across from each other, but she held his gaze in a way that he found a little off-putting, her incredible beauty notwithstanding.

The table of twelve began thinning out after an hour, as most of the attendees had kids at home, early starts the next morning, or both. A core group of hard-chargers stayed around for a third drink, but by the time the fourth round was dropped by the cocktail waitress, only Ryan, Baggett, and the woman everyone knew as Élise from Quebec City remained.

Ryan had spent the last forty-five minutes waiting for his opportunity to act. He was ready to move around to Élise's side of the table to make a play for her phone and he had a half-dozen ready-made excuses to make it happen, too, but first he needed to know the location of the device. Was it in a pocket, in her purse, in her hand? Even with his new sleight-of-hand skills, he couldn't very well sit down next to her and frisk her from head to toe, and because he'd seen no hint of the device in the ninety minutes since he'd arrived, he'd bided his time, waiting for her to reveal it.

The fact he hadn't seen it so far told him it was probably in her purse, so when she finally picked up her small silver clutch off the table and reached inside, he began moving into action. Just as he stood to head around the table to show Ralph and Élise something on his phone, he eyed her right hand. She held a phone in it and was checking it for text messages. But instantly Ryan realized the phone in her hand wasn't the one he had seen her with all week at Valley Floor.

Damn it. She'd switched phones. He knew he needed to pull data off the device she'd had at the facility, because that would be the most likely to contain the intel he was looking for.

Where was *that* phone? In her room?

Jack had no idea where she was staying. She hadn't offered the information and he'd not seen a natural opportunity to get it out of her. He felt certain she was somewhere on the Vegas Strip – all the other visitors to the NewCorp Valley Floor facility he'd run into had been – but without that knowledge he couldn't very well send another Campus operative off on a sneak-and-peek.

Jack excused himself to go to the restroom. The team could hear his every word, so he began speaking as soon as he was out of earshot from the table. 'Listen up, new sitrep. She's got a different phone on her.'

'Damn,' Chavez said. 'What the hell does that mean?'

Ryan said, 'I think it means Gavin was right. The other phone was for the operation. She got what she needed, so she's left that phone in her room. Or, hell, I don't know, it *could* be in her purse.'

Dom said, 'You've got to check her purse.'

Ryan fired back, 'And you've got to check her room.'

'Where is she staying?'

'Unknown.'

'Cuz, this is Vegas. There are one hundred twenty-five thousand hotel rooms in this town. You want I should start kicking in doors?'

Ryan grumbled a few cusswords of frustration, then

said, 'Okay, I'll find out for you, while I'm digging through her purse. You just sit there and take it easy in the meantime.'

Clark's admonishing low grumble came over the net. 'Gentlemen.'

Ding chimed in now: 'Ryan, it's okay. Check her purse, and if it's not there, tip us off by asking her about where she's staying. I'm online now, and Gavin's IT hacks have given me visibility into all the hotel records in town. You find out the name of the hotel and I'll get her room number. We'll send Dominic to break in while you watch the girl.'

Ryan agreed, although Ding made it sound easier than he imagined it would prove to be. 'I've got to get back. Baggett might try to kidnap her.'

Ding replied, 'That French spook would rip his balls off.'

Ryan returned to find Baggett gone, and Élise Legrande alone at the large table, checking her phone and clutching her purse in her lap.

Jack sat back down. 'What happened to Ralph?'

'He had to leave. He asked me to wish you a good evening.'

Ryan did his best to hide his pleasure, but Clark's voice entered his right ear and cooled his excitement. 'This is too easy. Keep your eyes open, kid, something's fishy.'

Clark was insinuating the Sharps intelligence officer might herself be operating *against* Ryan, but Ryan scoffed at this. He thought she was just interested in him and acting out of attraction. That she'd managed to clear Ralph Baggett's playing piece off the board was good news for

Ryan and his mission, not evidence that the woman had any objective beyond spending some time alone with him.

He watched her put her phone back in her purse, and while she did so he got a fair look inside. There was no other phone.

Ryan now knew he needed to find out the name of her hotel. He didn't have time to go slowly with this, so he started immediately. 'What do you think of the Venetian?'

He was hoping she would say something about the rooms – an indication this was her hotel.

But she just looked around her. 'It's nothing like Venice.'

'Not really, no. Still, it's pretty nice.' Jack went for broke. 'Where are you staying?'

She blinked once. Perhaps a little surprised at the question.

But she answered. 'Next door, at the Palazzo.'

'Really?' Jack said. 'That's funny. So am I.'

The Frenchwoman's eyes narrowed. Ryan could see she didn't believe him, and instantly he worried he'd screwed up. He wanted an excuse to stay with her a little longer so he could watch her while Dom worked, and if he claimed he was at the same hotel then they could possibly walk back together. Clark had warned Ryan she would have a good BS detector, but he'd pressed his luck anyway.

In his earpiece he heard Ding's voice, rushed. 'I'm getting you a room there now.'

'What room?' Legrande asked, clearly challenging his story.

431

Ryan raised his eyebrows. 'I'm sorry?'

'What is your room number at the Palazzo?'

Damn. He couldn't just pull a room number out of the air. She might continue challenging him, check for herself, and he'd be caught in a lie.

Ding heard the question. 'Gonna take a couple of minutes, Ryan! Stall her.'

Jack smiled. 'That's a bit forward, isn't it?'

'I am not saying it to be forward. I am saying it because I do not believe you are telling the truth. I don't really know what you are doing, but I think you just lied to me for some reason.'

Jack just said, 'You have trust issues.' He felt like a heel, but he was committed to this now, and he couldn't back away.

'I have trust issues because I have been around people who do not tell the truth. Like now, for instance.' Ryan could tell she was fully on guard. She prodded him for a minute, asked him where he was really staying, but he stuck with his story.

Finally, Élise said, 'Last chance to be honest, Jack. Where are you staying?'

Jack smiled. 'Let's go. I'll show you my room.' He held his breath.

'You're bluffing,' she said, a coquettish smile on her face. She truly didn't believe him, and she looked like she would relish putting him in his place. Jack felt sure she thought this was all just a ploy to get her dress off.

He *was* bluffing, he didn't have a room key. But Ryan couldn't imagine the poised and refined woman in front of him taking him up on the offer. Even if she didn't believe him. As bluffs went, he felt pretty good about this one.

He said, 'I think *you* are the one who is bluffing. You won't go.'

She did not reply to this. Instead, she said, 'I Googled you today.'

'Really? Did you enjoy the pictures of a fourteen-year-old me with goofy hair and braces?'

Without smiling she said, 'Very much so. Of course, I established you do work for Hendley Associates.'

'You didn't believe that, *either*?'

She didn't answer. Instead, she said, 'There is really nothing bad about you online, but I am surprised how little news there is about you since you got out of college. It's as if you went into the shadows after that.'

Now Ryan was beginning to get nervous. She was a spook, and spooks got suspicious easily. But he was surprised at the level on which she was challenging him. He wondered if she knew more about him than she was letting on, and if that had her concerned her intelligence operation had been compromised.

Jack just replied, 'There's not much news about me online for one simple reason. I am a bore. It works to my advantage. People get bored by bores.'

'You are asking a woman you do not know to come to a hotel room you do not have. That is strange, but I would not say it is boring.'

Ryan said, 'You *still* don't believe me?'

'Not for an instant. You need an excuse to follow me back to my hotel, so you claim it to be your hotel. You thought I wouldn't question this. Perhaps you thought we'd sit and have another drink together in the bar there, before I took you up to *my* bed.'

'Presumptuous.'

'Experienced.'

Finally Ding came over Jack's earpiece. 'Room thirty-nine-oh-eight. Junior suite. Clark's on his way to get your key at the front desk, and if you can stall her for twenty minutes Dom will have your shit moved from over here at the Mandarin into your room.'

Jack thought it was a bit hasty of Chavez to assume he was going to take this woman up to his hotel room. Hell, he didn't even have the key, and he didn't know how they could get it to him without her seeing the exchange.

Jack stood up and said, 'Room thirty-nine-oh-eight.' Not denying her premise, but challenging her none-theless.

For the first time, the woman smiled. 'Okay, Jack Ryan, Jr. Let's go to the Palazzo and see this room of yours.'

Jack hesitated. *Oops.*

Ding shouted into his ear, 'Not yet. Shit! We are *not* ready!'

Jack asked a passing waitress for the check, and he hoped like hell she was extremely bad at her job and took a long time producing it.

46

The very second his cousin announced he was staying at the Palazzo hotel, Dom Caruso leapt to his feet in the suite at the Mandarin Oriental, ran into Ryan's room, and began scooping up loose clothes, shoes, even his computer and peripherals, and he threw them haphazardly into an open rolling duffel on the floor. He then rifled through his cousin's closet, took pressed shirts and a suit, wadded them into a ball and crammed them inside the duffel, threw in a dopp kit full of toiletries, zipped it up, and ran with it for the door. He slung a backpack go-bag of his own over his shoulder and left the suite.

The valet downstairs had the keys to the Mercedes E-Class the team was using in town. The Mandarin Oriental was about a mile and a half south of the Palazzo on the Strip, a significant distance in traffic, so Dom didn't plan on waiting for the valet. As he rushed to the elevator he put the conference call with the rest of the team on hold on his phone, then dialed the saved mobile number to the head valet on duty tonight.

Clark had befriended the man, and a few of his coworkers, just after they had checked in.

The man answered and Dom spoke rapidly. 'Andy, this is Bobby, Mr Phillip's nephew.' The team all had cover identities, and Clark had issued a standing order forbidding any of the team to say Clark was their dad; therefore he was always Uncle Joe, Uncle Pete, or Uncle 'something' on their ops.

'Hey, bro. What's up?'

'I'll be there in three minutes. If my black E-Class is parked at your stand with the trunk open and the keys in it, I've got fifty bucks coming your way.'

'You got it, bro!' Andy said, and he hung up.

Clark was already in the Venetian, so he only had to head next door, which he did in a jog. It took him five minutes, and this got him there just five or six minutes ahead of Ryan and the Frenchwoman.

He went to the reception desk, skipped ahead of a couple of Japanese businessmen with several bows and professions of apologies, and picked up the two key cards to the junior suite on the thirty-ninth floor.

Ryan and Élise arrived at the front of the Palazzo at the same time a black Mercedes E-Class pulled up to the valet stand. Caruso climbed out just feet away from them, took his luggage out of the trunk, and followed them into the entrance.

Just inside the palatial lobby, Dom rolled by them and headed straight for the elevators like a businessman in some rush to get to his room.

In the main lobby, Ryan took Élise by the arm and stopped her. He nodded to a swanky lobby bar. 'The bartender here makes an incredible margarita.'

The Frenchwoman just shook her head with a smile. 'You've probably never set foot here in your life.'

Jack chuckled, still doing his best to give off the impression he was more fascinated by her mistrust than anything else. 'No drink first?'

She shook her head again. 'No, thank you. Are we going upstairs, or are you ready to give up on this charade?'

'Let's go up. I can't wait to see the look on your face.'

She shrugged. 'After you.'

Just twenty-five yards ahead of Ryan and the Frenchwoman, Dom raced to a huge bank of eight elevators around a corner. Eight of the sixteen elevators reached floors thirty-seven through fifty. Clark had just entered a car twenty seconds earlier, but he'd left a key in a planter for Dom and told him where he'd dumped it. Dom snatched it from the planter, took the first elevator that arrived, and stepped inside. He noticed the car bypassed floors seven through thirty-six. He pushed the button for the thirty-ninth floor, and the car shot straight up, not stopping at all along the way.

John Clark took his elevator up to the second floor, and on the way up he took a small piece of tape, affixed it to Ryan's card, and attached it to the buttons to the right of the door. As he did so he said, 'Listen up, Ryan. When you get to the bank of elevators, the last one will come down to you. Take it. Your card will be taped to the keys to the left of the door.'

John pushed the button in the car to send it back down, then stepped out.

As soon as Ryan and Élise arrived in front of the elevators, the last one dinged and opened. It went against Jack's sense of manners to enter before the woman, so he positioned himself on Élise's left and entered just a half-step behind her. He swiveled his body to cover the buttons and saw that the room key card was lightly taped over the thirty-ninth-floor button. Jack easily popped it off and pressed his floor with the same movement, all while turning around to face her.

His hand went down to his side, and he reached into his pocket with the card in his hand, then pulled it out and held it up.

She stared at it in disbelief.

The elevator rose to the second floor and the door opened. Jack and Élise stood there quietly looking at an empty tile floor. Jack looked at the gorgeous tall blonde and smiled. 'It's a beautiful hotel.'

'Seeing it for the first time?'

'No. Just mentioning it.'

The doors closed and they started heading up again.

John Clark bolted out of the third-floor stairwell, sweat dripping from his face and his chest heaving from exertion, and he ran toward the elevator bank. He reached it at a sprint and pushed the call button to go up.

As soon as he did so he heard the bell announcing a car was stopping on the floor. He quickly moved out of the sightline of anyone in the car.

The door opened just feet away from him and Clark held his breath so as to stop his heavy breathing. In the moment of silence, both in his earpiece and from the car itself, he heard a female speak with a pronounced French accent.

'Damn children.'

Ryan replied, 'Little bastards.' The door closed.

Clark let out a quick sigh of relief and said, 'I stalled them as much as I can, Dom. They'll be less than sixty seconds behind you.'

Caruso replied, his own voice affected by heavy breathing. 'Understood.'

Two minutes later Jack slipped the key card into the lock of 'his' hotel room on the thirty-ninth floor.

He held the door open, but Élise just stood there dumbfounded.

'I don't believe it,' she said softly, and only after a delay did she enter the room.

Jack smiled and followed her in, then he caught a surprised look on her face. He glanced across the room. Dominic had left a pair of Jack's red boxer shorts in the middle of the floor in the sitting area. Jack groaned inwardly, and told himself he'd kick his cousin's ass the next time he saw him.

Some other clothing was scattered about; there was a suit laid out neatly on his bed, and his computer was on the coffee table in front of the sofa. It was a little sloppy, but it looked legit.

'Sorry,' he said, scooping up his shorts. 'I hadn't planned on having company.'

Élise did not reply. Instead, she stepped over to the open bathroom door and peered inside. A couple of wet towels lay on the tile floor, the toothbrush was on the vanity next to an open tube of toothpaste, a mouthwash bottle open next to it.

The walls and floor of the shower were damp.

She turned away and stepped back into the middle of the room.

There was an iced bottle of champagne on the coffee table next to the sofa, and Ryan was both surprised and impressed that the hotel had managed to have that ready not more than twenty minutes after the initial reservation had been made. Jack walked over to it and pulled the bottle out of the ice.

Élise noticed the wine bucket now and she cocked her head quickly. 'Why the champagne?' she asked. 'Isn't that something that's normally done when you check in?'

Jack scrambled for a second, then said, 'It's a little embarrassing.'

'More embarrassing than your underwear on the floor?'

Jack laughed. 'The owner is a Republican. I don't throw my dad's name around, I'm not even using my own name on the reservation, but sometimes people recognize me. I guess he found out I'm here and he's giving me the royal treatment. Champagne every night.' Jack added, 'I didn't ask for it.'

'I see,' she replied.

Jack popped the bottle and poured two glasses, then he started to lead Élise toward the couch, but a voice in his ear caused him to change his plans.

It was Dominic, and his whisper was barely audible. 'Take her out on the balcony. *Now.*'

Christ, Ryan thought. Dom was somewhere in this room.

Jack said, 'Oh, I forgot. You *have* to see this view.' Jack led her to the balcony, the entire time hoping like hell he actually *did* have a nice view.

Dom Caruso slipped out of the closet next to the bed, shut the door behind him, and dropped down onto the floor. He belly-crawled across the carpet, keeping an eye on the balcony, and the backs of his cousin and, much more important, his date, the knockout French spy.

When he was certain her focus was firmly on the neon lights of the Strip from the thirty-ninth floor, Dom rose to his feet and left the room quickly and silently.

As soon as he was in the hall he said, 'I'm clear. Ding, vector me to her hotel room.'

Ding said, 'There is no reservation under her name at the hotel. Either she's using an alias, or a second alias, or she's using her real name, or she's not staying there.'

Dom stopped walking in the hallway. 'Well, damn. Okay, Jack, get back to work. Get it out of her.'

On the balcony, Élise turned away from the view and looked to Ryan. Her face had softened. She didn't seem as cynical or mistrusting.

She said, 'I'm sorry I didn't believe you.' She took a sip of champagne.

Jack took a sip from his glass. 'No big deal. So, now it's time for *you* to come clean. Where are you staying?'

'I told you. I'm staying here.'

Ryan took his time reading her face. Finally he said, 'I believe you.'

He heard Clark's voice in his ear now. 'Ryan is telling us she *is* staying there. Domingo, look for reservations under female names that came on the twenty-fifth of last month. That's the day before she started work at Valley Floor. There can't be more than a couple of women who have been here for two weeks.'

There was a pause for a moment. Élise and Jack stood out on the balcony and looked over the lights of Las Vegas.

Chavez called over the net now. 'Got it! Only three females who came on the twenty-fifth are still there. One of them is under the name Sophie Brochard from Ontario, Canada. Room thirty-one-twelve. That's *gotta* be our girl.'

Dom said, 'I'm en route.'

On the balcony of his suite, Jack turned away from the view of the Strip to find Élise going inside to retrieve the champagne bottle. She came back outside, refilled her own glass, then took his glass and did the same.

After she put the bottle down on the table on the balcony, she moved back to the railing, extremely close to Ryan.

Things were moving curiously fast, and now, far from worrying he'd have to find an excuse to keep the beautiful woman away from her hotel room while his cousin searched for the missing mobile phone, Ryan was less concerned about her wanting to leave and more concerned about her wanting to stay.

And then, as if on cue, she leaned forward and kissed him on the lips.

Jack was not caught totally off guard, he'd noted her attraction, but there was a difficult moment when she put her hand on the back of his head and pulled him close. The earpiece's battery supply hung behind his ear. It was out of sight, but it was not designed to go undetected if someone was mussing up the hair of the person wearing it.

Jack pulled away, a show of hesitation.

Clark spoke into his ear, his own voice soft. 'Jack, we are not receiving any transmissions from you. Everything okay in there?'

Élise said, 'Oh . . . I see. You are married.'

Jack smiled. 'If I were, I think you would have read about it on Google.'

'You're gay?'

'I guarantee *that* would have made the Internet.'

'Then?'

'I have to go to the bathroom.'

'Oh.' She smiled. 'No problem. I'll wait.'

Élise went back into the suite and sat down on the edge of the bed.

Ryan stepped into the bathroom, shut the door, and stood there. *C'mon, Jack, what's the fucking plan here?*

Ding spoke through his earpiece. 'Jack . . . Dom's going to need fifteen mikes minimum.'

'Yeah,' he whispered. 'Not a problem.'

Oh, boy.

Dom did not have a key to get into room 3112, but he didn't let that slow him down. As he stepped up to the door he pulled out a device built by Gavin Biery and his whiz kids at The Campus. It was a microcontroller just larger than a deck of cards, with a small cable that fed from it to a barrel connector.

Dom took the connector and knelt down so he could

see the bottom of the key-card door-locking mechanism. Here, hidden from view of hotel guests, was a tiny round port. He pushed his connector into the port and flipped a switch on his device.

Certain brands of key-card locks have these ports for the purpose of recharging the battery on the locking mechanism and uploading the hotel site code, a thirty-two-bit key that provides general access to all locks in the hotel. This is the master key that housekeeping and other hotel workers use so that they don't need an individual and ever-changing card to get into each room.

When Gavin powered up his microcontroller by flipping the switch, the lock sent the thirty-two-bit key from the lock down to the device, and then the device read and decoded it, and sent it back up to the lock.

The green light illuminated next to the key-card access slot in under a second, even though there was no key in the slot.

Dominic opened the door, unplugged his device, and slipped it back into his backpack.

Ryan stood in the marble bathroom of his junior suite, staring at himself in the mirror, trying to figure out what he was going to do about the woman on his bed.

He'd been surprised by how quickly Élise was escalating matters. They were both single, attractive people, and she had shown some interest, but it seemed more of a curiosity to her and less of a lustful nature.

Jack thought about kissing her. He'd not been able to properly enjoy it because of the earpiece and the chatter from his team, but otherwise it would have been a different story. Still, he was working, and this wasn't real. The thought of screwing some woman for the purpose of stalling her so someone else could ransack her hotel room made him sick to his stomach.

Clark thought the French spook was herself running some kind of op on Jack, either to compromise him or to gain information or influence, but Jack didn't see evidence of that himself. Clark was trained to think OPSEC and only OPSEC, while Jack had a lot of recent experience with members of the opposite sex showing interest in him.

He flushed the toilet, ran the water in the sink, and tried to tell himself this wasn't a harmless TV reality show, this was life or death. The woman in the next room was an enemy operative who was working on behalf of the damn North Koreans, and he didn't need to give a rat's ass about anything other than his mission.

There was no way to disengage without blowing the objective and revealing that he'd played her, and there was no way to keep her in this room without having sex with her.

'What's going on, Ryan?' Clark asked.

Ryan popped his earpiece out of his ear and slid it in his pocket, flipped off the water, and left the bathroom.

Time to go to work.

Élise was on the bed. She still had her clothes on, but her come-hither look told him he wasn't out of the woods. He took a step toward her.

And then her mobile phone rang in her purse.

There was a momentary look of surprise on her face. Jack wondered if the distinctive chirping ring meant the call was coming from a particular number. She stood up from the bed and picked her purse up from the coffee table. While doing so she said, 'Sorry. I'd better take this.'

'Sure,' Jack replied.

Hello?"

'It's Riley. Where *are* you?'

Veronika Martel could tell by the Englishman's voice that something was very wrong. 'Hi, Rebecca. Nice of you to call, but I am in the US at the moment. It's very late at night over here.'

'Listen to me,' Riley continued, as if she hadn't said a word. 'There is a man in your hotel room right now.'

'What? How do you know?'

'Not relevant. The point is I *do* know. What I don't know is just what the fuck he is doing, but I have men heading there now to find out. Wherever you are, you get your bloody ass back to your room right now!'

Ryan sat down on the bed and watched the French-woman turn away as she held the phone to her ear. After a brief conversation she turned back around, facing Ryan, and her face went from a guise of slight annoyance about the call that Ryan thought might have been feigned to an obvious appearance of anger that was both very real and very dark. Her eyes narrowed, staring directly at Ryan.

He didn't know what was happening, but he asked, 'Is something wrong?'

The woman hung up the phone and snatched up her purse. 'Who . . . *are* . . . you?' she asked.

'What do you mean?' He tried a little chuckle and stood

up, began walking over to her. *Don't leave,* he told himself. 'You Googled me, remember?'

When he was halfway across the small suite, she turned and stormed for the door.

'What's wrong? Wait.'

But she was gone, almost at a run, and the door slammed behind her.

'Damn it.' Ryan scrambled for his earpiece, digging for it in his pocket, but after a few seconds he gave up with the tiny contraption and dove headfirst across the bed. He grabbed his phone on the nightstand and unlocked it, then opened the conference call. 'Dom! Get the fuck out of there! She knows!'

47

Caruso had found the phone; it was in a wheeled roll-aboard whose lock he picked in twenty seconds after spending a minute checking it for telltales. Within three and a half minutes of entering the Frenchwoman's hotel room he had the device downloading to Gavin's specially designed unit.

And then, within seconds of his beginning the download, the frantic call came from Ryan telling him the woman was loose and on her way back to her room. Caruso was less worried about her showing up while he was here – to travel from the thirty-ninth floor to the thirty-first floor she'd first have to go down to the lobby to reach the other elevator bank – and more worried about how the hell she knew he was here in the first place. She'd gotten a call, Ryan said, so Dom assumed she had confederates in the hallway who had seen him, confederates who were somehow patched into hotel security cameras, or confederates who had bugged her room.

Whatever the case, it meant unknown parties were involved in this and aware of him, and this meant trouble.

Dom wasn't sure what to do, so he called out to Clark. 'John?'

'I'm in the lobby, watching for trouble heading your way. Don't see anyone, but get out of there. Could be someone already up on that floor.'

'This download is gonna take a few more minutes.'

Clark said, 'It's too late for covert. They know there was an intrusion. Just snag the phone and bolt.'

'I was hoping you'd say that.'

Caruso slipped the two phones joined with a cable into his backpack and started for the door. Her suite was similar to Ryan's; there was a small hallway that ran along the kitchenette and hid the front door from the living and sleeping area, and Dom ran for it, but once he turned into the little hallway of the suite, he saw the latch of the door slowly lowering.

It was too late to escape out the front.

Caruso turned and ran back into the suite, leapt over the coffee table and onto the sofa, then over the back of the sofa to the balcony door. He unlocked it and flung it open, then started outside.

There was a boom of a handgun discharge in the room behind him, then the crashing of glass right next to his head as the sliding glass door shattered. Dom took the eight-foot-deep balcony in two bounds, rolled over the side of the railing, grabbing the metal bar on the outside of the balcony, then scaling down quickly to the bottom of the railing. A second loud report from the room sounded closer than the first, and Dom struggled to hold on as his feet dangled thirty-one stories over Las Vegas Boulevard.

He heard Clark in his ear calling to him, but he concentrated on swinging his body back, away from the building, to pick up some momentum. He'd just started his swing forward when he felt his fingers slip off the metalwork of the balcony above his outstretched arms, and he looked up just in time to see an Asian man in a black hoodie leaning over the side, a suppressed pistol in his hands.

Dom swung to the balcony below him, let go fully now, and crashed onto a padded settee and then through a plexiglass bistro table. The crash knocked the wind out of him, and he knew he'd battered his arms and ribs, but he fought his way to his feet and looked back and up.

The Asian assassin could not see him from the balcony above, but he must have dropped to the floor of the balcony, because Dom now saw the pistol appear at the end of an arm that waved back and forth, pointing down to the balcony where Dom stood.

With a flash and a loud boom, the man fired. The round crashed through the locked glass door just three feet to Dom's left.

He dove to the ground on his right.

Another round barked; this one hit the glass closer to Dom.

Dom leapt back to his feet, grabbed a metal chair, and swung it up and out at the gun. He struck it as a fourth round fired, and he knocked the weapon from the man's hand. It arced out away from the building and fell from view.

Dom didn't want to wait around to see if this assassin had a backup, so he turned and ran through the shattered glass door. This room was empty, thankfully, so in seconds Dom was in the hall, and in seconds more he was in the stairwell. He raced down thirty floors in five minutes, adrenaline propelling him most of the way.

By the time he made it to the ground floor, Ryan and

Clark were out front, waiting for the valet to retrieve the Mercedes. Dom walked up next to them without a word, and when the car came he helped Jack get his luggage in the back.

They were back on Las Vegas Boulevard before the first responders pulled up out front with reports of shots fired high in the massive tower.

While Ryan uploaded the files taken from Élise's mobile phone, the rest of the team broke down the safe house. Dom called Adara Sherman and delivered news that she was more than accustomed to hearing these days. It was time to do another mad scramble to get the hell out of town.

The Gulfstream took off from Henderson Executive Airport, south of the city, at one-thirty in the morning.

Adara spent much of the first hour of the flight tending to Dominic Caruso. He had quite a few cuts and bruises, but no broken bones. Ryan thought his wounds looked pretty superficial, but Adara was the team medic and for some reason she felt the need to devote a lot of attention to Dom's injuries.

While Dom got treatment in the back of the cabin, the rest of the group sat up front and discussed the events of the evening. It was abundantly clear there was a unit of North Korean operatives, sanctioned to kill, shadowing employees of Sharps Global Intelligence Partners. It was unknown if the Sharps people were coordinating with them or not. It was also decided there wasn't a lot for the operators of The Campus to do other than return to

Alexandria and wait for Gavin Biery to unlock whatever secrets Élise's phone held.

Ryan had been compromised in all this, because an operative of Sharps's clearly knew, or else highly suspected, that he'd coerced her away from her hotel room at the exact moment someone was breaking into it. The original plan would have had no comebacks on Ryan, because Élise would have never known her phone had been compromised.

This wasn't good at all from a PERSEC perspective, but there wasn't much any of them could do about this now.

Soon after their debrief, the men lowered the backs on their cabin chairs and began nodding off.

It was five-thirty in the morning DC time, and two-thirty a.m. on the body clocks of the worn-out men in the Gulfstream, when the light on the cabin phone began flashing.

Adara Sherman had been sitting on the couch next to the bandaged and sound-asleep Dominic Caruso. She reached over and picked up the mobile handset. Softly she said, 'Aircraft.'

'Good morning, Ms. Sherman, Gavin Biery calling.'

'Hey, Mr Biery. All the guys are resting at the moment.'

'Aw. I bet they are just adorable. Let the others sleep, but throw some water on Ryan and hand him the phone.'

'Right away, sir.'

Adara declined the suggestion to use water, so Ryan woke to find her gently nudging him. When he opened his eyes fully and sat up, she handed him the phone.

Ryan looked at her. 'Biery?'

Adara nodded with a smile.

Ryan was angry for two seconds; then his face illuminated with excitement and he brought the phone to his ear. 'You can't possibly have anything for us yet, can you?'

'You forget how good I am, Ryan. Dom sent me the files he pulled from Élise Legrande's device. They were two-fifty-six encrypted, but with an off-the-shelf commercial security software we'd figured out a few months back. It's really not that hard when you take –'

'Gavin, that's great, but what did you find in the files?'

'Well . . . the device was a working Samsung Galaxy phone, so I found some games and stuff. A few ringtones, too.'

Ryan was annoyed, but he was glad to hear the man had a little of his swagger back after his disastrous experience in the field in Prague.

Gavin waited for a reply, and when none came he asked, 'Not funny?'

'What else, Gavin?'

'Oh, yeah, right. There is an application, apparently proprietary in nature. Clearly something that she downloaded from the NewCorp applications server.'

'What does it do?'

'The program is designed to do one thing and one thing only. It is set up to manage and operate a large series of froth flotation cells in sequence. I don't really know what those are, but that's not my department.'

Ryan had spent the past several days at the facility; he knew exactly what froth flotation cells were. 'That's the high-tech washing machines that the ore is put into. They separate the minerals from the rest of the powder. If you are saying this program is to run a bunch of them at one time, then it's basically the center of the entire refinery process.'

'Bingo, Jack. Apparently the North Koreans have got themselves a processing plant, but they don't have a brain for it. They sent this sexy French mademoiselle to the American processing plant and made a copy of their entire operation's system.'

Ryan said, 'As soon as we get back, we've got to get this intel to Mary Pat. She knows the big picture in all this much better than we do. Hopefully this will help her figure out what the hell to do next.'

48

The morning after his arrival in North Korea, CIA officer Adam Yao and his fellow Chinese mining technicians ate a breakfast of noodles and tea in the dining room of the Yanggakdo International Hotel, and then they were led into a banquet room on the second floor of the massive building.

After they had taken their seats, one of their minders stepped up on a riser and took his place behind a lectern. His Mandarin-speaking translator followed him up, and she picked up a microphone. Through the translator, the minder let everyone know they would be going back to the airport that afternoon for the hourlong flight north to Chongju, but for this morning, they would enjoy a lecture that would help them get acquainted with North Korea, its customs, its citizenry, and its rules.

Adam groaned inwardly.

The minder then ran down a list of dos and don'ts that everyone must abide by while here in Korea. Some of them seemed just a little picky. No spitting on the ground, for example. But others delved into the bizarre. They were told they were not allowed to fold, crumple, or discard any picture of the Dae Wonsu. This included newspapers, magazines, and other media, all of which had photos of the Supreme Leader on virtually every page. Adam wondered how newspapers were discarded, but he knew enough not to raise his hand and draw attention to himself.

It was explained that radios were outlawed, unless they had been converted to pick up only certain stations, all of which were controlled by the central government. There were only a few television stations, they broadcast only at certain times, and even their scheduled broadcasts were subject to interruption.

Adam wasn't in town to watch TV, but some of the others mumbled quietly in annoyance.

After the minder stepped down, a woman took the stage and began what turned out to be a fifty-minute speech about the Dae Wonsu, his father, and their special relationship with China. The North Korean leadership was spoken of in reverential terms, and the woman's eyes misted over more than once as she talked of the Choi family, claiming it was only through their action that 'big brother' China had been saved from wars and famine. She said North Korea had invented several technologies crucial in mining, computer technology, and even air travel, all of which the people in the audience benefited from greatly.

It was complete and utter lunacy, and the small crowd, mostly pulled from China's well-educated high-tech sector, sat angry and dismayed.

This was the first time Adam had seen up close and in person this level of brainwashing, and it was chilling. These people lived in a closed society, they had no access to the Internet, satellite TV, or even most radio.

Still, Adam's colleagues knew who was paying their wages, and they also knew who held the guns out in the hallway. While any one of these Chinese technical advisers could have stood up and announced that everything the woman said was wrong, no one did so.

When the lecture on the intellectual, cultural, and historical supremacy of North Korea was over, several armed men entered the banquet room from a door on the right, followed by an entourage of older men in business suits. In the middle of the group a small man emerged, flanked on both sides by uniformed guards. Adam craned his neck to see the top of a bald head. Soon the bald man stepped onto the little stage and up to a microphone.

He spoke in Korean, which the translator converted, but his voice was even and easy to hear, so Adam understood the gist of his words even before they were relayed in Chinese.

'Good morning, and welcome to the Democratic People's Republic of Korea. My name is Hwang Min-ho, and I am the director of Korea Natural Resources Trading Corporation. It was I who invited you here, so I am very glad to see you all.'

Adam thought the man sounded somewhat meek and pleasant, especially in comparison to the harsh voices from most of the guards and minders he'd been in contact with since his arrival.

Hwang spoke for a while about the mine, the history of North Korea's partnership with China on other projects, and his respect for both the nation of China and its abilities in the mining sector. His words seemed more literal, less jingoistic than those of the woman who had spoken before him, and Adam could easily read the crowd and discern their sense of relaxation.

Hwang then offered a surprisingly frank assessment of the conditions at Chongju. 'You will find this facility to be more rudimentary than what you are accustomed to. We ask your patience while we build a processing facility that is state-of-the-art. It will take time. For now, however, we will start slowly and grow to greatness.'

Yao was surprised that Hwang did not show the same near-psychotic level of reverence for his own nation's capability. Even the fact that Hwang was here addressing the Chinese workers in the first place was fascinating to the CIA non-official cover officer. He hadn't expected to see this man in person at all.

Hwang said, 'You are guest workers, but you are to be treated well. Your contract says you will work for eight weeks. Then you will be allowed one week for vacation, or, if you prefer, you can continue to work.'

A man near the front raised his hand and asked, 'What is there to do around the mine on vacation?'

The director at the lectern shrugged. 'Work.'

There was laughter throughout the room.

When he was finished with his presentation, Hwang Min-ho thanked everyone again and then asked, 'Are there any questions?'

Adam hoped that the rest of his group would be smart enough to keep their mouths shut, but several hands shot up at once.

A middle-aged man who Adam had been told worked with electromagnetic milling machines was called on by Hwang. He asked, 'Director, sir. Can you tell us about the electrical grid we will find at the facility?'

Hwang smiled a little. 'We have electricity from a

hydroelectric dam nearby. For times when the dam is not generating power, which is often, but not too often, we have oil generators from your country that can keep critical functions up and running. It is not Shanghai, all lights and electric trains, but electricity at Chongju is a priority during the workday.' He smiled again. 'At night you must all sleep so you can work the next day. You don't need light to sleep.'

Adam already knew the facility and even the entire city of Chongju were 'lights out' for about twelve hours a day because the electricity didn't run. He'd seen the sat images.

Another person asked the one question Adam most wanted to know the answer to. 'I understand the facility is still under construction. May we know when you expect to be operational?'

Hwang replied, 'Construction of the property is complete. We just received a shipment of computers that arrived last week. You all will be responsible for getting them installed and running at your various workstations. Also, there is a new shipment of industrial powder-processing equipment, and some milling equipment at the refinery that needs to be installed and tested. Other than that, there is one shipment of large equipment still on the way. It should be here very soon. My fervent hope is we will be producing refined metals within one month.'

After saying he would be spending a lot of time at the processing facility in the next few weeks to oversee the opening, Hwang left the riser to polite but genuine applause from the Chinese nationals.

*

The bus delivered the technicians to the airport and drove them directly onto the tarmac and up to their aircraft. Adam climbed out of the bus into a blustery wind that foretold a thunderstorm. He looked into the early-evening sky and saw thick dark clouds just west of the capital.

Adam found this ominous, even more so when he turned around and looked at the airplane they'd be flying to Chongju.

It was a Boeing 737 wearing the red, white, and blue markings of Air Koryo.

Adam had read somewhere that Skytrax, the world airline rating service, had reviewed and rated nearly seven hundred airlines over the globe, and they had given out but a single one-star rating.

Air Koryo, North Korea's national airline, was the recipient.

Adam didn't remember where he had read this fact, but as he climbed aboard the plane he wished he had forgotten it.

The Air Koryo flight was bad, but Adam had been on worse flights in the USA. It landed without incident at Kwaksan Airport in an evening rain shower, and the men and women were led onto another bus, and then were driven on surprisingly good roads to the city of Chongju.

On this bus ride, as on the other, several armed guards sat at the front, and an olive-drab truck full of troops followed close behind. Adam wondered if the North Koreans were fearful a Chinese technician would leap from the moving vehicle and run out into the hills around the road. It occurred to him that if these people really believed North Korea was the paradise the woman at the welcome meeting this morning had claimed it was, then it stood to reason they'd need to watch out for foreigners trying to break in to reap the nation's bounty.

The city of Chongju was all but blacked out, obviously because there was no electricity running this evening. Beyond the lights of the bus he could see only the illumination of a few other vehicles on side streets, plus cooking fires, the odd flashlight, and the glow of cigarettes from people on the sidewalks in the darkness.

There was one major exception to the darkness. The bus entered a large driving circle, and in the middle was a forty-foot-high statue of Choi Ji-hoon in his military uniform, holding a pair of binoculars in one hand and pointing northward toward China with the other. The entire statue was bathed in bright yellow light, and a tiny street market had been set up around it to take advantage of the glow of the Dae Wonsu.

The bus made a turn and Adam leaned into the window glass and felt a sudden lump in his throat as he saw the entrance to the temporary housing facility. He'd spent a great deal of time in the past weeks studying this very place in satellite images. To be rolling through the front gates of the complex – it looked like some sort of prison camp from a World War II film – made him feel so much farther from home.

Orders were given in Korean and then translated into Chinese by a minder, and soon Adam was lined up in front of the bus with the rest of his group. During a short wait in the darkness, Adam had a moment to recognize that the last time he'd looked at this parking lot in the center of all the metal trailers, he'd been sitting in a tidy and efficient conference room in the ODNI building in McLean, Virginia, with a Starbucks latte in one hand and a cinnamon roll in the other. Now he was here, queuing up single-file to be counted and checked in and given a cot.

Even for a NOC who'd played a lot of roles in his career, this felt surreal and otherworldly.

49

Three days before the arrival of the President of the United States in Mexico City, Iranian bomb maker Adel Zarif was driven back to the parking garage construction site on the corner of Vidal Alcocer and José J. Herrera.

It was seven p.m. and the evening rains had ended, dusk was falling quickly on the area, and the street market had closed. But the area was not quiet. The sounds and lights of construction were obvious as soon as he climbed out of Emilio's truck. Zarif had been told a group of six Maldonado men with experience in construction had been working at the site all afternoon; they had a cement mixer and some portable lights and would be kept away from him while he was here, but they would be all his when he needed them.

He'd already spent the entire day building his weapon at an auto repair yard a quarter-mile away in northern Tepito. He'd taken his three 105-millimeter high-explosive artillery shells, removed the fuses in the nose cones, replaced each with a homemade delayed-action base fuse, wired them to detonate, and attached a blasting cap to each device. The blasting caps were, in turn, attached to a signaling device.

At the beginning of the Iraq War, Zarif and men like him used simple electronic detonating signalers, such as garage-door openers, to command-detonate IEDs. Soon enough, however, coalition forces began taking measures to jam these signals, so Zarif and the others graduated to cell phones.

These worked for a while. In fact, Zarif still used these almost exclusively against insurgents in Syria, but cell phones were not a perfect solution, either. Their signals could be jammed or otherwise interrupted, and large parts of the world were without coverage.

But there was another way. Long-range cordless phones aren't popular in the United States, but in locations with spotty cell coverage the devices are ubiquitous. The Taiwanese firm StreamTel sold a popular model of phone that consisted of a base station that plugged into a wired phone network, and a handset with a range of up to dozens of kilometers. Two or more handsets could be paired to the same line, and this created a nearly unjammable long-range signaling device.

StreamTel sets were components of thousands of IEDs in the Middle East. The company boasted that forty percent of its world market share came from sales to Iraq, Afghanistan, and Pakistan, and the US military understood the reason behind the demand.

Zarif had a Maldonado lieutenant purchase a base station and two handsets from a telephone store in Guadalajara and ferry them into the capital city, and the Iranian built his device much as he would have done had he been in Mosul, Iraq, or Helmand Province in Afghanistan. It wasn't state-of-the-art, but the veteran bomb maker always believed the tried-and-true methods were the most reliable.

The entire IED was carried into the construction site

just after dark inside a large rolling tool chest the size of a steamer trunk, and then Zarif was left alone behind the orange tarp while the half-dozen other men poured concrete on the sidewalk on José J. Herrera and in the already built stairwell in the center of the site.

The open rebar wall frame that Zarif had found three days earlier had changed. The men today had built a lumber casing around the lower six feet of the wall and they had already filled it with concrete. Above this they had built another wooden frame to raise the wall up to its intended height of twelve feet, but a portion of the frame high on the wall was missing, following Zarif's instructions.

One by one Zarif took the pieces of his IED up a ladder and onto a scaffolding five feet off the ground next to the wall and he gently reassembled the device in the metal rebar grid exposed by the missing boards. The shells faced out toward the six-lane street on the other side of the tarp. They were positioned ten feet off the ground, and each one was slightly angled with wooden shunts so that they would project downward onto the street.

The artillery shells did not have full charges behind them, nor were they being propelled through long barrels that would spin them through rifling, so they would not launch like they would if fired from a howitzer. Still, Zarif had a design plan for his weapon to ensure that the explosives launched out to the street before detonating. He had two Maldonado men help him place three ninety-pound sheets of iron at the back of the device, behind the shells in the grid, using more wooden slats to hold them in position while he soldered them to the rebar. When he finished this, he had created a plate to deflect the back blast of the initial detonator charge, and thereby propel the artillery shells outward.

Zarif had created identical devices many times in the past, and he'd destroyed enemy armor with them at a range of up to fifty feet.

It took him nearly three hours to ready the IED high on the open wall, and then he covered the entire device with plastic bags, threading them through the rebar, wrapping them from the blast plate in back to the nose cones in front, protecting everything and hiding the bomb from the other Maldonado men. He and his helpers then cleared back the scaffolding and the ladder, and finally they called for the men to bring in the cement blower.

Three hours after this, the concrete was poured all around the device, and the next morning, when the quick-drying concrete had formed, workers began placing a thin sheet of stone veneer over the front of the wall.

By noon the next day the entire façade was complete. From Vidal Alcocer, the six-lane street down which the President would travel, it looked like a massive concrete parking-lot wall with a decorative façade, but in truth it hid the explosive force of three howitzer rounds, and on command, the rounds would launch out into the road in front of it and detonate.

But Zarif wasn't finished. In the afternoon Zarif had Emilio take him to a grocery store, and here he grabbed a basket and walked directly to the spice section. He picked up several containers of cumin and turmeric.

Emilio asked, 'Are you making dinner?'

'You'll see.'

They returned to the construction site. It was empty again, but now the tarp in front of the wall had been cleared away, and they walked around the wall and under the tarp on the José J. Herrera side. Zarif went to his wall, pulled out his containers of spices, opened them, and got down on his hands and knees. Slowly and meticulously he began pouring them along where the floor met the new wall. He used a lot right below the device, and then he crawled in each direction, sprinkling less and less until he had covered the entire floor.

He stood up, dusted off his hands, and walked over to a drain in the concrete floor of the parking garage. He knelt down and peered through the metal grating, then looked up to Emilio. 'One more thing. I need you to find me a dead animal.'

'What?'

'Really dead.'

An hour later a Maldonado runner arrived on the back of a motorcycle. In his hand he carried a white garbage bag. He handed it to Zarif, who opened the bag and recoiled from the stench. A putrefying cat lay inside.

Zarif walked over to the open drain, removed the grating, and dumped the dead cat out of the bag. It fell in just two feet before landing where the drainpipe turned.

He looked to Emilio. 'This will also affect the dogs" noses.'

Emilio nodded. 'What dogs?'

'The Americans will search this area before the

President drives by. I've seen it on YouTube. They will bring dogs that can smell explosives. But here the dogs will smell spices and dead cats.' He pointed up high on the wall. 'Even if they check the wall, they won't check up so high. No one will look for a bomb that points down.'

Zarif grinned at his own cleverness.

50

Adam spent his first day at the Chongju refinery installing his new computer terminal. Even though the machine was a new but run-of-the-mill PC, it had been shipped from France and had been loaded with a few off-the-shelf mining software programs he would use to operate the massive cone crusher. None of the software was terribly complicated, but the tools were very specific in nature, and even though Adam had learned the job in a couple weeks, no one in North Korea had the training or the experience to run the machine.

This meant Adam was the only person authorized to use the terminal, and this was extremely good news for Adam because the cone crusher operating program wasn't the most distinctive thing about this PC. Adam had been briefed and trained by the CIA's Science and Technology staff on how to use the terminal to send clandestine messages back to the Acrid Herald operations center at the Liberty Crossing Intelligence Campus.

Even though the device wasn't attached to the Internet, there was a text feature that was connected not to the computer's hard drive and motherboard but to another device that had been built into all the hardware. It was, essentially, a satellite phone without a speaker, just the components of the device that could make a connection via satellite and send a text message. The miniaturized pieces of the device were so well hidden within the rest of the computer hardware inside the tower that even if the North Koreans disassembled the machine, they would need a computer hardware expert to come to the conclusion that tiny pieces that didn't belong were attached to different parts of the motherboard and power supply. Even then it would be nigh on impossible to discern just what the equipment was, only that it wasn't needed.

But that wasn't covert enough for Science and Technology. The tiny components they did use were all Chinese in manufacture, made by the company Huawei, which, surely everyone in North Korean intelligence knew, had ties to Chinese intelligence.

Taking this extra step ensured that, even if the computer was revealed as an intelligence collection device, China would be the country blamed for spying on the Chongju operation.

That wouldn't do Adam one damn bit of good. North Korean counterintel would shoot him for being a Chinese spy just as quickly as they would shoot him for being an American spy, but at least America would be in the clear.

On his first day getting his machine up and running, Adam realized he couldn't have asked for a better desk. He had the lone workstation at a cubicle alongside a two-story-tall cone crushing machine. As far as secure locations went to broadcast his messages back to ODNI, he felt like he was in a comfortable place.

Several men worked on the machine in his proximity,

most of them on a catwalk above him, but Adam was the only man with any business in the back of the machine where his workstation stood. Further, the other workers were mechanical engineers and simple ore loaders, and Adam doubted they would notice anything amiss even if they did see him opening the texting program to contact ODNI.

This cone crusher had been here in North Korea for a year and a half, long before construction started on the refinery. The state-owned Chinese company Chinalco put the machine at the Chongju mine itself, a kilometer to the east, because the Chinese had planned on crushing the ore down to processing size so it could be transported in sacks on trucks, as opposed to larger rocks, which were harder to ferry. But the North Koreans had no problem trucking the ore the kilometer to the processing facility, so they brought the massive machine here, where the electricity ran more regularly than at the mine.

Right after a fifteen-minute break for tea and plant-wide government-mandated singing, stretching, and knee bends, Adam returned to his desk with plans to send his first message home. He checked his area to make sure there was no one around who could see what he was doing. This involved him simply looking back over his shoulder and then scanning overhead through the grating of the catwalk. When he was comfortable that he was clear, he restarted his PC, then went into the BIOS screen of the computer. Here he changed a series of settings, and then pressed enter.

He had two choices now. He could type a *1*, which would take him to the texting program, or he could type a *2*, which would send him to a satellite map of North Korea that had been hidden on the drive. In the case of an emergency exfiltration, Adam's minders had had the foresight to realize, he would need a good idea of the area and the ability to type in specific coordinates, so the function had been secreted on the drive.

Adam wasn't on the run now, and he hoped like hell he never would be, so he typed *1* and hit enter again.

The screen went blank except for a small blinking cursor in the lower right.

Adam had to admit, S&T had set this up so no one was going to accidentally find the clandestine software.

He took another glance around, then quickly typed out a message, all in Mandarin, so if it was somehow intercepted, the US would not be blamed for the operation.

SECRET

TO: FLASH FOR TIDALWAVE
FROM: AVALANCHE
SUBJECT: ARRIVAL ESTABLISHMENT
SOURCE: AVALANCHE

1. ALL NOMINAL. FULL REPORT SOONEST

2. FLASH – DIR. HWANG MIN-HO MET WITH AVALANCHE AND OTHER CHINA TECHS 2 DAYS PRIOR IN PYONGYANG – HE CLAIMS ONE (1) FURTHER SHIMENT OF LARGE EQUIPMENT TO ARRIVE BEFORE FACILITY ON LINE.

NO INDICATION OF TYPE OF EQUIPMENT. WITH NO
FURTHER CORROBORATION, AVALANCHE CANNOT
INDEPENDENTLY CONFIRM.

3. HWANG CLAIMS HE WILL BE PRESENT AT PROCESSING
FACILITY IN COMING WEEKS.

AVALANCHE

The final reference to his code name was the tip that he was not writing under duress. Had he signed off with anything else – or nothing at all – the control officers of Acrid Herald would have known the words on their screen could not be taken at face value.

Adam hit the enter key twice; this directed the satellite phone to send the digital message.

Science and Technology had warned him about this part. Back in McLean they let him know the sending could take a couple minutes, and some messages might have to be resent. As good as the technology was – and the eggheads from Langley promised it *was* the best – there were always atmospheric conditions that could come into play, as well as issues with other equipment at the Chongju facility.

They'd also given him one more interesting tidbit of in-formation. Most sat phones blast their signals to one of many commercial satellites, but this phone beamed to an NSA satellite in geostationary orbit over North Korea, parts of China, and Japan. He was assured the signal would broadcast, eventually, but was reminded to wait for a confirmation from the computer in the form of a long row of dashes that ran from left to right.

After a minute and a half he received this confirmation.

Adam was pleasantly surprised the boys and girls at S&T, who didn't have to be out in the field with the devices, didn't just put a big flashing 'MESSAGE SENT' graphic on the monitor.

51

As director of national intelligence, Mary Pat Foley was the chief intelligence officer of the United States of America, and with this role quite naturally came a tremendous amount of responsibility and a large number of draws on her time.

So the fact that she made a third trip down the George Washington Memorial Parkway to the offices of Hendley Associates indicated the importance of the intelligence product being generated by the sub rosa private outfit run by former South Carolina senator Gerry Hendley.

Today's meeting was not with the entire Campus operational staff. Instead, only Mary Pat, Gerry Hendley, and Jack Ryan sat in the conference room. Sam was still in New York, monitoring Sharps Partners. And there would be no after-action report today as they had done to explain their activities in Vietnam, so Clark, Chavez, and Caruso remained at their desks.

Ryan imparted the knowledge they had gleaned on the operation, without going into details of shootouts and breaking and entering. He was careful to avoid any more detail about the events of Las Vegas than was necessary.

Ryan explained how a Sharps agent copied the proprietary software, certainly to give to the North Koreans.

*

Mary Pat listened carefully. When Jack's presentation was finished, she seemed to consider how much she would tell the men around her, but apparently she decided on partial disclosure. 'Your information is helpful. We have our own intelligence source that picked up something that fits in with what you are telling me.'

Jack knew better than to ask 'What source?'

Mary Pat said, 'The Chongju refinery is expecting a shipment of material in the next few days. The source did not know what was coming in, only that the shipment would be very large.'

Jack said, 'Froth flotation cells certainly fit that description. The ones at Valley Floor are each probably the size of an SUV. They've got a dozen or more, so if Chongju is expecting a shipment of those, you can bet it would be big.'

Mary Pat said, 'If Chongju is expecting a shipment of flotation cells in the next week, they'd be on the water right now.'

Ryan and the other Hendley men assumed there wasn't much the United States could do about it if they *were* on the water. There was no law stopping the shipment of mining equipment.

Mary Pat returned to Liberty Crossing and immediately put in a call to CIA. Within minutes she had a team of men and women, all financial forensic specialists, trying to find any trace of either a sale or a shipment of froth flotation cells.

This was trickier than it might seem. While froth flotation cells were not exactly a common commodity bought and sold around the world, different versions of the units were used in many different kinds of industries. Additionally, it wasn't a sanctioned material, so the commerce of the items, as for most industrial products, was not necessarily recorded.

But the team was good, and they found four recent movements of the exact material in the first three hours of research. A Canadian company had just sold nine cells of the size and capability of that supported by the software. A Brazilian mine had gone out of business in the past year and all of its cells had been purchased some months earlier. An Australian firm had custom-built twelve cells just in the past month. And a Malaysian processing facility had upgraded to new tanks and sold its old cells off.

The economic forensic team began with the Canadian transaction. Quickly it was confirmed that the goods were still in Vancouver, and were to be shipped to Brazil, to another rare earth refinery. The company, its owners, and their known affiliations were double- and triple-checked, as the CIA looked for any evidence of a straw-man purchase for the North Koreans. But ultimately they decided the transaction was legitimate.

Next they looked at the defunct Brazilian processing plant. A deep scrub of the company and the sale showed them the cells were sold from one company entity to another, certainly to avoid losing the capital in bankruptcy proceedings. The analysts asked a CIA officer in São Paulo to fly up to Belo Horizonte immediately to go 'eyeball' the goods at the warehouse where the records said they were now being stored, but this appeared to be a dead end as well.

Ditto the Australian sale. Its custom-built froth flotation cells were on their way to the Lynas Advanced Materials Plant rare earth facility near Kuantan, Malaysia. This was one of the larger and more modern facilities in the world, and they processed much of Australia's rare earths. Even though the facility was just a few years old, it was not terribly surprising that they would upgrade their cells, because new developments in the field had heralded new technology, and LAMP was cutting-edge.

This left one more transaction. Where did the old cells from LAMP go?

The analytical team saw a red flag very quickly. The machinery had been sold four months earlier to a company that existed only on paper. That company went up in smoke, but before it went out of business it transferred its capital to a holding group registered in Singapore.

This turned out to be a dead end, at least in the short term, but the analysts knew their higher-ups were hell-bent on getting quick answers. They turned their attention to the location of the physical material. Lynas was an Australian company, so a conversation between CIA director Jay Canfield and his counterpart, the director of Australian intelligence, led to a conference call between CIA analysts and Australian businessmen, which led to Malaysian shipping clerks in Kota Bharu, a port on Malaysia's eastern shore. They confirmed a dozen large crates had been shipped in several trucks from Kuantan, warehoused in Kota Bharu, and then placed in four forty-five-foot high-cube shipping containers and placed on board a ship just fourteen days earlier.

That ship sailed to Manila, where the cargo was offloaded and driven away by private vehicles.

This looked like yet another dead end, but the analysts did not give up. They knew a CIA source – none of them were read in on Acrid Herald – had revealed the equipment was due to arrive in the next few days, so they began working the equation from the other direction, looking at shipping heading to North Korea. An Indonesian-flagged cargo ship, the *San Fernando Chieftain*, had begun a voyage in Marseille that would terminate in North Korea. On its way it made several ports of call, and one of those ports was Manila, just six days earlier.

The entire team began working on digging into the cargo on board, and within a short time they learned four forty-five-foot high-cube shipping containers from Malaysia, categorized only as machinery, had been placed on the manifest in the port of Manila. And the *San Fernando Chieftain* was now just thirty hours from arriving in the territorial waters of North Korea.

The economic forensics team delivered their findings up the chain, and they moved on to something else the next day, wholly unaware of the importance of the matter, or the full scope of their contribution.

When Mary Pat Foley received the news, she realized she had all the information she needed, but that in itself solved nothing. Finding evidence that a ship heading to North Korea contained particular items, if those items were not bound by sanction restrictions, did nothing to stop the items from reaching North Korea.

Still, Mary Pat decided, the President needed to know

that evidence led to the fact that North Korea needed but one more piece of the puzzle to begin production on their cash cow, and that puzzle piece seemed to be just one day away.

She called Arnie Van Damm herself and asked for an immediate slot to see the President. Arnie said he would be in and out of meetings all day preparing for his official visit to Mexico, but he worked her in immediately without protest.

Mary Pat Foley rolled onto the White House grounds fifty minutes later, and she was led into the Oval as she had been hundreds of times. She found the President on the sofa, laughing at something the distinguished-looking man sitting in front of him had just said.

Ryan stood and introduced Foley to Horatio Styles, the US ambassador to Mexico. He explained that Styles was up in Washington just for two days, and then he'd be returning with the President on Air Force One for his official visit.

After the introductions, the ambassador left the Oval Office on his way back to the Department of State. As soon as he was gone Ryan said, 'Hell of a guy. He served all over the world as a Marine officer, but he fell in love with Latin America. He retired a colonel, then got his Ph.D. in Latin American studies from Columbia. He's probably the most capable non-career State Department employee serving as an ambassador. If he spreads his wings a little he's got the makings of a hell of a secretary of state.'

'Yes, sir,' Mary Pat said, and the President sat back down.

'Okay, you're not here to listen to me brag about my brilliant ambassadorship nominations. What's up?'

She told him about the shipload of equipment heading to Chongju, and the fact it was likely the last major component necessary before the refinery became operational.

Ryan listened carefully. His first question did not surprise her in the least. 'This comes from our new source at the mine?'

'Partially, yes.' Mary Pat didn't mention that the President's own son had provided crucial bits of intel.

Jack looked long and hard at his director of national intelligence, trying to read her thoughts. He noted the ambiguity in her answer, and he was used to it. His people shielded him from things. He didn't much like it, but he understood it.

His mind switched from Mary Pat to the issue at hand. The UN Sanctions Committee refused to vote on increasing the economic sanctions against North Korea that Ryan knew were crucial to choking off the Hermit Kingdom's access to the hard currency it was using to obtain nuclear missile technology. Ryan had been thinking about what steps he was prepared to take unilaterally. He'd not yet come to a conclusion, but he'd now run out of time to mull it over.

He had to act.

'Mary Pat, from what we've learned in the past month, the evidence is clear, and it all points to the fact this Chongju facility is serving as a funding vehicle for North Korea's nuclear weapons program. I am going to go to the

National Security Council and authorize a Presidential Directive stating the Chongju mineral mine and processing facility in North Korea represents a clear and present danger to the security of the United States, and I will direct that our military, intelligence, and diplomatic efforts be engaged in keeping that facility from going into full production.'

He added, 'I'm not going to attack it, that would just send North Korean artillery and missiles raining down on Seoul, but I am damn well going to do everything short of that.'

Mary Pat had rarely seen her President more resolute. 'Yes, sir. Please be aware, though, that if you want the Navy to interdict that ship, they will have to do it within twenty-four hours, or it will be in North Korean waters.'

Ryan nodded. 'I understand. I'm going to call Burgess right now and tell him about the directive. By the time he gets forces in position to stop that boat, the paper will be signed.' Ryan rubbed his nose under his eyeglasses. 'We'll take heat for it, but it needs to happen.'

Mary Pat left the Oval minutes later. She had work to do. Perhaps less than the National Security Council, because they had just hours to draw up a Presidential Directive for POTUS to sign. But once this was done, Mary Pat knew the gloves were off. A Presidential Directive carried the full force and effect of law, and with it in place she and her counterparts in the Defense Department and the State Department would be directed to do whatever they could to see that the Chongju mine earned no more money for the North Korean nuclear weapons program.

And even though the battle would be fought in a co-ordinated fashion by the combined power of the entire United States government, the director of national intelligence was keenly aware that at the very tip of the spear in this endeavor was a young man in North Korea who was as alone as anyone could possibly be.

52

Dale Herbers of the US Secret Service was a week into his advance in Mexico City before he drove the presidential motorcade route from the airport to the Palacio Nacional. This was by design. He could have run the route earlier in his workup, but he felt his other responsibilities – securing the locations of the various static events of the President's trip to the city – were better taken care of first, and the motorcade route saved for closer to the actual day of. Things changed on the streets more than they changed in museums, restaurants, government buildings, and other attractions, and Herbers, like most advance-team shift leaders, wanted a game-time feel to the route the President would travel.

The forty-seven-year-old lead special agent and his senior staff of a dozen special agents, as well as several counterparts from various Mexican law enforcement agencies who were working the motorcade, all left Benito Juárez airport just after noon, the exact time of the President's scheduled arrival in two days. They drove together in a convoy of vehicles on the westerly route toward the Plaza de la Constitución, the massive central square where the palace stood and the President's motorcade from the airport would terminate.

One of the most important parts of the advance team's work was identifying the choke points and crowd gathering locations, the places where the motorcade would need to slow down to negotiate turns. Today his role was to assign American and Mexican law enforcement to these key portions of the motorcade, and to identify any other potential threats so as to deal with them now, before the President arrived.

In all the official events SWORDSMAN would attend here in Mexico, even those open to the public, every spectator and participant would be subjected to screening. This meant they would either pass through metal detectors or be wanded. And all bags would, of course, be searched. But it was impossible to secure the route, every window, rooftop, alleyway, every pocket of every civilian on every sidewalk, and every car on every side street.

Motorcades were a mess, but the Secret Service was accustomed to dealing with them. The President would be ushered along the way in 'the bubble,' a Secret Service term meaning a protective cocoon of close protection agents, a large counter-assault team that rode just behind him, and an array of static Secret Service men on rooftops and barricade positions along the route.

There were more than two hundred agents here in Mexico City for the visit, and virtually every last one of them had a role in the motorcade from the airport. And that was just the first line of defense. Mexican Federal Police would have another six hundred officers involved in roadblocks, motorcycle escorts, traffic control, and crowd overwatch.

And Herbers had one more thing going in his favor.

The Beast.

The presidential limousine was a highly modified and

customized Cadillac DTS and had acquired the name 'the Beast' because of its size and weight. But bullet-proof glass and thick armor plating were just two of the vehicle's features. Run-flat tires, night-vision equipment, an internal oxygen supply, and secure communications also made up the vehicle's security measures, and another, identical vehicle always ran in the motorcade so the President would have a backup if his primary broke down.

Herbers had been informed that SWORDSMAN had been asked to stay in the Beast for the duration of the drive by his lead protection agent, Andrea Price O'Day. This wasn't likely to be an issue; some Presidents liked to get out and glad-hand the crowd, but that wasn't really Ryan's style. While Herbers thought him to be a kind and approachable man, Ryan didn't possess the politician gene of so many of the other people he'd worked around in his twenty-three years on the service. Ryan didn't go out of his way to meet people unless it was necessary to win an election.

The convoy of advance-team men and women stopped many times along the route, and all of them would then climb out of their vehicles. Herbers would see a group of open windows that bothered him, or a troublesome building with balconies or other potential aggressor overwatch positions, or even just narrow side streets that ran close to his route that he wanted to look over to see if he felt it necessary to block them off.

This was an experienced group, and despite all the stops, they accomplished the first half of the route in good time. But then they traveled through the high-crime neighborhood of Tepito, and this part of the city required extra care.

When Agent Dale Herbers started his workup of the Mexico official visit, he and his staff quickly identified the short stretch of Eje 1 as a location that needed special attention. Every motorcade had to either go down this long, straight six-lane thoroughfare or else navigate the narrow two-lane streets of the Tepito and Centro districts. As much as the Secret Service tried to avoid taking the President on a predictable route, it had been decided that was preferable to taking him through a narrow warren of alleys surrounded by close-in buildings, subjecting the motorcade to twice as many turns and forcing it to travel much more slowly through such a rough district.

No, this stretch of Eje 1, called Vidal Alcocer, was undoubtedly the best route to take.

Which meant every motorcade from the airport used it, and this was a problem.

So now Herbers was here, looking over every block with a critical eye. He walked this vulnerable part of the motorcade route shadowed by four other Secret Service agents and four detectives from Mexico's Federal District police. They took notes on paper and on tablet computers, as Herbers directed the different organizations in how to prepare for the upcoming motorcade.

On the corner of Vidal Alcocer and José J. Herrera, Herbers noticed a construction site with a long twelve-foot-high wall running north and south along the sidewalk, and next to it a street market running west on Herrera.

A Mexican detective explained how they had planned

to barricade the market off from the motorcade route, and Herbers immediately crossed the street and ducked under the orange tarp at the southern edge of the site. The others followed him in.

He and his team spent a few minutes inside, walking around. He was looking for stashed weapons, a sniper's hide, anything out of the ordinary.

As soon as he headed over to the clean and newly poured concrete eastern wall of the site, he smelled the rotten stench of something dead. The other men smelled it, too, and it took less than thirty seconds for a Mexican Federal District officer to shine his flashlight in the sealed drain on the floor of the garage.

'*Gato,*' he said. Cat.

Herbers looked himself. 'Poor kitty must have gone down there before they covered the drain and got caught.'

He didn't give it another thought.

Herbers looked at the wall next. One of his men had a flashlight of his own and he walked the length of the wall, tapping it both at waist height and a little higher than his head, just to confirm there was no false compartment built into it.

A bomb-sniffing dog was led along the wall; she sniffed in the edges and immediately pulled her head back and sneezed. She kept walking, kept trying to sniff the area, and sneezed again.

Herbers glanced up to the dog handler for an explanation.

The handler just said, 'Construction dust. Masonry and loose grout.' He kept going. Within seconds they were moving into the next concrete staircase.

Herbers kept scanning the area for a few minutes. He saw a radio on a bucket, and he lifted the device and kicked over the bucket to make sure it wasn't wired to anything. He turned the radio on and heard a scratchy accordion-heavy tune. He flipped it off and replaced it on the bucket.

Herbers addressed both the Secret Service agents with him and the Federal District police detectives. 'I'll need this place sealed off with tape, and officers outside on the corner during the transit.'

One of the Mexican detectives said, 'I will have two cars behind the barricade outside on José J. Herrera. Four men watching the people at the market and the crowd that will form at the barricades so they can see the limo. I'll task two more men just to make sure no one tries to slip under the tarp to get into the construction site.'

'That's fine,' Herbers said, then he addressed his number two. 'Rick, I want a pair of our guys here as well.'

'You got it.'

'Let's put a long gun at the top of the stairs. It will give us a good view of the entire length of the street.'

Rick made a note.

They climbed out of the construction site and moved on to the next choke point, a turn to the west that would take them deep into the Centro Histórico toward the Palacio Nacional.

Herbers and his team had dozens of problem areas to check before the President arrived in less than forty-eight hours.

53

After waiting for two days in Las Vegas for instructions from the home office, Veronika Martel finally received orders from Edward Riley to fly to New York. She didn't even check into a hotel; instead, she drove right to the Sharps Global Intelligence Partners building, and there she was led into Sharps's fifth-floor office.

Riley was there, but he said surprisingly little. Sharps did most of the talking as he grilled her about her actions over her two weeks at Valley Floor.

Martel had made the decision early on not to mention her contact with Jack Ryan, Jr. Had she done so from the start she would be in the clear, but now she saw no way she could explain that he had been around her at the time she was operational at Valley Floor and that she had simply neglected to mention it. If she revealed his actions, actions she thought at the time were born from his interest in her, then she would look either incompetent or complicit.

And Veronika did not think for a moment Riley would believe she was incompetent.

She didn't see herself as such, either, but she wholly ad-mitted she had been greedy. Her desire to turn a mundane corporate intelligence operation into a one-woman attempt to recruit an important contact and in so doing leave her corporate work behind had been foolish, and she had been grossly overconfident.

Now all she could do was mitigate the damage. Bury any evidence of her attempt to recruit Ryan and leave Sharps behind, and portray herself as the unjust victim of a Sharps op that had been compromised somewhere else.

This worked surprisingly well. Sharps had allowed that an unknown actor had showed up during the New World Metals operation first in Vietnam, then during a phase that occurred here in New York, and finally in Las Vegas. Sharps said that while Veronika had been involved in Vietnam and Vegas, she had no knowledge of the operation in New York, so he was of the opinion she was not to blame for whatever leak had allowed the theft of the mobile phone and the compromise of the operation.

Martel gave a full-throated defense of her actions; she was careful not to cast any aspersions on Riley, because he was (a) her supervisor and someone she would have to continue working with, and (b) right here in the room.

She wondered later if she should have gone ahead and beat up on the Englishman anyway, because Riley had maintained his uncomfortable silence throughout the entire meeting, and Veronika took this as either some sort of culpability, or even weakness.

When it was over, Duke told Veronika that she would be required to stay in town, perhaps for just a few days, but perhaps for longer.

That afternoon she found a vacation rental on the Lower East Side. She wasn't operational, so she rented the property in her own name, but in a nod to her personal security she performed the transaction on the Internet and picked the key card up from a drop box so she wouldn't have to deal with anyone face-to-face.

The place wasn't home, and her unit was a small third-floor walk-up, but on the inside anyway it felt a little like Paris. It was better than a shoebox New York City hotel, and it was *much* better than a gaudy Vegas faux-wonderland casino hotel.

Sam Driscoll had spent a week and a half watching, filming, and reviewing every person who entered the offices of Sharps Global Intelligence Partners. He was across the street at an angle, north of Duke Sharps's building on Columbus, and sometimes he couldn't get great pictures of people entering. But virtually every person who exited the building got their picture taken, and these went into the facial-recognition program.

His boring work paid off on day ten, when the woman going by the name Élise Legrande entered the building. Ryan had made special mention of her, and he told Sam that anything he could do to track the woman after she left would be appreciated.

Sam had barely left his rented studio flat in a week and a half, so he was more than happy to take the opportunity to go off in hot pursuit. When she left the building an hour later Sam was seated on a park bench on the sidewalk next to the American Museum of Natural History, with a twelve-speed bike and a backpack next to him. The woman climbed into a cab and he took off after her, then easily tailed her a few blocks south to a coffee shop, where he saw her working on a tablet computer.

After an hour over a tea and her iPad, she climbed into another taxi. This time Sam had a difficult time tracking her, because she went all the way through Midtown, finally ending up on the Lower East Side. If he had been in a car or even on a motorcycle he would have lost her, but with his bike he was able to skirt traffic, and traffic laws, so he managed to keep her cab in sight until she climbed out on Clinton Street, put a code into a key box hanging from a railing in front of an apartment building, removed an electronic key card, and then carried her luggage up to the door.

Sam waited to see a light turn on on the third floor, and then he pedaled his bike all the way back up to 77th and Columbus.

The next morning Veronika rose early, dressed, and headed out on foot to a café for breakfast, and then she walked to a local market. She told herself she'd be here for a while, so she filled a grocery cart with food and drinks, and even flowers, and took it all back to her place.

It was a struggle to get everything up the three flights of stairs, but she managed, and she unlocked her door with her key card and struggled some more getting everything in and on the counter. After she had done this, she turned around and headed into her living room, and then she stopped cold.

She felt the expression of panic on her face, so she fought against it, and did her best to appear nonchalant.

She asked, 'How did you find me?'

Jack Ryan, Jr., sat on the sofa, his legs crossed. He wore a dark gray pin-striped suit and a burgundy tie, and he appeared utterly calm.

'Sometimes the old-fashioned ways work best.'

'You've been watching Sharps's office?'

'A colleague has.'

'What do you want?'

'Sit down, Veronika.'

Hearing her own name brought the panic back, but she did as instructed, and she tried again to feign an air of detachment. 'How did you get into the apartment?' When Ryan did not immediately speak, she said, 'Let me guess. You used the same site-code hack your people used to get into my hotel room in Las Vegas.'

Ryan replied, 'Sometimes the new ways work best.'

'Who do you work for?'

Ryan did not reply.

'Like father, like son? You are CIA?'

He shook his head. 'I know people. That's all. No law against that. Sometimes they need help. You are the one who has to explain herself.'

'Corporate intelligence is as old as corporations themselves. I've done nothing to be ashamed of.'

Ryan chuckled, and it angered her.

'What is it you think you have on me?'

'Veronika Aimée Martel, age thirty-eight. Born Rambouillet, France. You served in the DGSE for seven years, received high marks, very high. Then you had an affair with a deputy of the French National Assembly.' Ryan wasn't reading this, he had it memorized. 'Not a big deal in France, I don't guess, unless his wife happens to be the vice secretary of the Socialist Party.'

Veronika crossed her arms. A reflexive action to guard herself from danger.

'A bad decision on your part, but it shouldn't have affected your career as a spy. Still, you got banished from

494

the service, scooped up by Duke Sharps, and put back to work.'

'Very good, Jack. You have sources. That doesn't give you the right to break into my flat.'

Now Ryan uncrossed his legs and looked forward. 'My friends were there, in Ho Chi Minh City, the evening Colin Hazelton was murdered.'

Martel made no reaction. She didn't know the name, but she could guess who Hazelton was. Still, she gave nothing away.

'They got a good picture of you that night, and they have the ability to put faces with names, but nothing came up on you. My guess is either DGSE or Sharps had all files with your image erased.'

'Not all, obviously – otherwise you wouldn't be here.'

'You used your real name to rent this place. My friends searched for Veronika Martel, and they found some references to you. No image, but they didn't need the image once they had the name.'

'What do you want? I didn't kill this man in Ho Chi Minh City. I don't even know what you are talking about.'

'North Korean assassins were in Vietnam, in the Czech Republic, in Vegas, and right here in New York. People are dying to keep your mission up and running.'

'It's not my mission.'

'No. It's Edward Riley's mission. But you are his foot soldier, and now you are going to help my friends tie him directly to North Korea.'

She laughed now. 'Ridiculous. He isn't working with North Korea.'

'DPRK goons seem to turn up conveniently wherever he needs them. That's good enough for me.'

'If that was true, they would be here now, wouldn't they?'

'Believe me, there were concerns they would be. But I have friends all over your block, ready for them, and they swept your place for bugs. The North Koreans seem to have forgotten about you for the time being. My guess is you are sidelined, out of the operation after what happened in Las Vegas.'

'I hope that is true. If I am done, then I will return to Brussels and this will all be behind me.'

'You don't understand the stakes, Veronika. You are in danger as long as you are working with Sharps. If the North Koreans think for a second you failed them, they will do to you what they did to Colin Hazelton.'

Ryan crossed over to her side of the sitting area and knelt in front of her. He moved so close she thought he was going to kiss her.

'Help us, and we will protect you.'

'I need no protection. I do need you to leave.' Ryan didn't move back. 'You tricked me once, in Las Vegas. You won't trick me again.'

'This is no trick. I –'

'Are you going to arrest me? No? That is not the job of the CIA.' She smiled now. She had been off kilter for a while, but she felt like she had regained her ground. And now the man in front of her, so smug and sure of himself, did not know what to say. 'Get out.'

'Please, Veronika.'

'Out!'

Jack Ryan sighed, then he pulled out a pen and wrote his phone number on a magazine. 'My friends will keep someone in town. If you change your mind, or if you are in any trouble and need us, call me, and someone will be here in minutes.'

Veronika stood and pointed to the door. 'Get out.'

Ryan left the apartment, certain that the woman behind him had no idea how far the North Koreans were willing to go to see this to the end.

54

Presidential Directive or no, there was neither legal nor justifiable reason – as far as international law was concerned – for the boarding and inspection of the *San Fernando Chieftain*, an Indonesian-flagged container ship making fifteen knots in a roiling Yellow Sea.

True, it was on its way to the North Korean port of Nampo, southwest of Pyongyang. But the ship's stated destination was North Korea, so it had already been inspected by international proliferation experts, just before setting sail at Manila Terminal six days earlier. The cargo was confirmed to match the manifests; it was food aid and car parts and machinery for the nation's large coal-mining industry. The ship also broadcast its automatic identification system for its entire voyage, and there were absolutely no irregularities with its movements.

In short, the *San Fernando Chieftain* played by the rules, so the captain was furious now, standing in his wheelhouse, his binoculars to his eyes and fixed on a point three miles off his bow. Though it was late morning, a heavy squall darkened the skies and obscured his view slightly, but there was no mistaking the image in his optics. It was the massive American warship USS *Freedom*, and it had positioned itself in the path of the *San Fernando Chieftain*, blocking the way ahead.

The radio call left the captain even more confused and

angry. The Americans demanded to board, the captain asked them on what grounds they thought they had the right to do so, and the Americans cited UN Resolution 1874.

The Indonesian captain responded with outrage. The paperwork was on file and his transit had been documented. But the Americans were not listening to his reason. They informed him an armed boarding party was on the way, and for the safety of the captain, his crew, and his cargo, he needed to come full stop and comply with all demands.

The captain immediately called his home office. At this point there was nothing he could do but complain, because even though he was in the right, he wasn't about to fight the United States Navy.

At ten fifty-six Chief Daryl Ricks of Echo Platoon, SEAL Team 5, stood up in the Zodiac boat, spun his HK416 rifle over his back, and climbed up the pilot ladder that had been lowered by the crew of the *San Fernando Chieftain*.

Just like the interdiction his platoon had made that uncovered the rocket parts from France, his boarding today would be 'bottom up,' meaning from the water. Also as in that raid, this time his counterpart, Bones Hackworth of Bravo team, would be hitting 'top down,' from a helo already on station an eighth of a mile off the bow and closing.

This was not a typical sanctions enforcement. Normally he and his mates spot-checked cargo containers or cargo holds, with no specific intelligence on where to look or what, exactly, they were looking for. But for today's interdiction he had received specific intelligence about what he was looking for and where he could find it. From his understanding, the intel came from the Defense Intelligence Agency, although it had been filtered through channels and was delivered to him via sat phone contact with the intelligence officer of Team 5 in Seoul.

The IO had directed him to open and inspect four forty-five-foot high-cube shipping containers; he even had the hold number and location on the boat for where to find them.

There had been no information, oddly, on just what it was they were supposed to find inside the containers, but Ricks figured it didn't take much imagination to conclude he and his mates had hit this ship to grab another load of missile parts.

The last time there had been resistance, and Ricks knew he couldn't count on things going any easier for this interdiction, but so far, they'd seen no evidence that the crew was trying to hide anything or slow the SEALs down from taking a look for themselves.

Weird. This seems too damn easy, he thought, as he climbed onto the deck. But he kept his rifle up high, scanning for threats.

But there was no resistance from the crew. Ricks and his men took the wheelhouse while Hackworth and his team went for the engine room. In ten minutes the entire fourteen-member crew was covered on the deck by four men, and the rest of the SEALs headed for cargo hold two.

The containers were there, just as the IO had said; the numbers on the doors matched the report.

Greaser and Hendriks stepped forward and broke the seal on the first container. They opened the doors, and Ricks looked in with the flashlight on the end of his rifle. He scanned the beam up and down, and then left and right.

Hendriks stood behind him, and the Dutch special warfare operator said exactly what Ricks was thinking. 'Bad intel, Chief.'

There was no nuclear material inside the container. No missile parts, either. Instead, there were three huge round pieces of machinery lying on their sides that Ricks first thought were industrial-sized boilers.

There were invoices in pouches on the side of each massive unit. Ricks lowered his weapon and used the light on the side of his helmet now, and he saw the invoice said exactly what the equipment was.

'Froth flotation tanks.'

Greaser looked over some writing on the side of the unit. 'It's mineral refining equipment.'

The chief turned away without replying, headed to the next container to break the seal there.

Twenty minutes later Chief Ricks stood at the fantail of the ship with his sat phone to his ear. 'Typhoon Actual to Typhoon Main.'

'Typhoon Main. Go ahead, Actual.'

'No joy on the cargo.'

'Understood no joy. What did you find?'

'It's not WMD equipment.'

A pause. 'Understood. What did you find, Actual?'

Ricks explained. He waited a long time for a response, and he was about to check to see if Main had copied his last transmission, but then they replied.

'Typhoon Actual. Listen up. These containers are going to be offloaded from the ship. You will stay on board until a transloader arrives from Seoul, ETA to follow. You will oversee the transloading, and then you will release the ship and the rest of the cargo.'

Ricks cocked his head. 'Uh . . . Roger that. Just to clarify. I understand we are to confiscate this mining equipment, and hold the ship until we offload it?'

'Typhoon Actual, Typhoon Main. Roger.'

Ricks paused. 'Can we do that?'

'Chief, as far as you are concerned, you have been told that material is WMD-related. Do you understand?'

Ricks scratched the narrow portion of his neck between his body armor and the bottom of his helmet. 'Roger that, Typhoon Main. Actual out.'

Chief Ricks made his way back to his team in the cargo bay, where he found Greaser, Hendriks, and Hackworth. Echo Platoon was ready to hear the order to release the crew and dis-embark. Ricks said, 'Listen up. If anybody asks, we just found ourselves some more WMD.'

Greaser turned to his chief. 'Come again?'

'Nuke parts.'

Hendriks said, 'They look more like washing machines.'

'Fuck, Hendriks. I don't know. Maybe they use them to wash their ICBMS. I just know we are transloading this stuff to a ship heading over from South Korea.'

Hendriks said, 'So . . . this is kind of like stealing, right? We're pirates now?'

Ricks just shrugged. 'I guess national command knows what it's doing.'

Hendriks said, 'Doesn't sound to me like POTUS

knows what the hell he's doing. The North Koreans are assholes when we *don't* do anything to them. Stealing their shit might just send them over the edge.'

'Hendriks,' Ricks said, 'I can't wait till you're president. You've already got it all figured out.'

'I can't be president, Chief. I was born in Holland.'

Ricks turned and headed for the main deck to let the rest of the platoon know the plan. He called back in a sarcastic tone, 'Well, that sure is a pity, Hendriks.'

55

Sam Driscoll was just twelve hours into his surveillance of Veronika Martel's apartment building when a black BMW i8 pulled up in front and parked on the street. It was well past nightfall and a thunderstorm sent thick sheets of rain onto the street, so Sam couldn't make out the license plate from his vantage point, but he didn't need to.

He knew the vehicle.

He'd seen Edward Riley pulling into the parking lot under Sharps Global Intelligence Pártners more than once during his surveillance there, and he couldn't help but admire the man's choice in automobiles.

Driscoll's job here had been to keep an eye out for any North Koreans watching over Martel. Ryan didn't know if they'd come after her, but now that she seemed to be on the outside of the operation to help them obtain intel for their rare metals refinery, he worried she'd end up like Hazelton. It seemed unlikely, but he didn't want to leave it to chance.

Sam called Ryan, who answered quickly.

'Hey, Sam. What's up?'

'Wanted to let you know that Edward Riley just pulled up to Martel's apartment.'

'You sure it's him?'

'Have you seen his car?'

'No? What does he drive?'

'Beamer, i8.'

'Nice. Not exactly covert, but nice.'

'That coming from the guy who used to drive a canary yellow Hummer.'

'Touché. I wonder what he's doing there. I guess he's either going to give her another assignment or fire her. He's alone?'

'Yep. I checked the street for followers. It's raining up here, but as far as I can tell there are no sneaky North Koreans skulking around tonight.'

'Okay. Hey, by the way, you are getting some company.'

'Who?'

'All of us. Clark has us all heading back up to NYC. We don't have anything else to do but keep an eye on Martel.'

'I thought Sharps compromised the team in New York. You going to go mobile on the streets?'

'We think she's clear of North Korean surveillance, and we think the North Koreans were the ones who tipped off Sharps. We might be okay. Still, I have a feeling we won't be mobile very much. Most likely we'll all be hanging out at your place.'

Sam said, 'Awesome. Five dudes in a one-bathroom studio apartment eating pizza all day.'

'Just like college,' Ryan said, and Sam just grunted.

Riley arrived during a thunderstorm; he wore jeans and a black sweater, and he came empty-handed other than his umbrella and his mobile phone.

Veronika offered him tea, which he declined, so they

sat on opposite chairs in her living room. She could tell from his demeanor there was a problem.

'What's happened?'

Riley leaned forward. 'Last night our time, the United States Navy stopped the vessel delivering the froth flotation tanks to North Korea. They confiscated the material.'

Veronika did not reply. She was an intelligent woman. She assumed the Americans learned of the existence of the material from her download from Valley Floor.

And she also realized Riley needed someone to take the fall for what happened in Vegas.

'Just so you are aware, Duke is angry with you. He thinks you tipped off the Americans. The North Koreans are bloody furious as well.'

Martel rolled her eyes. 'That is completely absurd. Someone compromised the operation somehow. They broke into my hotel room knowing exactly what they were looking for.'

'And you have no idea who might have done this?' Riley asked.

She stared him right in the eyes. She knew the truth, but she also knew how to lie. 'None whatsoever.'

Riley clearly wanted her on the defensive, but that wasn't her style. She said, 'Perhaps you can help answer that question. You seem to be the one aware of the goings-on in my hotel room. You had me bugged? Did you have cameras on me? Is that it? Were you watching me change? Watching me sleep?'

Riley shook his head. Now her attempt to put *him* on the back foot had failed. He was utterly unruffled.

'Associates, on their own, were there in the hotel. There was a listening device left in your room.'

Martel recoiled in surprise. 'Associates?'

'Let's just say an interested party.'

'You mean the North Koreans? Who? RGB?'

Riley conceded this with a nod.

'So you are working *directly* with the North Koreans now? Not with New World Metals?'

Riley did not deny it. Instead, he said, 'Twelve trillion dollars. Can you get your pretty little head around that number?'

'That's the value of the mine?'

'Yes. There is an opportunity here to get in on the ground floor of an incredible enterprise. By the very nature of the enterprise, only a few people will be involved. There won't be competition for the mineral wealth in North Korea. Instead, there will be one state-owned company extracting it inside the country, and one foreign firm handling everything else outside of the country.'

Riley held up a finger. 'One firm.'

'New World Metals.'

'That's just the name this week, the operation to get the equipment and personnel into the country. Óscar Roblas has a hundred companies under him, and he'll create a hundred more. Shipping, materials, purchasing, marketing . . .' Riley smiled now. 'External security. Each venture will grow and grow until they explode in value, because he is North Korea's man. Once North Korea gets their shipment of flotation cells, nothing will stop them.'

'And how does any of that help you? You are Sharps's man.'

Riley waved away the comment. 'I'm my own man.

Duke is hell-bent on keeping his involvement limited to the business intelligence field. I see the opportunities as being much broader, and I see Sharps's ideas as being too narrow in scope. North Korea will come around to my understanding.'

Veronika nodded. 'So you went directly to the North Koreans and told them you were there for them. You would help them by going even further than Sharps. You'd help them kill people on the streets of America, if that's what they wanted.'

'I am doing both entities a favor. All three, if you count Óscar Roblas. Sharps gets plausible deniability. I work for Ro-blas and General Ri, North Korea's intelligence chief, directly.'

'And they cut you in?'

'That's the idea.'

Veronika thought over everything that she was hearing. She didn't understand why Riley was telling her all this. She could turn right around and tell Sharps that his number-two man was doing an end run around his clients.

She'd been in this business long enough to trust her instincts, and for a brief moment she wondered if she might be in some danger here. Was Riley here to eliminate her as payback for Vegas?

She leaned forward a little, ready to leap for the kitchen and the knife rack if he made any sudden moves. It seemed highly improbable, but the stakes had been rising on this New World Metals operation from the beginning.

Riley said, 'If you don't know it yet, you are done with Sharps. You are going down for the mistake in Las Vegas.'

'But –'

'Call him yourself. I'm here to deliver your marching orders.'

Riley added, 'But even though he can't use you any-more, I can.'

Martel understood, or at least she thought she did. She leaned back now; gone was any faint concern she had for her well-being, replaced now by anger and indignation. Riley was going to try to recruit her into his scheme, as if she were some sort of cheap agent who would flip at the drop of a hat. He thought he could control her by getting her fired by Sharps, so she'd have no choice but to ally herself with him.

Ridiculous. She'd been spied on by the North Koreans. Now Riley was extorting her to join him as an accessory to murder for a rogue regime.

That wasn't going to get her back to Paris. No, she wouldn't play ball.

She said, 'I will contact Duke. And I will demand a face-to-face meeting to explain myself.'

'You won't get it.'

'You really think I won't? Let's see. I bet I could get a meeting with him in his wife's bed if that's what I wanted.'

She saw the muscles in Riley's jaw tense and then release. His eyes narrowed to slits.

He stood and started for the door, and she followed, yelling after him, 'You are famous for blaming others for your mistakes, and for letting your ambition cloud your judgment. It happened in Italy, and it led to your downfall.'

He had reached the door and put his hand on the latch, but he turned back to face her.

She continued, 'You think the North Koreans will trust you over Sharps? You think Roblas will? Sharps isn't in charge of the operation. He is a figurehead. They know that. I am not in charge of the operation, either. Blame me for Las Vegas if you must. But whatever happened in Vietnam and New York had nothing to do with me. *You* are in charge. *You* will take the fall for that.'

She smiled now. She saw indecision on his angry face. 'I might not keep my job, but you will go down with me, Riley.'

He squared his body to hers, his breathing deepened, and his eyes widened out of the angry slits. His indecision receded, and he seemed ready to act.

'What?' she asked.

He took a step closer, and his hands raised toward her face.

Veronika thought he was going to pull her to him, to kiss her. She'd seen this look many times in her life, it was always the same. In the throes of an argument came the throes of passion. 'This turns you on? You think I want you? Are you insane?'

But he didn't pull her close. Instead, he laced his fingers around her feminine throat and tightened his grip.

She tried to push away. 'What are you —'

Her voice left her, replaced by a scream, and then a frightened shriek.

Riley threw his body on her, knocked her to the floor. He squeezed with all his might, her legs kicked and her arms flailed, but he'd positioned himself out of the way of the brunt of the blows.

While he choked the life from her, he leaned into her ear, so close her hair tickled his nose. 'Silly, Veronika. So tight and proper and cold. I told you why I was here. I can still use you. I didn't come to get you to join up with me. I came because I need someone to take the fall. The North Koreans are angry . . . so somebody has to die.'

Thirty seconds later she went limp in his hands, but he kept talking to her softly. 'This was your mistake. This was Sharps's mistake. But they know me. They appreciate my resolve. They see I'm not like Sharps.' He recognized she was dead now, so he let go slowly, and lowered her head onto the hardwood floor.

He rose. 'I'm a man who gets things done.'

56

Adel Zarif woke at first light, rolled out his prayer rug, and knelt facing Mecca. He said his prayers and then sat around waiting for Emilio to wake up. When the young Mexican finally did stir, it was another twenty minutes before he rose and knocked on the door to Zarif's room.

They ate breakfast in silence, and then watched some television. By ten a.m. a local news station was already covering the impending arrival of Jack Ryan. Zarif could not understand the reporter, but he watched the pictures of the National Palace and the airport, and Emilio did his best to provide running translations. From the reporter Zarif learned several things he already knew, like the time the President would arrive and his planned agenda for the official visit. Zarif also heard talk of a lot of things that he knew were never going to happen.

No matter how much the reporter gushed about the spread of the meal that would be served tonight, there would not be a dinner thrown in Jack Ryan's honor. And no matter how big and beautiful the Plaza de la Constitución was, Ryan was not going to go on a walking tour with the Mexican president there, because he would die before he got there.

But the Iranian did pick up one interesting tidbit. This was the first Zarif had heard that the First Lady of the

United States was not accompanying her husband today, but would instead fly down the next afternoon. The woman was apparently some sort of a doctor, Emilio didn't hear what sort, and according to the pieces Emilio translated into English that Zarif understood, she had important work to do in Maryland and would come down when she was finished.

Zarif told himself this woman would not be working all day today and tomorrow as she had planned. When she learned that her husband had been blown to a thousand pieces, she would probably never work again.

At eleven a.m. the two men were picked up by two more Maldonado operators from Guerrero who didn't know the city as well as they should, and they made a few wrong turns on their way to their destination. Emilio yelled at them from the back and the men yelled at him. Zarif was unnerved by the two men's disheveled appearance and their utter lack of knowledge of the city, and he worried his entire plan to make a new life for himself in the safety of North Korea could be derailed by these uncouth cowboys getting pulled over by a cop on the way to the assassination.

Zarif had nothing on his person that would incriminate him. He just carried his mobile phone, the long-range cordless phone he'd use to trigger the bomb, and the rechargeable batteries that went into it, which he kept outside the unit so that it did not accidentally send a signal and detonate the bomb too early. But he knew he might get questioned by the police if these fools drew attention to themselves, and the police would quickly find he was foreign and detain him.

Despite Zarif's concern, they made it to their destination without incident. At the scene, crowd-control barriers had already been erected, and at the street market on José J. Herrera, enough of a crowd had formed close to the barricades that Zarif decided he didn't want to get any closer. The police were already in place at the barricades, and although the Iranian didn't think he looked much different from the Mexicans around here – he was dark-complexioned and he wore a dark beard and mustache – he did not want to put this belief to the test and ruin his chance at a comfortable retirement on a beach full of beautiful Asian girls.

So Adel Zarif and Emilio stayed back and out of sight, but this was no threat to their plan, because they did not have to get any closer to detonate the bomb.

Another Maldonado man, Emilio said his name was Gordo, was already positioned across the street, close to the barricades at the other side of the intersection. He had a near-perfect position and line of sight on several blocks of Vidal Alcocer because there was a large parking lot to the north that gave him unobstructed views. He also had an iPad with which he would film the arrival of the presidential motorcade, and transmit it instantly to Emilio's iPhone.

Once the two presidential limousines were in front of the stone façade of the parking garage, Zarif would call the phone attached to the IED.

Gordo was going to die in the blast; Zarif had calculated this fact the second he saw the image on Emilio's phone, but he said nothing to Emilio.

While they were strolling around the market killing

time, Emilio said, 'The others will wait for the explosion to attack.'

Zarif did not understand. He cocked his head to the side. 'What others?'

'Twelve men from Guerrero are taking part in the attack. They are waiting in the area. They all have *cuernos de chivo*.'

'What is that?'

Emilio thought for a moment. 'Goat horns.'

The Iranian still had no idea what the Mexican was talking about.

'You know . . . AK-47s. A couple of guys have RPGs, too. Once the bomb goes off they will come out of the crowd and start shooting.' Emilio grinned. 'It's gonna be crazy.'

Zarif was furious. 'No one told me about this.'

'Relax. It is good. They will make sure Ryan is dead.'

'No, they won't. They will be seen in the crowd before the President comes, and someone will warn the Americans.'

Emilio tried to wave away the comment, but Zarif demanded to speak to the Maldonado cell leader. After a few minutes more trying to allay Zarif's fears, Emilio finally dialed a number on his mobile phone and spoke to the man on the other end for a minute. Finally, after a conversation translated by Emilio, Zarif persuaded the cell leader to have the Maldonado men back out of the crowd and move one block east of the motorcade route. He explained that once the explosion rocked the street, they could run one block and shoot up the scene to their hearts' content.

The cell leader put his men in four pickup trucks and parked them on Nicolas Bravo, with orders to wait for the big bang and then race to the scene. Two trucks would hit the motorcade from the southeast on José J. Herrera, and two more from the northeast on Nacional.

Zarif felt like these men were going to race up to the site where Jack Ryan already lay dead, and then do nothing more than get themselves massacred by the hundred or so cops and Secret Service agents who were still alive. But that wasn't his problem. He felt better now that there would be no tip-offs to the coming event, so he and Emilio stepped into a Starbucks, ordered iced coffees, and sat down to watch the video feed on his phone.

The Iranian had command-detonated devices by watching video cameras, but he was pretty sure this was the first time anyone had assassinated a world leader via iPhone.

57

Air Force One touched down at 12:05 p.m. The pilot brought the aircraft to a predetermined point on the tarmac and then the mobile stairs were driven up. Quickly a red carpet was rolled out, and members of a forty-man honor guard took their positions on either side.

Bomb squad personnel, K9 teams, counterassault SWAT officers, and hundreds of other American security forces representing a half-dozen federal agencies were already at the airport; they'd arrived more than a week earlier with the advance team or else on one of the four C-141 cargo aircraft full of men and equipment that had landed the day before.

Dozens of Secret Service agents fanned out around the aircraft, among them Lead Advance Agent Dale Herbers, who took a position watching the expanse of Benito Juárez International's tarmac along with the rest of the team. His advance work was now complete, and normally he would be moving on to his next location immediately, but the security needs here in Mexico required him to stay for POTUS's arrival and motorcade to the Palacio Nacional and then his hotel.

Twelve minutes after landing, Lead Protection Agent Andrea Price O'Day exited the aircraft and walked down the stairs. She took up a position at the foot of the stairs, and seconds later, President of the United States Jack

Ryan emerged from Air Force One and headed down himself. There was no music for him – this was not an official state visit but rather an official visit, which was one step down and less full of pomp and circumstance.

Still, Ryan was greeted at the bottom of the stairs by the Mexican foreign minister and a few other high-level functionaries, and while he stood there talking, mostly through an interpreter, US Ambassador to Mexico Horatio Styles quietly came out of the airplane and descended. He followed the President in the receiving line, and then headed for the limo with Ryan and O'Day.

The Beasts were parked back to front, and small flags of Mexico hung from poles on the fenders. It was de rigueur on foreign trips to display the local flag on the President's vehicle as a show of respect. The limo in front was positioned just beyond the honor guard, and the back door to the rear limo was lined up perfectly with the red carpet and the door was open. O'Day stood at the door while Ryan folded his six-foot frame into the vehicle, and after Ambassador Styles entered the back of the big black limo, she shut the door and ordered her team to the cars.

O'Day got in the front passenger side of Ryan's limo, next to driver Mitchell Delaney. Two agents rode on the running boards of the vehicle as it rolled forward in the motorcade, but they would hop off and get into a chase car at the airport's exit.

In front of the presidential limo was the other Beast, and in front of that a dozen black Chevy Suburbans carrying Secret Service, White House, and Department of State personnel. Ahead of these were Mexican police cars, some dozen in all, and at the very front of the convoy, twenty-one Mexican Federal Police motorcycles rumbled through the intersections, all of which had already been blocked off with more police.

Behind the President's vehicle came two Suburbans ferrying close protection agents, then three specially out-fitted Suburbans carrying the counterassault team. These vehicles all had open back gates full of armed men scanning both sides of the road, and they had hatches on the roof they could use to stand and fire from above. A fourth counterassault vehicle carried more heavy weapons and security equipment for the SWAT officers.

After this main security contingent came the Roadrunner, the unofficial name given to the Mobile Command and Control Vehicle, a Suburban filled with high-tech communications equipment that allowed the President and his team secure comms even while driving in foreign countries.

After the Roadrunner were two white sixteen-passenger media vans, then another twelve SUVs and sedans carrying more VIPs. All of these vehicles were already full, as the press and other staff traveling with the President had deplaned before the President.

The US contingent of the motorcade was thirty-five vehicles, but the Mexicans added more than eighty, most in the form of uniformed Federal Police on motorcycles.

In the lead media van, sixteen reporters from print, tele-vision, and wire services sat crammed together. In the middle of the first row behind the driver, twenty-seven-year-old CNN reporter Jill Crosby checked the service on her mobile phone. She was new to international travel, and although she'd been told she'd have no more trouble getting a signal in Mexico City than she would at the Washington Bureau where she worked, she needed to confirm it for herself.

She breathed a sigh of relief when her phone displayed four bars, a full-strength signal.

She'd never traveled with the President before and she had no plans to call anyone other than her boyfriend this afternoon, but she wanted to be ready for anything. That was her mantra, and it had gotten her this far. After all, you didn't make it this high in CNN at such a young age, assigned to an international flight aboard Air Force One, without working your ass off and leaving nothing to chance.

In the backseat of the Beast, Ryan and Styles drank bottled water and discussed protocol, but only for a short time, because the President wanted to hear another of the ambassador's old war stories. The Marine had been in Grenada, and in Panama, and he'd finished his military career fighting in the Middle East. He wasn't one to offer up long tales about past action, especially not to the President, who had his own fascinating history that was somewhat longer than the younger ambassador's, but Ryan had been a Marine himself, and he peppered Styles with questions about his time in the service like a fascinated college student.

It was 2:18 a.m. in Pyongyang, North Korea, but General Ri Tae-jin wore his full uniform, and he sat at his desk in his office in the Reconnaissance General Bureau. Across the room was a thirty-two-inch CRT television tuned to the American television news station CNN. With the general in his office was a female translator, herself in the green uniform of the Chosun Inmingun, the Korean military. She had been ordered here with no explanation of why she was to sit with the general throughout the early morning and provide running translations of US television news.

Right now the station was running its noon news hour, a story about flooding along the Ohio River. The translator gave the information to Ri quickly and confidently, but other than to verify her ability as a translator, the general wasn't interested. His mind was racing now, thinking about the importance of the next few minutes.

He had entered into this operation with doubt and anger, but as the scheme had progressed, as the pieces fell into place with the finding of the assassin in Syria, and as he'd heard reports back from his agents in Mexico City who were secretly monitoring the actions of the Maldonado cartel, he began to become cautiously optimistic about the entire enterprise.

And when the American President stole the mineral refinery equipment two days earlier, indicating to all he knew Ri's operation to build the processing plant directly correlated with the operation to obtain ICBM technology, General Ri knew Fire Axe – his operation in Mexico City – had to succeed for his operation in Chongju to succeed.

As if by curse or by fortune, one scheme folded into the other.

For Ri to live . . . Ryan had to die.

He held a hand in the air, stopping the translator's work

MEXICO CITY AMBUSH

in mid-sentence. Ohio could drown or wash away, Ri could not care less.

'You may pause until the important news comes on the air.'

The translator swallowed uncomfortably. 'Apologies, Comrade General. How will I know what is important?'

Ri's sad eyes blinked and brightened, and his nearly perpetual frown curved upward. 'You will know.'

As the Beast made a left off Costa Rica onto Vidal Alcocer, Ryan waved to a small crowd behind a barricade. Most seemed happy to see him, but a few angry-looking people, young males and females, waved a banner that he was not able to read.

Ryan turned to Styles. 'I bet the Maldonado killing in Acapulco gave you a few headaches.'

Styles said, 'Speaking as ambassador to Mexico, I confess it was a difficult time diplomatically, at least in our dealing with the general public, since the Maldonado brothers did enjoy some popular support around portions of the western regions of the country.'

Ryan nodded.

'But if I might be allowed to speak as a Marine for a moment.'

'Please do.'

'That son of a bitch needed to go.'

Jack nodded again.

Styles leaned forward. 'I understand totally if you are not at liberty to say, Mr President. But I sure would be curious to know if we, in fact, had operators on the ground in Acapulco.'

With a dry look Ryan replied, 'Can neither confirm nor deny, Ambassador.' And then he finished the line with a little wink.

Styles turned to look out the window. 'You just made my day, Mr President.'

Four blocks away, two men, one Mexican and in his twenties, the other Iranian and in his forties, sat at a small round table in the back corner of a Starbucks, both men leaning over a mobile phone. The older man held a white cordless telephone in his hand, but it was hidden under the table, resting on the backpack between his feet. Anyone paying attention might notice both men were perspiring, but the other patrons of the shop were engrossed in their own conversations and work.

Adel Zarif watched the video feed intently, hesitant to blink lest he miss the first limousine. Gordo moved the camera around more than Zarif would have liked, and the image shook and jerked as the crowd around the man at the barricade jostled him to get their own cameras up and into position.

But Zarif thought it was a gift from Allah that the image on Emilio's little phone settled down and centered perfectly just as a black Suburban passed in front of the wall, and the first big black limousine passed, its Mexican hood flags whipping in the breeze.

At the back of the Starbucks, Adel Zarif muttered softly to himself, *'Allahu akbar.'*

At the same moment, his tablemate, the Maldonado man Emilio, simply said, *'Come mierda.'* Eat shit.

Zarif pressed the button on the phone and connected the call.

Even here in the Starbucks, more than three blocks away, the explosion was deafening.

58

A dark gray cloud covered everyone and everything.

The entire street, the side streets around, the edge of the street market on the west, and the open parking lot on the east – everything in a twenty-five-yard radius from the blast site – was completely obscured by smoke and dust and tiny airborne particles of concrete.

Many outside the impenetrable cloud for another twenty-five yards in all directions were dead or dazed or disoriented by the force of the blast. Eardrums were stunned and ringing. Equilibrium was disrupted by the concussion.

Another twenty-five yards in all directions was consumed by wrecked vehicles or other confusion. Shrapnel this far out still caused death, windows were shattered, car alarms blared.

No one screamed for several seconds, the confusion and disbelief overpowering the natural sensation of fear.

Secret Service Agent Dale Herbers was one of five men in a Suburban six vehicles ahead of SWORDSMAN. The blast behind them had sent debris raining down on the roof of his SUV, but the driver looked back in his rearview and prepared to stomp on the gas. If they were under attack, the first rule was to get POTUS out of the engagement area as quickly as possible.

But the sheer size of the rolling cloud of destruction

behind him caused him to doubt standard protocol. Would the Beast even be able to roll out of the kill zone?

The driver called into his mike, trying to find out what he needed to do, but he did this simultaneously along with thirty other agents, and his transmission was walked over.

Herbers was the lead agent in the vehicle, so in the absence of any other instruction, he knew he'd need to lead the four men with him. He realized from the size of the blast that his vehicle might possibly be the closest to the President that had not been destroyed. But there was no way he was going to order his driver to back into the cloud to go looking for SWORDSMAN, because for all he knew, the President was lying injured in the street.

Instead, Herbers made a brave call. 'Pull over to open the lane, then everyone bail, cover, and evacuate!'

The driver raced the vehicle to the side of the six-lane road, giving as much open space as possible for any cars behind to continue on if they were able. The five agents then unloaded quickly, drawing their SIG Sauer pistols as they did so. This action put them in danger, of course, but there was no way they were continuing on without knowing if the Beast was operable or even intact. And all Secret Service agents knew their primary job was to cover and evacuate the principal, so Herbers and the others began sprinting toward the massive gray cloud.

Almost instantly Herbers saw his call to pull to the side of the road was folly. Nothing was going to be rolling to the south on Vidal Alcocer. They passed wrecked Suburbans, lying on their sides or perpendicular to the traffic lanes, windshields shattered, tires ripped apart and smoking. These SUVs weren't moving without a dozen men pushing them out of the way, and there was no time to stop for that until SWORDSMAN was safe.

Here and there a few men had climbed out of the damaged vehicles, but Herbers also saw bodies in the road and slumped over steering wheels.

On his right a crowd that had gathered behind the barricades on José J. Herrera looked like a massive tangle of prostrate bodies. Herbers slowed here to train his gun on any potential threats, but the only movement he saw was a little writhing and staggering by a few survivors in the midst of the stillness of death in the crowd.

A voice came through his earpiece, shouting something that seemed like it was a warning, but right now it seemed as if one hundred car alarms blared in a half-dozen different singsong keys, each bleat trying to shout over the other, and Herbers couldn't make out the call.

He saw no threats, so he turned away from the crowd and continued on toward the last known location of the Beast, running flat out in his dress shoes and business suit. His earpiece mike was alive now with calls, but he hadn't heard a word from O'Day, the President's lead agent.

Just as he reached the edge of the thick cloud of smoke and ran into it, he heard pounding gunfire behind him. Even before he turned around, he recognized the weapon from its distinctive sound. It was an AK-47, a rifle carried by no one in the Secret Service or in the Mexican federal forces. He shouted into his wrist mike at the same time as dozens of other men and women. 'Contact!'

Instantly he heard the high-pitched snapping of bullets

flying past him in the street, coming from the direction of the crowd.

In the back of the smoke cloud, an entire city block from where Herbers now stood in the street hunting for the source of the gunfire, Secret Service men who were still alive stumbled from their vehicles and began moving toward the cloud. They had no choice but to dismount, because burning vehicles in front of them blocked the way. The Roadrunner was down and on its side. No one had climbed out of it yet, though it had been a full thirty seconds since the massive blast.

The members of the counterassault team who had not died in the explosion or were not now wrapped up and disoriented in the dark cloud raced forward with their M4 rifles, desperate for any information, either through their eyes or through their headsets.

In the smoke, guns swung around in all directions looking for targets, and men reached out in vain, trying to find anyone or anything close by to help orient them.

Suddenly, seconds after the sound of AK fire south of their position sent the men scrambling, more gunfire erupted from the north, behind them. It was more automatic AKs along with staccato snaps from handguns as Secret Service agents returned fire.

The counterassault men at the northern edge of the cloud turned to engage two pickup trucks approaching from a side street, but the smoke and dust behind them enveloped them as the cloud grew.

Over the sound of the new multidirectional gunfire a

single screamed report filled every earpiece, headset, and vehicle radio of the massive Secret Service contingent.

'RPG!'

Jack Ryan opened his eyes and blinked away what he thought were tears. He brought his hand to his face and rubbed it, and he noticed his glasses were gone. He pulled his hand back and saw he was bleeding from his head.

He was wholly unaware there had been an explosion. He saw no flash, he heard no loud noise. He wondered if they had been in some sort of traffic accident. Right now he was only aware that he lay awkwardly on his right side, his legs higher than his head. Ambassador Styles's body was crumpled next to him. There was little light, which was odd, because the last thing he remembered from before he blacked out was that it had been a beautifully sunny afternoon.

The Beast was upside down, this became clear after a few seconds more, but even through the vehicle windows all he saw was a deep gray, as if they had somehow crashed into a dark lake.

That couldn't be. He wondered if he was dazed, so he shook his head to clear it, and only then did he feel the dull but pervasive pain on his right side.

'Mr President?'

'Yes, Andrea. I'm okay.'

He wasn't okay, but he was alive, and Andrea Price O'Day was in the front seat, herself upside down. She needed to hear his voice, so he complied.

Now Ryan reached forward and put his hand on the back of Horatio Styles. He was lying almost flat on the limo's ceiling, and he wasn't moving. Ryan meant to give him a shake to wake him up, but when he did so the man's head lolled to the side, facing Ryan's. His eyes were open and his pupils rolled back. Ryan could see his neck was broken.

'Styles is dead!' he called to O'Day, but she was transmitting on her mike and she did not respond.

Ryan heard gunfire outside the limo now, and it sounded like it was coming from two directions. A larger explosion, this sounded like an RPG hitting a vehicle, came from close behind.

O'Day said, 'We're staying in the vehicle. We've got oxygen and armor, and as long as we . . .' She stopped talking.

Jack rolled himself onto his left side now, and then onto his knees. He felt like his right arm was not cooperating, but it was there, still in his suit and not gushing blood, so he wasn't sure what his problem was.

He looked up to Andrea and then he saw why she stopped talking. Smoke began filling the interior of the car.

She turned to him. 'Listen carefully. Stay where you are. I'm coming around to your door.'

She didn't wait for Ryan to respond. Instead, she kicked open her front passenger door, rolled out onto the ground.

Ryan called out to the driver now. 'Hey, Mitch! You okay? We've got to go!' The man hung upside down from his seat belt. He turned his head toward Ryan, but he did not reply.

Andrea appeared at Ryan's window. She yanked hard on the upside-down door and it opened with a creak.

Ryan rolled out onto the street now; he was surprised to find the limo had been thrown all the way to the curb, probably twenty feet from where it had been in the middle of the road.

Ryan coughed out the smoke he had inhaled inside the vehicle, and then he began to stand. O'Day shielded him against the side of the limo, kept him on his knees, and he looked around for the first time. Two men in the tactical gear of the counterassault team came running through the thick smoke, their weapons high and their laser targeters cutting through the cloud like lightsabers. They formed on Ryan and they, too, made a cordon around him, and tried in vain to scan for targets in the massive amount of smoke and dust.

A third special agent, this one in a suit and tie, appeared. His face and leg were covered with blood but he was ambulatory, and he opened the driver's-side door of the upturned limo to help Special Agent Mitch Delaney out, but Ryan saw the man was heavily disoriented from the impact of the flipping limo.

O'Day was calling for a vehicle, *any* vehicle, to make its way slowly into the blast zone, through the half-dozen or so burning pieces of wreckage, and up to the Beast. She had to evacuate SWORDSMAN, preferably in something armored, but at this point she'd settle for anything with four wheels and a motor.

Ryan tried to pull out Ambassador Styles, but the agents around him kept him covered tightly. The smoke was obscuring their view of the attack that was taking place from two compass points, and this added to the confusion, but it was also obscuring the attackers' view of the blast area, so they couldn't possibly know the President was more or less out in the open, kneeling at the curb.

And then, from the south, came a racing, hissing sound that approached through the smoke. No one saw it, and no one identified it in time to do little more than crouch.

The RPG hit the side of the limousine and exploded, throwing everyone around it to the ground.

The two sixteen-passenger media vans had been well behind the explosion, but still the shock wave shook the vehicles on their chassis, and debris pounded them and cracked the windshields in several places. The windows along the passenger sides were shattered when the rearview mirrors were struck by flying debris and went flying into the sides of the vans. The incredible sound of the detonation and the subsequent impacts of shrapnel and car parts sent the passengers covering their heads and scrambling to get low.

The driver of the lead van was a member of the White House press office and not a trained security agent, but he'd been told what to do in an emergency. He was to get off the road, out of the way of security forces ahead of his van if the decision was made to retrograde out of the area, or of those behind the van if they needed to come up and assist.

Ten seconds after the explosion, however, he had not moved at all. Both of the van's front tires had been eviscerated by high-explosive shrapnel from the rear artillery shell that had torn across the road.

Four media personnel in the first van had been cut by

broken glass, and more were disoriented by shock, but CNN press-pool reporter Jill Crosby was unhurt. She was sitting in the second row of seats, just to the left of Fox reporter Jeff Harkes. Harkes caught a face full of glass, and while he grabbed at a vicious wound just over his right ear, Crosby climbed over his legs, grabbed the door latch, and flung it open. While others in the vehicle either tended to one another's injuries or tried to get out of the van, Jill Crosby ran toward the smoke-obscured scene ahead.

She'd just pulled her phone out of her pocket and dialed into CNN's Atlanta headquarters when the gunfire started. She arrived at a damaged Suburban that had been knocked ninety degrees and now faced west on the north-south thoroughfare. She ducked low and ran past the SUV, and on the other side of this she saw an identical Suburban fully engulfed in flames.

An explosion erupted near her, knocking her to the ground. She did not recognize that she had almost been blown apart by an RPG, so she climbed back to her feet and ran forward. All around her now there was more and more shooting.

She entered the thick wall of gray smoke just as her producer answered on the other end.

'It's Crosby! The presidential motorcade is under attack! We've got to go live!'

Two counterassault team officers raced past her with their guns at their shoulders, and then they disappeared into the smoke in front of her.

Herbers had given up on getting to the President; his job now was to suppress the hostiles in the two pickup trucks on the southern side of the engagement zone. The vehicles had pulled right into the crowd of dead and wounded. Herbers lay flat in the street and engaged the driver of one of the white pickups as the man shot his AK while crouched behind his car door, incorrectly thinking it to be suitable cover. Herbers and another agent dumped round after round of .40-caliber ammo through the thin sheet metal, killing the man.

He'd heard the transmission from O'Day saying she had SWORDSMAN at the Beast, but the Beast was down. She'd called to the second limo to have it come to her, but Herbers had yet to hear a response.

He didn't allow himself an instant to think about what had gone wrong. That would come later, much later, and it would come only for those who managed to survive the firefight. So he emptied his magazine at the threats on the side street, reloaded, and racked his pistol's slide to engage some more. Just as he brought it back up on a target, he saw a flash of light in the shade on the far side of José J. Herrera. Instantly the flash grew in size, and he realized he was looking at a streaking rocket-propelled grenade. It raced five feet off the ground, shot directly over his head as it passed into the smoke behind him, and then he heard the impact of an explosion.

He hoped like hell the RPG hadn't just hit SWORDSMAN's damaged limo with the President of the United States standing next to it.

Herbers opened fire at the source of the launch, a man standing alone with an empty rocket tube, sending the man to cover.

Then he started looking around for a vehicle. He knew

the President couldn't wait around in the kill zone any longer. A Suburban with a broken windshield was upright on good tires in the road, just fifty feet away. He saw a Secret Service agent slumped over the wheel, and another man lying facedown outside an open rear driver's-side door.

Herbers leapt to his feet and started running for the black SUV.

59

Ryan climbed back to his knees for the second time in the past forty-five seconds. His right arm hung by his side, the pain grew by the second, but through the pain he saw Andrea lying faceup on the curb, blood running from her forehead.

He blinked away the grit that had made its way into his eyes and crawled to her; she was just five feet away, but it felt like a mile.

All around him men fired weapons, alarms shrieked; a helicopter had flown so low that it whipped the smoke away in swirling vortexes. Two agents kept their hands on Ryan's back as they kept their weapons sweeping, occasionally firing, and hot brass clanged on the street. Ryan cradled Andrea's head in his hands. Her eyes were closed and her mouth was parted slightly. He put his head to her mouth and then to her chest, and he felt and heard nothing.

She wasn't breathing.

A counterassault officer tried to pull Ryan to his feet now, to bring him back to the relative safety of the upturned vehicle, but Ryan swatted the man's grip away with his left arm. Then he pinched Andrea's nose shut and began rescue breathing.

He'd been trained decades ago, but his wife had given him a refresher when Kyle was born, so he knew the fundamentals. He pushed away the chattering gunfire, and even a third detonation of an RPG against the wall of a parking garage nearby, and he continued short powerful breaths into her mouth, followed by one-handed chest compressions.

He was on his third round of breathing when he saw a response from her, just a quick inhalation and an expression of discomfort on her face, but he knew she was alive.

He was about to talk to her when a black Suburban raced backward down the sidewalk and screeched to a stop just ten feet away. Now several CAT officers pulled Ryan away from Andrea Price O'Day.

'Wait!' he shouted, but President Ryan was not in charge.

'We'll take care of her!' a young agent shouted, pulling the President toward the vehicle.

The back door opened and Ryan was pushed in roughly, while men with body armor surrounded him on all sides. He tried to get a look back over his shoulder at his longtime friend lying motionless in the street, but one of his protection detail was there, almost on top of him, and he shoved Ryan all the way to the floorboard and covered him with his own body.

Ryan screamed in pain.

The agent behind the wheel yelled to the other men, 'There's gunmen and wreckage ahead! Can we go back?'

The two counterassault men had come from behind in the motorcade. 'Affirmative! Wreckage on the road for fifty yards, then you are clear!'

Another man shouted, 'Punch it!'

The vehicle shot backward, the driver, Special Agent

Herbers, looking over his shoulder as he drove in reverse, doing his best to avoid slamming into the stationary vehicles. While he drove, another agent shouted into his headset.

Special Agent Davis Linklater broadcast on the Secret Service net. 'SWORDSMAN is mobile! Heading north, everybody get out of the way, and then fall in.' He looked up to Herbers behind the wheel. Herbers was in charge here. 'Where we going?'

Herbers didn't take his eyes off the road behind him. 'Airport!' The Suburban sideswiped a burning counterassault vehicle lying on its side, jolting all in the SUV, but it kept moving backward at speed.

Everyone in the Starbucks three blocks away had either run outside to see the scene at the far end of the street market or else pushed themselves up to the window glass to look outside.

With two exceptions. Emilio and Zarif walked out onto José J. Herrera and turned left, away from the blast, although the young Mexican walked backward, marveling at the massive cloud of smoke.

'*Dios mío,*' he mumbled in awe. Zarif didn't know what the kid expected, but it clearly wasn't anything like what had just happened.

He turned back to Zarif and picked up his pace. 'My God. That was big, man.'

Zarif didn't hear any shooting until they had walked another half-block, but when the crackling gunfire came he was pleasantly surprised. He knew the sound of an AK, and he heard multiple Kalashnikovs open up; their

539

machinelike cyclic thumping mixed nicely with the dozens of car alarms and the thundering of helicopters overhead.

A scene of utter chaos had erupted, and that was even before the first crash of an RPG explosion.

Both men were picked up in the truck by the two Maldonado cowboys who had dropped them off over an hour earlier, and they began driving back to the safe house to the north.

Secret Service Agent Davis Linklater straddled the President of the United States in the backseat of the Suburban. He ran his hands all over Ryan's body, under his coat, and along his back. Ryan winced when Linklater felt his right shoulder, and the seasoned special agent saw the President's pupils lose focus.

'Where do you hurt, Mr President?'

Ryan looked around him, and turning his head caused a blinding pain in his right shoulder. 'Yeah,' he responded.

'*Where*, sir?'

Ryan looked down at his left wrist, it was swollen. 'My wrist.' After a moment he said, 'I think I broke my shoulder, too.'

Linklater felt a little more, this time closer to Ryan's clavicle.

Ryan cried out. 'Damn it, Link!'

'Collarbone,' Linklater said.

Ryan nodded distractedly. 'Andrea? How is Andrea?'

The agent replied, 'I honestly don't know, Mr President. We're going to take care of you, get you to the aircraft, and get home.'

'We can't leave Andrea and –'

'There are hundreds of law enforcement and first re-sponders back at the scene. They will take good care of her, I promise.'

'I want you to find out.'

'I will . . . when we are on board Air Force One.'

Lead Secret Service Agent Dale Herbers was behind the wheel, and he was damn glad he'd been here in town for a week already. He knew his way back to the airport without even having to look at the GPS, and this was good, because the GPS had been knocked off the windshield and was now nowhere to be found. He was well off the motorcade route, trying to skirt around the heavy traffic that had been created when the route was reopened to traffic after the motorcade had passed.

He raced through intersections at high speed, honking his horn. This vehicle wasn't armored, but it did have strobing blue lights, and he ran them continuously as he drove.

Herbers made a hard right to move parallel to gridlocked Eje 2 Norte Transval, and immediately he heard about it from Linklater.

'Smooth, Dale! He's got fractures! Unknown internal!'

'Okay!'

There were four armed men in the car in total; Herbers, two shooters from the counterassault team, and Davis Link-later, one of SWORDSMAN's protection detail. When they left the ambush site, Linklater and the two shooters had been in back with the President, but one of the CAT agents had climbed up into the front passenger seat, kicking all the other agents in the head with his shiny black combat boots in the process. Now he rode shotgun with his assault rifle over the dashboard scanning left and right, and in the back, the other black-clad agent with a carbine was on his knees next to Link-later and SWORDS-MAN, facing the rear window and watching for any threats on their tail.

While Linklater attended to SWORDSMAN, Dale Herbers found himself running comms as well as driving, which wasn't optimal at all, but he wanted the shooters in the car concentrating on watching for threats.

Herbers had called out his location to the rest of the detail, and by now mobile Secret Service agents were racing to catch up with him from behind, fortifying the protective bubble around Air Force One, or else in vehicles heading out of the airport to meet the Suburban along the way.

Over a dozen Mexican Federal Police motorcycles had managed to keep up with the black Suburban as it left the blast zone, and two more Suburbans full of special agents were a few hundred yards back and blasting through lights and stop signs to stay with the evac.

In the backseat Linklater had finished his initial assessment of his protectee, and he called it in to the aircraft so Ryan's personal doctor, Maura Handwerker, would be ready for him when he arrived.

When Linklater finished with his transmission, Ryan reached out and grabbed the lapel of his suit coat. 'How many dead, Davis?'

'I don't know, sir.' He shook his head. 'A lot.'

'Tell me what you saw.'

'I was in the chase car two back from you. It was an IED. The SUV in front of me was down. I didn't see anyone bail. I saw Ambassador Styles. He appeared deceased. The driver of your vehicle . . . he was deceased.'

Jack shut his eyes. 'Delaney.' Mitch Delaney had been on his detail for two years. He'd been alive when Ryan saw him, but that was before the RPG struck the Beast.

'Yes, sir.'

'What else did you see?'

'CAT came up and wasted a bunch of fuckers. Sorry, sir. Just a little adrenaline.'

'It's okay, Davis,' Ryan said as he patted the man's lapel back in place. 'Whoever they were, they were most definitely fuckers.'

60

Jill Crosby had spent the past minute and a half lying flat on the ground next to the Mobile Command and Control Vehicle that everyone called the Roadrunner. A fierce gun battle raged all around her. She'd been on the other side of the vehicle when the Suburban raced backward along the sidewalk to the upturned limousine and then continued backward behind her, so she'd seen none of that.

But even if she had not been shielded from the SUV, she still might have missed it, because her eyes were fixed firmly on the wreckage just seventy-five feet away. It was the Beast, it was split in half and burning, and smoldering, charred bodies sat in the backseat.

This was Crosby's first time in the presidential motorcade, and she had no idea there were actually two identical limousines. She was certain the vehicle in front of her was the one the President had been traveling in.

The gunfire and explosions abated after two minutes, and almost immediately after that she saw Secret Service men in dark suits and sunglasses race to the burning limo in the middle of the road and begin spraying it with fire extinguishers. Other CAT men appeared and covered them, unsure if there were any more threats in the buildings.

The fact there was such an effort to put out the fire

convinced her of what was going on. She had no doubt in her mind she was looking at the bodies of US Ambassador Horatio Styles and President of the United States Jack Ryan.

She filmed it all with her camera phone, but when she heard a voice on the phone's speaker, she quickly brought it back to her mouth, ending the shot.

She'd wanted to send a live video feed from her phone to be broadcast, but the producer told her to just record for playback so they could control what made it on the air.

The anchor in Atlanta set up the phone call quickly on live TV. 'CNN's Jill Crosby is on the phone with us from the scene in Mexico City, where the presidential motorcade has just come under attack. Jill, are you there?'

'I'm here, Don. I am in the center of a continuing, protracted ambush of the presidential motorcade. There was a bomb or a missile, some sort of massive explosion, and that was followed quickly by more shooting and smaller explosions. The motorcade stopped moving, so I left the press-pool van to try and get through the smoke to see the President. I saw wreckage and bodies, and then I had to take cover where I am right now.'

'Are you able to see the President?'

She filmed again for a moment, then brought the phone back to her mouth. The sounds of sirens, shouting and screaming, and the low-flying helicopters meant she had to yell. 'The limousine is on fire. There are two bodies in the back of the limousine that I can see. At least one in the front.'

'Let's be very careful. Are you certain the President was in that limousine?'

Jill didn't understand the question. Where else would the President be but in the limo?

She answered authoritatively. 'I saw Ryan and Ambassador Styles get into this vehicle. I believe I am filming their bodies right now, Don.'

The anchor in Atlanta cautioned the audience that there had been no confirmation, and reports from the scene were apt to change quickly.

But it didn't matter. Within three minutes and twelve seconds of the IED's detonation on the corner of Vidal Alcocer and José J. Herrera, a reporter on live national television proclaimed that the President had been assassinated.

General Ri Tae-jin wanted CNN to show video, but instead he saw an American man with black skin sitting at a desk and talking. He then heard the breathless voice of a woman shouting English above the sounds of sirens, and he listened to his translator's rendition of the woman's words. He nodded, over and over, as the unconfirmed report came that the attack had been successful.

Within seconds the video came, but it was from a helicopter. The translator said that it was from Mexican television and was being fed into CNN. There was a huge cloud of smoke over a sunny street. In the distant haze the massive sprawling city lay out across the bottom of a valley. The camera zoomed to show the burning wreckage of several vehicles, some more cars and SUVs tossed about haphazardly, and rushing first responders moving in every direction.

Ri was satisfied. There was a massive zone of destruction. He'd been military intelligence, not infantry, but he had done his share of battle damage assessments, and he noted the zone was much larger than that from the impact of a round of field artillery.

No one in the middle of that would survive.

Ri felt certain the assassination had been carried out, but there was one more critical component to Operation Fire Axe that he would need confirmation of, so even though it was well after three in the morning, he knew neither he nor his translator would be leaving his office for some time to come.

The American Secret Service liaison at the airport had told the Mexican Federal Police official in charge that the vehicle carrying the President would come through the north VIP gate in five minutes, and if anyone at the gate tried to stop it, the men in the vehicle would open fire.

The Mexican authorities at the airport had the good sense to stay out of the way, but as it happened, Lead Special Agent Dale Herbers drove in the middle of a motorcade of fourteen vehicles, some containing other members of the Secret Service but most driven by Mexican police, who were fully involved in the evacuation of the American President. Together they all raced through the gate with sirens and lights blaring, and they all screeched to a halt at the aircraft. Though most of the US security force was still on its way back from the ambush site, there were still more than twenty-five armed Secret Service men around the plane, and every last one of them had a hand-gun or a long gun in their hand and their heads on swivels as they checked the area for threats.

Linklater, Herbers, and the two CAT agents helped the President out of the back of the vehicle. Two Air Force chief master sergeants who served as stewards on the aircraft were waiting with a stretcher, but the President walked on his own power to the stairs. He moved hunched over slightly, his right arm hanging and the expression on his face pained, but he was strong enough to make it all the way up to the cabin door of the 747 with only minimal help from the stewards at his side. Ryan was trailed up the stairs by a phalanx of men with assault rifles on their shoulders, all of whom walked backward and trained their holographic weapon sights on the distant terminal or the fields around the airport.

Once inside the plane, Ryan reached out to the wall to hold himself up, and his knees gave way.

Dr. Maura Handwerker was waiting at the entrance and she caught him. She had already moved many items out of the small but well-equipped medical office right next to the hatch and into the President's suite in the nose of the aircraft just a dozen feet away. Here there was more room for SWORDSMAN to lie down, and more room for Handwerker to do everything she needed to do short of X-rays, which, if necessary, could be done in the medical office.

Ryan was carried gingerly into his suite, and then laid on his back on the bed. His face was ashen from the pain and the mild shock, and blood was smeared from scratches on his forehead. Immediately Handwerker and her nurse for the trip, an Air Force critical-care nurse, began cutting off his suit with fabric shears.

Arnie Van Damm wasn't along for the trip. Instead, his

assistant chief of staff, a fresh-faced thirty-three-year-old named David Detmer, stood far back out of the way of the medical professionals. Still, he was in earshot, so when Ryan started shouting out his name, Detmer leaned his head into the suite.

'I'm here, sir!'

'Secure phone!'

'The Vice President has been told. He's on his way back to Washington from California.'

Ryan shook his head, causing him a fresh jolt of pain. 'I need Arnie. Then Cathy.'

Dr. Handwerker glared at Detmer, because she couldn't glare at the President. She did say, "Mr President, I need you to lie right here for now and relax. You have a broken collarbone, and likely a broken wrist. We'll want to give you an MRI to see if you have a concussion, but that can wait till we're back in DC For now we will go under the assumption that you do have a concussion, so we'll want you to stay flat on your back.

'We'll immobilize your arm, and this will help with the shoulder pain.'

'Okay, but I need to make some calls.'

'Sir, first I need to debride your wounds and clean them up. I need to better immobilize –'

Arguing with the doctor had the effect of clearing Ryan's head a little. 'Doctor, I won't stop you from doing your job, but you have to let me do mine. Right now President Volodin in Russia, as well as a few other crazies, need to know I am still on the damn job!'

Handwerker took cold compresses from a chest she'd rolled into the room before the President arrived. She wrapped them around his left wrist. Without looking up she said, 'Someone hold the phone for him, he can't use either of his hands right now.'

A headset was attached to the secure cabin phone, and Detmer connected with Arnie Van Damm. He struggled to make his way around the Air Force nurse and put the headset on Ryan's head.

Jack coughed, then said, 'Arnie?'

'Jesus, Jack, how are you?'

Ryan winced with the ice-cold compresses on his injured left wrist. 'Andrea's hurt. Mitch Delaney's dead. Ambassador Styles, too. That kid that just joined the detail . . . Philip something.'

'I'm sorry. How are –'

'Philip Weingarten. Couldn't have been thirty years old. I saw him facedown in the street.'

'How are *you*?'

Jack answered distractedly. 'I'll be fine. What have you done?'

'Your National Security Council is convening in the PEOC. The Vice President is on his way back from California.'

The PEOC was the Presidential Emergency Operations Center, a nuclear strike – proof bomb-shelter version of the Situation Room.

Arnie continued, 'A CNN reporter on the scene said you were dead. It went live on air and it's all over social media, but no one else has taken the bait. As soon as I heard you were alive, I contacted the head of their news division on his cell phone and said he needed to walk that back right now. He thought I was spinning him, the son

550

of a bitch. I told him he either retracted that bullshit story or I'd see he was blamed for the attack if the Russians decide to spin up a full-on invasion of central Ukraine.'

While Arnie was talking, Ryan could feel the aircraft accelerate on its takeoff roll. He didn't think they could have closed the hatch three minutes prior, and already they were hurtling down the runway. No one in the room around him bothered to strap themselves in, they were all too busy working. He had the sense that his legs were cold, and he thought that meant his pants had been removed, but lifting his head to look down would have been too painful, so he just lay there, staring at the ceiling.

Arnie said, 'MSNBC is reporting that the Muslim Brotherhood, the Islamic State, and the Taliban have all taken credit for the attack.'

Ryan replied, 'You need to make a statement. Let everyone know I'm alive.'

Arnie said, 'Getting the press in the briefing room. I'll go on as soon as I get off with you.'

Just then, a mobile phone was passed into the President's suite from the hallway. One of Ryan's young aides called out, 'It's the First Lady, Mr President!'

Jack told Arnie to hold and he waited for someone to remove the headset and hold the mobile phone to his ear. He turned his head to get situated better, and he hissed with the new onset of agony in his shoulder. Covering quickly, he said, 'Hi, honey. I'm fine. I was just about to call you, I'm sorry.'

'I needed to hear you, Jack. I love you.' Ryan could hear the pain and terror in Cathy's voice. 'Now put me on with Dr. Handwerker.'

He wasn't surprised his wife wasn't going to rely on him to relay his condition. She knew Jack wasn't a physician, and she also knew he would sugarcoat any serious issue. Before he sent the phone on he said, 'Do the kids know?'

He was talking about Kyle and Katie, but Cathy would know this. 'They don't. They were on a field trip when it hit the news up here. The Secret Service has them on their way to the White House. I'll need to tell them something when I get there.'

'Tell them I'm coming home.'

'Who did it, Jack? Was it Maldonado?'

'Not a clue. I don't even know what happened. We were riding along, and then I woke up in a heap. I've got to run. Passing you to Maura.'

He turned his attention back to Arnie now. Though he'd been on the verge of shock just minutes earlier, the familiar aspects of doing his job, managing crises, delegating responsibility, all cleared his head. His pain had not dissipated, but his brain had something else to focus on. 'What are the Russians doing?'

'Full alert.'

'That's it?'

'They have bombers skirting Alaskan airspace, but that happens on a good day.'

'Yeah. I want a briefing from SecState and SecDef within the hour.'

'It's all taken care of here.'

'No, Arnie. They need to be on the phone with their counterparts in the UK, Russia, China –'

'Jack! They've already started that. We're taking care of

the immediate fires here. The world is going to hang on while you get patched up.'

Jack all but ignored him. 'I want you to make a list. I will work the phones all day and talk until I lose my voice. I need to let everyone know I am strong and in charge.'

Dr. Maura Handwerker said, 'I'm sorry, Mr President. But you are going to need to rest.'

'I need to make a statement, too. Live. On camera. We can't wait to land, we need to do that from the plane.'

Ryan saw his doctor above him glance over at the nurse. They didn't say anything, they focused on placing compresses on his shoulder, but he understood the look.

Ryan forced himself to look down. His shoes were on the floor and his black slacks had been sheared off, bloody gauze covered his lower right leg. His suit coat and dress shirt were gone as well, and his right arm was being held close to his body by the nurse, who was prepping Ace bandages to wrap it. His left arm was by his side, covered in compresses. He could feel the scratches on his face that had gone unattended because they were down at the bottom of the priority list.

He looked to the nurse. 'That bad?'

She said, 'If you order us to clean you up, we will do it, but you really need to rest, and your collarbone needs to stay right where it is, which means we can't put a shirt on you.'

Jack addressed Arnie Van Damm again. 'You go live now, and I'll do an audio statement. We'll get one of the press people up here to record it.'

Detmer had been standing back, but he said, 'Sorry,

Mr President. Secret Service didn't let any press on the plane before we took off.'

'Shit,' said Ryan.

'I can record you,' Detmer offered.

'Yeah,' said Jack. 'Coming from the White House, some will say it's faked, but that and a picture of my face will have to do till we land.'

Maura said, 'I'll put a bandage on your forehead. We'll make you presentable.'

61

Emilio, the two Maldonado cowboys, and Adel Zarif arrived at the safe-house apartment thirty-five minutes after the attack. As they climbed the stairs all four men looked to the south and saw the thick hanging cloud of smoke. It was diffusing now, but it, and the half-dozen helicopters circling around, would remain in the air over the city for some time.

Zarif was looking forward to watching the news broadcasts while he waited for nightfall. The plan was for the Maldonado men to take him all the way into Guerrero, where they would then fly him from Acapulco to Cuba. There, North Korean agents would be waiting to take him to Pyongyang.

And Zarif couldn't wait to get out of here.

One of the rough-looking men unlocked the door and stepped into the apartment, followed close on his heels by his partner. Emilio entered, and then Zarif followed him in.

All three Mexicans headed for the kitchen to get beers, but Zarif walked straight down the hallway to the bathroom in the back. He hadn't taken the time to piss since he'd left hours earlier, and the TV would have to wait while he took care of business. He didn't even take off his backpack before he unzipped his fly, but as soon as he did this, he heard a shout from the living room, and then a second shout, this time from Emilio.

He leaned out of the bathroom and looked up the hallway into the living room. Three Asian men in the blue coveralls of sanitation workers had entered the apartment right behind Zarif and the Maldonado men. In their hands were black pistols with long silencers. While Emilio and the other two stood by the television with beers in their hands, the three men opened fire, shooting each Mexican several times.

Their bodies spasmed and spun and dropped to the blood-spattered carpet.

Zarif leapt back into the bathroom, he shut and locked the door, then he climbed into the bathtub. Above the tub was a window high on the wall. He reached up and pulled it open, and then he struggled to heft himself up to it.

Behind him the bathroom door splintered with a dozen bullet holes. Zarif pushed through the window as hard as he could, then fell outside onto a small overhang. He rolled to the edge, then tipped over the side and dropped down one floor to a dusty parking lot.

As he looked back over his shoulder he heard scuffling in the bathroom, and then more gunfire erupted from the window, pocking the parking lot around him. Zarif dove between a parked Ford Bronco and an old Winnebago and crawled as fast as he could to the other side.

He then rose to a crouch and sprinted into the street, racing through moving traffic. On the far side he ran along the sidewalk for blocks.

And as he ran, his dream of the Asian girls and the beach house evaporated. He had no idea where to go or what to do, so he just ran on through the city, still in disbelief that he had done everything asked of him and the infidel North Koreans had sent killers anyway.

In his Pyongyang office, General Ri sat patiently waiting for the call from his RGB director in Mexico. Once the word finally came that the Iranian bomber had been killed, he would go home and sleep for a few hours before returning to work. He expected to be contacted by the office of the Dae Wonsu, invited to the Ryongsong Residence and congratulated personally, and he wanted to be fresh for this event.

While he bided his time he had the woman with him keep up the running translations from CNN, and he watched the feed with rapt fascination. There was footage now of a burning limousine, and although the image had been obscured to cover burning bodies in the middle of the wreckage, his translator said the reporter was claiming the dead to be the President and the ambassador.

The translator kept talking over with the English words: '. . . devastating attack on the motorcade carrying President Jack Ryan. We have been told there are casualties, a significant number of casualties. Perhaps in the dozens, perhaps many, many more.'

Ri had tuned out. Now he was thinking about how to pay quiet honor to Zarif. The bomb maker was likely already dead, killed under his instruction. Still, something was in order for the man's contribution to the North Korean people. There could be no official announcement, of course. If ever word made it back to the United States that North Korea was complicit in the assassination of their leader, then the Americans would fire every last one of their nuclear missiles. They were a warlike people who had been looking for the right time, and the right excuse, for seventy years.

Ri worried any mistake in his operation would give them that excuse, but he had confidence in his plan, and as the TV screen in front of him now showed an overhead view, from a helicopter, perhaps, of an entire city block of wrecked and burning vehicles, shattered shop windows, and debris in the streets, General Ri allowed himself to feel even more confident.

The television feed switched to the White House now. The translator said a press secretary was due to make a statement. Ri smiled. This would be the announcement he had waited for. The man who walked out was in his sixties and bald, and he wore small glasses that made him look like a professor. Ri could tell the man had never served in his nation's military, and to the general that alone was reason for derision.

Never mind that he was American.

The translator said, 'Comrade General, this man's name is Arnold Van Damm. He is the principal adjutant to the President, and his closest adviser.'

Ri chuckled. 'If he was his closest adviser, he would have been in the car with him.'

'Yes, Comrade General.'

The American appeared somewhat rushed and irresolute, and he took a moment to control his emotion, looking down at a small sheet of paper in front of him. Finally he looked into the camera. 'Ladies and gentlemen. Approximately forty minutes ago, at twelve thirty-five local time in Mexico City, one thirty-five here in

Washington, a vicious and cowardly attack was perpetrated not just against the United States of America but also against the entire free world. The motorcade carrying the President was ambushed by unknown individuals using explosives, rifles, and rockets. President Ryan was traveling in an armored vehicle that was disabled by the initial explosion, and several other vehicles were also disabled or destroyed.'

A male reporter all but screamed: 'Is the President alive?'

Arnie Van Damm nodded instantly. 'The President is very much alive. He is currently on Air Force One and returning to Washington.'

Ri snatched the translator by her arm and yanked her closer. 'Alive?'

'Yes, Comrade General.'

A female reporter on television shouted now, and the translator spoke in Korean. 'Is he injured?'

'The President was slightly wounded, it appears he has some fractures. He is in good spirits. His injuries were tended to on the aircraft by his personal doctor.'

'Can he speak to the press?'

'Due to the security situation at the airport, the press pool was either not able or not allowed to board the aircraft. I understand he will record an audio message, and as soon as I get that I will send it out to all the media contacts.'

A young male reporter from MSNBC called out now. 'Why not a video message?'

Arnie said, 'Honestly, we don't have the time to set up a secure video conference with Air Force One.'

'Arnie, how can we confirm it's really Ryan talking if we can't even see him?'

Arnie looked at the man for a long time. 'You just announced to your viewership that the Taliban has accepted responsibility. Did you confirm that, or did you just run with it?'

'Well, we –'

'I don't care if you believe it's Jack Ryan on the audio. Just run it. He'll be back in Washington in a few hours, and I'm sure we'll prove any skeptics wrong.'

Another question came from the front row. 'Who is in charge?'

Van Damm said, 'John Patrick Ryan is the President of the United States. That has not changed.'

In the office in Pyongyang, General Ri looked at the uniformed woman next to him now, not at the television. 'He is alive and on his airplane?'

'Yes, Comrade General.'

Ri shook his head. Slowly at first, and then more quickly. 'It's a lie. His body is on the airplane. They are buying themselves a few hours. Once the plane lands in Washington, and they all have their stories straight, they will claim the President died in flight.'

'Yes, Comrade General.'

Ri stood and began pacing his office. Within seconds his phone rang, and he stormed over and snatched it up. 'Yes?' He nodded. '*What?* Zarif is alive? Damn you! Find him now, or your family will be in Chongjin by the end of the week!' He slammed the phone down so hard the translator cried out.

*

In New York City, the entire Campus team had just arrived to help Sam Driscoll with his surveillance on Veronika Martel. She had not left her apartment yet today, but the team expected movement soon because it was already early afternoon.

Clark had gone out to rent a second vehicle, but the rest of the men had been sitting in the living room on a conference call with Gavin Biery. Suddenly Clark came through the door, almost in a run. Ding, Dom, Sam, and Jack stood quickly, confused and concerned by his manner. He shut the door, then he looked at the television. When he saw it was turned off he headed straight through the living room toward the hall to the bedrooms. On the way he said, 'Ryan, follow me.'

Ryan stood, looked around at the other guys. 'What the hell did I do?' Clark had already stormed down the hall.

Ryan entered the bedroom seconds later. Clark moved close to him. Jack had been concerned he was in trouble, but he could see something else in Clark's eyes, something that gave him even more reason to fear.

'What is it?'

'Son, your dad's motorcade was attacked in Mexico City. It's all over the news.'

Ryan's mouth opened slightly, but he did not speak.

'Nobody knows anything yet. I called Gerry and he's on it, but we're going to learn more from the media that was down there.'

Clark didn't mention that one of the cable outlets had already announced the assassination of the President. Instead, he said, 'You need to call your mom.'

Just then Ryan's phone rang in the living room. He raced back in and stared at it for a moment, then he picked it up and looked at the number.

It was his mother.

His hand shook. 'Is he dead?'

'He's hurt, but Maura says he'll be okay.'

Jack felt his knees weaken, and he gave in to it, dropping onto the couch and leaning forward. Quickly he held a thumbs-up for Clark, but the other men still had no idea what had happened.

Clark grabbed the TV remote.

'Who did it?' Jack asked.

'He doesn't know.'

'If it was in Mexico it had to be Santiago Maldonado and those psychos under him.'

'Can you come to George Washington Hospital this afternoon? I know he'll want to see you when he gets home.'

Ryan turned his head away from the phone when an ambulance siren raced up the street, and when the ambulance stopped in front of the small apartment building directly across from them, he walked to the window. The other Campus operators followed.

'Jack?' his mother said. 'Are you there?'

'I have to call you back.'

'Are you coming to the hospital?'

'I'll be there.' He hung up the phone as two paramedics ran up the steps to the building and were let in by one of the residents.

Clark looked to Sam, and Sam moved without being asked. He ran down the stairs and crossed the street.

Already two neighbors walking their dogs had stopped by the ambulance. A woman came down from the apartment building a few seconds later, and they started chatting.

Sam stood back, but he was close enough to hear.

Five minutes later he was back in the apartment across the street.

'The super found the body of a woman in three-A. The tenant.'

Ryan was back on the couch. CNN was on TV, Arnie Van Damm had just spoken. He couldn't take his eyes from the images on the screen, but he also couldn't believe Veronika was dead, just one hundred feet from where he sat.

Sam Driscoll did not hesitate to place blame for Martel's murder. 'It wasn't the North Koreans. If you go through the back door of that building you have to pass up the alley next to it, and you can see that from here. I've had cams running twenty-four-seven and the only person who came or left since the last time I saw Martel alive was Edward Riley.'

Chavez said, 'Riley murdered his own agent? Why?'

No one knew.

Ryan sat alone with his face in his hands for a minute, suddenly tired and overwhelmed. Finally, he stood. 'Sorry, guys, I've got to get back to DC'

Clark stood as well. 'I'll drive you to the airport.' He turned to the rest of the crew. 'I want the rest of you guys looking for Riley. Sharps knows about us, so it's going to be a challenge to operate back on these streets, but I don't think Sharps was involved in this. He's way too slick to be whacking his own people in New York. This, whatever it is, is something else.' He looked to the TV for a moment. He wished he was down in Mexico on the hunt for the perpetrators of the ambush, and he knew his crew was thinking the same thing. He needed to keep them on mission. 'Stay focused. Ryan . . . let's go.'

62

President Jack Ryan asked those around him in the presidential suite in the nose of the aircraft to help him up. Even though this recording would be audio only, he couldn't give a speech lying on his back and staring at the ceiling. The import of the moment required him to, at the very least, sit upright. His doctor and the Air Force nurse first tried to talk him out of sitting, but they saw the determination in his eyes, and they quickly became his confederates in the endeavor, helping him up and into one of two chairs by a tiny desk.

Once Ryan was in the chair, his right arm cinched across his chest and his left arm wrapped with compresses, Dr. Handwerker and the Air Force nurse stepped back and sat down on the bed he had just vacated, and David Detmer, assistant to the chief of staff, entered the room. He had a small digital recorder he'd borrowed from a secretary, and he held it up to the President, kneeling in front of him.

At first Jack struggled to concentrate. Any adrenaline that had helped mute his pain had dissipated, the discomfort was increasing by the minute, and the intense dull ache in his shoulder and neck now felt like a million pins and needles, with intermittent quick jolts of sharper pain.

*

But he fought through. To Detmer he said, 'Needless to say, I don't have a prepared statement for this. It's going to be off-the-cuff a little, so I hope the historical record will cut me some slack.'

'Be yourself, Mr President. That will be fine.'

Ryan cleared his throat and said, 'This is President Jack Ryan. Right now I am speaking to you from Air Force One. We are flying with fighter escort and are minutes from US airspace.'

In truth, they were a lot of minutes from US airspace, actually over an hour, but he assumed by the time this was disseminated to the media it would be accurate, and the entire focus of his speech now was to quell the fervor of America's more opportunistic enemies.

'I was banged up a little bit in the attack, but much more important, some colleagues and dear friends of mine have been killed, and many others have been injured. I do not know the full scope of the loss of life yet, but if you pray, I hope you will join me in praying for those who died needlessly today, and for those who were hurt.'

He felt tired suddenly. He took a moment to force strength into his voice.

"I want to stress to the American people that although I don't yet know who is responsible for this, I personally witnessed many Mexican citizens, members of their Federal Police and other law enforcement agencies, risk their lives to protect the presidential motorcade. I am sure the loss of life among the innocent Mexicans will be as great or greater than ours. Whoever perpetrated the attack today, and I remind everyone that that has not yet been determined, remember that good Mexican men and women fought and died to protect the . . . the continuity of the United States government. As soon as I can I will call President Lopez personally and thank him and his fellow countrymen. His nation has been going through some difficult times, and I want him to know I'm going to go home to get patched up, and then I'm going to come back to Mexico City and see him as planned.

'And now, to the people responsible for today's action. Your objective was the decapitation of the US government. Hearing my voice, you now realize that you have failed. I suspect you will do what your kind always does. You will run, and you will hide.' Ryan took a calming breath. "Just as you failed today, you will fail in that endeavor, because we *will* find you. And whatever quarrel you *thought* you had with America will seem like nothing, because you have made a true enemy today, and America will not rest until you have been dealt what you deserve.

'I look forward to a video press conference as soon as I get back to Washington. In the meantime . . . God bless the United States of America.'

Ryan nodded to Detmer, who ended the recording.

A digital camera was brought into the room, Ryan's face was framed in the lens in front of the presidential seal on the wall of the suite, and a picture was taken. There would be no record of the fact he'd just made one of the most important speeches of his career in his underwear.

As soon as he was prostrate on the bed again, Ryan called for Detmer. When he appeared over him, Ryan said, 'David, as soon as you get that recording to Arnie, you have one job, and one job only. I want you to find out the condition of Andrea Price O'Day. If she's at a hospital in Mexico I want those doctors to know they can have anything they want or need from us. Do you understand?'

'Yes, Mr President.'

Jack closed his eyes and tried to think of anything but the pain in his right shoulder.

Arnie got the recording to the news media within a half-hour of its being made. The Dow had dropped 1,000 points in the first hour after the attack, stopping trading for an hour. After Ryan's 'proof of life' went out, trading was restarted, and the Dow rebounded 619 points. It would still be rocked for the day, but not nearly as bad as Wall Street had feared initially.

Adel Zarif found a bus station within an hour of the attack by the North Koreans at the safe house, and with little understanding of where he was going, he boarded a coach for Toluca. It was about forty miles away, west of the capital, so he arrived in the afternoon, just as the daily shower began.

He walked through the crowded downtown district in the warm rain until he found a cheap hostel, and here he booked a private room for the night. There was no request for an ID or passport or credit card, and the old man behind the counter took no notice of the fact the man's English was spoken with an accent.

Zarif's room was flea-infested and smelled of mold, but he felt safe enough here, so he sat at the little card table in the corner, put his head down, and tried to come up with a plan.

It took him an hour, but it would have taken him longer if he had other options. As it was, he had very little money, no Spanish-language skills, and not a single friend in the entire country of Mexico.

There were two things, and two things only, that he *did* have. He had contact information in the form of a phone number and an e-mail address to a North Korean intelligence agent in Cuba, and he had information that, if revealed to the world, would likely get North Korea burned to the ground by the USA.

So Zarif's one option was blackmail.

He started a video recording on his phone, placed the phone on the desk, and scooted his chair back to put himself in the picture. He spoke in English.

'My name is Adel Zarif. I was living in Damascus when I was contacted by the Reconnaissance General Bureau of the Democratic People's Republic of Korea. I was hired to assassinate Jack Ryan in Mexico City. I was offered asylum in the coastal city of Hamhŭng once the job was complete . . .'

His entire recording lasted only four minutes, but it laid out the entire operation. He sent the video file to the e-mail address of his North Korean contact in Cuba. And then he sent a text message right after this.

I will e-mail this recording to every newspaper and television station in America. You have one hour to call me to hear my demands.

The call came in less than twenty minutes. Zarif demanded from the North Koreans $2 million and a face-to-face exchange in Mexico. The RGB agent said he would call the Iranian back as soon as arrangements had been made, but Zarif just laughed in his face, telling him he would destroy his phone before it could be traced and then call the RGB man back from another phone in eighteen hours.

Zarif had not made it through a half-dozen Middle Eastern wars by being a fool. He did what he said he would do, shattering his phone with a brick behind his hostel, before heading out to find another phone and another place to stay the night.

He didn't know what he would do with $2 million, he still had no documents and no friends. But he determined he could get a lot further with the money than without it, and he suspected he could make it out of Mexico eventually, and find someplace to hide.

It wasn't a perfect plan, but those were problems for another day, because he knew the North Koreans would try to kill him if they got the chance.

63

Adam Yao woke this morning, as he had every morning he'd been in Chongju, to the sounds of roosters crowing. He looked to the clock on the wall of the temporary housing trailer and saw it was only five-thirty, but he was wide awake so he rolled out of bed and headed to the toilet.

A few minutes later he stepped outside the unit he shared with eight other men and women, and he stretched on the asphalt parking lot. It was a misty, cool morning, still dark outside, but the moon glowed through the vapor. The cooks wouldn't have the breakfast of tea and noodles ready until seven, and the Chinese technicians wouldn't climb in the buses for the twenty-minute bus ride to the refinery until eight, so Adam decided he would take this opportunity to glean some intel the only way available to him right now. He would go for a morning run inside the perimeter of the fence surrounding the compound, and he would see what he could see.

As he jogged he saw several bored and tired North Korean guards who just glanced at him and then went back to their conversations and their cigarettes. As he passed the hotel adjacent to the temporary housing compound, he saw several black cars and vans. These he knew belonged to Hwang Min-ho, who had arrived the previous evening from Pyongyang.

Adam knew something important was going on. The

day before at work he'd been ordered to reduce his daily quota of powder. On the three previous days he'd been directed to work until he had produced eight hundred kilograms of crushed ore, which took him twelve hours. But yesterday this was changed to just one hundred kilos.

He had not asked any questions, he simply complied, but in the break room other Chinese technicians had been talking about the changes in their own work spaces, and one man relayed how the North Korean shift supervisor had told him the separation equipment that was due to arrive any day had been delayed. Adam knew this intel was secondhand at best, and he had no way of judging its accuracy, but the fact Hwang himself came in that evening made him wonder if the North Koreans had some sort of a crisis on their hands.

On his second lap around the inside of the fence he was surprised to notice another runner slowly jogging in the distance around the unfenced portion of the parking lot. He was too far away and it was too dark to see him clearly, but Adam assumed the man must have been a guest at the hotel.

Adam slowed his jog. For a moment he thought the runner might have been Hwang himself, because the man was small and slight, but soon he discounted this possibility because Hwang was bald, and the runner definitely had hair.

On his next lap he tried to time his run so he would be on the fence line at the same moment the runner approached on the other side of the fence. Adam was more curious than anything, because now he had put together the likelihood that the runner might be one of the foreign guest workers from Australia. Adam had seen them at the refinery, although none of them had business in his part of the plant, and he knew they were staying in the hotel.

He timed his lap perfectly. As he neared the approaching runner on the other side of the fence he realized he had been mistaken. This was not a man, this was the red-headed Australian woman he'd seen a few times before.

She smiled and waved as she approached. Adam waved back and kept running.

When she was still in front of him and closing, she called out to him. '*Ni hao.*' Hello.

Surprised to hear the white woman speak Mandarin, Adam slowed. He nodded to her. '*Ni hao.*'

She stopped fully now. '*Ni hao ma?*' How are you?

Adam stopped as well. '*Wo hen hao. Ni ne?*' I am fine, and you?

She continued in stilted Mandarin. 'I am good. I am Dr. Powers, from Australia.'

'Shan Xin. From China. You speak very good Mandarin.'

'Thank you. I went to university in Shenzhen. My husband is from there.'

In truth her Chinese was fair at best, it was heavily accented with an Australian twang, but Adam felt his heart pounding. Perhaps he could get some information from this woman, and do it without revealing anything about his true identity.

But he knew he needed to go slowly and carefully so as not to arouse suspicion. He started with some idle conversation. 'You run every day?'

'There is nothing else to do,' she said. 'What is your job at Chongju?'

'I am the computer operator of the cone crushing machine in the powder-processing department. I arrived just last week. And you?'

'I am a geologist. I have been here for over a month.'

Adam smiled and nodded. 'Very good.'

She shook her head. Even in the darkness, Adam thought she looked sad.

He said, 'You are far from home.'

She didn't hesitate to open up. 'I have two children. A boy and a girl. I miss them.'

'I understand. I have a boy and a girl, too.'

She brightened a little. 'Really? How lovely. What are their names?'

The woman was obviously bored and lonely. Adam made up names, ages, and even personalities of two children. It was called mirroring, and it was probably the oldest social engineering trick in the book, but it was also supremely effective.

'You have pictures?'

Adam let his shoulders droop. 'They took all our personal belongings in Shanghai. They were just pictures. What does it matter? Now I cannot look into the eyes of little Lanfen, my daughter, before I go to sleep at night.'

Adam was a good actor. Powers bought it hook, line, and sinker. He felt bad for the deception – she was probably a nice woman who'd made a bad decision in coming here – but he had a job to do, and bad acting in his job would compromise his mission and *could* get him killed.

Powers said, 'I regret coming. I would go home in a

minute, but they won't let us leave until the facility is producing.'

Adam saw an opportunity. He was rushing things, he knew, but this was too good to pass up. 'I worry about when that will happen. Yesterday they told us the refinery will not start on time. Some equipment was supposed to arrive, but it has been delayed. You want to leave, but I do not. There are no jobs in mining where I come from. I am afraid they will send us home if it doesn't come soon.'

Powers waved away Adam's concern. 'The arrival of the flotation cells was held up. Don't worry. Hwang will get more here soon. He has to.'

'*Has* to?'

'It's all about money. The North Koreans don't get paid until the refinery starts producing. On the day the refinery goes on line, North Korea stands to get five hundred million US dollars from their foreign partner.'

'I see,' he said. 'How do you know all this?'

Instantly he saw he'd gone too far with his questioning. She hesitated in answering, and she looked around to make sure they were not being watched. Dr. Powers was concerned about what she had just said because, Adam assumed, it was something she was not supposed to know.

As a NOC, Adam knew how to put sources at ease. He laughed. 'Maybe you shouldn't say anything else to me.' He smiled. 'I am just a computer technician. I am happy you think the facility will go on line soon. That is all I care about.'

She relaxed, and a minute later the two of them had

jogged off in separate directions along opposite sides of the fence line.

Three hours later Adam sat at his terminal, typing out his report for the operations center of Acrid Herald. He did not use Dr. Powers's name or even make any reference to her, because if his mission was discovered he did not want her implicated, but he reported her claim that North Korea would receive a $500 million payment on the day the refinery went live.

From what Adam knew about where that money was going and what it was being used for, he hoped like hell that day never came.

64

Óscar Roblas de Mota had been asleep in his suite at the Pan Pacific hotel in Singapore when the attack on Jack Ryan occurred in his hometown ten thousand miles away. He slept in the next morning, and it wasn't until one of his personal assistants roused him at nine that he heard the news.

From nine a.m. till ten a.m. he sat in his white bathrobe on the sofa and watched television, both US and Mexican satellite stations. By now there was video of the ambush from cell phones, helicopter news crews, and security cameras. A virtual glut of moving pictures of the entire attack from multiple angles.

He called a half-dozen friends in government in the district; he was as dialed-in as anyone could be there, after all. Everyone was saying the attack was the work of Santiago Maldonado, but Roblas didn't buy that for a minute. The Maldonados had claimed responsibility, but they weren't an active group inside Mexico City. Sure, they could have driven into town for the attack, but Roblas didn't see them as competent enough to pull off anything of this magnitude. He knew they had recently failed in an attempt to kill the mayor of a small city in Guerrero, and here they were, supposedly taking out dozens of trained security and wounding the President of the United States?

Not a chance.

In the back of his mind Roblas thought of General Ri. The North Korean intelligence chief would have people who could have done this, and he would also have contacts within the Maldonado clan. There was no question as to motive. Ri's schemes had been thwarted on the mining front and on the ICBM front, in both cases by the man who narrowly escaped death the day before in Mexico City.

At eleven a.m. Roblas tore himself away from the screen and showered, then he dressed for a lunch meeting with bankers, but as he did so he became more and more suspicious that the North Koreans were responsible for what had happened.

He was not angry that they had tried, he was angry that they had failed, and he was *very* angry that they had done it in 'his' city.

He was just about to head with his entourage down to his limousine when a secure call came for him on the satellite phone. Just receiving word of the call itself convinced him he was right about what had happened.

'*Bueno?*'

It was one of Ri's translators, speaking English. 'Good after-noon. Comrade General Ri for you, sir.'

Roblas offered no greeting. Instead, he said, 'What has happened in my city?'

Ri replied, 'At this point, I only know what is in the international press.'

'I don't believe you. Maldonado did not do this. It was either you or the Russians.'

'Then it was the Russians.' The translator waited a long time for a reply from Mexico.

Finally, Roblas said, 'If you *did* have anything to do with this, I hope, for your sake and mine, that you cleaned up your mess.'

There was a long pause. 'There is some mess left to clean up.'

'What the hell does that mean?'

Ri said, 'A man has reached out to us. He appears to be responsible for what happened yesterday.'

'I am listening.'

Ri explained the extortion demand of the Iranian who was now, apparently, somewhere in Mexico.

When Ri was finished, Óscar Roblas said, 'This is not my concern. Why should I involve myself in this? I am not responsible for what you have done!'

Ri answered back calmly, and the translator spoke almost robotically. 'You may not be responsible, but this does concern you.'

'What does that mean?'

'You have invested a great deal of time and effort into Chongju. You are very close to reaping a return on your considerable investment.'

'Is that a threat?'

'Not at all. But let me put it to you like this. Do you think there will be a valuable mining operation at Chongju if America comes to the erroneous conclusion North Korea tried to kill its president yesterday?'

Roblas understood. If there was war, North Korea would lose. And if North Korea lost, Roblas would lose as well.

It was a simple business proposition. Risk versus reward. As he thought about it, he felt the reward potential was favorable. The potential for risk in sending someone to silence the assassin was high, but not as high as the potential for reward if the mission was successful.

And Ri was right. Roblas had already invested a lot into this endeavor. A phone call now was just one more small thing.

Ri asked, 'Do you have access to someone who can deal with the problem in Mexico?'

Roblas looked down at his hands and saw they trembled. He was furious for being dragged into this.

But there *was* a man. Not a Mexican; Roblas wouldn't send his own people into this hornets' nest of culpability. He needed to do what he could to maintain a veneer of plausible deniability. Instead, he would have his people contact Edward Riley. He was Sharps's man, but while Sharps would balk at this and run for cover, Riley would do it willingly. Riley would do anything.

He would clean this up.

Roblas said, 'Give me a number for one of your agents. I will hand that number to a man, and I don't know what will happen after that. As I told you, I am not involved in this.'

Ri said, 'Sometimes matters outside of our control must be dealt with so that misunderstandings are not made.'

Roblas hung up the phone on the director of North Korean foreign intelligence.

Jack Ryan, Jr., shaved his beard off in the ninety minutes he spent in his Alexandria condo before being picked up by White House personnel for the ride to the hospital. He looked like a new man, or at least he felt he looked the same as he used to before growing the beard, and that was the idea. He didn't want his meager attempt at a natural disguise outed to the world if someone happened to get a photograph of him. The beard would grow back, but if that became the new publicly known image of him, the beard would do him no good.

This was to be a private family visit, but Ryan knew how the media operated, and there would be a lot of photogs around the hospital trying to get a money shot of the shell-shocked presidential family. Ryan would do all in his power to stay off tonight's TV and out of tomorrow's newspapers, but he returned his appearance to the non-Campus version of Jack Ryan, Jr., just in case.

Just before nine p.m. he was ushered into the hospital through a back delivery entrance and then taken to a private waiting room. Here he was reunited with his sister Sally, his mom, and his younger siblings, Katie and Kyle. There were also dozens of police and Secret Service, but they had the good manners to give the family some space to be alone.

At nine-thirty they were brought into the President's hospital room. Jack had been told over and over that his father would be in a great deal of pain for a few weeks but his injuries were not life-threatening, and in truth he looked good considering the pictures the younger Ryan had seen of the flipped limo, but Jack Junior was still shocked by his father's weakened state. His fit, vital, and bright-eyed dad now lay there sound asleep in a hospital gown, an oxygen tube in his nose and a large bandage on his forehead.

Dr. Maura Handwerker was by his side as she had been since he staggered aboard Air Force One, and she immediately apologized to the family, saying she'd had to give the President some pain medication before they arrived and he'd be out of it for the rest of the night. She said the President had fought for hours against the meds, but finally relented when she explained to him he wouldn't sleep a moment in so much discomfort, and the next day he would be utterly useless.

Without Jack Senior to talk to, the family just stood at his bedside and caught up. Jack hadn't seen his big sister in months, and Katie and Kyle lamented that it had been ages since he'd visited them in the White House.

Jack caught his mom's eye; he saw worry on her face, not just about her husband, but also about her son, as she wondered what he was involved in that had made him so remote recently. He did his best to reassure her with a hug, because there wasn't much he could say.

As the conversation moved away from Jack Junior and on to other things, he stood over his father, looked at his bandages and his predicament, and wondered about the son of a bitch who had done this to him.

Everyone was pinning this on Santiago Maldonado, but if Jack had to bet right now, he'd say it was the president of Russia, perhaps using Maldonado as a proxy.

Just then his phone vibrated in his pants pocket. He excused himself and stepped out of the room into the hallway. Two Secret Service agents stood there by the door, and Jack knew they weren't going anywhere, so he walked a few feet farther.

The caller ID let him know it was Chavez on the line.

'Hey, Ding.'

'Sorry. I know you are with your dad.'

'It's okay.'

'How is he?'

'Tough.'

'Damn right he is.'

'Is something wrong?'

'Something's *weird*, I'll say that. We've been hunting for Riley all afternoon with no joy. Went to all his haunts. Finally, we turned to Gavin – we should have gone to him first, to tell you the truth. He traced the LoJack security feature on the guy's BMW.'

'Smart.'

'Yeah. Turns out Riley drove to Teterboro Airport about two hours ago and parked his car in a long-term lot. We spent another half-hour trying to figure out the destinations of the aircraft leaving shortly after his arrival. There were about a half-dozen corporate planes that he could have been on, but we ruled out all but one by looking into the owners, the destinations, and then deciding neither Sharps nor Riley had any known dealings with them.'

'So . . . where do you think he went?'

'Jack . . . we think he went to Mexico City.'

Jack turned his head toward his father's room. He watched through a glass partition as Sally lifted Katie up onto the edge of the bed. The little girl was fighting back tears as she leaned over and kissed her sleeping father.

Ryan's voice dropped an octave. 'What would he be doing down there?'

Ding said, 'We don't know, but we thought we'd go find

out. He's on a plane owned by a shell company set up at an Antiguan bank. Gavin researched the CIA's Intelink-TS database for financial forensics, and it led him to Grupo Pacífico. It's an oil, gas, and mineral company owned by a Mexican billionaire named Óscar Roblas de Mota. Grupo Pacífico isn't an overt client of Duke Sharps's, but Sam's facial-recognition work in front of Sharps's Upper West Side digs turned up a pair of Grupo Pacífico execs paying old Duke a visit.'

'I'll be damned,' Ryan said. He didn't know what it meant. That there could be any connection to Riley's trip and the assassination attempt was still too much of a stretch to seriously contemplate. But the fact that Riley was heading to Mexico City the day of the attack, and the day after committing a brazen murder in New York, seemed particularly troublesome to say the least.

Ding said, 'We're heading down tonight. Not even sure how we'll track him once we're there, but we've got a couple ideas. Clark says stay where you are if you need to be with your dad, but if you are able to get away –'

Ryan was already moving. 'I'll be at the airport in an hour.'

Ding said, 'Roger that. Tell your old man we're thinking of him.'

65

Edward Riley flew from Teterboro Airport in New Jersey direct to Mexico City's Benito Juárez International Airport in the back of an Embraer Phenom 300 corporate jet owned by one of Óscar Roblas's shell companies. He landed just after three a.m. and was driven by a hired car to a hotel in the posh Polanco neighborhood of the city.

He'd worked on his plan for most of the flight, so he caught a few hours' sleep in the early morning, and then, just after nine a.m., he was visited by an RGB agent named Kim who explained that he himself had just arrived from Havana the evening before. Kim had been the one in contact with Zarif, and he came over to Mexico once it was clear Zarif was attempting to blackmail North Korea for $2 million.

Riley thought the sum to be relatively small, but he understood why Zarif chose this amount. The bomb maker wouldn't have easy access to banks, so the cash had to be carried, and two million US dollars was about the largest amount easily transported by a single person. He could have carried a lot more in euros, but either Zarif did not know this or else he felt dollars would be more useful here in the Western Hemisphere.

Kim had spoken to Zarif just before arriving at Riley's hotel. The Iranian had demanded to work with a middleman, someone who was not Asian, someone who spoke

English. He'd explained that this person would make the transfer at eight p.m. that evening at the Cinépolis movie theater in Toluca.

Riley would be this man.

It had already been decided by North Korea that there would be no blackmail money paid to Zarif. Having him alive and able to reveal details of Operation Fire Axe was not a suitable option, so Kim had made no attempt to collect the funds.

Riley agreed with their assessment in general, although Roblas's people had given him the phone number of a local banker he could call at any hour if he needed cash to buy back evidence. Even though Riley knew Óscar Roblas could have easily come up with the money to buy the man's silence, there could be no guarantees Zarif wouldn't just reveal his knowledge about the North Koreans' involvement in the attack anyway.

So the solution was simple: Zarif had to die.

But Riley knew this wasn't a situation where they could just shoot him dead on the street. The man had allegedly created a video detailing North Korea's involvement in the assassination attempt, and Zarif would have to be a complete and utter fool to arrive at the location for the exchange without leaving an ace in the hole. No, the bomb maker would have secured a copy of that video with someone, or he would have mailed it to an address, or saved it on a computer that was not on his person.

Riley needed to know what Zarif had done to ensure his safety, and there was only one way to get that in-formation.

The Englishman pictured a long and uncomfortable night of brutal torture.

He needed a secure location to do this, and his Polanco hotel room would hardly suffice for what he had in mind. He told Roblas's banker he needed only ten thousand dollars, and he expected to return that to him when the operation was complete, but what he needed more was a location somewhere in the area where he would not be disturbed for twenty-four to forty-eight hours. The banker put him on hold for several minutes, presumably to contact either Roblas or someone below him, and then he returned to the line with an address. He said it was a private villa in Cuernavaca, a city in the mountains an hour south of the capital. The banker promised Riley no one would bother him there.

Next came a discussion between Kim and Riley about how to get their hands on Adel Zarif. Riley had transported cash for blackmail payments before in his career. He knew one million US dollars, if acquired in hundred-dollar bills, would easily fit into an average-sized school backpack. He went to a nearby department store and purchased two dark backpacks, then stepped into a used-book store and bought enough cheap paper-back novels to fill the packs.

Once he had his decoys, he and Kim drove together to Toluca, where they reconnoitered the movie theater and the streets around it. It was just after three p.m., so he knew Zarif would probably not be in the area, but Riley wanted to figure out why he had decided on this location for the drop. Once they circled the block a couple of times, he had his answer.

He explained his conclusion to Kim. 'There are a lot of ways out of that cineplex. Each of the six screens has its own fire escape, and there is a main entrance and a back way out of the lobby. He's worried about a double cross. We need all the exits covered.'

'How do you propose we do that? There are two of us, and you will be inside.'

Riley said, 'I can hire a team of local muscle, but that's going to take more time than we have.'

Kim understood this would be his responsibility. 'I can get RGB men here from Mexico City.'

'No. If Zarif sees Asians, he'll run.'

Kim thought for a moment more. 'I have a better idea. Let me make a call.'

In the late afternoon, ten operatives of Cuba's Directorate of Intelligence arrived in two Jeep Cherokees. The North Koreans had good working relations with the Cubans, and the DI men had a large operation here in Mexico. Kim had to go all the way up to General Ri to secure this in extremis operational partnership, but Riley liked the arrangement. Zarif was an Iranian with no experience in the Spanish-speaking world, so Riley felt certain a crew of Cubans on the streets around here would not raise alarms the way North Koreans would.

The Cubans were all armed, and though they weren't from the Toluca area, they at least knew how to blend in here in Mexico.

They didn't know about the North Koreans' responsibility in the attack on the US President; as far as they knew, they were simply helping their communist friends catch a kidnapper during a ransom exchange and hold him until he revealed the location of his victim.

At eight p.m. Riley walked through the theater entrance with one backpack over his shoulder and the other in his hand. He bought a ticket to the first movie advertised on the marquee above the cashier's head, and he stood at the concession stand, as ordered by Zarif, for five minutes. He assumed this was so that Zarif, who was somewhere here in the large multiplex, could identify him.

After his five-minute wait, Riley entered the theater where his film would be playing, and he walked up the stairs and found a seat in the top row.

Almost immediately the lights lowered, and soon after that Riley saw a lone man climbing the stairs toward him.

Zarif sat down and looked at him strangely. Riley replied, 'You said you didn't want to see any North Koreans, and you wanted someone who spoke English.'

The Iranian nodded. 'I thought you would be Mexican. Who are you?'

'I am a business associate. Nothing more. There was a misunderstanding yesterday, and it's my hope I can put it right.' He patted the two backpacks stacked on the chair next to him.

'Let's see the money.'

Riley reached into his shirt and pulled out the bound stack of one hundred hundred-dollar bills. He tossed it into Zarif's lap nonchalantly, like there was a hell of a lot more where that came from.

'Ten thousand. The rest is here.' He patted the bags.

Zarif looked it over and stuck it into his pocket. 'Hand it over to me.'

'No. I want the phone first, and any other recordings you made.' Zarif handed it over and Riley looked to find the video the man had made. It was there, so he slipped the phone into his pocket.

Then Riley leaned close. 'We need to know you didn't do anything else with that video.'

'There is one more copy in a safe place. When I get the money and get away, I will call you and –'

He stopped talking because Riley was shaking his head back and forth. 'That's not on, mate. Tell you what. You keep the ten thousand. I'll keep this one-point-nine-nine mil. When you are ready to give me what I want, *everything*, then give me a call.' He smiled. 'Buy yourself a phone with what I gave you.'

Zarif tried to stop him, but Riley stood. He left the theater via the main entrance. As soon as he did so, he called Kim. 'I expect he'll be running out one of the back exits.'

'The Cubans are ready.'

Adel Zarif left the theater where he met with Riley and walked into one of the other theaters in the cineplex, heading for the fire escape. He was confused and scared now. The exchange looked like it was going to go off without a hitch, but suddenly the Englishman just got up and left.

It was only at the moment when he pushed through the fire exit that he realized it had all been a trick. There was no more money, because the entire meet was simply to make sure that he was there in the theater.

He saw two young men in leather jackets standing in the alley, just feet away from the exit. They looked Mexican to him, like everyone else he'd seen on the street around the theater, so he was not alarmed at first. But as he passed under a streetlamp and continued down the street, he saw their long shadows following him.

A black Jeep Cherokee came from the other direction in the alley, then pulled to a stop right next to him. Zarif turned to take off in a run, but now there were four men around him; they tackled him to the ground on the sidewalk and they dragged him into the Jeep.

A pillowcase was put over his head and his arms were pinned behind his back and secured with electrical tape.

He thought he heard a conversation in Spanish, and then a man speaking English with a British accent, clearly the same man as in the theater. 'Where did you send the file?'

'I uploaded it.'

'That's a bloody lie, mate. I checked your phone. You didn't e-mail it or text it to anyone but our mutual friend in Havana.'

'I used a cable, I uploaded it on a computer.'

'*What* computer?'

Zarif hesitated. 'Just give me the money and I'll tell you.'

'There is no more money. There is only the chance to save your life, and that is fading away like the money did. Talk!'

Zarif thought over his options, and there were none. He could tell them, and they would surely kill him because he had no more leverage. Or he could not tell them, and they would torture him. Eventually he would die, or he would talk and then he would die.

From somewhere in the vehicle a fist was thrown and it connected with his jaw. The Englishman screamed: 'Where is the bloody recording?'

Zarif decided his only chance was to stall and hope Allah saved him.

He spat blood out of his mouth; it wet the inside of the pillowcase.

And then he said, *'Allahu akbar.'*

'Oh, bloody hell. Take him to the villa. We're in for a long night.'

66

The operators of The Campus had been on Riley's trail for an entire twenty-four hours. They landed in Mexico City at six-fifteen in the morning, and the Gulfstream purposefully taxied to the same fixed-base operator that Riley's Embraer jet had used a few hours before. Ding Chavez spoke with the manager on duty and asked about the earlier aircraft. The man wasn't terribly forthcoming at first, but after a pair of hundred-dollar bills changed hands, he seemed to remember some details about the Embraer. From this Ding ascertained the name of the limousine company that had picked up the one passenger on board. A call to this service brought out the same driver – precious few limousines ran between three and seven a.m., after all – and a ride into the city led to a friendly chat that was made more friendly with two more Ben Franklins, and just like that, Chavez was taken to the same Polanco hotel where the Englishman had been dropped earlier in the morning.

By ten a.m. the entire Campus team was in position around the hotel. Caruso and Ryan were on rented motor-cycles, Clark and Driscoll drove in a nondescript 2010 Dodge Durango, and Chavez had access to a rented C-Class Mercedes that he'd parked with the valet. The men were spread out, but wired together via earpieces. Chavez remained in the lobby; he wore a business suit and he sipped coffee while reading *El Día*, the local newspaper.

There were a lot of Asians in the building – the hotel was popular with foreign businessmen – so a call from Clark for everyone to keep their eyes open for possible North Korean Riley accomplices turned up nothing conclusive.

Finally, Riley himself came out of the elevator at noon with a fit-looking Asian whom Chavez immediately pegged as RGB. The RGB man picked up a Lexus SUV from the valet stand, and both men climbed in and headed off.

For the next hour the five Americans leapfrogged in a four-vehicle mobile surveillance, tracking Riley and his colleague all the way to Toluca, an hour west of the city. They watched the men circle a theater very slowly, and then drive to a café, where they spent an hour talking on their phones. Soon after this Riley did some shopping at a department store and then a bookstore, where he purchased a curiously large number of paperbacks.

In the early evening the Lexus pulled into the parking lot of a shopping center, and soon a pair of black Jeep Cherokees stopped next to it. By now the Campus men had dispersed themselves hundreds of yards away to stay out of sight. Dom and Jack were parked on an overpass, Chavez was in his Mercedes in an adjacent parking lot, and Driscoll and Clark stood in the atrium of an office building across the street. They were far from their targets, but they all had binos or other optics and could see the team of ten Hispanic-looking males meeting with the Englishman and the North Korean.

As Riley and the Asian conferred around the vehicles

with the new arrivals, Chavez called Clark on the net. 'John, you've been around the longest. Any guesses at all as to what's going on?'

'Nothing good. That's a dozen men in total. I see side-arms printing under their jackets. The new arrivals all seem to be taking orders from Riley. Meeting in a parking lot like this . . . looks like a pre-operation briefing. I'd say something's about to go down.'

Caruso added, 'Something that Riley and his buddy from Pyongyang couldn't pull off without more muscle.'

Clark agreed. 'Yep. All we can do is keep tracking. And stay the hell out of the way if those guns come out of their waistbands.'

Soon the entourage led by Riley drove in a three-vehicle convoy toward the center of the city, and within ten minutes Clark called their destination. 'They're heading back to that theater they reconned earlier.'

And they did just that. Riley climbed out of the Lexus a few blocks from the entrance and then the Lexus rolled on, and the Jeeps peeled off and headed up side streets. Dom tracked one of them to a lot two blocks to the south, and Ryan found the other idling on a side street two blocks to the north.

While the rest of the Campus team took positions on all compass points and waited, Chavez went into the theater and bought a ticket.

Soon Riley came inside and stood at the concession stand without buying anything. Chavez saw the two back-packs, and at first he thought they might have held explosives, but almost immediately he remembered the big purchase at the bookstore.

It came together quickly for him. He transmitted into his earpiece mike. 'Unless Riley is the newest member of the Toluca walking bookmobile, he's here for an exchange. He's got a couple of packs that I think are supposed to look like money bags.'

Clark said, 'Loaded with the paperbacks?'

'Yep.'

Sam Driscoll asked, 'Why do you need a dozen guys for a handoff?'

Clark answered that. 'Because either you *think* it's going to go bad or you *know* it's going to go bad.'

'Meaning they are planning on whacking somebody?'

Ding said, 'Or maybe just grabbing them. Don't know. This should be interesting. Maybe I should buy some popcorn.'

Twenty minutes later The Campus tailed the Lexus and the two Jeeps out of town to the south, and every one of the American operators wondered about the identity of the guy Riley and his goons had just kidnapped off the street.

President of the United States Jack Ryan had spent a miserable day pretending he wasn't miserable. Everything he had done since waking up this morning had been an act. An act for his doctors, telling them he didn't need any painkillers heavier than anti-inflammatories, because he didn't want to be doped up; an act for the reporters from Fox and *The Washington Post* who shared a staged and controlled five-minute visit with the President, to show just how well he was doing twenty-four hours after the attack.

An act during his quick phone call with Patrick O'Day, husband of Andrea Price O'Day. She was still in Mexico City receiving care, and her husband was by her side. Her condition had been downgraded from critical to serious, but she was in a medically induced coma, and American doctors were consulting with the Mexican neuros on how to proceed. Jack knew the last thing Pat needed was to listen to him complain about his own aches and pains, so he lied and told Andrea's husband he was fine and then they prayed together for her recovery.

An act for the world leaders he spoke with on the phone and the dozens more he communicated with via videotaped message, all meant to convince America's allies that all was right with the good ship Ryan.

And an act for his wife, Cathy, so that she wouldn't worry any more than she naturally would, and a greater act for his kids so they wouldn't be terrified about the monsters out there in the world who would want to hurt their dad.

But there was one person and one person only to whom Ryan spoke the pure, unvarnished truth. Arnie Van Damm got that duty, and a difficult duty it was. When the doctors and nurses were out of earshot, when the family had returned to the White House to finally get some sleep, when there were no more reporters or well-wishers or lookie-loos, Ryan bitched and moaned at Arnie.

'Nurse Ratched over there has got this goddamned dressing too tight! She and Maura are trying to shove these fucking elephant tranquilizers down my damn throat. Do they think I can be a chief executive and a zombie at the same time? I'm going to get AG Murray to investigate them to see if they are Russian spies. And those Secret Service guys yesterday . . . let me tell you. I know they had a job to do, but those young wild asses slung me around into that car like a rag doll when I was trying to help Andrea.'

Arnie listened to every last complaint and concern, and there were a dozen more; he took notes where needed, and nodded sympathetically throughout. When the tirades were finally over, he nodded more and said, 'Jack. If you aren't hurting and bitching, then you aren't living.' He smiled. 'Clearly, you are living, and considering the alternative and how close you came to that alternative yesterday, I'd say that's a pretty good deal.'

'Did you listen to a *thing* I just said?'

'Yes, and I think you are just pissed because the Russkies didn't attack. You thought your presence was the one thing holding back the red tide against America, but now you see that even when they thought you were out of the picture, they still have to consider it a bit before kicking off an invasion.'

'Funny, Arnie.'

'On a serious note, Mary Pat is outside.'

Jack nodded. 'Bring her in. She knows me well enough to know my happy face is a put-on. I don't have to fake anything for her.'

Mary Pat Foley entered a moment later, and Arnie stayed in the room. She asked about Jack's condition, about how he felt and how the doctors were treating him, and Jack grumbled a little, but all the venting he'd done to Arnie had let enough steam out of the kettle so that he no longer needed to blow his top.

Finally, she said, 'I thought you'd want to know where we are with finding the culprit for the attack. We're only a day into the investigation, but we've turned up a little.'

'What did you find?'

'Dead Maldonado operatives at the scene. A dozen guys. Only four known cartel goons, but the others all had Maldonado tattoos and IDs linking them back to Guerrero state, where that clan rules the roads.'

'What about the explosive? I don't remember a damn thing about a bomb. I woke up thinking we'd been in a traffic accident. Everybody says it was a hell of a blast.'

'Hundred-five-millimeter howitzer shells. Three of them. Looks like they came from the Mexican military.'

'Holy hell,' Ryan muttered. He'd seen what a 105 could do in the Marine Corps, and it wasn't pretty.

'One of the high-explosive rounds impacted directly with the front limousine. Killed the four Secret Service men riding in it. A second shell hit right in front of your vehicle. If you were fifteen feet ahead it would be all over, Jack.'

That sank in for a moment.

'That knocked you upside down. Ambassador Styles broke his neck in the flip. He died instantly, mercifully. The last shell hit behind your limo. It took out a counter-rassault team vehicle and the vehicle next to it.'

Jack looked down at the wires, tubes, and bandages that seemed to be holding him together. 'Arnie?'

Van Damm had been looking down at his phone. 'Sir?'

'Come here and shake my hand.'

Arnie stepped over and lightly squeezed the fingertips on Ryan's immobilized left hand, because his right hand was wrap-ped to his chest and completely covered in cotton bandages.

'Forget everything I just said. I'm the luckiest guy in the world.'

'Forgotten, Mr President.'

'You know I yell at you because I can't yell at anybody else.'

'Of course I do.'

Ryan said, 'When we leave the White House you have my permission to write a kiss-and-tell book about what an ass I can be. You'll make a mint. Hell, I'll write the foreword.'

Van Damm and Mary Pat both smiled. Arnie said, 'When I get out of here all I want to do is go to some tiny quiet college in New England, teach a class in conflict resolution or something, and decompress.'

Ryan cracked a smile himself. It was his first authentic smile in the past day. 'That sounds pretty good. I might take that class.'

'That would make me uncomfortable, Mr President, because you will be a recurring case study.'

67

It was nearly eleven p.m. when Edward Riley and his entourage neared the Cuernavaca address given to him by Roblas's banker. There were no lights on this winding hilly road, but the houses they'd passed in the past few minutes had all been palatial mansions in gated grounds. This seemed to be some sort of neighborhood for the elite, and Riley knew they were near enough to Mexico City that this was probably a getaway for the city's wealthiest inhabitants.

He had expected the banker to give him access to a remote rustic farm, but when he arrived at the actual address he found something altogether different. Like the other properties on the road, it was a massive gated compound on a wooded hillside, and high on the distant hill at the center of the parcel he saw an ultramodern space-age building bathed in dramatic outdoor lighting. It was a private mansion with a pool that surrounded it almost like a moat, and from the road it looked like a big white-and-glass spaceship hovering in the nighttime sky and looming over the valley.

They pulled up the two-hundred-yard-long winding driveway and parked in front of the house. Riley ordered that Zarif be kept in one of the Jeeps surrounded by four of the armed Cuban DI agents while Riley and Kim headed up to the front door of the mansion. The door, like the gate back down the hill, was unlocked. Inside, all the lights were on and ceiling fans slowly rotated high over a massive cylindrical-shaped great room, which, through two-story-high floor-to-ceiling windows, overlooked a beautifully landscaped backyard pool complete with waterfalls and fountains.

The majority of the décor inside was as white as the building itself. Zarif was brought into the great room and tied to a chair, and even though Riley had been told there would be no one around, he had the Cubans fan out and check the grounds and the buildings from top to bottom. They found a pool house, a detached guesthouse, a garage, and a few other outbuildings, and after searching through everything, they confirmed they were indeed alone.

RGB agent Kim had two pairs of Cubans begin patrols of the grounds, and the other six men he placed around the main building: three outside on the wraparound second-floor balcony, and three inside with the prisoner.

Zarif had said nothing during the hourlong drive, and he said nothing when Riley pulled off the pillowcase. It took him a moment to adjust to the light, but when he did he just gazed at the opulence all around him with some confusion.

Riley sat down on the sofa in front of him. 'Well, then, let's get started, shall we?'

The Campus had struggled to keep sight of Riley's caravan while remaining undetected, and this was a difficult mission, but all four vehicles in their surveillance package were driven by experts in vehicle tails. Just outside Toluca,

MANSION IN CUERNAVACA

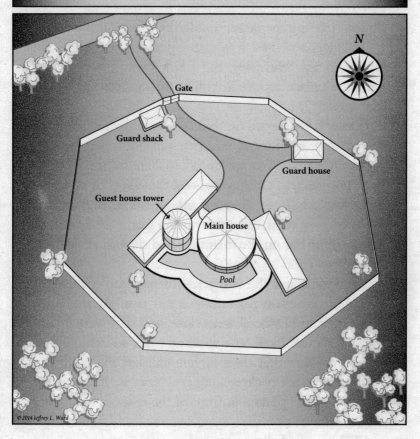

N

Gate

Guard shack

Guard house

Guest house tower

Main house

Pool

© 2014 Jeffrey L. Ward

when it appeared that Riley and his entourage were leaving the suburbs and not heading back to Mexico City, Caruso and Ryan peeled away and accelerated beyond their targets, and they raced forward to probable turnoffs ahead. Each time Riley and his three vehicles passed them, another vehicle in the Campus detail would make a move, by either going down adjacent roads to avoid being seen or directly passing the target if absolutely unavoidable.

The darkness and a gentle but steady evening rain helped in this endeavor, but Clark knew they couldn't continue on for too long without being detected by the men ahead.

Finally Riley turned off the highway and into the city of Cuernavaca, and he and the other vehicles rolled through the city itself. The Campus men lost them for several minutes. Fortunately, Chavez noticed three sets of taillights ascending a hillside off to the side of the road, so with a lot of coordination and a few wrong turns, The Campus regained the eye on the man they had tracked all the way from New York.

The Lexus and the two Jeeps turned into the gate of a modern mansion just after eleven p.m. At the time, only Clark and Driscoll were close, and they were a hundred fifty yards back on a winding road, so initially they missed the fact that their targets had left the road. But with some quick backtracking they saw the lights of the vehicles as they parked in front of the space-age building on the hill.

Clark notified the team, and then he called Gavin in Alexandria and told him to find out who owned the property and to call back the second he had something. With this done, he notified his men of the game plan. 'I want two guys inside the grounds, head for the back. The objective is a photograph of the unknown subject they picked up behind the theater. Riley came a long way to get that guy, and I want to know who the hell he is.'

Driscoll and Ryan were given the overwatch job, based solely on the equipment in each man's backpack. Driscoll had the best camera, and Ryan had a dark hoodie and a night-vision monocle. Both men were carrying small Smith & Wesson pistols in their Thunderwear holsters, but neither had any intention of getting into a gunfight with a dozen men.

Especially on behalf of some victim who meant nothing to them at this point.

They jumped the fence from an adjacent property thirty minutes after Riley and his crew arrived at the mansion, and they found themselves in a grove of pecan trees. Ryan spent a few moments scanning through his forty-millimeter night-observation device to make sure there were no dogs or men in the area, but once they were clear, they were slowed down some by pecans on the ground. Every step seemed to make a loud noise for the first twenty-five yards as the shells cracked underfoot.

Finally they reached some open ground. Here Ryan scanned the house again, and he saw a man on a tower looking in his general direction, so he and Sam backed into the trees and moved laterally along the fence, farther toward the back of the property.

They found a decent hide after ducking a pair of two-man patrols, and they ended up low in a copse of cohune palm that grew alongside a little pond in the back of the property, halfway between the fence and the pool house at the back edge of the main building. From here they had a good vantage point that gave them a view of the entire back of the main house.

Driscoll brought out his Nikon, attached a 500-millimeter lens, and centered on the movement in the expansive and bright main room of the house. As soon as he focused he could see Edward Riley pacing back and forth. He snapped a few pictures. Also in the room was the Asian man they had first seen around noon at the hotel in Mexico City. Sam photographed him as well. With them were three Hispanic-looking tough guys, and seated was the unknown individual who Riley had picked up in Toluca earlier in the evening.

Sam spoke softly into his earpiece microphone as he snapped some pictures of the man. 'This poor guy has taken a beating. Looks like the North Korean is tuning him up, trying to get him to talk, I guess.'

Clark was still outside the property in the Durango. 'Is Riley the one asking the questions?'

Sam saw Riley speaking at that moment. Soon the Asian man backhanded the bound victim again.

'That's my read on it. Sending the headshot now to Gavin.'

Gavin had been given the heads-up in Alexandria to expedite the processing of the image just as soon as it came through.

The conference call that kept all the men connected to one another by their headsets received a new guest just five minutes after Sam sent the image.

606

'Hey, guys. It's Gavin. I just loaded the image. Expect it to take a half-hour or more, if there is a hit at all.'

'That's fine. What about the property?'

'Owned by a Mexican bank. Did some digging through CIA, and traced it back to Grupo Pacífico.'

Ryan said, 'Just like the plane Riley flew down on.'

'Bingo,' Biery confirmed. 'Owned by Óscar Roblas. Doesn't look like it's a personal address. More like a place he loans out or throws parties in. Typical rich-guy stuff that the rest of us don't ever –'

There was a pause on the line. Clark said, 'Gavin? Did we lose you?'

'Uh . . . no. But you won't believe this. Facial recog is complete.'

'You're kidding.'

'No, I'm really not.' Gavin seemed stunned himself. 'Oh, I see. I set it up so it would first run through the FBI and CIA's database of wanted subjects. It saves time that way because it's not just looking over a general database of –'

Jack Ryan, Jr., interjected over Biery's explanation. 'Who the fuck is it, Gavin?'

'Oh. Sorry. According to the FBI Most Wanted database, that man's name is Adel Zarif, he is a forty-eight-year-old Iranian from –'

John Clark spoke for the rest of the team. 'We know who he is.'

And it was true. Everyone in The Campus was aware of one of the most notorious terrorist bomb makers of the past fifteen years.

Caruso spoke next. 'You know what this means, right?'

Clark did. 'The IED yesterday.'

It sank in slowly to the five men surrounding the mansion. The perpetrator of the attempted assassination of the President of the United States, Jack's father, was right in front of them.

And this clearly meant Riley and the North Koreans were involved as well. No one knew who the other ten men were, but if this had something to do with the attack on Jack Ryan, Sr., it seemed likely the Hispanics in the mix were Maldonado gunmen.

Clark said, 'We are *not* calling this in to Mexican law enforcement.'

A universal agreement was reached immediately on this. No one was confident the Mexicans could take this place down before the men inside escaped. Then Clark added, 'We could call Hendley and have him notify Mary Pat. She would contact Justice and they would put together an FBI package. Surely they have assets staged in Mexico City after what went down yesterday.'

No one spoke. ———

'Or we go after him now. There are a dozen men in there. Riley I'm not too concerned about. The RGB trains some decent combatants, but we've dealt with several in the past few weeks.'

Ryan said, 'The other guys must be part of the Maldonado cartel. As a fighting force, they suck.'

Clark replied, 'We don't know who they are for sure. Best possible scenario is they are Maldonado men. If that is the case, I like our chances hitting that residence.'

Sam was the first to speak up. 'We don't know who all Riley is working with. All it's going to take is for him to call up a friendly helo to land on the lawn to fly that guy away. That happens, we're left with pictures only.'

Jack Ryan, Jr., had already decided he was going to hit that house in front of him, with or without the rest of The Campus. Those men had tried to kill his father, and they'd come damn close. The discussion on the commo net among his colleagues was academic to him, although he knew that without any help his chances for survival would be nil.

Clark said, 'Okay. We are going to take that building down. We don't have breaching charges, body armor, long guns, intel on the OPFOR, or an exfil plan. We probably don't have much time, either. We *do* have pistols, the element of surprise, and a need. I want to hear everyone's ideas, and I want to hear them now.'

The team spent the next five minutes on a plan. While they were doing so, Dom Caruso dropped over the eastern wall of the property, two hundred yards from Ryan and Driscoll on the northern side.

He found excellent cover by low-crawling through some flowering jacaranda. When he was in position he called over the network, 'How are we going to cross all that open ground?'

Domingo Chavez answered this. 'You need a distraction, and I've got an idea.'

Edward Riley was impressed with the Iranian's ability to deal with pain. Certainly by now his jaw and nose were broken, the orbital bone of his skull looked like it had been cracked, and several of his teeth had been knocked out. Blood flowed easily from his mouth and nose and the swollen blackness under his left eye. But he'd said little more than *'Allahu akbar'* and some words Riley took to be curses.

The Englishman looked at his watch. He wanted to have this entire episode behind him in a day, but it wasn't looking good. Even if the man talked right now, and that didn't look likely, Riley would still have to go check out the location of this alleged computer where Zarif uploaded the file. He didn't know if the man had any confederates here in the country, or if he'd simply gone to a library or an electronics shop, or even if he had loaded the video onto a mobile phone and mailed it to some random address. Somewhere, Riley was convinced, was evidence that could link North Korea to the assassination attempt the day before.

Suddenly there was a disturbance upstairs. Someone was calling out in Spanish from the balcony over the front door. Riley looked to the Cubans around him.

A Cuban who spoke English entered the room and addressed Riley and Kim. 'They say a car is approaching up the drive. Mercedes. The driver is the only occupant.'

That didn't sound like a threat to Riley, but it did sound like something he needed to deal with. He headed to the front door with the Cuban who spoke English. Zarif would remain out of sight because the front door was in a large entryway with wraparound stairs that shielded the expansive living area.

Riley opened the front door in time to see a well-dressed Latin man in his mid-forties climb out of his black Mercedes with his keys in his hand. His necktie was loose and his shirt was unbuttoned, and he staggered a little as he climbed up the steps.

'May I help you?' Riley asked.

'*¿Qué?*'

The Cuban spoke to the man. He was all the way in the entryway before he responded.

The Cuban said, 'He's asking where his uncle Óscar is.'

'Óscar Roblas?'

'*Sí,*' said the man. He was clearly drunk; Riley could see his Spanish was slurred. '*Tío Óscar.*'

'Tell him Óscar Roblas loaned this house to us tonight. He can call him if he wants, but I invite him to do so outside. We have an important business meeting under way.'

Riley put his hand on the man's chest and started to push him toward the door. The man staggered some more, and then said something.

'He asks if he can use the bathroom before he leaves. He says it is an emergency.'

Riley looked at the man for several seconds. Finally, he said, 'Yes. Of course he can.'

The Latin man nodded and began heading toward the hallway to the back rooms; he had made it about ten feet when he heard the distinctive click of the hammer of a pistol two feet behind his head. The sound echoed in the sterile and spartan entryway of the modern house.

'Good evening, Mr Domingo Chavez. How lovely of you to drop by.'

68

Chavez turned around slowly, his hands in the air. Riley faced him now, an excited smile on his face and a Beretta 92 pistol pointing at Chavez's chest. Riley had apparently taken it from the man next to him.

From the moment Chavez walked into the house forty-five seconds earlier, two very bad things had happened. One was obvious; Riley had recognized him, though Ding didn't know how the man knew about him in the first place.

But the other was potentially worse. The instant the Hispanic man began talking in the doorway, Chavez realized he was not some poorly trained cartel cowboy from Mexico's west. No, he was Cuban, he was educated, and by virtue of the fact he was here involved with North Korean spies, Iranian terrorists, and a New York – based privately contracted British operative, there was no question in Chavez's mind but that this man and his nine buddies were DI, Cuban Intelligence Directorate. Ding knew the Cubans turned out some skilled shooters, and he also knew his team of four men outside would be walking into a buzz saw.

Riley brought Chavez into the main room and stood him next to the seated Zarif. He then looked to the two other Cubans standing around. 'Secure the building, tell the others. This man is CIA, and he probably has friends close by.' There were two men with guns left, both pointed at Chavez: Riley, who stood just six feet in front of Chavez, and the Cuban who answered the door, who had pulled a small backup pistol and was now ten feet away on Chavez's right. The North Korean was also there, standing by the sofa, but Chavez did not see a weapon in his hand.

Riley addressed Kim now. 'This man was following me a couple of weeks ago in New York. He was with others at the time. American operatives. If they are here, then we need to go.'

Kim said, 'Let's get in the cars.'

'First, we must deal with Zarif.' Riley pointed his gun at the badly beaten Iranian. Zarif seemed only peripherally aware of what was going on. 'Running out of time, mate. I'm going to start shooting now. Kneecaps. Ankles. Privates. Then the head.'

He aimed his gun at Zarif's knee. The Iranian cried out in fear, and Chavez leapt forward for Riley's gun.

Riley realized Chavez was coming for him, closing the distance in a single step, so he tried to swing the Beretta back in Chavez's direction. Chavez grabbed Riley's wrist and turned it away, pointed it toward the other armed man in the room, and the jolt of the move caused the Englishman to squeeze his hand. The gun fired a nine-millimeter bullet across the room at 1,100 feet per second, and it hit the Cuban high in his right shoulder, spinning him around and causing his gun to discharge into the wall over Chavez's head.

Chavez head-butted Riley now, sending him to the cold tile floor, and he pulled the pistol out of Riley's hands as he fell. Chavez raised the weapon toward the North

Korean, but once he saw the man was not going for a gun of his own, Chavez swung around toward the second-floor landing. Above him he saw an armed Cuban leaning over.

Chavez realized Zarif was directly behind him, and likely in the Cuban's line of fire. He turned and knocked over the Iranian in his chair, and while doing so fired back over his shoulder to keep the Cuban's head down.

Out of the corner of his eye Chavez saw the North Korean making a run for the stairs that led from the living room to the upstairs landing, with Edward Riley right on his heels.

Chavez grabbed Zarif by his collar and started to pull him across the floor to cover from the second floor as a second Cuban arrived. Chavez saw both men rise over the railing of the landing and aim down toward him, and a third and a fourth man came through the entryway. Chavez knew he wouldn't be able to engage all threats in a four-on-one gunfight.

Jack Ryan, Jr., and Dominic Caruso came through the doorway to the kitchen, their Smith & Wesson pistols snapping and smoking. Both men in the hall to the entryway dove for cover, but only one made it back to the safety of the wall. The other dropped on his back as blood splattered across the white tile.

The men upstairs fired down, but now Chavez had sighted in on one of them. While he continued to try to pull Zarif around the couch and out of the line of fire, he shot one of the men on the landing; then he dove behind the heavy couch as more men appeared from the entryway.

*

Sam Driscoll leapt from the branch of the pecan tree onto the second-floor balcony at the western side of the house. His landing was silent enough, so he drew his Smith and moved stealthily the first few feet for the back door, but when the gunfire erupted downstairs, faster than anyone on the team had anticipated it would, he picked up the pace.

There had been a man at the back tower, but when Sam moved around the corner to engage him he saw the man had passed through the sliding glass door, presumably to check on the source of gunfire in the house. Sam made it through the glass doorway, then moved quickly across an empty guest bedroom. He ducked his head quickly into the hallway to take a mental picture of what was there. To his left were several doors and a darkened hallway, to his right the hall ended at the landing. Protracted gunfire came from there, but from his sliver of view here he could see no one.

He stepped out into the hall at the exact same moment the Cuban who'd left the balcony earlier came out of the room to Sam's left. The two men saw each other simultaneously, four feet apart, and as they both brought their pistols up, the weapons slammed into each other and bounced free.

Sam swung at the man's face, but the Cuban stepped out of the way and drew a knife. Sam had a blade of his own, but he didn't reach for it. Instead, he closed the distance and locked on to the other man's arms. The two men slammed against both walls of the hallway, then crashed onto the ground. Sam ended up on top of the man, facing up, away from him. The Cuban pulled his knife down to the American's torso, but Sam still had his hands on the Cuban's wrists, and he pushed the knife back with all his might, desperate to keep it from plunging into his chest.

Ryan was with Caruso, firing from the kitchen, across the living room, and into the entryway, where several attackers had congregated. Ding was on his knees behind the couch in the center of the room, and Zarif was still taped to a chair on his side next to Ding.

Ryan knew Sam was all alone upstairs. They had accounted for all of the combatants, killing two men on patrol silently with knives and then moving toward the house when the other patrol was around front, but no one had figured on the North Korean agent and Riley both running upstairs. If they had weapons already, or if they picked guns up from fallen men on the landing, that would leave Sam seriously outnumbered on the second floor.

Ryan chanced a run for the stairs, but he had to cross the open ground of the living room. With only four bullets left in his nine-shot subcompact, he darted behind Chavez, exposing himself to fire from the men in the entryway. Chavez and Caruso both saw what Ryan was doing, so they exposed themselves to draw some attention from the shooters, then fired one round each before dropping back to cover again.

Ryan leapt onto the stairs, slamming into the wall to get out of the sightline of the gunners in the entryway, and then he began running up, his pistol high and sweeping back and forth.

*

John Clark slammed on the Durango's brakes right at the front door to the mansion, and he rolled out onto the gravel drive as his vehicle started taking fire.

It had been his job to drive the getaway vehicle, but when Chavez started the gunfight early he knew the plan had not survived first contact with the enemy, so he decided to interject himself into the direct-action portion of the operation.

He rose up from behind the hood of the big SUV, and fired left-handed at a man on the balcony, striking him in the forehead and sending him tumbling over the railing and crashing on the roof of the Durango.

Clark then ran for the front door, and while doing so he called his position to his team so they didn't shoot him upon entry.

Riley and the North Korean RGB officer had ducked into the first room next to the landing. Riley then prized open a window, but the North Korean wanted a weapon in case they met resistance outside. He ran back to the landing and saw both Cubans dead, lying still on their backs. They had been shot from the living room below. He grabbed one of the men's pistols and headed for the upstairs hallway. He was looking for a window he could use to escape or, at the very least, a room where he could barricade himself to fight back the American agents.

He entered the hallway and saw movement ahead. He raised his gun to fire, and as he did so he saw a bearded American roll off a dead Cuban agent while scooping a gun up from the floor of the hallway. The man lifted it, turned toward the North Korean's direction, and raised the pistol in a blur.

The North Korean fired. Instantly he felt the impact as a round slammed him in the chest, knocking him flat onto his back. He tried to breathe in but nothing happened. He felt his mouth fill with blood and his eyes began to feel impossibly heavy. Just before they closed he forced himself to lift his head, to look past his feet down the hall, and doing so gave him some peace, because the bearded American was down on his back as well, his own chest covered in blood.

Sam is down! Sam is down!" Ryan shouted into his earpiece as he leapt over the dead North Korean, stumbled over the dead Cuban with the knife in his chest, and then dropped to his knees next to Sam Driscoll. Sam's eyes were closed and his mouth slightly open. There was no movement at all on his face or in his body.

'Sam!'

Ryan put pressure on the gunshot wound. It was right over the heart, and his training and his common sense told him it was unsurvivable, but he kept pressing down, called into his earpiece for some help.

The gunfire downstairs lasted another minute. When it ended, Caruso was the first man to Ryan, then Clark and finally Chavez, who had Zarif standing now and in tow, with the pillowcase back over his head.

Sam Driscoll was dead. John Clark made the determination, though it was obvious to all. Caruso and Ryan carried the body downstairs and loaded it into the Durango without a word, while Chavez hog-tied the Iranian and put him in the back.

They drove off, remaining silent for the first few minutes, till Caruso broke the stillness to call Adara Sherman to let her know he needed the jet ready to go in thirty minutes.

The emotions ran the gamut from sadness to fury to the jacked-up remnants of adrenaline that always coursed through the men post-op, only to be replaced by utter exhaustion soon after.

When a member of the team finally did speak, it was Ryan. He made no mention of what had just occurred, he only asked the question that no one had the answer to, and everyone wanted to know.

'What the fuck happened to Riley?'

Edward Riley ran down the darkened hillside, fell, climbed to his feet, and stumbled again. His forehead was bleeding, his clothing was shredded, his arms and legs were bloody and battered from the brush that he tore through and the fence he climbed over and fell from.

He figured he'd gone a mile or more already, although in truth it was much, much less. He had a phone somewhere on his person, and he'd use it, but now he was still in self-preservation mode, that base and primal desire for survival, nothing more.

He'd almost been killed, he'd most definitely been compromised to the extent he could never return home to the US, and he had nothing to show for his mission, because his mission had failed.

He ran on, down the hill, only because he could think of no other course of action to take.

69

Ri Tae-jin did not yell or scream or threaten. Instead, he made no reply at all. He simply hung up the telephone and blinked once, his hangdog eyes giving away no expression. He was alone in his office, for now anyway, so he could have said or done anything he wanted, but his only desire at present was for a moment of quiet.

The assassin was in the wind. Probably in the hands of the Americans.

He had failed. The President was alive, and North Korea's involvement would soon become obvious.

Fire Axe had turned into a disaster.

He blinked again, and his eyes shined a little with new resolve. He picked the phone back off the cradle and waited for his secretary to answer.

'Yes, Comrade General?'

'I need to talk with someone in Technology.'

'I will get Director Pak. One moment –'

'No. I want someone in Technology Outfitting. Special Projects. Not a director. Just someone with access to material. It is only a small technical question I have about a piece of equipment.'

'Yes, sir. Comrade Li serves as Assistant of Provisions and Supplies.'

'Li will be fine, then.'

While he waited for the connection to be made, he

looked down at the medals on his chest. Sometimes he straightened them as an affectation, but they were perfect now. All lined up in columns and rows.

'Comrade General? Comrade Li Hyon-chol here. How may I serve you?'

General Ri arrived home in his armored car a little later than usual, but his wife made no mention of it. She already had dinner on the table and the two children were washed and in their chairs. Ri paused in the driveway to give a wave to his driver, and his wife thought this was odd, but she made no mention of this, either.

He entered the house and she reached to help him take off his tunic, but he said he had been feeling cold this afternoon and would keep it on. When she tried to take his briefcase he said he had some papers in it he would need to look at during dinner.

She smiled and bowed, and then the two of them came to the dinner table.

He placed the briefcase below the table and he kissed his boy and he kissed his girl, and he listened to them both tell him about their day at school. They had gone to see a new painting of the Dae Wonsu at the national art museum, and it was even more magnificent than their teacher had promised.

Ri smiled and nodded, and then he sat down, glancing at his watch as he did so.

Every night before dinner they did what virtually every family did, they sang a song to their Dear Leader. Normally his wife chose the song, and she assumed, even though Tae-jin was acting strangely, tonight would be no different. 'Dinner is getting cold, so how about a short song?' Smiling at the kids, she said, 'I know you remember "Don't Walk on the Cold Snow, Dear Leader." Don't you?'

The children smiled and clapped. It was a favorite of theirs.

But Ri shook his head. 'Not tonight. Tonight let us hold hands, and sit together, and think of our family. Of ourselves. Not the Dae Wonsu. Not tonight.'

The children cocked their heads, and his wife looked at him with confusion.

A knock came at the front door. Ri's wife stood to answer it, but he told her to sit back down.

'But it's the door,' she said.

Ri smiled at her, then he smiled at his children.

And at that moment the door burst in on its hinges, splintering the door frame. Armed soldiers in green, guns high and voices loud, charged into the home.

The children tried to leap to their feet, but Ri held them by their forearms. His wife cried out in shock and fear but remained in her chair.

Quickly, Lieutenant General Ri's left hand released his daughter's forearm and he put his hand under the table. He closed his eyes, pulled hard at something hanging from the handle of his briefcase, and one second later the entire home exploded outward as two kilos of Semtex plastic explosive detonated.

The dogs of Chongjin would go hungry again tonight.

Director Hwang Min-ho sat in a makeshift office on the second floor of the Chongju rare earth mineral production facility, and he stared at the envelope in his hands. A courier from Pyongyang had just arrived and delivered the envelope, telling Hwang it was a letter from General Ri.

This was curious. Ri could have simply picked up the phone and called. Hwang opened the sealed packaging, and then a sealed inner envelope, and he unfolded the single sheet inside. He was surprised to find it was a hand-written message from the general.

> *Comrade Director Hwang:*
>
> *We have accomplished much in the past year. Our shared inspiration for the endeavor propelled us forward, but motivation alone would not have brought us to the cusp of success where we now find ourselves. Our plan was sound and our execution more than could have been expected of anyone — we can be proud that we came this close given the considerable obstacles in our path.*
>
> *I regret I will not be in position to provide continued support to the development of the mine at Chongju. When my replacement is appointed, I hope you will find him to be superior as a partner in the endeavor.*
>
> *I wish you good fortune.*
>
> *Ri*

Hwang did not understand. Ri could not simply *choose* to stop his operation to bring Chongju on line. With a slight tremor in his hand he picked up the phone and dialed Ri's direct office line in Pyongyang. While it rang he checked his watch. It was mid-morning; the general should have been at his desk.

A male secretary answered. Hwang said who he was and asked to be put through directly to the general.

'I am sorry, Comrade Director. General Ri died last night in a gas explosion in his home.'

Hwang did not speak for some time. Finally he asked, 'And his family?'

'They all perished, unfortunately.'

Hwang nodded to himself, thanked the man, hung up the phone, and put his head down on the desk.

The bastard had killed himself, this Hwang did not doubt for an instant. Hwang knew nothing about the attempt on the life of the President of the United States other than what had been announced on state-sponsored television, and they'd mentioned nothing about America's claim that North Korea had been involved, so he did not know why the head of the RGB decided he'd blow himself and his family to bits. But he spent little time considering Ri's motivations. Instead, his focus immediately turned to his own precarious situation.

Hwang thought of his options, and quickly determined that there were none. Ri had been correct in his letter. They had accomplished much in the past year, and they had come close to success. But now that Ri was gone, there was no chance Hwang could mine, process, ship, and market rare earth minerals. He needed the active engagement of the RGB to work with Óscar Roblas overseas through all phases of the product cycle.

The mining director had worked tirelessly over the past year, and even with the recent setback of the confiscation of the froth flotation tanks by the Americans, he'd still been able to see a way forward. But now, in this instance, he knew it was over, and with this realization came the deep sadness of hopelessness.

He would die for his failure, and he was thinking of this, but more than anything he thought of his children. They'd done nothing wrong, they had celebrated and honored the Dae Wonsu with every fiber of their being, and soon the Dae Wonsu would nevertheless order them put to death.

They would die for their father's failure.

It seemed so utterly unfair.

He lifted his head off the desk slowly. No. Hwang had not failed. General Ri had failed, and then he had taken the coward's way out. Why should Hwang's children pay for that?

Hwang's eyes fixed in determination. He would *not* just sit here and wait to suffer the consequences of failure for someone else.

The fifty-four-year-old director snatched up his phone and called his own secretary.

'Put me through to the Agricultural Bank of China, Singapore branch. Vice President Chang Lan.'

While he waited for the connection to be made, he thought over his new plan. Chang Lan was Chinese, and when he'd last visited Pyongyang, Hwang had been notified by a member of his staff that the man had been asking pointed questions about the private lives of certain North Korean government officials. Hwang's employee wondered if he should notify internal security about the man's actions, but Hwang had ordered him to keep his mouth shut. Chang Lan's bank was important to the Chongju mining operation, and the last thing Hwang needed was paranoid state security minders harassing an executive of an important financial institution because he'd solicited a little idle gossip.

Hwang didn't think the man was a member of Chinese intelligence, but he surely had connections back in Beijing that could connect him with their Ministry of State Security. And although Chang Lan was no friend, he was a colleague, and he might be able to put Hwang in contact with others in China who could help him do the only thing that would save Hwang and his family now.

Defect.

The director of the CIA's National Clandestine Service knew where he could find the director of national intelligence. The last three times Brian Calhoun called the office of Mary Pat Foley, he'd been told she'd gone downstairs to the Acrid Herald command center. This time he called the third-floor office suite directly, and she took the call in a private room off the main room full of computers and communications gear.

'Hi, Brian. I guess you caught me skulking around behind the scenes in Acrid Herald again.'

Calhoun replied, 'Your title gives you the right and the duty to skulk around any part of that building you like. I'm glad I reached you, though. We just got some time-critical intel.'

'Tell me.'

'As part of the wider investigation into the foreign accounts used by North Korea, we've been monitoring activities at a branch of a Chinese bank in Singapore. The CIA station there has a joint program with NSA to intercept communications of some of the bank's key officials. It's a new program that hasn't paid dividends to date, but I think we just hit the jackpot.'

'Go on.'

'North Korean mining director Hwang Min-ho has contacted an exec at this bank, apparently someone he's had a long-standing relationship with. He is expressing a desire to defect to China.'

'My God! Why?'

'We don't know for sure. We didn't hear Hwang directly, and the banker did not say. He only relayed the fact Hwang wanted to get out of North Korea with his family as soon as possible. He says he has no way to get to China himself, but he will be meeting with Chinese mining officials in Pyongyang next week.'

Mary Pat began furiously scratching notes on a pad. She said, 'The failure to get Chongju up and running must have him looking over his shoulder.'

Calhoun agreed. 'He thinks he's going to get the firing squad. I can't think of any other reason he'd want to bolt like this.'

'Any idea why he's reaching out to China specifically?'

'He knows them, nothing more. What he *doesn't* know is this banker acquaintance of his in Singapore doesn't want to get involved. He hasn't communicated with the Chinese yet. We found out when he, I'm speaking of the banker, called a colleague in Beijing and asked for advice. The colleague told him he needed to take it directly to the MSS, to not use the phone or the Chinese embassy in Singapore, so the man will be flying home on Saturday.'

'Hwang thinks the Chinese will just come get him?'

Calhoun said, 'Not sure what he thinks, but as soon as the Chinese know about Hwang and his desire to defect, the ball will be in their court. I'm wondering if we can somehow take advantage of this three-day window before they find out.'

Mary Pat had an idea, and although she knew it was thin, she also knew the greatest intelligence coups often began with an opportunity that, at first blush, seemed impossible to capitalize on. She said, 'I want you over here at the Acrid Herald command center as soon as possible. We're going to put a plan together to get Avalanche involved in this.'

'I'm on my way.'

70

Adam Yao had genuine concerns he would be sent home from North Korea, and the fact that this concerned him almost – *almost* – made him laugh. For the past three days he had been ordered to produce no powder in his cone crusher. The ore he had prepared for the froth flotation tanks sat in rail cars alongside the refinery, protected from the rain with plastic sheeting. There was no room to store more powder, so Director Hwang had ordered Adam's portion of the refinery shuttered to save electricity. Some other de-partments were still up and running – geology, maintenance, metallurgy – but no one needed any more crushed rock, so Adam had no job to do.

Adam had seen Hwang twice during his time here, once walking through the facility and once walking with his family from his SUV to the hotel. He thought it strange the man had brought his family with him here, but not overly so. He was the director, after all, he could do whatever he wanted. Both times he saw the little man, he appeared positively distressed. It had pleased Adam because it probably meant he was having difficulties getting his operation up and running, but it also created problems for Adam, because since he'd not been at his computer terminal he had not been able to communicate with Acrid Herald control for the past three days.

He had tried to use this downtime to get some more intel from Dr. Powers; he saw her each and every morning during his jog, sometimes just for a minute, sometimes for much longer. She was as stressed as Director Hwang, but for the opposite reason. She informed Adam, still in stilted Chinese, that there would be a new shipment of flotation tanks, though she did not know when. Each day she had revealed more about her desire to get the hell out of here and never look back, and the fact the tanks had not yet arrived had brought her to the edge of despair. She wanted to get production started on the plant so she could go home.

Adam decided to take a chance today. He told his shift supervisor he needed to run some diagnostics on his machine's computer and, no, it could not wait another day, because if the machine needed physical repair he had to do it now in the downtime. His shift supervisor talked with the floor manager, and it was agreed that Adam's entire section would get twenty minutes of generator power so he could use his computer.

The truth was, Adam just wanted the opportunity to check for any messages from the Acrid Herald ops center.

When the lights came up on his floor he was already waiting at his terminal. He fired up his computer, made certain he was alone, and then opened his communications device in his system's BIOS. He followed his memorized sequence of actions, and soon enough he saw there was, in fact, a message waiting for him. He was certain it would be a worried request for an update because he had not reported in, but instead, when he clicked to open it, he found it to be something altogether different. He read it once all the way through, and then again, more slowly the second time because he just couldn't believe it.

As he read he felt his heart pounding inside his coveralls.

Under his breath and all but inaudible, but nevertheless in English, he spoke. 'Oh . . . my . . . God.'

SECRET

TO: FLASH FOR AVALANCHE
FROM: TIDALWAVE
SUBJECT: POSSIBLE DEFECTION OF HWANG MIN-HO/
PERSONNEL
RECOVERY/EXTRACTION
SOURCE: SIGINT SINGAPORE STATION

1: ACCORDING TO SIGINT INTERCEPTS THROUGH STATION SINGAPORE, MINING DIRECTOR HWANG MIN-HO HAS EXPRESSED WISHES TO INTERMEDIARY TO DEFECT TO CHINA. INTERMEDIARY NAME IS CHANG LAN – A CHINESE BANKER AND ACQUAINTANCE OF HWANG. UNKOWN MOTIVATION, BUT ANALYTICAL SOURCES SUSPECT HE IS CONCERNED RE PERSONAL SAFETY AFTER PROBLEMS WITH REFINERY PRODUCTION TIMETABLES. CHINESE GOVT HAS NOT YET RECEIVED REQUEST FROM INTERMEDIARY, BUT WILL WITHIN 48 HRS.

2: REQUEST AVALANCHE MAKE CONTACT WITH DIR. HWANG IN NEXT 24 HOURS UNDER COVER OF CHINESE INTELLIGENCE OFFICER. CONFIRM HIS WISH TO DEFECT.

BOLSTER BY INFORMING HIM OF DANGERS OF
REMAINING IN PLACE. BRING HIM TO GRID
39 45'58.04" – 124 50'50.21" NOTE – HE INFORMS
INTERMEDIARY THAT HE HAS HIS FAMILY WITH HIM
IN CHONGJU. YOU ARE AUTHORIZED TO BRING OUT
HIS FAMILY IF ABLE.

3: YOUR ARRIVAL WILL BE MONITORED BY SATELLITE,
AND YOUR RECOVERY WILL BE EFFECTED BY AIR.

TIDALWAVE

Yao looked at the date of the message. It was sent yesterday. The forty-eight-hour timetable was just cut in half.

A file had been sent along as well, and he opened it. It was a satellite map of northwestern North Korea to the Chinese border, with his extraction location marked. It was at the end of a long straight dirt road west of the city of Sonchon, just west of where he now sat and near the coast.

Expanding the satellite map as large as possible, he saw at the end of the road something that looked like a poultry farm.

So, Adam said to himself, *I'm supposed to go knock on Hwang's door and say, 'I hear you want to defect. Let's go. Can we take your car?'*

Sure, that's going to happen.

And then what? Extraction via air? Really? What, a helo is just going to come flying straight up the middle of North Fucking Korea and land at a chicken farm?

*

632

Yao closed the message and it automatically erased. He was just about to type out a new message when he heard footsteps on the other side of the cone crusher.

A Korean spoke in Mandarin: 'Your time is up, Shan. Generator power goes out in one minute.'

Shit. He shut down his machine and walked away as the lights went out. Acrid Herald would see that he received the message, but they wouldn't hear what he wanted to tell them, that there was *no fucking way* he was getting Hwang out of North Korea.

Adam slept little, but the morning came anyway. He rose from his cot at five-thirty and went outside, and after a short stretch he started his daily jog.

Dr. Powers was there, and they stopped to chat. She seemed sadder and more sullen than ever, but nothing new had happened. She was just becoming more and more depressed that she had no idea when she would be allowed to go home.

Adam had spent the evening thinking over his next move, and he knew now was his one chance to get it right. 'I need a small favor from you.'

She nodded. 'What is it?'

He looked around to make sure they were alone, and then he placed a folded sheet of paper through the fence wire. She took it.

'Don't open it,' he said. 'Can you give it to Director Hwang? I don't know if I will see him at the factory today.'

Despite his instructions, she opened it. It was written in Chinese. 'I speak Mandarin, but I can't read it. What does it say?'

Adam was pissed, but this was part of NOC work. Misjudging how someone would react. Last night in bed he'd put it at seventy-five percent that she would do what he asked without question. Clearly now, he'd made the wrong call. He said, 'I can't tell you. It's about the factory. Concerns we have about the conditions. He will not be mad at you. You can't even read it.'

She was on guard. 'Who are you?'

'You know who I am. Shan Xin.'

She seemed very suspicious now, and Adam worried he'd overplayed his relationship with the Australian woman. He reached a hand through the fence. 'You know what? Never mind. I'll give it to him myself.'

But Powers put the sheet in her pocket. 'I'll see him in the lobby before he leaves for work. He has breakfast with his family in the restaurant there. It's a luxury we foreign contractors do not enjoy. Spending time with our families, I mean.' She paused. 'Let me guess. You would like it if I didn't let anyone see me hand it to him, wouldn't you?'

Adam just nodded.

'And it's about conditions at the factory?'

He nodded again.

'You think he gives a damn?'

'Probably not.'

She shrugged. 'Okay. I'll do it. If you are lucky, they will send you home for complaining. Hell, maybe I should try it.'

Adam said, 'Let's see how it goes for me first.'

'Good idea.'

71

Duke Sharps lunched alone at a back table at Nice Matin restaurant on Amsterdam Avenue on the Upper West Side, but he wasn't very hungry. He picked at the turkey-and-avocado sandwich in front of him and he sipped a gin martini, very dirty, while he read *The New York Times*.

The above-the-fold article was about the assassination attempt on President Jack Ryan three days earlier, and this article had positively ruined his appetite.

The US government claimed to have evidence tying the attack to North Korea. They weren't revealing the source of their intel, and at this point it looked like some unsourced and unsubstantiated leak out of the White House, but the *Times* was running with it.

Sharps thought it was probably a lie, but even so, this lie could end up costing him a great deal of money. The Ryan administration was doing everything it could to beef up sanctions on North Korea, apparently even taking the extraordinary step of fingering them in the Mexico City massacre. It was incredible to Sharps that Ryan would blame Pyongyang for the killing of one US ambassador, nine American Secret Service agents, and thirty-seven Mexican nationals, and the injuring of more than a hundred fifty, dozens critically.

Who knows, thought Sharps. *Maybe they did have something on North Korea.* But whatever they had, it would be tangential, a stretch. America was blaming who they wanted to blame for the attack, and it pissed Sharps off because his contract with Óscar Roblas's New World Metals depended on North Korea getting a fair shake on the international markets.

Sharps stopped reading suddenly, and then he slowly lowered the newspaper in front of him, looking over the top as he did so.

John Clark sat in the chair on the other side of Sharps's table. His face was placid, his legs were crossed, and he leaned back. Sharps hadn't heard him sit down. The old bastard could still skulk around like the snake eater he used to be.

Duke saw the confidence on the man's face, and he fought a sudden and unfamiliar feeling of uncertainty. He tried to make himself sound self-assured. 'To what do I owe this pleasure, Mr Clark?'

'No pleasure for you, Duke. You are sitting with the grim reaper.'

Sharps folded the paper and placed it in his lap, and then he leaned forward. 'I beg your pardon?'

'If you had any thin fantasies of continuing on after today, you should probably go ahead and abandon that hope, because your life is over.'

Sharps chuckled. 'I ran you out of town a few weeks ago. Circumstances not unlike this, if I remember correctly. If you think you have something on me, something big and bold and brash enough to where you can come back to my city all chuff and tough . . . well, then, let's hear it.'

'I'd much rather you saw it.'

Duke Sharps blinked. '*Saw* it?'

Clark lifted his hands from under the table. In them he clutched a stack of eight-by-ten photographs.

'These are all time-stamped, but I won't bore you with those details.'

'What are they?'

He slapped them down, one by one, and as they dropped on Duke's turkey-and-avocado sandwich, Clark narrated. 'This is you with your man Edward Riley.' It was a photo of the two men leaving Sharps Partners together. He dropped another photo. 'This is your employee Veronika Martel entering your building.'

More photos dropped in quick succession. 'This is your man Riley going to Martel's apartment, and this is Riley leaving Martel's apartment. This is Martel being carted out in a body bag.'

Sharps cocked his head. He started to say something but John Clark did not pause to let him speak. 'This one is your man Riley in Mexico, at the property owned by your client, Óscar Roblas de Mota.'

He tossed down another picture, it spun around to Sharps's chest, but he caught it. 'This is your man Riley with a North Korean intelligence agent.'

'What in the hell is —'

'And this is your man Riley, a North Korean intelligence agent, and a poor fellow tied to a chair. That man is Adel Zarif, the would-be assassin of the President of the United States.'

Sharps did not even try to stammer an explanation or a quip. He turned white, looked back up to Clark, opened his mouth, then closed it again.

Clark leaned close. 'Nothing? Okay . . . let me help you. Say that the photos are fakes.'

Duke cocked his head.

Clark nodded. 'Go ahead.'

'Well . . . they *are* fakes. Complete forgeries. My attorneys will prove that —'

Clark leaned back in his chair. 'Zarif is alive, he's in US custody, and he is singing like a bird. He's fingered Riley, and we have video. Mexican police have two Cuban intelligence officers in custody as well, wounded but talking, and they will confirm coordinating with your employee in Cuernavaca. Apparently they are pissed, because it wasn't till they were down there and under fire that they realized they had been co-opted into a plan to capture and kill the would-be presidential assassin before he could reveal the ringleaders of the plot.'

The stammer came now, and it was even more pathetic than Clark expected it to be. 'John . . . you *have* to believe me. I had *nothing* to do with *any* of this. No knowledge whatsoever. Riley must have gone behind my back to —'

'It's over, Sharps. Everything. You'll go to prison or you'll spend the next decade and all your money trying to stay out of prison. No one in this town, in this country, on this earth, will associate with you, because doing so will bring them nothing but hell.'

'What . . . what do you want?'

Clark chuckled now. 'To watch you swing. Nothing more.'

'Come on. *Come on!*' Sharps shouted it now, and the entire restaurant turned to the two older men in the corner.

Clark said nothing.

Finally, in an excited whisper, Duke Sharps said, '*Riley*. I can give you Riley on a platter.'

'Necessary . . . but not sufficient.'

'He's gone off grid. He's gone off grid, but I will find him.'

'How?'

'He's trying to do a deal. I heard about it from Roblas.'

'What deal?'

Sharps hesitated, but only for a moment. He was a beaten man. Full cooperation was his only play. 'In Thailand. Some processing equipment for the North Koreans. He's trying to go behind my back to do it, but I heard. Russian cargo planes. It goes down tomorrow. If you hurry you might be able to –'

Clark held up a finger to silence Duke, and then he finger-motioned someone over. A man appeared from the sidewalk-seating entrance of the restaurant. He was young, with dark hair and a trim beard. He wore a dark blue suit and sunglasses.

He pulled out FBI credentials and flashed them.

'Wayne Sharps, I'm Special Agent Caruso, FBI. On your feet.'

Sharps hesitated. Everyone in the restaurant stared.

John Clark just sat there with his legs crossed and a satisfied smile on his face.

'I'm not going to ask you again,' Caruso said. 'You stand, or I put you face-first on the floor with a knee in the back of your neck.'

Sharps stood now, and Caruso turned him around and cuffed him.

*

Adam Yao sat on the catwalk of his cone crusher with three of the other technicians. It was six p.m., another full day without power on his floor, but there were candles and flashlights, and the four men had spent nine hours sitting here on their cold and dormant machine, smoking and talking and wondering if the North Koreans were ever going to get their act together and turn the factory back on.

A man walked alone up the dark walkway in the middle of the powder-processing floor. All four cone crusher employees stood and came down from the catwalk when they realized it was Director Hwang. He'd never shown any interest in this part of the facility at all, but now he appeared fascinated by the cone crusher. He walked around it, seeming to inspect it in the dim light.

Yao stood in a line with the three others.

Hwang looked the men over now. In Mandarin he said, 'Which one of you works with the computer?'

Adam stepped forward. 'Shan Xin, Comrade Director.'

Hwang stared at him a long time. Adam just stared back, hoping like hell Hwang didn't screw this up.

The director said, 'I have questions about the software we need to buy to update the machinery. Are you the man I need to ask about this?'

'Yes, Comrade Director.'

'Then follow me.'

Adam followed the man back into an administrative section of the building. He'd never been here, and he was surprised when, after climbing up a staircase, he saw Dr. Helen Powers coming out of a room with her lab coat on. She nodded to Hwang and looked at Adam with surprise, but she said nothing.

They stepped into an office and Hwang closed the door. He looked nervous, like his demeanor before had been a put-on and now he was letting true feelings show.

'Have we met before?' he asked. It was a weird thing to say, but Adam knew the man just wanted to establish that Adam was, in fact, with Chinese intelligence.

'No, Comrade Director, but I believe we have a mutual friend. Chang Lan.'

Hwang blew out a sigh of relief, but afterward he appeared no less worried. He shook Adam's hand.

'I had no idea you were here, inside the operation, the entire time.'

Adam kept his conversation in Mandarin. Hwang seemed to speak it well enough. 'I understand you have your family with you.'

'Yes,' the director answered quickly. 'Can we go tonight?'

'Better we do it early in the morning. When you leave for work. We can take your car.'

'And we will go to the border? Do you have a way across?'

Adam wasn't sure what to say. He decided to stick to as much truth as he could think of. 'We will travel by air. I am to take you and your family to a location near Sonchon, and we will be picked up.'

Hwang said, 'But we must leave now. You do not have the time you think you do.'

'What do you mean?'

'The Chinese technicians will be leaving tonight.'

'What?'

'The processing facility will go dormant and the workers are being sent home.'

'Why? What has changed?'

Hwang blinked in surprise. 'You don't know?'

Now Adam said, 'I don't know *what*?'

'General Ri of the RGB killed himself yesterday.'

Oh, shit, Adam thought. He knew he needed to look like he was in charge, so he just nodded, then asked, 'What did Ri have to do with Chongju?'

Hwang said, 'Ri was the only chance we had to make the refinery work. We will never get the froth flotation tanks now. My only hope is to escape with my family to China.'

Adam thought it over for just a moment, because he realized every second was important now. 'Okay. If they decide the refinery won't work, they might have you shot. We'd better go tonight.'

'With my family,' Hwang added.

'Yes. It is arranged. We can accommodate all three of them.'

'Five.'

'Five?'

'My parents are coming.'

Adam shook his head. He kept speaking in Mandarin, though it was a challenge. 'Your *what*? Parents? Hell, no. I can't take everybody.'

'It's no problem, I have them staying at a vacation cottage near the water. Just twenty minutes' drive from Chongju.'

'We can't bring your parents.'

'Then I cannot leave.'

Adam found himself wanting to punch a wall. After thinking it over a minute more, he said, 'Okay. We take your car to the hotel. Pick up your family, go to the cottage, grab your parents, and head for the extraction.'

'What about your other agent?'

'What other agent?'

'Dr. Powers. The Australian.'

'She isn't an agent. She just gave you the note.'

'My aide saw her do it. They will think she was involved.' Hwang looked away.

Adam said, 'Internal security will kill her, won't they?'

'Oh, yes. Of course they will.'

'Goddamn it.' Adam mumbled it in English.

'What?'

'It's English. It means "The more, the merrier."'

72

Five minutes later Hwang went back to his office and explained to his staff that he would drive himself back to the hotel and then go visit his parents. They assumed the director's parents were home in Pyongyang, and he did nothing to dispel their assumption.

While the director was taking care of this and other matters, Yao was in the geology lab with Helen Powers. They were alone, which was a good thing for them both, because Adam decided he would speak English.

He didn't think she would think much of her chances if he told her he was a Chinese spy. She put together on her own who he worked for the moment he dropped his accent fully. 'Dr. Powers. Do you really want to get out of here?'

'I . . . you are American?'

'You tell anyone and I will be killed. You will be suspected, at best, and stood up against a wall right next to me, at worst. You understand that, don't you?'

'Why the blazes would I tell anyone? You think I like these people? They are mad bastards.'

'Hwang and I are leaving, and if you stay, you will be in danger.'

'Let me get my purse.'

Adam drove behind the wheel of a silver Pyeonghwa Pronto, Hwang's seven-passenger SUV. Hwang sat next to him in the front, and in the middle row sat his wife and two small children. They were all confused, but they were quiet, because they were obedient, and Hwang told them everything was fine.

Dr. Helen Powers sat in the third row, doing her best to keep her red hair under a black cap so it didn't draw any more attention to the vehicle than necessary as they drove through the North Korean backcountry.

As they neared the cottage, Hwang spoke in Mandarin to Adam.

'*Go-you.*' Hwang said it softly.

Adam turned to Hwang. He wasn't sure what the Korean was talking about, or even if he'd heard correctly. '*Go-you*' meant 'dogs' in Mandarin. He knew the Korean word, so he checked.

'*Gae?*'

'Yes.' Hwang continued in Mandarin. 'Dogs.'

'What about dogs?'

'You said Choi would have me shot. You are wrong. He *wouldn't* have had me shot. He would have fed me to starving dogs.'

Adam turned back to the road. He squeezed the steering wheel tighter. 'We've heard about that. Most of our analysts thought it was just an exaggerated rumor.'

'No rumor. General Gang of foreign intelligence was killed in this manner last year.'

Mother of God. 'How do you know?'

'Because General Ri told me. He was there.' After a pause he said, 'Ri killed himself and his family so they would not suffer the same fate.'

Yao shuddered. He wished like hell he had some way to

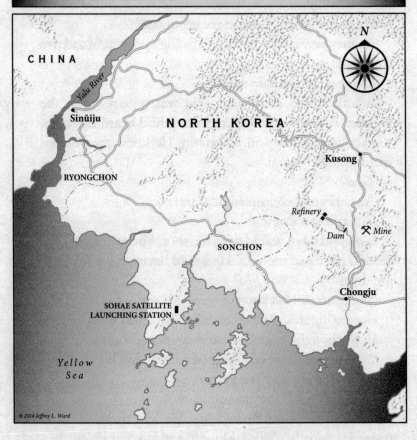

NORTHWEST NORTH KOREA

CHINA

Yalu River

Sinŭiju

NORTH KOREA

Kusong

RYONGCHON

Refinery

Dam

Mine

SONCHON

Chongju

SOHAE SATELLITE
LAUNCHING STATION

Yellow
Sea

© 2014 Jeffrey L. Ward

talk to Acrid Herald control and let them know he was on the way. They said they'd be watching from above, which meant satellites, probably the KH-12 that Adam knew monitored North Korea, but now that he was picking up strays along the way, he could only hope the helicopter they were sending was big enough to handle everyone.

They arrived at the cottage at seven p.m. It wasn't remote at all, just one of hundreds of cookie-cutter little homes with postage-stamp fenced yards that overlooked the coastline in a massive complex. A cool wind blew in from Korea Bay, and the moon provided enough light for Hwang to pick out the right unit. While many of North Korea's citizens starved, a few thousand elite owned vacation cottages. Hwang's family was one of the 'haves,' and while it didn't look like much to Yao, in this country it was an unfathomable luxury to ninety-nine percent of the population.

Adam said, 'Okay, just like we planned it. Quickly. Don't answer questions, just get them moving. No luggage. Just the clothes on their backs and any medicine they need in the next twenty-four hours.'

Hwang just nodded.

Everyone stayed in the vehicle except for Hwang, who climbed out and went to the front door. He knocked, and waited.

Adam rolled down the driver's-side window. He was only twenty-five feet from Hwang at the door, and he wanted to listen to how Hwang told his presumably elderly parents that they had to leave right this minute.

An elderly man and woman stepped out and onto the

stoop in front of the door. Hwang's father put his hand on his son's shoulder. He leaned on unsteady legs. Adam thought the old man was just using his son for balance, but quickly he realized he was leaning close to his son to say something.

'What is it, Father? We must hurry.'

This worried Adam. How would the old man know they were going somewhere?

The father mumbled something. Adam couldn't understand, and he saw Hwang couldn't make it out, either.

'What, Father?'

'Disgrace. You are a *disgrace*! You bring dishonor on us!'

Adam was moving in a half-second, opening the car door, leaping out into the little driveway, running up to the door. 'Hwang!'

The old lady shouted now. 'The Dae Wonsu will have his revenge for your deceit!' She threw a bony, weak fist at her son's face. It glanced off him, but he reacted as if he had been decked by a heavyweight.

'Mother!' Hwang shouted in shock.

Adam pushed between them as both the old man and the old lady began throwing blows. Most of them hit Adam on his back. None of them hurt at all.

'Let's go!' he said in Mandarin.

'Traitor!' Hwang senior shrieked. *'Working with the* jung gug-ui*!'* The Chinese.

Yao saw the tears on Hwang's face, the incomprehension that his own parents had turned against him.

But he wouldn't leave.

Adam shouted, 'They turned you in! We have to get out of here!'

648

Hwang just stood on the little stoop; his parents were still within arm's reach and they swung and scratched at him. Adam fought them both off with one arm, but he'd taken a blow just over the eye and the old couple seemed to grow stronger with adrenaline. If he had his way he'd deck them both, just drop them with a couple of jabs, but he knew that would just anger Hwang and jeopardize a mission that already had enough going against it.

'Forget them!' he shouted at Hwang. He saw Hwang's wife climbing out of the SUV now. He yelled at her in Korean. 'Get back in the car!'

'No!' Hwang cried openly now, his face tight, eyes squinted but tears managing to find their way through and down his face.

'Hwang!' Adam shouted. 'Your children! Min-hee and Du-ho won't stand a chance if we don't run right now!'

The fifty-four-year-old Korean turned to Adam, opened his eyes a little. Finally he turned and started back to the car.

Adam took one last look at the parents. They were impossibly small and rail-thin, but the anger in their eyes made them look like wild animals.

Hwang walked across the driveway, his parents running after him. Adam got behind Hwang to where he couldn't see him, then spun around with his fist balled and high. He had no plans on beating an eighty-year-old couple, even though he thought it likely their actions might well get him, this family, and the Australian geologist killed.

He jumped back behind the wheel and jammed the vehicle in reverse, backed out of the little dirt drive, and put it in gear. He stomped on the accelerator, and the four-cylinder shot dirt and fishtailed, then raced on.

Headlights appeared on the tiny road ahead of him. Multiple sets of high beams. Adam kept racing right toward them as fast as he could, hoping like hell they would move out of the way. At twenty yards he could tell they were troop trucks, so he swerved off the road and began crashing through the low fences of the tiny postage-stamp yards in front of the cottages. One after the other he smashed through wooden and wire fences, then bounced up into gardens, back down the other side, and then crashed through the next stretch of fence.

As they passed the trucks he heard the booming cracks of rifle fire. Everyone in the SUV screamed for their lives, but the vehicle bounced on, reached the end of the neighborhood, and peeled hard to the right, accelerating down a hill.

'You called your parents! You told them we were coming. Didn't you?' Adam asked.

Hwang just nodded, tears streaming down his face. Behind him his wife screamed at him, and his kids were on the verge of hyperventilation. Dr. Powers was doing everything she could to calm the children, but she didn't speak their language, so it was an impossible task.

A pair of helicopters flew low overhead.

'Hold on!' Adam said it in Korean, then jacked the wheel to the right.

The mud and rocks slapped the undercarriage of the vehicle as it bounced down a hill in the dark.

He shouted to Hwang. 'Where does this road go?'

'It leads to a stream. Straight ahead at the bottom of the hill.'

'How deep?'

Hwang thought. 'At this time of the year it is very shallow. Almost dry in places.'

Adam didn't much like his plan, but he felt he had no choice. He reached up and flipped off the headlights.

'What are you doing?'

'I'm hoping they don't have night vision!'

He fought the strong urge to turn the lights back on, and the even stronger urge to slow down. Finally he felt the hill bottom out, and he turned to the right, away from the ocean to his left. He slowed a little, but kept as much speed as he dared. The SUV bounced wildly over the rocks in the dry streambed.

Adam saw the lights of the helicopters in the distance as the SUV drove on. The helos would follow the road, looking for the SUV, and as long as Adam and the others stayed at the bottom of the little valley, moving in the dry streambed, and as long as there was cover from the flora above them, they would be safe.

'Are you okay?' Adam asked Hwang.

The North Korean was still crying, but he nodded distractedly. Though Hwang's family was in the car with him, Adam saw that the man felt totally alone after his parents turned on him.

Adam said, 'You *had* to do this. Choi was going to kill everyone in your family.'

Hwang turned and pointed at Adam angrily. 'You are an inferior *jung gug-ui*! You do not say the family name of the Dae Wonsu!'

Christ, Yao thought. *This one is brainwashed like all the others.*

73

President of the United States Jack Ryan wasn't fit to travel, especially halfway around the world, but he was doing it anyway. The trip was against the advice of his doctors, his wife, and anyone with a shred of knowledge of broken bones and soft-tissue damage and the dangers of exhaustion, but Ryan was the President, and he overruled them all.

He'd been making his calls to world leaders two days earlier when President Ling of China had offered to meet with him at any time to discuss the disintegrating relations with North Korea. Ryan sensed that the offer was more than just the typical platitudes that came along with telling someone he was glad he'd not been murdered, so Ryan told Ling he would very much like to get together in China for a private talk.

Ling had said 'anytime,' so Ryan proposed three days hence.

The translators had to triple-check that the American President was talking about arriving in Beijing on Saturday. *This* Saturday.

Within hours of the phone conversation Mary Pat Foley all but burst into Ryan's hospital room to tell him an Iranian bomb maker had been captured alive near Mexico City, and he had details of an interesting trip to Pyongyang he'd made just prior to his attack on the presidential motorcade. With incontrovertible proof North Korea was involved, the Ryan administration leaked a rumor to take the heat off the Mexican government. Ryan ordered Justice and DNI to hold most of the details they had, because he wanted to exploit the information at a time and place of his own choosing. It was statecraft, and Ryan figured if he had to get blown up, he might as well get something out of it for America in the process.

Ryan and Foley decided Ryan would use this trip to Beijing to pass the intelligence about North Korea's involvement directly to Chinese President Ling. Ling would be terrified – he would know any action taken by the United States against Pyongyang would destabilize the Korean Peninsula, and he would worry about a war, a refugee crisis, and his own country's exposure to 'guilt by association,' since even though China and North Korea were in the middle of their worst relationship of the past seventy years, North Korea still had no closer friend than its large communist neighbor to the north.

Ryan wanted Ling to be scared about what actions the US might take for retribution. The more concerned China was about threats to its own national interests, the more inclined they would be to partner with the United States against the criminal regime in Pyongyang.

Then Mary Pat read President Ryan in on Acrid Herald. What had started out as an opportunity to learn about a North Korean mineral processing facility had turned into a major intelligence coup. Right now Hwang Min-ho was on the run in North Korea, attempting to defect, he thought, to the Chinese. If this worked, Ryan knew, he would have someone who could reveal to the world how North Korea's mineral wealth was being used not for the good of its own people but instead to build up their nuclear missile arsenal. If it all worked as planned, if Hwang made it out and revealed what he knew, then Ryan knew his meeting with President Ling tomorrow would be an opportunity for the two superpowers to work together on a mutual problem.

In the meantime, Ryan just wished he wasn't such an invalid at the moment. Although he could walk and talk, his left hand was in a cast and his right arm was in a sling. With all the attendants at his disposal, there was no one around here in this office on Air Force One, and he needed to scratch his damn nose, and this put him in an exceptionally foul humor.

Adam Yao drove the North Korean – made SUV slowly down the long, straight dirt road at midnight. He went all the way to the end, some mile and a half from the main highway, until he reached the poultry farm. Here he turned off the engine and listened carefully.

Nothing. A few chickens clucking in a coop, the sound of wind through the pine trees thick on the adjacent hillside, but no sound of helicopters racing in.

Adam was scared now, but the kids behind him were asleep. Hwang and his wife spoke softly back and forth. She was frightened still, but Hwang seemed to be doing a better job of calming her than himself, because he appeared to be scared shitless.

Min-hee, the nine-year-old girl, sat up suddenly and looked around, and soon Du-ho did the same. Within seconds Adam heard it as well – it was a high-pitched buzzing, very faint but growing in volume.

It didn't sound to Adam like an airplane, not even a small one, and it was definitely not a helicopter. Still, he told everyone to get out.

Once they were on the dirt road they heard it better. It was definitely a propeller, and it hummed almost like a lawn mower.

Adam saw it first, but he didn't know what he was looking at. A winged apparition moved low over the trees, darker than the night sky behind it.

Then Hwang saw it. 'What is that?'

It passed directly overhead, then banked tightly, and lined up on the road upon which they stood.

Adam said, 'It's a UAV. A drone.' It was a Predator, which was unquestionably American, but it was doubtful Hwang or his wife would know this. As it neared, Adam was glad to see there was no US flag on the side.

'What is it doing here?' Hwang asked.

'I have absolutely no idea.'

Du-ho pointed into the sky. 'There is another one.'

Both Predators landed on the road, one after the other, and then taxied to within fifty feet of Adam Yao.

To himself he said, 'You've got to be kidding.'

It occurred to him there might be a message or a piece of equipment on the aircraft, so he walked over to the closer one. He saw a large basket hanging from the bottom. It was the size of a loveseat, and it had a pneumatic hatch with a marking that read PULL.

Adam did so, and the device separated like a clamshell, the bottom lowering down about a foot and a half.

Adam looked inside. There was LED lighting glowing to help him.

He saw two sleeping bags and a satellite phone.

He snatched the phone and saw that it was blinking; there was already a call coming through.

Adam moved away from Hwang and his family and whispered. 'Avalanche.'

'Hello, Avalanche. You are speaking with the tactical operations center on board the USS *Freedom*. This line is being broadcast to op center TIDALWAVE, and we are watching you from a KH-12.'

'Understood.'

'What is the status of your cargo? We see three adults and two children in addition to yourself.'

'I have six pax total. Three adults including precious cargo and two children.'

'Who is the other adult?'

'I had to bring out an Australian woman. Dr. Powers. She was compromised and in danger.'

There was a pause. 'Copy.'

'Is this basket what I think it is?'

'It is a personnel recovery device. Place the adult male in one basket with the male child. Put the two adult women together with the female child. We didn't know about the Australian. We are expediting the backup UAV to your poz, but be advised, you'll be waiting there five mikes.'

Adam spoke even softer now so Hwang and his wife could not hear, although they did not speak English. 'Is this shit gonna work?'

'Affirmative, Avalanche. Those UAVs are top secret.

Code name Freebird. They are tested at three hundred pounds per aircraft, well over the weight requirement needed. The baskets are not pressurized, so the ride will be low and a little bumpy, but it won't be too bad.'

'Oh . . . okay. Any chance I can squeeze in?'

'Unless your new friend weighs less than forty-five pounds, I do not recommend it. The aircraft becomes unstable above three hundred twenty-five pounds.'

Adam started to speak, but the male voice told him to wait. After a few seconds he came back on the line, his voice more agitated.

'Be advised, Avalanche. We are monitoring military helicopters moving into your sector. Twelve minutes out at current speed. Get that cargo on board, seal the hatch, and go find some cover. We'll do the rest, sir.'

'Okay.' He was more resolute this time with his reply, not because he now felt much better about flying in the Freebird, but rather because now that he knew DPRK helos were inbound, he felt much worse about standing around here pondering his options.

He ran over to Hwang and spoke in Mandarin. 'Quickly. You and your family will fly in these airplanes.'

'Those aren't airplanes!'

The man did have a point, Adam conceded to himself, but he knew he had to appear steadfast. 'They are perfectly safe. We do this all the time.'

'Where are the pilots?'

Adam would have said the pilots were sitting safe and comfortable, maybe thousands of miles away, because he didn't like this idea one bit, but he needed Hwang to comply.

So instead he said, 'You'll meet them when they land. These are remote-controlled UAVs.'

'I . . . I don't know.'

'Dae Wonsu's helicopters will be here in ten minutes. Do you know what will happen if the Army catches you and your family?'

Adam knew his argument was convincing, but he was surprised by the quick one-eighty. Hwang said, 'We should go now.'

'Exactly.'

The children were actually the easiest part of the equation. They let Adam pick them up with no complaints. He placed Du-ho into one Predator, and then Hwang climbed in behind him. Adam put Min-hee into the other Predator, and then Dr. Powers climbed in along with Mrs Hwang.

There was room for one more child in Hwang's aircraft. But there was not enough room for a CIA officer.

Adam pushed the buttons to close the two baskets. He wanted to say, 'Good luck,' but decided against it. Instead, still in Mandarin, he said, 'See you in a little while.'

The first UAV taxied around, facing away from the direction of the approaching helicopters, and began accelerating up the straight road. The second turned and followed, not one hundred yards behind.

They climbed into the air one after the other. Adam felt the squeeze of tension in his stomach as they rose toward the green hill.

They disappeared into the night in under a minute.

He heard a voice on the sat phone, which he had

lowered while watching the extraction. 'Repeat last, *Freedom*?'

'Be aware, third UAV approaching from south. Get off the road so it can land.'

'Copy that.'

Adam ran over to stand next to the SUV, and he listened for the arriving Predator. When he heard it he could tell it was flying a lot faster than the others, because the pitch was much higher.

The aircraft banked over the hill next to the road, lined up on final approach, and increased its descent.

And then it exploded in a fireball.

Adam shielded his eyes from the light and shouted into the sat phone. '*Freedom*, you just lost the UAV!'

After a quick pause the reply came. 'Roger, Avalanche. Inbound helos took it out with an air-to-air missile. You need to get out of there now!'

Adam dove into the SUV and turned the engine over. He stomped on the gas and raced up the road. Two attack helicopters came over the hill on his right, swooping down at nap-of-the-earth height. They flew over Adam, then banked around hard, and came back in his direction.

He floored it. As he accelerated up the road, the two helos passed on a gun run. Shells rained down on the road right in front of him, but they landed long.

Adam knew he wouldn't survive another pass. He had a half-mile before getting to the highway, and they could pick him off there just as easily. He had to get out of the SUV and into the trees.

He pushed the engine as fast as the Pronto would go

on the straight dirt road, then he popped the transmission into neutral. He opened his door and dove out into the low grass by the road. The SUV continued on.

Adam tumbled end over end, slamming his knee into a rock as he bounced on the earth. As soon as he stopped rolling, he climbed to his feet and limped into the hillside forest.

He heard the helos fire again at the vehicle, and then he heard a huge explosion. The SUV had taken a hit to the gas tank, and now it burned in the road behind him.

He hoped like hell no one would look for him for the length of time it took them to discover no bodies inside the burning SUV.

Even though he was injured now, he was starting to feel very lucky, considering how close he had come to death.

But then he realized he'd left the sat phone in the SUV.

He dropped down into the grass, pounding the ground in frustration. It was more than twenty miles to the Yalu River. China was on the other side, and it was hardly welcoming, but it was all he had to shoot for. He pulled himself back to his feet and hobbled up the hill, blood running down his leg.

74

The two Freebirds flew out over Korea Bay, then south to Inchon. There the UAVs were shadowed by a pair of US Navy Seahawk helos in case of mechanical problems over water. The UAVs had no problems, however, and landed at Osan Air Base without incident ninety-five minutes later, marking the first and second operational use of a Predator Freebird.

When the baskets were opened by CIA personnel at the airfield, everyone was alive, awake, and aware, although Hwang and his daughter had both vomited repeatedly in transit.

Hwang dropped to the tarmac, then helped his son out of the basket. Once Du-ho was on firm ground, Hwang ran over to his wife and daughter and hugged them both.

It was only then that he realized he was surrounded by Americans.

Twenty minutes later he sat in a conference room in an administrative building at the airfield. He'd been given a change of clothes and a bottle of water, but no one had spoken directly to him until an American woman in her sixties entered the room with a Korean woman wearing the uniform of the United States Air Force. The Korean woman informed Hwang that she would be his translator. He nodded, but his eyes were on the other woman in front of him. 'I want to speak to someone in charge.' The translator relayed this in English.

Mary Pat Foley replied, 'I am the director of all the combined intelligence agencies for the United States of America. Will I do?'

Hwang looked to the translator, then back to Mary Pat. 'Yes. You will do.'

She spent twenty minutes establishing who Hwang was, what he knew, and what access he had. Afterward, she left the room for an hour.

When she came back, she said, 'Here are our terms. We want every piece of information you have. Everything about your operation. If we are satisfied with what you give us, in return you will receive political asylum in the United States. If you would like to relocate to South Korea, I feel confident we can see that this happens, but that is ultimately up to the South Koreans.'

Hwang nodded slowly. He considered asking if he could go to China, but he did not. 'I agree to your terms.'

'Good. Let's begin with your debrief immediately.'

He was surprised by this. 'I am very tired. Could we begin later, after I rest?'

Foley shook her head. 'Absolutely not. Lives are at stake, Mr Hwang. Your wife and your children can rest. You and I have a lot of work to do.'

Hwang sighed.

National Geospatial-Intelligence analyst Annette Brawley had spent the first part of her day looking over train cars in Pyongyang, searching for evidence that the North Koreans were moving any of their mining equipment

662

north, salvaging parts from copper or coal mines with the intention of transporting them up to the strip mine at Chongju.

She hadn't found anything interesting on the North Korean rail network, but she was holding out hope that some new sat images due in the next few minutes might give her a clearer picture of the mine itself.

She glanced at the time, and looked up from her computer monitor to see Colonel Mike Peters storming her way.

'Hi, Mike.'

'Come with me.'

'Sorry, boss, I can't go right now, we're about to get the latest Chongju images from NRO.'

'This isn't a request. You and me have been ordered to go to the bubble on five.'

'Holy crap,' Brawley said, standing up from her desk as she did so. 'Are we in trouble?'

'Dunno. I know we *will* be if we aren't there in about two minutes.'

Brawley and Peters were led into the secure communications room, known as the bubble. They sat down in front of a monitor that displayed the image of an empty desk. Behind it was a sign that said OSAN AB.

After a minute they saw some moving shadows off to the side of the desk on the monitor. The two NGA employees looked at each other in confusion.

After a minute more Peters uttered a tentative 'Hello?'

Almost instantly, Mary Pat Foley, the director of national intelligence, sat down at the desk. Her eyes were to a point off screen, and it quickly became apparent someone was talking to her. She nodded, then looked at the monitor in front of her. She seemed rushed and concerned, and this made Annette Brawley absolutely terrified.

Foley said, 'Okay. Sorry, I don't know your names.'

Peters spoke for both himself and his employee. 'Madame Director. I'm Colonel Michael Peters of NGA and this is Annette Brawley, an analyst in my office. How can we be of service?'

'Your desk has developed the information on the rare earth mineral mine and processing facility in Chongju, DPRK?'

'Yes, Madame Director,' Peters said.

Brawley detected nervousness in her boss's voice.

Someone off camera spoke to Director Foley, and she nodded.

'I am told you, Ms. Brawley, know more about this area than anyone else in the US intelligence community.'

Brawley had no idea if that was true, because she had no idea what other operations were going on in that area. She only knew about the mines. She replied, 'I have focused on the north-western mountains and foothills of DPRK for over two years.'

Foley nodded. 'What I am about to tell you both is code-word-classified.'

Brawley nodded slowly; she felt sweat dripping down the back of her neck.

Foley said, 'We had a CIA officer on the ground in Chongju. Last night he was compromised during extraction. Right now he is in the wind, and we think it is possible he is injured.'

Brawley's lips moved, forming the words *Oh my God*, although she made no sound.

Peters asked, 'Do we know anything about what type of vehicle he is driving?'

'He was in an SUV of local manufacture. That vehicle has been destroyed by helicopter gunfire.'

'Was he inside?'

'SIGINT says the North Koreans are tearing up the countryside looking for someone. We hope it's him. We were tracking him with a satellite, but we lost him after DPRK helicopters destroyed the vehicle he was traveling in. We caught a heat register of a lone individual nearby after the attack, but we lost the signature.'

'No comms, I take it,' Peters said.

'Unfortunately, we have no communication with him at this point. We do not know his location. All of his extraction options, it appears from NRO's and CIA's reading of the satellite images available to us, are closed off. We don't know what he can do, and we don't know what he will do.'

Brawley nodded. 'We should have the newest daylight images in less than five minutes. If there has been anomalous police, government, or military activity in the area, maybe I can find evidence of it. Use that as a starting point to know where to look for . . .' She searched for the term. 'The officer.'

Foley said, 'The officer's code name is Avalanche. He is an American citizen of Chinese descent.'

Brawley raised a hand. 'If we find him, or evidence of where he is . . . is there something that can be done for him?'

Foley's lips tightened, a pained expression. 'Frankly, Ms. Brawley, I have no idea. Our options are extremely limited. But if we can't even find Avalanche, I can guarantee he has no chance whatsoever.'

Brawley nodded. 'I'll find him.' She didn't know why she said it, but once it came out of her mouth she knew she had to come through.

Adam Yao pedaled the bike with his right leg while his left stuck out in front of him. The swelling in his knee made it impossible to bend his leg, so slow, painful, one-legged biking was all that was available to him.

He'd stolen the bike in a tiny suburb of Sonchon City by picking the lock on a bike rack, and then he'd ridden as fast as he could with one leg, mostly on dirt roads, and even on fields and hillsides. It was slow going, he might have been averaging three miles an hour tops, but he had no choice but to push on.

He knew his only chance was to get to and then over the Yalu River. Getting to it would be tough. There were patrols on the highways and in the little towns, and he had spent the early-morning hours ducking helos that crisscrossed the sky. Once daylight came in a few hours, it would be even tougher for him. If he wasn't in a good hide site by sunup he wouldn't have a chance in hell.

And getting over the Yalu would be even harder. There were bridges, but they would be well guarded. The current was known to be impossible to swim, and any ferryboats, even the kinds used by smugglers, would most likely be known to the North Korean government, and therefore monitored now that the DPRK knew there was an enemy agent in their area.

His leg was bleeding from a gash next to the knee. He needed stitches for sure, and he needed to elevate it and apply pressure, but he'd done nothing more than tear off a piece of his shirt and tie it over the wound. It continued to pump blood, and Adam wondered how long it would take for him to weaken from the blood loss.

Adam was a smart guy, which meant he knew he was fucked. But what choice did he have? He just kept pumping the pedal on the right side of the bike, up and down, trying to get as far north as possible before daylight.

Annette Brawley sat in the bubble, in front of the monitor that connected her via videoconference to Osan Air Base in South Korea, and looked at her laptop. Mary Pat Foley sat on the other end of the connection, a laptop in front of her as well, and together they looked at a series of satellite pictures resident on their computers. Annette could make notes on her computer with a stylus, and Mary Pat would immediately see the notations on her images.

Annette said, 'Look here. A police car and several people standing around.'

'What is that?'

'That's a bicycle rack outside an apartment building. This is on the outskirts of Sonchon, not far from where Avalanche disappeared. I think someone stole a bike. Theft in North Korea like that is highly rare, because stealing a bike over there will get you executed. My assumption is Avalanche took it as a means of transportation. And from here he went north.'

'How do you know that?'

'West is the ocean. East is the entire nation of North Korea. South is the majority of the military in pursuit of him. North is the Yalu River, but on the other side of that is China. He has bad options in each direction, but nothing will look more promising than north.'

Mary Pat said, 'Okay. Go on.'

'We estimate his rate on a bicycle on the back roads to be seven miles an hour. I base this on the movements of other men around his age and their progress when moving north. Actually, the average is closer to ten, depending on the bicycle, but we know Avalanche would be avoiding checkpoints and population centers, so we shave off thirty percent.'

Annette Brawley moved the image far to the north, then enhanced the image even more. It was some sort of an open field, a dirt road running to the south of it, that much was plain.

Foley saw nothing in the field. 'What am I looking at?'

'The fact that this is empty. This is at seven a.m. Well after the time we would expect him to arrive if he was coming here.'

'Why do you think he would be coming here, specifically?'

Brawley switched the image. 'Because of this.' It was the same location as the last image, with one exception.

Foley looked at the picture. 'Is that a bicycle? Lying in the field?'

"It's a bicycle in a rice paddy, on its side. And it's not just any bicycle. This is a Kalmaegi – they are made at Life Detention Settlement Number 25, up in North

Hamgyong Province. It's the highest-quality local brand used in North Korea. There is a waiting list for these bikes, three or four years, and that's if you are lucky and you have the money. I can't say no one in North Korea would ever leave a Kalmaegi lying around like this, but I will say no one in this poor mountainous area would.

'And there's more. This showed up between eight and nine a.m. Much later than we thought he would arrive, even considering his environment.'

'What does that mean to you?'

'Significant injury,' Brawley said gravely.

'So . . . where is he now?'

'If he had been captured we would expect to see vehicle tracks leading into this rice paddy. I checked, the paddies aren't flooded, but the ground is very wet from the spring rains. Truck tires would remain for weeks this time of the year. Even if he was picked up by a group of men on foot, we would see some disturbance. But there's nothing.'

'If he walked off, would we see that?'

'No. The resolution won't pick up a single set of footprints.' Brawley smiled. 'I wish. No, it won't even pick up the disturbance of one body going through waist-high foliage or crops. Even if it was hundreds of yards of trail, it's just too narrow and subtle to show up.'

'So, I'll ask again. Where is he?'

Brawley used the laser pointer to touch a crescent-shaped grove of trees at the edge of the Yalu River. The roof of a tiny fishing shack was apparent at one side, but there was no sign of life anywhere else in the area.

"I think he is in these trees. I've checked the Chinese side of the river and it is crawling with border guards. I don't see indication that anything exciting is happening as far as they are concerned, so he hasn't crossed.

'That leaves these trees. If he is healthy enough to try it, he might be waiting for nightfall to cross. But there are whirlpools and relatively strong currents this time of year.'

'How do we know that?'

'There are links on Map of the World. Americans have traveled the Yalu and then reported it. Just adventure travelers in rafts and kayaks, not spooks. Crazy if you think about it, but there are some crazy folks out there, and we benefit from them. If he does try to swim or float across . . .' Brawley hesitated. 'If he tries, I don't think Avalanche will make it.'

Mary Pat Foley said, 'This is really incredible work, Ms. Brawley.'

'Thank you,' Annette replied. 'I just wish I could do more for Avalanche.'

'Someone else needs to do something for Avalanche now. If we get him out, it will be because of you.'

One hour later Annette Brawley was shutting down her computer for the night. She wanted to get home to make dinner for Stephanie. Her daughter would complain about it, but Annette knew the best thing she could do to help Stephanie through her tumultuous teenage years – years made more tumultuous by the death of her father – was to be there for her, even if she didn't appreciate the effort.

Just as she stood and reached for her purse, the phone on her desk rang; maybe this would be Stephanie, letting her know she wouldn't be home for dinner. She liked to wait until right before her mom left work to tell her.

Annette answered her phone. 'Brawley.'

'Please hold for the President of the United States.'

'Excuse me?' There was no response. Her heart skipped a beat, but quickly she came to her senses. 'Colonel Peters, that's not funny. I've got work to do.'

Just then the unmistakable voice of President Jack Ryan came over her line. She looked around the room, motioning frantically to two coworkers still in the office, but neither noticed her.

'Ms. Brawley. Jack Ryan here.'

She cleared her throat. 'Mr President.'

'Quick question. In about ten minutes I'm going to be sitting with the president of the People's Republic of China. It is crucial that I give him good information regarding the CIA asset on the ground in the DPRK. Director Foley told me your conclusions, and they sound solid to me, but I'm going to put you on the spot here. How certain are you that he's right where you say he is?'

Annette realized her hand was shaking the telephone receiver. She pushed it tighter against her ear. She looked at the picture of Ryan she kept on her desk. 'Mr President, I believe he went into those woods. One hundred percent. And I don't believe anyone has gone in to get him. Again, I'm one hundred percent confident in that. The only unknown is whether or not he is in the Yalu River. I truly hope he is still in those trees, but the only way to know for sure is to go in there and look for him.'

The President's reply came quickly, like he was rushed. 'You've done some good work. I wish I had had some of the technology you possess back in my analyst days, but I know enough to know more noise doesn't necessarily mean more music. You've got a ton of things you have to work through, and I'm impressed.'

'Thank you, sir. It is wonderful to be appreciated.'

'I know what you mean. Thankless work most of the time.' He paused. 'So . . . thanks.'

'I'm sorry about Mexico. Are you feeling better?'

'Every day. Gotta run. Good-bye.'

The line went dead in Annette Brawley's hand, and within seconds she began questioning whether or not the conversation had even taken place.

75

President Ryan had spent less than ninety minutes in direct talks with Chinese president Ling, but already he felt he had accomplished more substantive work than he had in his past two years of bilateral dealings with the often obstinate and sometimes belligerent superpower.

He had not met the new president face-to-face until now, and he wanted to ascribe much of the progress of the past hour and a half to his good working relationship with the man, but he suspected Ling wasn't terribly different from most of the other high Chinese Communist Party officials that the party extrudes into leadership positions. No, the success of this meeting had much do to with the fact Ryan came bearing both threats and gifts.

The first order of business had been to detail to the Chinese president North Korea's involvement in the attack in Mexico City. Ryan brought no evidence with him – this wasn't the type of meeting where two men would look over photos and witness statements together. Ryan instead offered to send Ling every shred of intelligence the US had gleaned from Adel Zarif over the past three days.

Ling was astonished, and Ryan was pleased to see the seventy-year-old Chinese Communist Party leader seemed to be every bit as worried about how this would affect China as Ryan had hoped he would be.

Ryan then delved into details about Choi's obsessive quest to obtain nuclear missiles that could reach the US mainland. Again, President Ling's face registered the gravity of the threat this posed to his own nation.

Ryan could see that Ling knew what was good for him and his country. He would play ball with America in the looming crisis. The last thing in the world he needed was a war between nuclear powers on his border, and Choi Ji-hoon's aggressive quest for intermediate-range missiles and his targeting of world leaders were leading the region inexorably toward war.

With the threats laid out in stark terms, Ryan offered his gift. He told Ling of the defection of Hwang Min-ho, the director of Korea Natural Resources Trading Corporation. The man was in US custody, but Ryan offered China access to him, and the opportunity to put him on national television and radio. Hwang was prepared to speak about how the North Korean Supreme Leader had initiated the process to squander many trillions of dollars' worth of desperately needed riches for his nation by expelling Chinese miners, all because he wanted to obtain a nuclear weapons delivery vehicle that would reach to the US It was an endeavor that might well have led to the destruction of the entire Korean Peninsula in the process, and the citizens of North Korea needed to know about this.

Ryan knew the Chinese had media, mostly radio broadcasts, that could reach into hundreds of thousands of homes in North Korea. Not to the proletariat, these people only had the government radio sets that blocked all but officially recognized channels, but to the elite of the nation, virtually all of whom listened to modified radios that allowed them to pick up Chinese transmissions, often translated into Korean for their benefit.

Within hours Hwang could be on a flight to Beijing with an American contingent. It was crucial he spread the word about Chongju to the people of North Korea as soon as possible, because Choi had been showing his volatility. The impounding of his mining equipment, the accusations he was involved in the assassination plot, the capture of his ICBM technology, and now the news that his intelligence chief had committed suicide. Choi was a wounded animal and everyone expected him to act as such.

And Choi had lived down to these expectations. In the past day he had launched two short-range rockets into the Sea of Japan and shelled a pair of South Korean islands.

Ryan knew the only sure bet was for Choi to be deposed from within, and the best chance for an internal uprising was convincing the elite of the nation that Choi had adversely affected all of their fortunes with his reckless obsession with nuclear missiles.

And on this Ryan and Ling were on the same page. They both felt their nations would only benefit if Choi was knocked from power. Ryan explained to Ling he knew the rare earth mineral mine's value and its potential value to Ling's nation. 'If you could get your mining industry back inside North Korea, it would be a tremendous boon to your nation's economy.'

Ling nodded, then asked, 'How do you propose we convince Choi to allow this, without offering him missiles that would reach your California?'

Ryan said, 'China has a lot of positive influence over North Korea. Hwang's speech might force the hand of the people of the nation to sack Choi.'

'That is possible. We do maintain many friendly contacts with people in positions of power.'

Ryan knew this, and he knew the answer to the question he posed next, but he knew it only through intelligence intercepts from China. He couldn't reveal this, of course, so he played dumb.

'Ji-hoon's uncle, I forgot his name ... he was the ambassador to China, wasn't he? Whatever happened to him?'

Ling nodded. 'Choi Sang-u. We had a most excellent relationship with him. His nephew thought the relationship was too good, unfortunately, so Ji-hoon threw Sang-u in prison.'

Ryan said, 'It sounds like it would benefit China if this man was put into power in place of Ji-hoon.'

Ling agreed. 'This would be the best possible outcome.' After a pause he added, 'Depending, of course, on his present health and condition. You might know there is an attempt to reeducate those in prison. Not so much in the internment camps, but still we would have to evaluate him to see if he could take over the reins of power.'

Ryan said, 'If this works, you might just have to take your chances. God knows he'd be better than Ji-hoon in power.'

Ling nodded thoughtfully. 'You make a fair point.'

Ryan felt like the matter was dealt with. Hwang would tell the North Korean elite that China should be in North

Korea operating the mineral mine. And that wouldn't happen with Choi Ji-hoon in Ryongsong.

Ryan switched gears suddenly. 'Mr President, there is another matter I need to discuss with you.'

'Unrelated?'

'No, it's related. I would like to ask for some help. A citizen of my country is, at present, in North Korea. He is wounded, and it is critical we retrieve him.'

Ling listened to the translation, then asked, 'Do you mean to tell me you have an American secret agent inside North Korea?'

Ryan shrugged a little. 'I am not prepared to say what the man's occupation is. But I hope you will appreciate the fact I refuse to lie to you.'

The president of China nodded slightly.

'What is it you want?'

'He is less than a kilometer from your border on the southern side of the Yalu River.'

'You are asking us to open our border crossing?'

'No, Mr President. I am asking more than that. I am asking you to send some men in to get him.'

'I am afraid what you are asking is out of the question. Despite the other matter to which we have just agreed, it is important for my country to maintain good and open relations with the DPRK. The potential for scandal in this matter is too great.'

'The success of the first matter depends on the positive resolution of the second.'

The president of China turned to his translator and had him repeat himself. Ryan saw the man was confused by the wording, but he let him figure it out on his own.

Finally President Ling spoke and the translator turned it into English. 'Do you mean to say the entire deal depends on this one man?'

Ryan did not hesitate. 'Yes, that is exactly what I am saying. It is in both of our nations'' interests that this man is rescued, alive.'

Ling was still astonished, but Ryan could see the gears turning in his head. The man saw an opportunity. 'If I agree to your request, I would like the opportunity for my intelligence officials to sit with this individual for a short interview.'

Ryan had been ready for this. 'The information he has is related to the issue at hand, nothing more.'

'Be that as it may, I request —'

'It is likely this man is gravely injured. I want him delivered to us, here in Beijing. I will delay my departure, if necessary. If you do that, you have my personal assurance that an interview will be granted, provided he is in condition to give an interview and only if my own people are allowed to be present during the interview.' Ryan smiled. 'I expect this man might be very confused by everything.'

Ling asked, 'When do we need to rescue your agent?'

Ryan said, 'Within the hour would be ideal, Mr President.'

Ling just stared at his translator in shock.

76

Adam Yao lay in a thick copse of trees alongside the Yalu River, some fifty yards from the gravel road behind him. He heard trucks passing on the road, back and forth, over and over, for most of the day. They couldn't see him, he was well hidden, but he knew that as soon as the army thought to dismount some troops to check the wood line he would have to crawl to the river or lie here and await capture.

And the river was too cold to ford, especially in his weakened state.

Adam's knee was swollen like a grapefruit, and the huge gash was showing signs of infection just twenty-four hours after he dove out of the racing SUV. He had crawled the last fifty yards through a muddy rice paddy after he fell off the bicycle, and an hour earlier when he tried to stand up he had been unable to put any weight on the leg at all.

He knew he wasn't going anywhere. It had been a bone-chilling and wretched evening, and he told himself he was ready to die. Freezing to death had always seemed so awful those few times in his life he'd ever thought about it, but now he found himself accepting his fate. At peace with it.

Occasionally he thought he heard voices, never right on top of him but certainly on the road and perhaps even on boats passing on the Yalu River. He'd not understood any of the words, and after a while he started to wonder if his mind was not just playing tricks on him.

Though he had heard the footfalls of individual men traveling on the road far below him, he did not hear the men in white at all until they were right on top of his position. He opened his eyes suddenly, aware of a presence close by, and he saw a group of armed men in white snow camouflage surrounding him here in the trees.

It was too dark to tell anything else about them, but Adam assumed they were North Korean Special Forces.

One of the men knelt down at his head while two more began working on his leg wound. The others, Adam saw, had taken up positions in the woods, their guns up in defense of him.

What the hell was going on?

In Mandarin the man at his head said, 'Yao?'

How did they know his name? He shook his head. '*Wu.*' No.

'Your country sent us.'

'I don't believe you.'

'Believe whatever you want. We are putting you on a stretcher and taking you over the river into China.'

And Adam Yao just let them do it. He was in no position to argue.

Edward Riley stood on the fifth-floor rooftop of the apartment building across from Mae Fah Luang – Chiang Rai International Airport in Chiang Rai, Thailand. With his binoculars in hand, he looked over the entire length of the tarmac, his eyes wide to take in the scant electric lighting; his binoculars were all but useless in the evening darkness.

Where are they? They were supposed to be here hours ago.

Once he was clear of immediate danger in Mexico, Riley had contacted Óscar Roblas and told him he was still in play. He exaggerated his abilities and influence, and he asked Roblas what he needed to do to prove he was still an asset to the operation.

Riley had been almost surprised when Roblas answered him, giving him the specifications of the froth flotation tanks, relaying the size and weight of the equipment, and filling him in on the special logistical problems involved in moving the huge industrial devices into North Korea.

Now Riley was here, in Thailand, and he had moved mountains to accomplish the one thing the North Koreans and Ro-blas had not been able to do for themselves. In the past five days Riley had played every last card in his deck. He'd used contacts, made deals, traded on old friendships, and called in every last favor he'd ever been owed by anyone. With this intangible currency he'd made it out of Mexico, over to Asia, and he'd negotiated with Russian cargo companies and Thai businessmen.

If he could pull this off he could show both Roblas and Pyongyang that he was worth the risk and an asset to their lucrative enterprise. Though compromised to the Americans, wanted as an accessory after the fact to the damnable thing that happened in Mexico City, he still could come through with the goods, and they would keep him under their wing.

He'd arranged for a pair of Russian Antonov cargo aircraft to land at the airport here, and once they arrived, he'd only have to contact Roblas, who was trying to secure the delivery of a new set of froth tanks that were on the water from Brazil. If the planes showed up as arranged, Riley could fly the bloody equipment into North Korea and bypass the Americans and their blockade.

But so far, the fucking Russians hadn't shown.

He'd work the phones, he'd make sure the tanks were on the ship and on the way, and he'd make sure the payment from the North Koreans made it to the seller.

But if the Russians in their cargo planes didn't make it to Thailand, then this deal was dead in the dirt.

He tried the binoculars again. Nothing. 'Where are those bloody planes?'

He lowered his binoculars and turned to head back to the stairs.

He stopped suddenly when he saw a man standing there in the low light, forty feet away.

'Who are you?'

'Someone who's come a long way for this.'

Riley did not recognize the man, though he could tell he was American. Riley didn't have a gun, but the other man showed no hint of a weapon, either. 'FBI?'

The man shook his head.

'Who, then?'

'My name is Jack.'

Meant nothing to Riley.

'A friend of Chavez.'

Oh.

'A friend of Veronika's.'

What?

Riley thought about running for the stairwell, but this

man looked prepared to stop him. He could just put down his head and charge forward, throw punches, and hope for the best, but Riley wasn't any kind of fighter.

'What is it you want?'

'I'm taking you back to the United States.'

'All by yourself you are? Or did you bring your friends? The friends from Cuernavaca.'

The man called Jack said, 'I have a lot of friends, but to tell you the truth, I think I'll do it all alone.'

Riley nodded almost to himself, seemed to think it over dispassionately, and then he charged.

Not toward the man by the stairs. But in the other direction.

Toward the building's edge.

There was another apartment building next door, but that structure was separated by an alleyway fifteen feet wide. The neighboring rooftop was one story lower, and Riley thought he could make it. He charged on, picking up as much speed as possible, knowing his one avenue of escape was a massive leap between two buildings some seventy-five feet in the air.

Jack Ryan, Jr., thought he might be able to stop the man before he threw himself over the side of the five-story building. He could shout something and run for him, either catch up or hope the man hesitated near the edge. But Ryan just stood there, watching, while the Englishman leapt. The man kicked his legs and flailed his arms; then he disappeared over the side of the apartment building. Ryan did not hear him land on the other rooftop. Instead he heard a long, shrieking scream that grew more distant.

He heard no impact, but immediately his earpiece came alive.

'Ryan! I saw someone fall! You okay?' It was Chavez.

'I'm fine. Did you see him hit?'

'Facedown in the middle of the alley.'

Jack said, 'No better than he deserves.'

'Yeah.'

Clark's voice came over the net now. 'Works for me. Let's pack it up. If we leave now, we'll be back in time for Sam's funeral at Arlington.'

Ryan nodded to himself on the rooftop, and then he headed for the stairs.

Epilogue

Adam could have flown on another plane, but the CIA wanted him out of China as soon as possible, and the next US government aircraft to depart Beijing was the big white 747 known as Air Force One.

President Ryan delayed his departure two days to make this happen, and it had been an interesting time, indeed. The coup in North Korea took less than twenty hours, beginning with Hwang's speech to the North Korean people and ending with the reports on Korean state television that the Dae Wonsu had taken ill and was going to spend some time recovering in the mountains of his birthplace.

The kid had been born in a hospital in Pyongyang, so it was anybody's bet where he was, but Jack Ryan didn't think it was anywhere good.

It wasn't bloodless: Choi's bodyguards put up a fight, but they were up against the Chosun Inmingun, and it was a matter of hours, not days, before the tide turned and the power shifted in North Korea.

The Chinese made it happen, all would say, and while the Chinese had great influence over the North Korean military and certainly controlled the media access that had allowed Hwang to reveal the scope of Choi's corruption to his own people, few would ever know America's role in uncovering the Chongju mine scandal or the effect a single American agent had in the affair. The rumor would come out that the Chinese had someone at the mine, and this would be helped along by an Australian geologist, who, back with her family in Melbourne, allowed that her intermediate knowledge of Mandarin played a small role in saving the Korean Peninsula from a madman.

Dr. Powers was just glad to be home. She'd keep quiet about the American agent, her ride in a remote-controlled aircraft, and her arrival at a US air base.

The CIA moved Adam Yao onto Air Force One out of sight of the press and even traveling administration personnel. Almost no one on board knew that a man on a stretcher had been carried onto the aircraft after the curtains were closed. The only personnel aware were the CIA officers and medical staff who brought him from the embassy, along with two Secret Service agents who checked everyone extra carefully these days, even Adam Yao, though he was flat on his back with a bandage around his leg.

For his part, Yao had been sullen since he'd regained consciousness in the clinic in the embassy. He'd responded to direct questions from his doctors, but he hadn't said much else. No one had even tried to debrief him yet. CIA had a serious protocol for debriefs, and the officer's health was paramount. Apologies were made to the Chinese that they couldn't speak to the man, but the Chinese had their hands full with the goings-on to their south, so they'd not made much of a fuss.

Air Force One was well out over the Sea of Japan when President Ryan entered the medical office and sat down next to the injured CIA NOC. Adam tried to pull himself higher on his pillow. He couldn't have stood up if his life depended on it, and even though he knew it would have been respectful to do so, he also knew better than to try.

But he did raise a weak hand with an IV tube running from it.

Ryan said, 'It's an honor to meet you, Mr Yao.'

'Likewise, sir.' His voice was weak, a result of the drugs and exhaustion, but he was aware. He looked over his President. The cast on his left arm, the sling on his right arm. 'Oh my gosh. Are you okay?'

Ryan smiled. The kid had missed a lot of happenings over the past week.

'I'm okay. And I am told you are going to be fine. Little frostbite. Broken kneecap, a laceration, a mild infection that should clear up in a few days.'

Adam just nodded. He said nothing else.

Ryan thought he detected a problem. 'Is there something bothering you?'

'I'm sorry for asking this, Mr President. I don't want to sound ungrateful, but I have to know. Did we make some deal with the Chinese to get me out?'

Ryan did not hesitate in his response. 'None at all. I added you onto the end of a deal that had already been made. A deal in both our nations'' interests.' He shrugged. 'Hell, a deal that worked out for everyone. Ultimately, even the North Koreans, although I don't expect a thank-you card and a tray of cookies anytime soon.'

Adam blew out a long sigh, utterly relieved. With a smile he said, 'They would be awful cookies, I can guarantee that.'

'That's good intel,' Ryan joked, and he patted Yao on the arm with his cast. 'Can I get you anything?'

'I have everything I need now. Thank you.'

Then Ryan turned serious. 'The work you have done has made an incredible difference. Hwang is talking to us, and he made a statement that went out all over the world about the rare earth mine. It's hard to predict what will happen inside the DPRK now that Choi's gone. We expect chaos in the short term, but in the long term, we think it will have a positive effect.'

'What about the foreign nationals working at the Chongju mine?'

Ryan said, 'Hwang has provided that information to us, and we will be passing it on to the Australians, French, Canadians, and others before he speaks publicly. These countries will need to appeal directly to the North Koreans. It's all we can do.'

Ryan added, "We cannot thank you enough for what you've done. You've sacrificed a lot.

'It was my call that put you in North Korea. I knew when I complained to our intelligence execs that the HUMINT wasn't acceptable that they would redouble efforts to change that. And I knew that meant some young man or young woman would be going into harm's way. I don't take that lightly, at all. I know it must be hard to appreciate that the old people running this country really do care about the young people they cajole into the dangerous missions. But I was there once, in your shoes. A long time ago.'

'I know you were, sir. And I hope you know I'm happy you sent me. I'm glad I got to make a little difference.'

Adam coughed and Ryan got the impression he wanted to say something else.

'What is it?'

Adam said, 'I met your son. A great guy.'

Jack chuckled softly. 'Should I ask where you met him?'

Adam shrugged. 'I wouldn't.'

Jack let it go. Finally, he stood. 'Get well, Mr Yao. Your country needs you.'

'Yes, Mr President.'

Jack Ryan went up to his office on Air Force One to make some calls. Andrea had come out of her coma and she was talking now; she was due to fly back to the US the next morning with her husband and young son, and Ryan wanted to speak with her immediately to thank her for everything she'd done. As much as he wanted to hear her voice, he knew she'd want to hear his as well, because even though she was in a hospital bed five thousand miles away from her President right now, he was still her protectee, and she would feel the unease of not having seen him get to safety in Mexico.

Ryan sat down at his desk with a wince, and he asked his secretary to place the call. While he waited, he looked at the photos of his family on his desk. He had a few years more to devote to his country, and then he would be able to give himself back to his family fully, and as he looked at a picture of his entire clan, he thought about a day when they wouldn't have to worry about the possibility of getting a call like the one Cathy had gotten last week.

Ryan smiled. That day was coming.

But then he looked at Jack Junior in the photo. His

smile faded. That day wouldn't come for Cathy so soon, after all. His son had pushed himself headlong into danger and danger had pushed back, more than once, this Ryan Senior knew. He also knew that, someday, he might get the call that the husbands and wives and parents of all those Secret Service agents got last week, giving him the news that his son had been killed in the line of duty, and the thought of it utterly chilled him, so he did the only thing he could think to do.

He shut his eyes and prayed for peace.

He just wanted a decent book to read ...

Not too much to ask, is it? It was in 1935 when Allen Lane, Managing Director of Bodley Head Publishers, stood on a platform at Exeter railway station looking for something good to read on his journey back to London. His choice was limited to popular magazines and poor-quality paperbacks – the same choice faced every day by the vast majority of readers, few of whom could afford hardbacks. Lane's disappointment and subsequent anger at the range of books generally available led him to found a company – and change the world.

'We believed in the existence in this country of a vast reading public for intelligent books at a low price, and staked everything on it'
Sir Allen Lane, 1902–1970, founder of Penguin Books

The quality paperback had arrived – and not just in bookshops. Lane was adamant that his Penguins should appear in chain stores and tobacconists, and should cost no more than a packet of cigarettes.

Reading habits (and cigarette prices) have changed since 1935, but Penguin still believes in publishing the best books for everybody to enjoy. We still believe that good design costs no more than bad design, and we still believe that quality books published passionately and responsibly make the world a better place.

So wherever you see the little bird – whether it's on a piece of prize-winning literary fiction or a celebrity autobiography, political tour de force or historical masterpiece, a serial-killer thriller, reference book, world classic or a piece of pure escapism – you can bet that it represents the very best that the genre has to offer.

Whatever you like to read – trust Penguin.